Praise for *Fraud Catcher*
a novel based on true cases

"An enthralling book, *Fraud Catcher* is a gripping read with enjoyable characters and a highly original plot. The authenticity adds an extra dimension to this must-read thriller."

~ Lissa Oliver, broadcaster, award-winning international journalist and author

"An exciting, enjoyable read . . . authentic, intriguing cases, interesting characters. 'Baltimore Bear' is my favorite chapter. Simply stated, this is a very good book. I recommend it."

~ Tom Keller, insurance investigator since 1981

"Fraud Catcher is a splendid read—exciting, fast-paced, enjoyable and often very funny, with lots of twists, written by an actual fraud investigator. Tom Cooper knows first-hand what he's writing about. His hero, Tom Brabazon, is great—a guy whom I'd want to solve cases for me. There'll be a TV series from this, mark my words."

~ Lucy Clare, Woodford book reviewer

Fraud Catcher

By Tom Cooper

TINGLE CREEK
2012

TINGLE CREEK, 2012

Copyright © 2012 by Connaught Pendil

First Edition

Library of Congress Control Number: 2012953233

TINGLE CREEK ISBN: 0-615-72381-0

Edited by R.E. Hall

Published in the United States of America by Tingle Creek, P.O. Box 910039, Beaumont Station, Lexington, KY 40591

www.tinglecreekbooks.com

Printed in the United States of America

To my lovely & wonderful daughter, Catherine, make your passion your career. Always maintain your integrity, honor and independence. Never be a borrower or a lender.

***

To Barbara, my best friend for 27 years, the best and nicest person, plus the most brilliant horsewoman I've ever known.

***

To Pinky, who saved my life.

~Contents~

Chapter 1   THE INTERVIEW

Pauleen Farrell was right, yet again. Tom Brabazon got a second chance for a new life.

"Just talk to the man," she said. "Dr. Stone wants you to. What else have you got to do?"

Nothing. That was his problem. Tom's track records and career as an Olympic athlete were history, the medals won, the cheering finished. Washed up at 29, what was he going to do for the rest of his life?

Run and duck, as it's turned out.

Catching criminals and creating justice.

But one day, when his luck ran out, Tom Brabazon
was stabbed.

****

Wearing sunglasses, the man spoke to Tom after shaking hands with Pauleen and Tom:

"You're right for this job," he began quietly. "We investigate frauds and swindles. We've tried ex-cops, ex FBI
agents, ex military and journalists. Most wash out–they
can't handle this job."

The man waited while the waitress poured coffee before he continued:

"We solve frauds, all kinds of frauds. We catch cheats,
embezzlers, fraudsters, con artists, swindlers, investment
crooks and business thieves. We find missing people,
finding people who've disappeared on purpose and don't
want to be found." He waved to the waitress for milk.

"Figure out how, then who, when and where. Don't
waste time with their motive; the why is simply greed,
always greed."

He paused before adding, "We do it quietly, no police,
no media, no headlines. Each job is different. We do it
right, do it fast, no mistakes. I need, want, independent
thinkers, problem solvers, people with stamina, tenacious,
able to connect the dots, work without committees, people
who can duck and swerve and accelerate."

Another pause before he added, with hard conviction:
"You've got what it takes. Dr. Stone says so."

"But I'm just a runner. That's all I know," Tom disagreed.

"You *were* a runner," the man replied with a firm and
correcting emphasis on the past tense. "Now, like most

retired athletes, you're a has-been. Life's rough now. I know what you're going through. That's typical for ex-athletes. You've got no passion now, no goals, you've lived and won your dreams, but you're lost now. I was in your shoes after I quit running sixteen years ago. I know how you feel. We'll train you. You'll be a winner again." The man's eyes remained glued to Tom's.

"I want you to be a fraud investigator for me," the man said. "You'll find this job to be a new passion and worthwhile. This is good work, noble work, satisfying, meaningful, just like winning gold. As good as winning a gold medal. We catch the bad guys. We create justice. This air tastes even better."

He moved out of shadow, calling to the waitress for a coffee refill. Pauleen and Tom gasped. He was George Hancock Alexander, twice an Olympic gold medalist, a superstar, Tom's hero when he began running. Tom realized that Alexander was asking him to accept a future that he found irresistible. He needed a challenge, a new beginning. This, he decided, was it.

Tom Brabazon accepted Alexander's offer and began a rollercoaster race, sometimes dangerous, always interesting, sometimes strange, and always intriguing. Problem solving.

Trouble is, sometimes the bad guys get mad.

Chapter 2   DUBLIN, IRELAND

Tom Brabazon never forgot the thrill the first time someone threatened to kill him. That thrill replaced running to become his second obsession.

For Tom, it had all begun as a simple favor to Don Melville, a friend of his coach Dr. Bill Stone, the day before flying to Ireland for an international university athletics competition.

For Don Melville, this story had actually started during the summer of 1942 when playing polo in Wichita, Kansas while serving in the U.S. Cavalry in his first effort to win World War II. The colonel commanding Don's unit in Kansas was still practicing for another mounted war against the Kaiser, even though the cavalry had been officially disbanded in 1918. News traveled slowly in those days.

Don became friends with Bill Stone, a tough horse vet from Virginia also serving with the regiment, when Stone treated his lame gelding on that dusty polo field in Kansas. Thirty-five years later, their friendship found an unexpected bonus in Tom Brabazon.

Without Don Melville asking a favor which would start his career, Tom would never have gone on to catch dozens of criminals, fraudsters and swindlers, solved scams and frauds ranging from minor all the way to multi-million dollar international swindles or found missing people all over the world.

Many crooks have wished Brabazon dead.

Dr. Bill Stone coached athletes after retiring as a vet because a stallion had crushed his arm. He didn't know Brabazon well, only as another college athlete on a sports scholarship, smarter than most, aloof but oh-so-determined during training and in races, neither the fastest nor the most naturally gifted but certainly the most dedicated runner.

Dr. Stone didn't know and wouldn't have cared about Tom's weird background but he was impressed by the boy's concentration and detected something special in the young man.

In a rare moment of being sociable, the hard-nosed and usually distant Stone invited Tom and six teammates to a hunt 'breakfast' party, held one afternoon less than thirty miles away near Upperville, Virginia. It was the first day of the Piedmont Hunt's foxhunting season, in Northern

Virginia's hunt country, fifty miles west of Washington D.C.

In September of 1942, the Army decided to transfer Don Melville from his cushy life playing polo to serious training and iron discipline in Georgia in order to become a paratrooper.

He dropped by parachute behind enemy lines near Omaha Beach on D-Day, June 6, 1944, luckily avoiding being hit by the Nazi soldiers shooting into the air. Captured by the Germans after heavy hand-to-hand combat two weeks later and transported to Germany, he escaped as a prisoner of war, returned to England and was quickly re-assigned to fight in the Pacific where he lost a leg. After the war ended, he'd moved to Upperville where he farmed two hundred acres and renewed his friendship with Dr. Stone who lived in nearby Middleburg.

The old man had been foxhunting with the Piedmont Hunt the day he met Tom. Foxhunting was his greatest joy in life and a necessary refuge from his sorrows, his wife having died in a skiing accident several years before and their son killed in Vietnam. His one major worry left, what had happened to his sister-in-law in Dublin, was about to be sorted when Dr. Stone, his old polo buddy, introduced him over hot apple cider and salmon sandwiches to the quiet, secretive young man without an accent.

Don Melville didn't, couldn't have, known that he'd picked the right athlete from the group, the only one who could succeed in solving his mystery.

"Bill here says that you're going over to Ireland tomorrow to race for the University. Have you ever been in Ireland before?" Don asked.

"Yessir," came Tom's reply.

"Well, young man, I'd greatly appreciate your doing something for me over in Dublin, between races, if you'll have the time."

"What's that, sir?" Tom asked politely.

"I haven't heard from my sister-in-law, Olive Wiley, for four years. She's probably dead, none of us are getting any younger but I'd like to know. She hasn't answered my letters and I checked but her phone was disconnected a while back. I can't understand why she'd cash my checks for her birthdays and Christmas but not write and thank me." He took another sip of hot apple cider laced with brandy.

"Young man, I'd like you to find out where she's buried and put some flowers on her grave. My wife Mary was her sister. I escaped from a camp in Germany with a pilot from Seattle called Steve Lewis. We were both shot as we were crossing the border into Switzerland. Mary was living in a nearby village called Les Gloches and saved my life but Steve died that night. I married Mary after the war ended."

"I'll be happy to do what I can, sir, if you'll give me her address."

"Olive Wiley, Park Avenue, Sandymount, a suburb of Dublin," the old man replied and wrote the full address on a piece of paper for Tom.

"She'd be 77 now. Her husband died many years ago. They had a daughter named Margaret who was engaged the last I heard. Olive's son George was killed in Northern Ireland in 1969. He was a lieutenant in the British Army. There is no other family." The old man was sad. "I'll pay you for your time and reimburse your expenses. Here is one hundred dollars for a start."

"Thank you, sir."

"Don't go cheap on the flowers, son."

****

Dublin in the 1970s was poor, very different than today's busy, wealthy, cosmopolitan city, which is the result of much investment from European Union money and global technology companies like Intel, Dell and Microsoft in the energetic capital of the roaring "Celtic Tiger."

The Tiger lost its claws, many might say its legs were amputated, during the great global recession which began in 2008. Back in the 1970s, Ireland was in the early period of a nasty twenty-year economic depression, which began with the introduction of a wealth tax by the socialist government placed on foreigners retired in Ireland.

Nearly all of the rich foreigners left quickly to avoid the tax. Dozens of families, disappointed with Ireland breaking an international tax treaty, were saddened to leave a country where they loved living as guests, spending plenty of money, knowing that their money was welcome even though they were sometimes not.

The next blow to sleepy, peaceful Southern Ireland was the oil crisis in 1973, which created huge inflation and serious unemployment. High levels of emigration continued. It would be a rough quarter century for Ireland, one which created much pain before the Celtic Tiger changed Ireland forever.

The Anglo-Irish landed gentry, having inherited large estates from their ancestors granted to them by Cromwell in the 1600s, still ruled Southern Ireland economically and socially through the 1970s. The other 95% of the population was Irish Catholic, most of whom lacked education and did the work while the Anglo-Irish aristocracy continued to live the comfortable lifestyle of the Victorian age, unaware that their era of superiority was nearly over and would finally end in the 1990s.

The civil war, called "The Troubles," which began in Northern Ireland in the late 1960s, was a distant world away from life in the South.

Tom Brabazon, who'd used other names but had been christened Stephen Lester Walwyn, had lived in Ireland long before attending Manassas University in Virginia. His was a strange, often harsh, childhood and he never belonged nor was he ever accepted in Ireland.

Born in another country, which was one strike against him, and arriving aged eleven he also didn't fit in because he was neither Anglo-Irish nor Irish Catholic. Nobody in Ireland cared to which church anybody went, the differences weren't religious but economic and traditional.

These were two separate groups in Ireland, which never mixed socially while both regarded incomers as suspect. Tom, or actually Steve, didn't refer to himself as belonging to any ethnic group or a particular nationality, but both groups regarded him as an outsider. His often charming, sometimes cruel stepfather was Anglo-Irish and treated Tom badly.

Tom believed that he'd always be an outsider everywhere in the world, especially in Ireland. Just the way it was—no roots anywhere, his mother and father both murdered, no brothers or sisters, his stepfather long since avoided. He'd run away from Ireland at seventeen, away from his stepfather and school and was now twenty-four.

He had become an independent, self-sufficient young man who'd seen too little of a good life but too much of the bad.

Tom decided not to mention to his teammates that he'd been in Ireland before or that he'd been asked to do an errand for Don Melville. He assumed that Dr. Stone had recommended him personally. He'd learned to keep his thoughts and background to himself, neither be friendly nor unfriendly, not get too close, but be popular with everyone, and never to answer questions about himself.

His teammates and classroom acquaintances supposed that he was an Army brat, moving often from base to base, which might explain why he was different, evasive but not remote, why he hadn't grown up like them in a small town or big city, with a high school anybody recognized.

His girlfriend Sarah Silver thought it odd that Tom never mentioned a prom, never called anywhere home, never told stories about his life or family and never revealed well . . . anything. Tom was strong, reliable, decent and kind, but mysterious. She was reasonably sure, believing herself to be an excellent judge of character, that Tom wasn't a mass murderer but it upset her that he wouldn't open up to her. She wanted to know him. After all, wasn't that what relationships meant, sharing each others' dreams and feelings? Tom never did.

He wouldn't even explain to Sarah why he had started growing a beard a month before the team's trip to Ireland. The truth was he didn't want to be recognized. He knew that he and his team would be photographed and he didn't want any questions asked. The past was past and he preferred it to stay that way.

He remembered that the Brabazons were a famous sporting family in Ireland, headed by legendary steeple-chasing jockey Aubrey, but for this trip he had to use the same name he used at the University. He deflected attention in Ireland after explaining–lying–that his male ancestor with the rare Brabazon surname had been exported as a convict to America. That shut people up, even the Irish journalists.

Fortunately, none of his opponents in Ireland identified him from their school days, although he recognized several of them.

His school days in Ireland hadn't been happy ones, but that's when he'd learned to be comfortable being solitary. Running and hunting alone was what he preferred, to be self-reliant. Football, rugby, cricket were team sports, which meant relying on each other, dependent on others. He was self-sufficient, having learned to be independent in an odd, unusual but not altogether unhappy childhood. He preferred the solitary style of a runner.

After winning both the 1500 meter and the 3000 meter races–he was no sprinter–by sheer determination that rainy day in the huge Phoenix Park in Dublin, winning because he *had* to win to satisfy his sense of purpose, he went looking for the old man's relative, Olive Wiley.

He didn't expect it to be a big deal, just a few questions, find the old lady's final resting place, buy flowers and write the sad news to Mr. Melville when he returned to Virginia. Then he'd continue running, the one thing that he loved and trusted besides hunting in the woods. He was about to learn that tracking people in the city was the same as following animal tracks in the woods, just less muddy.

Tom knew his way around the decaying thousand-year-old city of Dublin rather too well, having survived on its streets for three days as a fifteen-year-old runaway from boarding school. Pure bad luck, when recognized in a bookmaker's shop by his Latin teacher, had returned him to school.

His chief memories of the school had been the cold. Cold runs every morning across a mountain, followed by cold showers, cold porridge and cold boiled potatoes, which occasionally had been scooped up off steep steps after being spilled when carried up from the kitchen, rugby in the rain and the mud, more cold showers.

He'd finally escaped for good, reaching Florida on his eighteenth birthday, wanting a new life, with a fake birth certificate and passport. His main criterion for the future was for no more frozen temperatures. He'd changed his mind about freezing to move to Manassas University in Virginia, despite the cold winters, because of its excellent track and field program.

No, he didn't want to be recognized on this athletics trip as a former student.

He caught the double-decker bus headed towards the front entrance of 400-year-old Trinity College where his stepfather had earned a degree. It was slow, passed the world famous Guinness brewery, then the 'penny ha'penny bridge' and travelling along the 'quays' of the river Liffey which slices Dublin in half. The bus then did a fair bit of meandering and he hopped off at St. Stephen's Green, right at the top of Grafton Street, long famous as the best street for retail shopping in Dublin with Switzers and Brown & Thomas its most famous shops.

Tom looked around, memories of long ago returning. He'd never expected to be back in Dublin, having escaped Ireland for good all those years before. Nothing looked different except for him with his beard. Strange what he recalled now, small episodes that he'd guessed were forgotten forever.

He remembered walking down Grafton Street from St. Stephen's Green one rainy afternoon years earlier on his way to meeting his mother at the wonderful Bewley's Café with the great scents of roasting coffee beans. Bewley's was the best cafe in all of Ireland, a coffee, cake and bun establishment totally opposite in style from Starbucks, where two main groups congregated– university students from nearby Trinity and elderly ladies.

When the rain cascaded down that distant afternoon, Tom decided to purchase an umbrella so went into a men's shop, bought one and returned to the street. After about fifty yards, a sudden gust of wind inverted his new umbrella and smashed the steel frame into limp, crumpled bits. Tom did a u-turn, returned to the shop and politely asked for either a refund or a new umbrella.

The sales clerk made the mistake of blaming Tom for the damage, saying without joking but with a peculiar type of typical Irish logic, "You shouldn't have used it in the rain," and initially refused a refund until discovering Tom's unyielding insistence for his money back. Tom received his refund but was instructed never to return to the store.

Tom laughed as he remembered a story, insisted as true by all who told it, that a Dublin City councilor had proposed, after honeymooning in Venice, that a gondola be purchased for the lake in St. Stephens Green. After a spirited debate, it was decided to vote on the issue. When a resounding 'yes' carried the motion, a second councilor suggested that the council purchase a second gondola "so that we can breed them."

He decided not to walk down Grafton Street, a shorter distance to the bus stop he needed to reach. Instead, he walked parallel to St. Stephen's Green but on the opposite side of the street towards the famous Shelbourne Hotel, where generations of rural Irish landowners had enjoyed their visits to Dublin. Tom smiled at his memory of when he'd last passed this spot a dozen years before.

There had been an expensively tweed-clad, upper class, elderly Anglo-Irish lady doing her bit for charity by raising funds for the Society for the Prevention of Cruelty to Children. Calling out for donations and becoming bored, the lady had shortened her pleas in stages until she shouted, "Give to cruelty to children," just as Tom's mother, with an American accent and dragging him, passed her.

Hearing that impassioned plea, Tom's mother whipped out a coin, dropped it into the can held by the tweeded woman and, tongue-in-cheek, called out in a cheerful voice, "I'll gladly give to that. I hate the little buggers," and strode past with a straight face. Tom and the by-standers enjoyed the charity collector's horrified expression.

Tom walked towards the Shelbourne until he reached Nassau Street, turned left and downhill, reached the wall of Trinity College and walked around past the back gate until he was on the opposite side of campus. That's where he jumped onto a #3 bus to Sandymount, a village about three miles away. It all took plenty of time, but Tom was in no hurry.

The Wiley house on Park Avenue was literally at the end of the line, a half mile beyond Sandymount, where the driver parked, switched off the engine and bluntly told his final passenger to get out. Dubliners are never as friendly to each other as they are to tourists and the driver naturally assumed that Tom was a local, probably a rich student, certainly not a tourist, so courtesy wasn't part of the ride.

Tom stepped off the bus, surrounded by the mid-afternoon silence of an empty middle class suburb before school got out. From the bus' upper level, he'd spotted the house, an ivy-clad rambling brick place on the corner of the grassy area where the bus had stopped, the driveway affording privacy from the street. The name Wilson was on the green mailbox with the number confirming the correct address.

He walked up the driveway, enjoying the beautiful lawn and rhododendron filled gardens, observing that everything was neat and tidy. Plenty of money spent here, he could tell, assuming that Ireland's economic mess and massive unemployment had obviously not reached up this driveway. He knocked on the massive wood door, heard a dog barking inside and then footsteps.

An elderly housemaid opened the door, looked surprised at the stranger and asked what he wanted.

"I'm looking for Mrs. Wiley," explained Tom.

"Well now, she doesn't live here any more, young man. She moved away before I came to work here but I'll take you through to meet the Reverend, Reverend Wilson." She waved her hand.

"Please follow me to the sitting room," the white-haired woman said as she allowed the dog, a dachshund, outdoors before leading Tom into a comfortable sitting room. She asked him to sit on a settee for a minute and offered tea. Everyone in Ireland drank tea in those days and to refuse it was as unthinkable as it was usually undrinkable, having simmered on the Aga cooker since daybreak. She left him alone.

Tom was observant by habit and noticed new, high quality furniture and two valuable paintings hanging on the opposite wall, certainly not hand-me-downs but recent auction house purchases. Tom knew nothing about art or art fraud back then, yet they didn't look counterfeit to his untrained eye.

The room confirmed his first impression that the country's troubled economy hadn't invaded this household. On the mantelpiece was a photograph of a racehorse winning at Leopardstown, which Tom knew was on the edge of southwestern Dublin and Ireland's second leading racecourse. Looking closely, he read: *Embezzler*, three-year-old colt by Mill Reef ex Night Special, winner of the Gr. 3 Switzer Stakes, 10 furlongs, owner Mrs. Gerald Wiley Wilson, trainer Trevor Baxter, jockey Tony O'Brien.

The door opened and a dark-haired man in his forties, about five-foot-six, carrying a paunch and wearing a clergyman's collar, strode in. He introduced himself to Tom as Reverend Wilson, no first name offered, and asked what Tom's visit was all about.

"I'm trying to find Mrs. Wiley, Reverend."

The Reverend wanted to know why, a reasonable request, but asked suspiciously. Tom wasn't an open book himself but had planned to bat straightforward until he thought he saw Reverend Wilson's hands twist nervously.

"Well," he chose his words cautiously, with a suddenly strong American accent, hoping that his host wouldn't notice the switch, "my name is Colin Mitchell and I'm from San Antonio, Texas, not far from the border with Mexico. I'm over here in Ireland looking up any relatives because my granddad emigrated to the States from Dublin and talks often about his sister Olive Wiley."

"What's your grandfather's name, Mitchell, and how old is he?"

Tom had to think fast. He knew he had only one chance. "Donald Melville, sir, my mom's dad. He's in his seventies, he fought in the war."

"Well, young man, Mrs. Wiley is dead. I don't know why you came here. Indeed, I somehow don't believe you." The housemaid came in with her tray with tea and biscuits, what Americans call cookies.

"Mary," added Reverend Wilson, "there's no need for tea. This lad isn't staying. In fact, he's leaving now," he said firmly.

Switching back to Tom, without ever having taken his eyes off him, the Reverend told him to leave immediately.

The maid was baffled and suggested that Mrs. Wilson, who was sorting flowers in the kitchen, could easily answer the nice young man's questions about where her mother was. Then she stopped, worried and surprised when her boss glared at her. A now-angry Reverend Wilson was not pleased with the maid's slip, not at all.

"May I speak to Mrs. Wilson then?" asked Tom.

"No, she's unavailable. Leave. Now." The Reverend, acting less than spiritual, escorted him to the door and told him to never return.

A woman, presumably Mrs. Wilson, entered the corridor as they reached the front door, raised her eyebrows and began asking questions but the minister firmly told her to return to the kitchen. She obeyed silently.

Tom walked down the driveway and when he turned back to see the man still staring at him, he deliberately broke off some flowers and dropped them onto the gravel. Reverend Wilson shouted, but Tom doubted that the police would be called and walked calmly to the bus stop.

While waiting at the bus stop for the #3 bus, he had plenty of time to think. Even in his young life, he'd heard that many men disliked their mothers-in-law yet didn't overreact like that. The reason must be that the Reverend was hiding something.

Why was he nervous? The racehorse and the art showed that he was obviously living beyond his means, as everyone knew that the struggling Church of Ireland wasn't prone to paying high salaries to their men of God. Maybe he'd won the Irish Sweepstakes. But probably not. Still, that didn't explain his rudeness.

Maybe the shy Mrs. Wilson had inherited but Don Melville had said that Olive Wiley didn't have much money. That was why he'd mailed her regular checks.

Tom had learned to observe people's expressions over the years, watching their eyes and mouths. He thought that he could tell when somebody was lying, hiding something or was afraid. While he didn't understand why Reverend Wilson might be afraid of him, a mild-mannered unassuming young guy simply looking for an old lady, Tom Brabazon was certain that Reverend Wilson was afraid.

The big question was why. 'Why' was a mystery to Tom.

The young man's main interest in life was minding his own business . . . in his spare time, it was his hobby. But Wilson's surprising treatment of him rankled and Tom disliked mysteries.

After all those years in Ireland hunting with hounds and listening to old Sean O'Sullivan, the retired con artist's many stories, he had a nose for scent. He could smell Reverend Wilson's scent and he suddenly felt like hunting it. Tom didn't want to unravel a family's mysteries, he just wanted to find an old lady who meant a lot to his coach's friend, a World War II hero, who, after all his war experiences to save freedom, deserved a promise to be kept.

Tom had promised to find Mrs. Wiley, probably dead but maybe alive. He would do so.

****

The next morning after training, Tom asked Dr. Stone for time off, explaining that he was searching for Mr. Melville's sister-in-law.

Permission granted, Tom hopped on another bus downtown to the office of the *Irish Times* on D'Olier Street and searched through the obituaries of the past five years. In those days before computers and even microfiche, this required searching through each day's paper and was tedious. Tom was quickly bored but, being determined by nature, stayed three hours and found just two Olive Wileys.

Neither was possible. One was a lady twelve years too old, who'd died in Co. Meath, in 1975, but had had no issue and the other was a twelve-year-old girl who'd been killed by a bus in Limerick City the previous month.

Tom guessed that his Mrs. Wiley was Anglo-Irish Protestant. When you have lived in Ireland, even for a short time, you know who's Anglo and who's Catholic. Wiley spelled that way meant Anglo-Irish. Irish Catholic priests are celibate, as everyone knows, and in those days very few Catholic girls married a Protestant. It was a very rare event so Tom ruled out the possibility of Mrs. Wilson being Catholic.

So, after consulting the phone book, he went to the Church of Ireland's head office to check on Wilson, taking yet another bus. He asked for a list of all their dead members in the past half-decade. Both Olive Wileys were listed but not his.

For added measure, he checked the curriculum vitae of Reverend Gerald John Foster Wilson, TCD B.A.1956, Dr. of Divinity 1962 and rector of Ballsbridge, Dublin, the suburb next to Sandymount and a much wealthier and higher class part of the city. Respectable people of solid middle class with some money lived in Sandymount. The wealthy lived in Ballsbridge, home of the Royal Dublin Society where the famed R.D.S. horse show is held every August. That's also the home of the rugby ground at Lansdowne Road where Ireland fights its international rugby matches and many embassies including the ugly U.S. embassy. Ballsbridge, not Sandymount, is where racehorse owners lived.

He found that Wilson's father was also a Church of Ireland minister, currently a Bishop out west in County Mayo with a still living wife. Young Wilson had obviously not yet inherited whatever meager amount dad and mum had saved.

Tom then returned to D'Olier Street and checked out Mrs. Wilson's racehorse Embezzler in the *Irish Times'* newspaper's office, where he was helped by the resident librarian, an aspiring young journalist named Cathy O'Toole.

Embezzler, she told him, was trained at The Curragh in Co. Kildare, by Trevor Baxter. The now three-year-old colt had cost 15,000 guineas—a guinea being five percent more than a pound—as a yearling, a high enough price before prices went through the roof in the Thoroughbred racing world. The horse had run in that year's two most important races placing fourth in the Irish Two Thousand Guineas and sixth in the Irish Derby, and had won his final start of the season, the Switzer Stakes.

Tom had been to the races in Ireland a few times absorbing quite a bit of knowledge about the sport over the years. Even he knew that the sire Mill Reef had been a champion and Derby winner in England and that his foals were expensive.

"The colt isn't top class but is above average," Cathy judged. "He's a good type but lacks enough acceleration to beat the best horses. He won't race again here this year because our flat racing season's almost over. The final flat meeting will be next week. Embezzler will probably end up in America because he'll find it impossible to win a top race here."

Cathy then discovered that the Wilsons owned two other racehorses, another trained by Mr. Baxter and one steeplechaser trained by a different man.

Three racehorses cost a lot of money to maintain. Few people anywhere can afford that much, let alone a minister. So how was Reverend Wilson managing it?

He asked for details of the trainer.

"Mr. Baxter," Cathy replied, "is a nice man and successful trainer. He's a jolly-natured Englishman who trains for the aristocracy and for pleasure, not money.

He's somebody choosy about selecting his owners." She added: "Would you like his address and phone number?"

"No, but thanks," Tom replied.

A Church of Ireland rector and his wife were unlikely candidates, Tom assumed, to rate as important in the racing world or to qualify to be an owner of Trevor Baxter, let alone be able to afford to own a Derby colt. Even though their rhododendrons were lovely, Tom couldn't understand how they could afford to buy a horse for 15,000 guineas. That's a lot of rhodo bushes.

The puzzle was the money.

It usually is, as Tom would discover over the years in his investigations.

Find the money and you've found the missing piece of the jigsaw puzzle, the missing person, their hideaway, the crime. Motives don't matter except in the courtroom and on TV. Criminals—and their lawyers—always justify their own actions. Motives are in the eye of the beholder. The real reason is because they can do the crime and get away with it, or think they can. Find the money and you'll discover how, when and where. 'Why' is for the movies.

So Tom asked himself: Where did the money come from to pay for the paintings and racehorses? Still irritated by the minister's rudeness, surprised by the man's nervousness and now puzzled by what was, he admitted, none of his business, Tom felt himself pushed, not simply to find Mrs. Wiley for somebody he barely knew, but by a new emotion . . . that he wanted to solve this mystery.

Tom returned to the bus stop at the southern end of Sandymount the next afternoon to wait for the maid, reasoning that she'd be unlikely to be a live-in (that tradition had stopped in Ireland in the 1950s), wouldn't have a car and couldn't afford to live nearby, so the bus was the only viable option for her to get home unless she had a bicycle.

Buses came and left while he cut hedges nearby, using a trimmer he'd bought at lunchtime, watching from a safe vantage spot out of sight of the house. His hedge trimming was to prevent anyone becoming suspicious about a young man hanging around doing nothing.

Two hedges were well-trimmed before the maid finally walked to the bus stop. Tom walked over, reasoned that her employer wouldn't have discussed their conversation but guessed that the maid, like most house servants the world over, knew exactly what was happening in the house. Tom knew that employers and customers foolishly tend to believe that the cleaning staff is deaf and blind, and sometimes their error is costly.

The irony is that the worse they are treated, the better the employees hear and remember, sometimes to their bosses' later discomfort, willingly enough to tell "secrets" to strangers. Lots of best selling 'tell all' books, embarrassing their ex-employers, are written by former employees of Royal families, important C.E.O.s and celebrities.

So Tom sat down one seat in front of the maid, turned with a smile and remarked at his surprise to see her again. Though uneducated, she wasn't stupid and realized that this meeting wasn't a coincidence. She apologized, embarrassed at Reverend Wilson's rudeness.

Mary, the maid, wanted to talk so Tom listened. She said that she thought that Tom looked like a nice young man.

"Do you," she asked, "know my son Peter who lives in America? He's in Boston." The Irish typically assume that everybody knows everybody else in the United States, believing that both countries are nearly the same size.

"No, sorry," Tom replied. "Texas is a long way from Boston."

Mary was surprised. She then announced that she had just quit because her boss had refused to raise her wage by a pound a week, claiming that he couldn't afford it and that she should be grateful to have a job because there were many unemployed people who'd love hers.

Mary said that the Reverend, while a lovely man to his parishioners, was nasty to his wife, who was afraid of him and that he spent her money.

"I know where Mrs. Wiley is," Mary announced with a triumphant smile, all loyalty to her former employer having evaporated with her resignation.

"She isn't dead at all, young man. She's living under the false name of Eileen O'Neill in St. Michael's Catholic nursing home in Dundrum."

Dundrum, Tom recalled, was a suburb several miles away in southwest Dublin, not far from Leopardstown racecourse or his old school.

Mary continued that Mrs. Wilson was forbidden by Reverend Wilson to contact her mother, but wrote letters anyway, which Mary mailed, and that the charming Minister of God grabbed all mail addressed to Mrs. Wiley.

Tom thanked Mary, got off at the bus stop in front of Trinity and hopped on the next bus to Dundrum. He walked for five minutes before turning onto the correct street, found St. Michael's nursing home and entered. He asked the first nun he saw for permission to see his aunt Mrs. Eileen O'Neill saying that he was the son of her brother, Don Melville, in Virginia. The nun said that Mrs. O'Neill was suffering from dementia.

"In fact, young man, you've wasted your time coming here," the nun told him. "She won't recognize you. She hasn't recognized anyone since her daughter stopped coming and the doctor says she's crazy. She certainly lies all day and blasphemes, saying that she's not a Catholic, says she's an atheist. Such horrible things that she says."

Tom didn't move. He wasn't going to leave without seeing her.

"You're better off not seeing her, young man, but since you've come from America," she relented. Then she continued chattering, "Have you met my brother Frank Prendergast? He lives in New York, that's close to Virginia, isn't it? I'm surprised you don't know him, thought everyone in America did. Well, here's her room."

Tom saw an ancient and thin woman in dirty nightclothes, rocking back and forth, with tattered grey hair, angry eyes and spitting at the TV, moaning incoherently, smelly and disheveled with deep scratches down both arms. He was shocked. There were restraints on her legs and she was locked under what looked like a seatbelt.

As if speaking to an imbecile, or a 'gombeen' or 'eejit' as the Irish would say, the nun introduced the visitor very slowly to the woman, who twisted her neck and stared at Tom. He winced when she spat as he was named as her nephew.

"I have no nephew. Who the hell are you?" She was unimpressed and disbelieving. The nun pulled on Tom's arm to leave but he leaned forward and spoke slowly, clearly, in the old lady's left ear.

"Mrs. Wiley, your brother-in-law Don Melville in Upperville, Virginia, asked me to find you. You never answered his letters. He said to say 'Les Gloches,' that you'll understand."

Hearing the names of Don Melville and the Swiss village, the woman suddenly began crying, threw out her arms and called out, "How is Don? Thank you for coming. Sister Clare, this is my nephew from America. Young man, please get me the hell out of here. Now!"

Tom got Mrs. Wiley discharged within the hour and gradually discovered the whole story.

The Reverend Wilson had stolen her house, taken her money and got her committed to the Catholic retirement home telling the nuns that she was a crazy woman incapable of telling the truth. He intercepted her mail, cashed her savings and all her checks spending it on racehorses and art. The social cachet of being a racehorse owner and spending time with the really rich excited him. His wife Margaret was petrified of him.

Tom took Cathy O'Toole out to dinner that night. The young journalist got her scoop, broke the story in the *Irish Times*, front page, and a promotion. The embarrassed Bishop, Wilson's boss, couldn't explain to Cathy and her readers why nobody in the Church—he, to be precise—had wondered how a rector with a non-working wife could afford three racehorses.

Cathy won her dream of becoming a sports correspondent and, a few years later, interviewed an athlete at the Olympics who somehow reminded her a lot of the young man who'd helped her break her first big story but had had a beard and a different name, Mike Dickinson, in Dublin.

Reverend Wilson was stripped of both his parish duties and his ministership, arrested and served four years in jail for embezzlement and other charges. He was forced to sell his horses. The price he received for Embezzler went straight to his lawyer to pay his legal bills.

After Tom and Mrs. Wiley had told their story at the Dundrum police station, Tom went with two detectives to

Park Avenue in Sandymount to watch the arrest. After being handcuffed, Wilson shouted at Tom:

"I'll kill you for this, you bastard. I promise you."

Detective McGrath quickly rabbit-punched Wilson in the right kidney, kicked the back of his right knee and gave him another kick in the kidney as the holy man collapsed onto the gravel. McGrath then opened Wilson's mouth, shoved some stones in and forced him to swallow. It was over so quickly that Tom barely saw it happen.

The detective announced firmly that Tom had seen nothing and added: "This bastard will have a stomach ache for the next day or two. It'll teach him that crime doesn't pay."

Tom laughed at Wilson. "I'm not worried, you thief. You're in handcuffs, you're going to jail and you don't know who I am."

"How did you guess? Nobody else did," Wilson gasped.

"You were rude for no reason and your hands were shaking," Tom replied. "That and Embezzler's winning race photograph on the mantelpiece. The name was the real tip-off."

McGrath looked around the beautiful gardens with the large, two-storied rambling house in the background and commented drily, "To pay for this, Reverend, I'd be supposin' that you charge plenty for confessions. Is that when you started stealing?"

****

Tom couldn't sleep that night. He'd enjoyed this. This was a buzz, as good as winning races.

The next morning at breakfast, his team was impressed by the lead story in the *Irish Times*.

"Didya see this yet?" asked the squad's best sprinter, George Hawkins. "This Yank is something else, a real good guy. Makes us all look good, doesn't he?"

Tom poured his coffee.

"Hey, where were you yesterday, Tom, after training? You took off. Where didya go?" Hawkins was friendly, unsuspicious.

"Just wandering around town, being a tourist, seeing the city a bit," Tom answered quietly. He noticed Dr. Stone's quick smile and was relieved when his coach kept silent.

Mrs. Wiley was reunited with her daughter at the police station. They never saw Tom again.

Six months later, the day after they watched the former Reverend but-now-convicted-criminal Mr. Wilson standing scared in the dock to receive his sentence, they flew west to a new life in Upperville, Virginia.

Chapter 3   SARAH and TOM

Sarah Silver was frustrated because Tom, her lover, wouldn't open up to her.

What about pillow talk, she wondered, as she gazed at Tom's sleeping face, trying to understand what made him tick. Where did he come from, why wouldn't he talk about himself, why was he so . . . Sarah searched for the right word . . . so secretive . . . so, almost un-American.

Tom refused to talk about himself.

Americans expect openness. Make an appointment to see a doctor and you'll be handed a very long questionnaire and all questions must be answered. Some small animal vets require a Social Security Number, not for their patient, but for the owner. Rent a TV and you'll be asked for a complete autobiography, plus the names of five friends. No wonder social networking is so popular in the United States.

Politicians wanting to be elected for office are pretty much required to give every detail of their lives to the public and media. Even their tax returns and health records are made public. No records, no chance of winning, because that's the trade-off. Their lives are publicly traced back to infancy.

One presidential candidate in the 1990s stood a reasonable chance of being nominated as the Republican candidate until a first grade classmate told a journalist about the candidate's temper tantrum one day in the classroom. The resulting furor somehow extinguished the candidate's chances of being nominated.

Such openness is also expected among ordinary citizens in their daily activities. Anyone secretive and unwilling to "reveal all" is regarded with suspicion. Maybe that's the way it should be, who knows? Secretive people in the United States are thought to be hiding something.

The something is automatically assumed to be bad because, otherwise, the belief is that the person would be open. Secrets are unfashionable and unwelcome in modern America.

Sarah Silver had a dilemma. A psychology student, with the primary and immediate ambition of obtaining a Mrs. Degree, she was worried about her relationship with Tom. While his mystery was attractive, his refusal to tell her about himself and his feelings upset her.

What was he hiding? He kept deflecting her questions—aloof, polite but vague.

It was maddening. She hated mysteries and read the final chapter of Agatha Christie's novels before the first page. Sarah thought that the saying "curiosity killed the cat" was simply for cats.

Sarah wanted a completely open relationship with Tom and had revealed almost, but not all, to him about her family, schooling and dreams and hoped that he'd reciprocate in kind. But he didn't. She kept her dream of marriage to him a secret.

She'd slept with him, partly because he was sexy but also to get him to talk. After five months and twelve days of making love, their relationship seemed no further advanced. He was still secretive, she knew no more about him than when they'd first had sex and it was driving her crazy. Tom just wouldn't tell her anything.

He didn't get huffy about it although he was becoming privately irritated by her need for "openness." Both her other lovers, now history, had prattled on constantly about themselves. They'd annoyed her because they wouldn't let her talk.

Why was Tom different? Weren't men all the same?

Sarah was proud of Tom, how he excelled on the track and in the classroom, felt protected by him, his strength and manliness. He was gentle, reliable, punctual and sometimes moody–his mind far away, never sharing his thoughts.

His eyes were kind, but wary and deep. She could never find subtitles.

Once when he was quiet, she offered him: "A penny for your thoughts," hoping to catch him momentarily un-guarded. He wasn't caught out, replying: "For God's sake, why? Save your money."

She knew that he would protect her and always listen to her problems. Sarah loved being recognized on campus as his girlfriend, as the girlfriend of the star athlete, the best runner and potential State champion, people talking about maybe the Olympics one day.

She didn't understand why he hated having his photograph taken for the college paper or their town's weekly, why he didn't encourage the sports media, why he preferred to be left alone to run and study. She'd disliked his beard, the one he'd grown before his trip to Ireland, and was mightily relieved when he shaved it off after his return. Its absence had been a nice present, she thought.

Sarah joked that his eyes were shut in every photograph whenever Tom couldn't avoid the camera. She wondered why he hated parties, dancing, fireworks, all loud noises, crowds. She wanted an explanation.

Sarah wouldn't have believed the truth.

Tom knew that Sarah wouldn't understand even if he'd told her. He didn't want to. Sarah had yet to learn that nothing in this world—not money, not blackmail, not even sex—could make Tom Brabazon do anything against his will. He wasn't hard-nosed but he was a survivor, on his own strange terms.

He didn't open up to her, because he couldn't, not with her, not with anybody, really. Sarah was too ordinary, too decent, starry-eyed and clear-minded, a middle-class suburban American girl from Richmond, Virginia, who'd never suffered or experienced any real pain. She'd had a happy, normal childhood.

Tom hadn't.

Not getting a new car for her 18th birthday didn't rate, Tom reckoned, with his life's experiences. Sarah was a nice girl, he liked her, but she was way too nice, too carefree, too . . . there's that word again . . . too open for him. He'd seen too much, too much ugliness, stared into the crater, had demons, ones he couldn't shake. They owned him and gave him nightmares.

Sarah Silver was a perfectly pleasant girl, who'd make an excellent wife, life partner, friend and confidante for someone, someone like her who needed her, who'd grown up like she did with a happy, comfortable life, but it couldn't be him. Tom knew that Sarah couldn't understand, because of her background and because he didn't understand himself.

All Tom knew was that he wanted to run. Needed to run, keep running, every day, it was his obsession. Run faster, faster, to win, the only way he knew to be independent. Girls were fine, college was fine, jobs to pay the bills were fine, but the only love he still had remaining for anything was running.

He was a runner.

He had to run. It was his compulsion.

To be a runner he had to be independent, reliant on only himself. The coaches helped, his favorite being Dr. Stone, but it was his sweat when he was out pounding on the track, not depending on anyone's support, doing it himself, alone. He preferred that, needed that.

When he ran, he had to concentrate on his running, didn't–couldn't–think about the past, the bad times, being let down, the horrors, the dreadful images, which returned in his nightmares, the awful murder of his mother and so much else.

Tom had seen so much more than the carefree students giggling in his classes and in the cafeteria. He was too uncomfortable to join the crowd even when they admired his running. Nobody could touch or damage him while he was running or get inside his mind when he was on the track.

He didn't need anyone now and had learned to depend on nobody. It wasn't safe, or wise. He'd learned the hard way that if you love somebody, they either let you down . . . or they die.

****

Tom was an ordinary enough kid, with an ordinary enough life, until the afternoon of his 11th birthday. When his father didn't arrive home for his birthday party at their ten-acre property in Woodbine, Maryland, about an hour's drive from Baltimore, Tom's feelings were crushed.

Dad had promised that, no matter what, he'd be there, wouldn't work overtime. He wouldn't miss his son's birthday party, even though he'd been away at work all Christmas Day, especially since the family was still reeling from his brother Billy's death a few months earlier.

He'd learned that his dad, his best friend, his hero, his hunting companion and teacher about life and wildlife, had to be away at work on holidays, weekends and nights despite other dads having normal 9 to 5, Monday to Friday jobs.

Tom understood that, but when you're eleven and it's your birthday, well, you just want your dad to be there. His friends could count on their dads being at their birthday parties but he couldn't even explain to his friends why his dad wasn't there, because his parents had sworn him to secrecy about his dad's job.

People, they'd said, would treat him differently if they knew that his dad was a police officer. People, his parents told him, disliked cops. He didn't understand why.

He never forgot getting angry at his dad for being late, then not showing up for his party at all. He never forgot his shame at being angry. He never got a chance to say he forgave his dad, or even to say goodbye.

At about the time Stevie Walwyn, for that was Tom Brabazon's name at the age of 11, was blowing out his candles, upset that Daddy didn't love him enough to be there, Daddy was being shot by a suspect in a slum in the city of Baltimore.

Tom's father was a detective, chasing a thief in a nickel-and-dime robbery gone sour. While little Stevie was unwrapping his presents, his dad was bleeding to death in a gutter on a street in the ghetto, a soon-to-be forgotten hero in the unceasing war on crime.

****

They had gone on many hunting trips, just the pair of them, camping in the Blue Ridge Mountains of Virginia and in the Poconos of eastern Pennsylvania. Their favorite spot was some woods near Sperryville, Rappahannock County, Virginia, only a few miles from his grandparents' farm. They'd camped there the night before his birthday.

His dad, Dick Walwyn, who'd taught him so much about hunting and the outdoors, had grown up, poor and barefoot, in the foothills of the Blue Ridge Mountains in north central Virginia, an hour's drive southwest of Washington D.C. on a hilly, rocky and thinly-soiled farm, which was split by the boundaries of Rappahannock and Culpeper counties.

He'd quickly learned that there was no free lunch, no real handout from a distant government. "The War on Poverty" was a Washington slogan which meant nothing to his family and neighbors, where the only way to survive was by hunting and catching your own meat.

Dick grew up an expert on tracking animals, outguessing their movements, understanding their behavior. A lover of wildlife and the woods, he passed on his knowledge to his son.

That was all the inheritance Tom would get and, while it proved valuable many years later, he received it far too early. He was only eleven years old.

Chapter 4   OXFORD

It was every parent's nightmare. Their child was missing and had been for four months.

They begged Tom to get her home by Christmas.

He expected it to be a fairly routine search but he was wrong.

He fell in love. He didn't expect that. That scared him.

Different girls. Identical twins.

On a snowy afternoon in December during training on the campus of the University of Manassas, athletics coach Dr. Stone called Tom into his office to have a quiet chat.

He'd be grateful, he said quietly, if Brabazon would help another of his friends with a similar problem.

Tom preferred to be left alone to run, that being his interest and focused ambition, but the gruff, tough, old World War II veteran was not the type of guy to be refused. Brabazon assumed that Stone wouldn't walk him up the garden path again without a back-up plan, so he agreed.

Besides, catching that clergyman embezzler in Ireland had been satisfying. Dr. Stone had shaken his hand during the flight home to Washington and said: "Well done." His coach's compliment had been as pleasing to Tom as his joy at finding Mrs. Wiley.

Dr. Stone hated interstates and heavy traffic so, instead of taking the quicker way on the traffic-strewn 1-95 beltway around Washington D.C., he drove a scenic, meandering route that evening, driving them up to Delaware from Manassas, southwest of Washington D.C., north through quiet countryside to Leesburg and across Maryland, passing through Tom's original hometown of Woodbine. Tom had moved away from Woodbine at age 11 after the murder of his father and this, 13 years later, was his first return.

Woodbine appeared to have changed very little. Tom wondered what he would have become had he grown up there and how different his life would have been. Would that have been him among that group of young men he saw walking down Main Street, he wondered. What if his father had survived? What if both his parents could still have been alive now?

He kept his thoughts, typically, to himself.

They crossed the state line into Delaware.

Best known for being the official headquarters, for tax purposes, of many of America's largest corporations, Delaware is the ancestral home of the wealthy du Pont family. The family's wealth originally stemmed from gunpowder manufacture before quickly diversifying into the production of many types of chemicals.

The Du Pont Company was one of America's great family-owned business enterprises for a long time and continues as a multi-billion dollar corporation today.

Their destination was a grand old estate, in du Pont ownership for generations, a few miles outside the state capital of Wilmington and their hosts were a distressed middle-age couple and their beautiful 20-year-old daughter, whom Tom immediately wanted to ask out.

This couple was facing every parent's nightmare.

Mr. du Pont Scott explained that their twin daughters had gone to Europe for their summer vacation during college recess but only one, Jennifer, had returned home in August.

The other twin, Sophie, had stayed behind after she and Jennifer had argued about a guy, which was nothing new, but this particular guy had turned out to be trouble. Although identical twins and the best of friends, they were unwilling to share boyfriends.

Sometimes they enjoyed teasing and fooling men about which sister was which. Only their mother was 100% correct all the time. Not even their father was always able to distinguish them—but whenever they'd both fallen for the same fortunate young man, well, they'd argue.

They'd both lost their virginity on prom night, Jennifer with her date but Sophie, who was somewhat wilder in temperament, had ditched her beau and ended up in the back seat of a Mercedes, belonging to a boy she knew only vaguely from tennis at the country club.

Their parents, having not forgotten their own celebrations at that age, were suspicious about the prom night's outcome but hoped that they were wrong. The good news was that neither girl had gotten pregnant.

In Oxford, England, when they'd argued over the young man, Jennifer told Sophie that she was returning home. She took the train to London and the underground to Heathrow, postponed her flight to Philadelphia for two days, hoping that Sophie would appear at their London hotel or the Pan Am check-in counter but finally gave up, jumped onto a plane and flew home.

She and her parents were sure that Sophie would return soon but as the weeks came and went, college resumed without her and the weekly postcards came regularly at first then fortnightly and finally stopped altogether. Worry began to overtake irritation at Sophie's adolescent and irresponsible behavior.

Now, months later, just two weeks before Christmas, her parents were justifiably scared. They'd had no luck with the American Embassy in London who just didn't care about a runaway rich girl even one that possessed one of the greatest names of American aristocracy.

They had good reason to be worried even though there was no proof of kidnapping or foul play . . . no ransom notes or fingers in the mail, so the FBI (who lacked jurisdiction in Britain) couldn't do anything.

Her parents had flown to England but, not surprisingly, they'd found no trace of their beautiful American daughter. There was no indication of a crime and she was of age. Scotland Yard, after assigning a pair of young detectives to the case, who checked hospitals and morgues without progress for two days, shrugged and suggested private detectives instead.

The du Pont Scotts then hired private detectives with no success, only receiving endless envelopes of invoices and receipts for expenses. A client with the du Pont name was the opportunity of a lifetime for a private investigator and none of their choices declined the opportunity to milk their bank account.

None admitted—perhaps they didn't understand—that an American in Britain or Europe stood less chance of being told the truth by locals hiding dark secrets or simply disliking Yanks than of finding an invited Arab at a Jewish wedding.

Even though the Americans had rescued Britain and Europe from the Nazis and the brilliance and foresight of General George Marshall had restored their economies with his Marshall Plan after World War II, it was curious how seldom the British and Europeans acknowledged American help. Perhaps it wasn't a lack of appreciation but more a desire to forget the War and all its misery.

The fall-out came when American tourists and businesspeople visited what is now called Europe—from Galway to Greece to Berlin—to discover that the welcome mat was often less than the Americans expected, the motto being "Don't talk to outsiders."

"How," asked the worried parents, "can a girl just disappear, leaving no trace?"

Tom Brabazon wasn't surprised about the Scotts' lack of progress. Having grown up in Ireland, he knew first-hand the locals' unwillingness to help foreigners.

Nor was he surprised that a young person could just disappear. He himself had done exactly that seven years earlier.

Tom decided to accept the du Pont Scotts' offer of "we'll pay anything; we just want our darling Sophie back." He was sure that the private detectives had heard the same, to their considerable advantage. After all, he'd received no better offers for the holiday season except for Sarah's, which he'd declined.

Sarah had insisted but he'd held firm. Thanksgiving at her parents' house had been fine but Christmas would suggest that an engagement was expected and he wasn't ready, interested or willing to get married to Sarah.

Or to anybody. He was a runner.

Tom didn't know England well but, as a college student, he figured he knew where to start looking for a lost college girl. After that, it should be almost the same as tracking a deer through the woods in Virginia or a lost hound in Ireland except that he'd be tracking people in towns.

Patience, observation, listening and pretending to be the quarry were in his blood. He'd been taught by experts. The difference was that animals told no lies, the woods were easy to understand, there was no dishonesty there, just life and death and survival, survival of the fittest.

Tom believed that he knew the value of his skills and time and gave his price to the frantic parents. Unlike the private eyes, he didn't care how rich they were or how important they were in society.

"That's fine. Don't worry about the cost, Tom," replied Sophie's father.

"We love her. We want her home. Please, please find her," added Mrs. du Pont Scott.

He was intrigued by the challenge of finding their daughter: it would be a hunt. He could be alone after the forced, unavoidable throngs of other students at University. He felt uncomfortable in large groups of people.

It turned out that Tom wouldn't be alone on this trip, because Jennifer announced that she'd accompany him. He initially refused because he preferred to be alone when possible–that was another aspect of his personality that psychology student and wannabe wife Sarah Silver couldn't understand–but he was persuaded that he was wrong this time.

Jennifer pointed out that she could show him exactly where they'd been, probably find some of the people they'd met, that she felt guilty for having left Sophie behind and, besides, she could be there when they found her sister. Jennifer didn't add that she thought that Tom was cute.

"Don't worry, Mom and Dad, I won't disappear, I promise," Jennifer added. "I'll help Tom and he'll protect me."

"Honey," said her less-than-relaxed mother, "One missing daughter is bad enough." But Dr. Stone agreed with her idea so Jennifer's reasoning won.

Mr. and Mrs. du Pont Scott told Tom that they'd buy two plane tickets and book hotel rooms for them in London.

During the long drive back to Virginia the next morning, Tom and Dr. Stone discussed the meeting and planned trip.

"For God's sake, Tom," said Dr. Stone, "don't let Jennifer vanish. That is an order."

The old vet then probed into Tom's background but the young man gave away nothing other than his university activities. He expected Dr. Stone to get offended, huffy or even angry but was relieved when he didn't. Tom preferred to keep his unusual and chaotic life story secret. He liked his coach and realized that there was more, much more, to this old man than appeared on the surface. Tom liked that: he was the same but, surely, for different reasons.

Unlike the students who attended university with Tom, Dr. Stone's generation, formed by the Depression then World War II, didn't prattle about its feelings and angst.

Tom did manage to get Dr. Stone reminiscing about his life as a horse vet in Virginia before the war changed everything. He was riveted by his amusing stories and extraordinary characters, the old-fashioned, pre-antibiotic treatments, so very similar to the stories of another vet, James Herriott, set in the Yorkshire Dales 3,000 miles away.

Tom had a gift for getting other people to talk. They thought that he was a great listener but this habit of being silent and asking questions, created by patience and to suppress his painful memories, allowed him to prevent revealing himself.

He wouldn't do that for anyone, not for Sarah or Dr. Stone or anybody. It hurt too much and couldn't be changed or fixed, so why talk about it, he reckoned. He actually enjoyed hearing about other people's lives and their experiences, finding most of them more or less interesting and informative.

He reckoned that he'd never know when some of it would prove handy and he got to hear about lots of new parts of many lives. Tom had learned early in life that nearly everybody, no matter their age, background, successes or place in the world, nearly everybody enjoyed talking about themselves.

Sit beside a stranger on an airplane or a train and get them to open up.

They seldom stop until the trip is over and rarely stop talking about the subject they rate as the most interesting in the world. It's not sex, not even money but themselves. Sometimes some of their stories are true. Tom had figured out that when people were talking about themselves, they asked him very little about himself.

Tom's bottom line was not to reveal any truths about the real Tom or Dick or Steve or whatever the hell his real identity was. Tom loved listening, learning, was always amused that this stranger had lived an entire life, with its ups and downs, excitement and sadness, with no connection to Tom and that neither party had known of each other's existence until that serendipitous event when they were issued seats next to each other.

Tom always enjoyed the small pleasure that his traveling companion, male or female, would never know any more about him when they said goodbye than they'd known before they'd met.

Jennifer du Pont Scott proved a challenge to Tom's determination to keep silent.

A week later, on the flight from JFK in New York to Heathrow in London, Jennifer proved the opposite of Sarah Silver on the shrewdness level. While Sarah was naïve, trusting and as open as a book, Jennifer had been taught throughout her life to be cautious and that men, gold diggers, would flock to her not because of herself but for her wealth and name . . . and for the money and glamour she would provide.

Jennifer had been raised "privileged" but possessed the rare virtue among the children of the ultra rich: that although spoiled and kept away from the nastiness of the real world, she was not blind to reality or arrogant or obnoxious. There was a lot of depth in Jennifer, which appealed to Tom.

An hour into the flight, Jennifer revealed that though she loved her grandmother, the old lady had always preached to the twins that men would only be attracted to their money, never to them. As a result, Jennifer admitted, both girls were insecure.

Jennifer announced that she wanted to travel for a few years, using her mother's maiden name, being anonymous, taking odd jobs, something not allowed in her family and discover the world while being treated just like any above average 20-year-old girl.

She explained that her parents would require her to marry someone as rich as them, another Ivy leaguer with a private school education, homes in Vail and the Bahamas, racehorses and yachts, servants and large stock portfolios managed by personal retainers on Wall Street.

She wasn't looking for rebellion, didn't want to revolt for true love or life in a suburban 2 up and 3 down with a mortgage. She just wanted to live in the real world for a while, not in the grittiest parts of the world, no south Chicago, Haiti or south Philadelphia, not that extreme. Just something normal before she married someone she liked well enough and produced two children, who would be raised just like her.

"Tell me about yourself, Tom," she finally asked after they'd awoken from broken sleeps, her head resting on his shoulder. A murky dawn was breaking.

"I'm just a college student, studying languages." He hoped that was vague enough to make her lose interest.

"Where are you from?" she continued politely.

"Lots of places, my dad traveled a lot."

"Where's home?"

"Nowhere, really. Never stayed anywhere long enough. My dad is dead, he was killed in an accident."

"Oh, I'm so sorry," came Jennifer's reply. "What about your mom? Where's she?"

"Dead as well, there's just me left." Tom was hoping she'd stop asking questions.

"What do you want to do?"

"I'm a runner, a miler, 2 miles, 3 miles."

The cold wet coastline and checkerboard stone-walled, dark green fields of County Sligo in the west of Ireland appeared tiny through the rainclouds and they both peered through the window, Jennifer with excitement.

Tom remembered the week he'd spent in the town of Sligo on a school field trip, a happy memory. The students had wandered through villages and along country lanes, interviewing the locals about the area's geography and history. He'd had many good times in Ireland but the bad ones had been worse. Those were the horrors that gave him nightmares.

"No," Jennifer continued, "I mean, what do you want to do for a career? Languages, does that mean diplomacy or international business, United Nations, what?"

Tom replied that he didn't know, hadn't decided. He was a runner, why couldn't she accept his answer, drop the subject, stop asking him questions and talk about herself again, like most people.

"Why," asked Jennifer with an insight that surprised Tom, "if you're just an ordinary college student as you say, why does Dr. Stone think that you can find my sister?"

"Dunno," replied Tom, who was beginning to realize that she wasn't just a very pretty, very rich face and that perhaps he needed to find the answer himself.

"Are you in the CIA?" Jennifer continued with a laugh, as the plane began its descent over Somerset where King Arthur and his Knights had played a millennium before.

"No, of course not."

"But that would be sooo exciting. James Bond is so sexy," she added dreamily.

"He was MI6, not CIA," Tom corrected before adding, "I can't, won't, take orders so the CIA wouldn't be my style. Besides, most of them are nuts, according to the movies and TV shows, aren't they?" Every few years the public discovers new versions of the CIA's peculiar color of insanity.

"But languages would be good in the CIA."

"I'm sure they would but I'm equally sure that the CIA isn't for me. Maybe I'll become an archaeologist, I dunno." Tom realized that it was past time to have a good, simple, better, pat answer to people's questions about his future.

He decided to choose optometry as an impenetrable cover. Few would ask enough probing questions for him to trip over that choice but he realized that he'd have to switch his major to science for anybody to believe it.

Jennifer continued to press, just to make conversation, be friendly.

Tom didn't mind, well he did actually but Jennifer's probing didn't bother him as much as Sarah's or other people's questions. He didn't understand why but most people asked questions just to be polite, to pass the time, he reckoned. He hoped that they couldn't spot the worry in his eyes.

He was sure that Jennifer didn't have designs on him as a husband as he didn't qualify–he had zero stock portfolio, let alone an eight digit one and he sure didn't possess blue blood. He was the son of a dead Baltimore police officer from a hardscrabble farm in Virginia. Jennfer's parents would always consider him a servant even if, then he corrected himself . . . *when* he brought home their lost daughter.

"I'm a runner. I just want to be the best runner in the world."

"But why does Dr. Stone think you can find Sophie when everyone else has failed?"

Tom guessed that it was because of the minister and the old lady in Dublin but had no intention of breathing a syllable about that. He didn't have any insight into why Dr. Stone had selected him for the Irish job, although he assumed that it was no coincidence.

"Well, maybe," he sighed, knowing that she wouldn't stop until she got an answer, "because I do a bit of search and rescue in Virginia, in my spare time." This was true.

"I like finding missing people." This was also true. "I enjoy figuring out mysteries, the challenge. I'm good at them. I like helping people in trouble."

Tom stopped, annoyed that he'd revealed too much of himself, couldn't understand why Jennifer could get him to talk when his girlfriend and others couldn't. He was suddenly nervous that, having opened up a bit to her, Jennifer would manage to peer down and find the horrors, which he had promised to himself that he'd never reveal to anyone.

Jennifer nodded and was quiet for a while.

After landing the plane, the captain announced over the loudspeaker while taxiing to the gate that the temperature and weather were respectively 42 degrees Fahrenheit and cloudy, a comparatively tropical day for London in December.

At that news, many of the passengers who'd never before spent a day in England in December and were used
to sub-zero temperatures at home whooped with pleasure
and removed their heavy winter coats. When the door
opened, allowing a blast of London's winter-chilled, damp
air into the plane and freezing the passengers, they were
shocked, chilled to the bone and scurried to put their
coats back on.

While standing and waiting to leave the plane, Jennifer asked more questions.

"Well, thank you, Mr. Tom Brabazon, for being willing
to help me and my family. But why *are* you helping us
and at Christmastime? Where are you going to spend
Christmas?"

The answer to the first question was easy. Tom repeated: "Because Dr. Stone asked me, he's my coach. I
respect him. He's a hard man to refuse." He paused.

"He's also going to help me become an Olympic champion." Again, he felt an irritation that he'd let his guard
down, revealing too much.

"Second, I like you and your parents and feel sorry for
what the three of you are going through. I don't care
about your wealth or any of that."

Tom didn't answer question two. He didn't know. Had
he known then how he'd spend Christmas Eve, he'd have
found an alternative.

Jennifer gave him a kiss. "Well thank you again and
when we find my sister, I'll sleep with you. As my personal thank you. OK?"

That sounded like a great paycheck to Tom. Jennifer
was very attractive, not stuck up but sensible and very
appealing. He wasn't, what was the word, betrothed or

committed to Sarah Silver, so sleeping with Jennifer wouldn't be wrong, not a sin, he thought.

Besides, he hadn't found Miss Sophie du Pont Scott yet. But he would, he was sure. He found what he hunted or went hungry. He was only worried that when he found her that she might not be alive.

The reality was worse than death.

After Immigration where the official didn't spot anything wrong with his forged passport—that rascal Mark Moulton in Dublin was damn good at forgeries—and Customs, Tom and Jennifer took the train into central London. Then they took a taxi to the luxurious five-star Connaught Hotel, far too fancy for Tom but that's what Mr. du Pont Scott had booked and it made him most uncomfortable. There was plenty of Scottish and Yorkshire blood in him. He hated spending money.

What's a Scotchman with every ounce of generosity squeezed out of him? A Yorkshireman.

Tom had never experienced luxury before and he disliked spending other people's money unnecessarily. A mattress at a youth hostel was good enough for him. Jennifer, however, laughed at his complaint and disappeared into her room, laughing at his mulishness.

After showers and naps in separate rooms, they re-emerged post jetlag, feeling much more alert in mid-afternoon, grabbing a quick lunch before catching an unheated train to Oxford. The cold froze their toes and fingers.

On the plane across the Atlantic, Tom had quizzed Jennifer for every detail of her summer trip to England. Now, on the train, he made her repeat her story with particular emphasis on the guy who'd split up her and Sophie.

She admitted that she'd slept with him but that he'd made her uneasy. She wouldn't explain precisely why but Tom decided that, if he pressed—and he would—her distrust of Frederick would be revealed. She didn't have a photo and didn't know his surname.

Tom frankly found it odd that Jennifer would have sex with a man whose surname she didn't know. The right atmosphere and plenty of charm, he supposed. Tom asked plenty of questions about Sophie.

Both girls had stayed in Oxford with a friend who shared a flat above a shop near the corner of Brasenose Lane and St. Mary's Passage, sandwiched between the Museum of the History of Science and Brasenose College. Jennifer said that Frederick had lived elsewhere in a house in Headington, several miles to the east of the city.

Frederick had described himself as a student. She didn't remember which subject. Tom felt that was odd, also.

****

Both Tom and Jennifer were keen to start hunting the minute they left the train station in Oxford. Never having been there before, however, he decided to get his bearings by walking—no taxi—through the ancient city, whose first college was founded in 1167. Jennifer led the way.

Tom believed in scouting the territory on foot, getting a feel of direction. The cold seeped relentlessly into their bones despite walking quickly.

"Let's check every place where you saw Frederick," suggested Tom. "He's the key to finding Sophie."

"OK," Jennifer replied.

The first place they checked out was the Ashmolean museum on Beaumont Street, built in 1683, where Jennifer said she'd gone with Frederick the first day they'd met. The museum contained an extraordinary collection of . . . almost everything collectible. It was fascinating but they were disappointed. Frederick wasn't there.

They ate lunch in the turf tavern in Bath Street, another popular place for students, a fascinating old pub which made hot buttered rum punch in winter heated in a huge tureen. Jennifer explained that one glass removed the pain of the cold and wet while two glasses stopped you walking. They decided against drinking any. They didn't see Frederick there either so Tom insisted that they move on.

Tom asked Jennifer to show him where Frederick had first met the girls, exactly how and what and where everything had happened. He had to find the trail and pick up the scent. This wasn't a TV show and he wasn't Inspector Clouseau. This was real.

Frederick had introduced himself to the twins in a student-packed pub on St. Michael's Street, so after lunch they went straight there after checking into a youth hostel. Tom insisted.

"We're not going to find either your sister or this creep Frederick if we eat afternoon tea in or stay at Oxford's equivalent, if it has one, of your fancy Connaught Hotel."

When Jennifer complained, Tom asked, "Did Freddy meet you at a fancy hotel or where there are lots of students? Did you see any students at the Connaught, except for us?" This time, Tom won.

They walked past dozens of identical bicycles and through the door into the pub, a place that seemed a cross between a café and a common room for the prefects at his boarding school in Ireland. Every chair was filled, bags were strewn nearly everywhere, talking filled the room, the smell of marijuana and beer overpowered the food and there was nobody over the age of 25.

When Tom scanned the room the thought occurred to him that, if these kids were the finest of their generation and would become the future presidents, prime ministers and other rulers of the Earth, maybe it might be wise to move to a different planet and the sooner the better.

They just looked like normal college kids back in Virginia, probably a lot smarter and a bit softer, but ordinary people.

He'd always been in awe of Oxford because he'd been taught at school by equally awed teachers that Oxford was the pinnacle of education, that only the brightest and best were selected to attend there.

The crème de la crème, the smartest of each generation, the best A level stars from each private school went to Oxford but he saw no immediately obvious budding Sir Winston Churchills or Bill Clintons in this place.

Several Rhodes Scholars may have been inside that modest, teeming café that afternoon but if they had been, Tom didn't spot them. He detected no brilliance or dazzles as he looked around. Just a bunch of kids, identical to those back at Manassas University except for wearing scarves in a futile attempt to defeat the frigid English air. They weren't starving to death but instead were trying to pick up a bedmate to beat the cold.

"He's not here, either," Jennifer reported with disappointment. Tom had guessed that it wasn't going to be that easy.

"We'll keep looking until we find them both," Tom reassured her. "We're not going home without your sister. The trail begins here in Oxford."

They took a taxi to a house in suburban Headington, several miles away, where Frederick had taken Jennifer but nobody was at home. Next door, however, there was a family who'd never heard of him. The woman said that only an older man lived there but sometimes his son visited. Another dead end. Tom was patient. You learn to be patient in the woods and on the streets.

As their taxi was pulling away, after they'd climbed back in, Jennifer deflated again, they heard the woman shouting at them. Tom asked the taxi driver to stop and the woman ran up to them, her right hand outstretched with some mail.

"These," she panted, "came today. We share the mailbox and the neighbor isn't home yet." Tom supposed that the woman read the mail before passing it along, but that didn't matter to him. He thanked her without asking why she'd hand her neighbor's mail to a stranger. He wasn't going to give her the chance of snatching it back.

Jennifer got excited again and Tom, despite his natural skepticism, felt a glimmer of hope inside. It slowly subsided, however, as they poured through the bits and pieces. There were bills, all addressed to the same man but the only mail to anybody named Frederick and the only piece Tom kept, was from a dentist's office in Geneva, Switzerland, reminding him of his next appointment which was on December 24th at 11.00 a.m. Tom had been in Geneva once before.

"But," Jennifer complained, "Frederick told me he lives in Paris so this Geneva postcard must be a mistake, somehow."

The thought occurred to Tom that Frederick might be a liar. He turned out to be much worse.

They returned to central Oxford in another attempt to locate Frederick, this time in another students' hangout.

They stopped off at a shop to buy a backpack, which Tom suggested in order for Jennifer to look more like a student, before going to the Student Union where Tom asked Jennifer to mingle. He wandered unnoticed through the crowd, watching Jennifer and those who spoke to her and how they reacted to her, hoping that the scent would pick up again. It always did. Just needed to be patient, quiet, observant and watchful.

Tom enjoyed being able to semi-vanish in a room or in a crowd and he melted into the room. Jennifer looked but couldn't spot him watching her and those who spoke to her and how they reacted.

Nothing much happened. Several guys tried to pick her up but none resembled her description of Frederick. Jennifer didn't spot the due-next-week-in-Switzerland dental patient and after half an hour, she began looking for Tom. When Tom wanted to avoid being seen, he could do it well but became better skilled as the years and decades passed.

He watched her searching the room for him without success and eventually tapped her on the shoulder.

"Where were you? Where did you go?" Jennifer asked.

"I was here the whole time, watching you, as I promised. No sign of Freddy boy?"

"His name's Frederick, not Freddy boy," she replied in an annoyed tone as if she wouldn't have ever slept with an ordinary Freddy but only with a Frederick. A Sir Frederick would, Tom supposed, have gotten her clothes off easily.

Tom decided to let it pass.

"What's next?" she asked.

"You said that he took you to Blenheim Palace. That's a few miles out of town so let's go there for the afternoon. Retrace your steps, pretend that I'm Freddy . . . I'm sorry, Frederick . . . and we'll see what happens."

"What are you hoping will happen?" she asked. That was a perfectly reasonable question so Tom answered cheerfully enough.

"What I'm trying to do is retrace where you saw and went with him, what he told you, who saw you, what you did together . . . "

She stopped him

"Everything?" she asked.

"Yes, of course."

"I don't want to tell you everything."

"Well, why not?" he replied abruptly. "I'm trying to find your sister who disappeared, as far as we know, with a guy named Frederick. When we find Frederick, then possibly we'll find your sister. I need to know everything, hope that we meet people who saw you together, who'll tell us more about him." He stopped, slightly exasperated.

"I need clues, scent and footprints to track him down. There'll be dead ends, wild goose chases and wasted time but there'll be real clues in the same bag. We just won't know which they are at the beginning. We've got to find Frederick so don't hold anything back if you want me to find your sister."

"What if she isn't with him?"

"If she's not, he'll know where she went," Tom answered. "Then we'll discover how much he's lying and we'll re-find her scent. This isn't like TV. Well, I don't know about TV but I know how to hunt and search and track."

"And rescue. Search *and* rescue," she said with emphasis.

"Actually, when I hunt animals, it's usually to kill . . ." he added quickly, "but only in order to eat."

"But," Jennifer answered, "Tom, you're searching for Sophie, my sister, a human being, not an animal, not for food."

She paused before saying, nervously:

"You're not, I hope, not planning to eat her, are you?" They both laughed, which eased their tension.

"Search and rescue is different for people. It's not the same as hunting."

Tom began to speak and then bit his tongue just in time. It would be a mistake to voice the possibility that Sophie was dead. So far, two of his five search and rescue team searches had resulted in discovering dead bodies. No need to say it. Jennifer and her parents were aware that Sophie might be dead but couldn't, wouldn't say it out loud.

"Same technique or anyway, ah," Tom stumbled, "it's how I do it. I'm a hunter. Other hunters have their own methods." Tom added, "I need you to recreate everything you know about Frederick, where you went, what you did, every detail."

"I'm not," Jennifer replied blushing, "going to tell you *everything*."

Tom finally received her message and understood. He blushed too.

"Okay," he relented. "Not everything, I know you had sex with this Frederick so I don't want to . . . ah . . ." Tom was embarrassed so he stammered, "know those details but please tell me everything else you remember."

"Let's go to Blenheim Palace," Jennifer suggested.

They took a bus out to the little town of Woodstock and then walked to Blenheim Palace, the birthplace of Sir Winston Churchill in 1874 and for three centuries one of Britain's most palatial houses. Tom insisted that they follow the exact route that Frederick and the then smitten but now un-smitten Jennifer had taken.

They were the only tourists on that cold, damp December afternoon. Their guide said that she'd shown very few people all day–if you could call a pair of students a group, then they were her third group of tourists.

Nothing unusual happened but Tom didn't mind. He didn't expect a quick solution, a sudden TV moment.

The scent was pretty much gone but it was there, it had to be, he'd find it, he repeated to himself, just be patient and stay observant. If success in life was really 99% perspiration and 1% inspiration, then hunting was all about no perspiration but 50% patience and 50% observation.

After finishing inside the palace and crossing the long famous bridge, they returned to the village and waited for the bus back into Oxford. They filled in the time by browsing in the only shop still open in the village. Jennifer purchased a scarf and some small knickknacks for her parents while Tom bought a horse brass with leather mounting and two brasses, the upper in the shape of a small horseshoe with a horse's head inside and the one underneath was a star with the thistle of Scotland.

The shop lady explained that ploughmen put brasses like that on the halters of their plough horses, the Clydesdales and other breeds, when they went to summer

FRAUD CATCHER

shows. Tom knew that from his days in Ireland but feigned ignorance.

He had no desire to explain to Jennifer why he recognized the brasses.

Realizing that they were Americans, the lady explained that brasses were hung off the walls of traditional British pubs but that the plough horse and the horses that pulled the beer trucks were almost extinct. Tractors and trucks had replaced the old horses.

They paid, thanked her, exchanged Christmas greetings and hopped onto the rickety, cold bus back to Oxford.

Tom went running that evening, alone.

He ran to Headington to Freddy boy's lair, his den, where he'd had sex with Jennifer, the lucky guy. Tom liked Jennifer, admired–appreciated–her brains, enjoyed her looks and realized that she was special. But she irritated him because she could make him talk, talk about himself, open up. He found it hard not to talk more to her; he sort of wanted to but also didn't want to. This confused him.

It was against his grain, his intuition and his self-taught survival skills to reveal anything but Jennifer was better than Sarah at coaxing it out of him. He wanted to sleep with her, of course, all college boys want to have sex with girls, he enjoyed being with her but she was crowding him too much. He needed distance, to be alone.

He ran with lots on his mind. Why couldn't old Doc Stone let him be a runner, why couldn't he just let Tom run? Doing search and rescue was something Stan Davies, a running teammate, had told him and Dr. Stone about. Tom enjoyed doing that although he was only part of a large team at S&R and he was better at hunting solo.

But this missing girl business was something else. Sophie hadn't gotten lost in the woods, fallen, twisted an ankle, broken a leg or gotten confused.

The woods were where he was most comfortable, where he could spot broken branches, track a scent, pretend to be the missing person who wasn't in a thousand-year-old university town.

He couldn't pretend to be a rich 20-year-old girl. He couldn't act that role. Sophie was different than Jennifer, sillier, an identical twin sure but not as smart, not as analytical; she was rasher and, he knew in his bones, in trouble.

The British cops hadn't found Sophie du Pont Scott. Neither had all those private investigators nor had the Embassy people. Why did Dr. Stone think that Tom could do it? Finding the old lady in Dublin was easy, nobody else had searched for her and anybody with a few brains could have found her.

But a flighty, hot-headed, rich, unworldly American girl who had fallen in love with a guy in Oxford and just hadn't returned home—why had Doc Stone dragged Tom Brabazon onto this cold trail? Why not an ex police officer, a retired detective? There must be many of those sitting around with a pension and plenty of time.

Why me, Tom pondered. I'm not sure that I can find this girl. Dad could have, sure, but he was a real detective, he worked robbery, a trained detective. I'm not. What if I can't find Sophie? Then what, he wondered, as he pounded along the footpaths in the cold, damp darkness.

He found the house, returned the unread mail to the mailbox, knocked on the door and waited, stepping aside so that he was safe in case the person opening the door had a weapon. He'd learned that trick in Northern Ireland, he believed, but he was wrong.

This was a cop's trick. His dad had taught him that, had taught him self-defense, boxing and taught him how to survive and hunt in the woods.

When a balding man in his 50s opened the door, Tom asked to talk to Frederick. The man welcomed him in, explaining that Frederick was out and that he didn't actually live there but just rented a room. Tom followed him up a steep flight and turned to the left at the top of the stairs.

There was quite a large room, quite tidy even though it was quickly apparent that no self-respecting female lived there. The man introduced himself as George Jarvis, a council worker.

"I'm divorced, those are my kids and ex-wife," he added, pointing to photographs on the wall of a once happy family. Tom gathered that the man was explaining that he wasn't a homosexual.

"When do you expect Freddy, I mean, Frederick, back?" asked Tom, looking around at the rest of the room.

"Well," came the answer, "he comes and goes. I never know when to expect him." Jarvis chattered on.

"He's got a key and he always pays me cash a month in advance. He brings girls here, a different one every time. I can't see it but whatever he's got, the girls love him for it. I wouldn't mind some of that and them. They find his charm irresistible, a different bloody girl every time. And, you know what, they're all knockouts. Bloody hell, he's amazing."

Mr. Jarvis stopped before adding: "He never brought any chaps here. Now what I mean, he's definitely no poofter but I mean that this is his pad, his sex pad. He doesn't take them to where he lives, maybe his landlady won't allow girls."

Tom smiled, agreeing that that was probably the case.

Jarvis continued: "I don't know how he does it. I mean, I'd pay big money to know his bloody secret but maybe he's just better looking than me. You know, he once had twins, one after the other. Lucky bugger. I couldn't tell them apart until I messed up his wicket when talking to the second girl." He laughed at the memory.

"When I called her Sophie, she said that her name was Jennifer." Tom inhaled quickly. This was his first solid scenting and, excited, his heart raced but Jarvis failed to notice.

"It was kind of funny. She asked me how come I'd called her Sophie and how did I know her sister's name?"

George continued: "When I told her that she'd been here two nights before and I'd chatted with her then and 'what the hell, don't joke, your name's Sophie and you take your coffee black with two sugars and you're from America and now you tell me your name's Jennifer?

"'What's your real name?' I asked her, thinking she was having me on." George stopped to offer Tom a drink. "She repeated angrily that it was Jennifer and that her sister was Sophie."

"Oops, old boy," George Jarvis said, "I told myself, 'George, you've really screwed up Freddy's fun this time.' This girl, Jennifer, number two, she was furious. Pissed off you could understand, I'm sure. She was hot, I mean, bloody hot." He paused briefly.

"She didn't finish her coffee but carried her cup back into Frederick's room—he was still lying in bed—and she poured her coffee over him, screeched like a peacock, got dressed and left. Didn't even put her bloody make-up on."

Mr. Jarvis was laughing. Tom couldn't help himself and starting laughing, too. He tried to picture the scene. Jennifer outraged, two-timed, well, he sure as hell wouldn't two-time her or any girl, actually. He thought that Frederick deserved his coffee shower.

"What happened next?" Tom asked.

"Well," George Jarvis continued drily with a big smile, "Frederick doesn't drink coffee. He prefers tea. Anyway, after Jennifer/Sophie/whatever her name stomped down the stairs, he came out here soaked in coffee, his hair, his face, his body. He was as naked as the day the doctor smacked him on his backside. He asked me if the girl had left, what had happened out here and then laughed."

The man paused, laughing at the memory.

"Freddy said that he couldn't tell the twins apart and had been puzzled about the one who turned out to be Jennifer. He said that that now explained why they were different in bed, the first was really hot but this one—Jennifer—was good, too, but more subdued and traditional.

"He laughed again, said they were identical with their clothes on and off, that he'd thought he could tell them apart by the way they talked but it was obvious now that they were different. He said, 'God, Sophie was better,' then went to the bathroom and cleaned himself up.

"Crikey, he's a cool customer and you know what, he's been back since with several other girls. But, no more twins." George paused. "Maybe lover boy's learnt a lesson. I'm sorry that I rocked the boat but how could I have known?"

Tom reckoned that it was just as well Jennifer wasn't with him. No wonder the girls had argued over the target of their affections.

He realized that this was his first scenting of Frederick, lover boy, who must be quite well known around Oxford with his kind of magic. Tom hoped that he could track down other jilted girls or at least discover where they were picked up.

The answer to that should be simple: the student's bar was one likely place. That was where Jennifer had met Freddy.

"Let's hope," Tom suggested, "that Freddy doesn't meet any triplets."

George Jarvis chuckled: "Hadn't thought of that, lad. Anyway, do you want to leave a message for him?"

"No, thanks, I guess I'll find him around the town." He paused: "Do you know which college he's in?"

"No, I don't, lad. In fact, I kind've think that he's not a student. He's here any old hour, he never talks about exams or lectures. He doesn't act like a typical student, d'you know what I mean?" Jarvis stroked his moustache.

"He travels a lot too, to Europe, goes there every few weeks. Nasty bloody place, that. I haven't been there for years. It's full of foreigners talking silly strange languages. Why the hell can't those sods speak English like we do? I'm an Englishman, lad, and proud of it."

Tom half-expected Jarvis to start singing the national anthem and asked where Freddy boy went.

"Well, lad, he takes a girl with him every time, I know that and he's always away for just a few days, not more than a week. Always brings a new girl here every time, though, except those twins. Lucky bastard. Wish I could get his leftovers.

"Ha!" he laughed again at the memory of Jennifer's coffee. "I know that he goes to Switzerland, he talks about Geneva. I don't know where else except . . . sorry, dunno.

He must travel well, that ferry made me sick, bloody Frogs. I don't trust 'em."

Tom said: "But Freddy is French, you know."

"No, he's bloody not, lad. He speaks French but he's as English as me, born and bred at the Duke . . . Duke of Stackallan and Lord Pendil's Bula Abbey. He lived there all his life until his bloody mother ran off with a bloody Frog. Bula's in Wiltshire, lad, of course, how come you don't know that?"

Tom shrugged but stayed silent and let the man talk.

"His dad and I worked together on the estate looking after Lord Pendil's deer. His mum is a cleaner in the big house, the Abbey. Well, she ran off with some joker who was working at Lady Pendil's horse stud, taking Freddy along. Went to bloody France. His mother returned a year later and Sam took her back—that surprised me—but Freddy didn't return with her.

"Imagine my surprise when he knocked on my door in March and said, 'Hello, I'm Frederick Wells.' Not Freddy, mind you, but Frederick." The man snorted.

"All grown up, he was too. Sam had told him that I'd moved to Oxford after my divorce. Freddy wanted a pad for girls but he's also got his own place near Magalan College. Got loads of money, too, for a student, plenty of tens and twenties. Not like any other bloody students except for the aristocrats, those bloody toffs."

It was time for Tom to leave. He thanked Mr. Anti-European Jarvis and began to walk downstairs. He heard George calling as he was closing the door, looked back up the narrow stairs with the bare walls to watch him throw down a postcard.

"Give this to the lucky bugger. I need to tell his dad about that sex pistol son of his, when I see him again."

It was a postcard from Geneva with some interesting information but no return address or sender's name. All it said was: "I want another one before Christmas." Well, Tom knew that he shouldn't expect too much. That would be greedy.

Tom had fresh energy as he began his return run to the city centre. He was excited. This was how he'd felt in Dublin. Damn, he felt good. He almost floated back to town, not even breaking a sweat but perhaps the chilly night air helped. His gloom was lifted as he felt the same good flicker of excitement.

The wind was dropping, the temperature rising, Frederick's scent was improving. Tom almost bayed like a foxhound. More like a bloodhound.

Lover boy Freddy was almost in sight.

****

They returned the next morning to the student's bar. Tom instructed Jennifer to keep her eyes open and let him know when she recognized anyone who might know Freddy, ah Frederick.

He sat quietly at a table in a corner, sipping coffee and eating chocolate croissants for over an hour, watching Jennifer, the people coming and going. He was distant, the outsider among these students—he'd always been unwanted, reminded daily of it, in Ireland years before, both at boarding school and, oh bloody yes, every single damned day at home, too.

He always tried but failed to convince himself that being an outsider didn't hurt. But, it bloody did.

A tall, skinny guy with ridiculously long sideburns–the British call them 'mutton chops'–and a feeble moustache walked in and went up to Jennifer and said hello. It was obvious from her response that yes, she recognized him but no, it was not Sir Frederick. Jennifer removed her glasses and promptly put them back on. This was her signal to Tom to approach. Keeping them off would be the sign that it was the great lover himself.

"Tom," Jennifer said when he arrived again unseen– she was beginning to find his habit of suddenly reappearing a bit spooky–"this is Charlie Prescott. We met here in the summer. He knows Frederick."

The boy looked harmless enough to Tom. They did the superficial "howarya" routine. Then Charlie dropped a bombshell.

"Jenny, if you're looking for Frederick, I saw him just a minute ago. He was locking his bike outside the bank." That was across the street, a few doors down.

Time was suspended as both Jennifer and Tom forgot to breathe.

"Is Sophie with him?" the rich girl asked.

"No, she's back in the States isn't she? That's what Frederick told me ages ago. He's got a new girlfriend now, my sister Harriet. They're leaving today for the weekend."

"What's he wearing?" asked Tom.

"Dunno. Let's see–hat, scarf"–not much help as everybody with a grain of sense in Oxford in December and most of them in Oxford are pretty intelligent, wear a hat and scarf–"oh yes, his cashmere coat, yes, that's right. Always wears that."

Had Tom had time to laugh, he might have blurted out, "Well, he doesn't in bed," but Jennifer was pulling him and Charlie through the crowd and out onto the street.

"There he is," shouted Jennifer with excitement. "Frederick," she called out, "Frederick, hi, it's me. How are you?"

They ran, leaving the mystified Charlie Prescott behind. He wasn't accustomed to girls being so obvious. Certainly his own girlfriend had never shouted to him in a street.

Frederick the great lover got a great shock when he saw Jennifer du Pont Scott.

At first he believed that it was Sophie, who shouldn't have been there at all. He didn't recognize the chap running with her but decided to run. His air of charm and nonchalance forsook him. He turned tail and fled.

He really, really, really didn't want to meet Sophie Scott again. It was impossible. He knew where she was and she couldn't possibly have returned to Oxford. These unnerving thoughts were ricocheting inside his brain. He didn't have time to unlock his bike so he ran.

Unfortunately for the lover boy, it was his bad luck that Tom Brabazon was the guy chasing him and was a much faster runner. After all, Tom was training for the Olympics. Probably nobody in Oxford that day could have outrun Brabazon, even Oxford's own hero Sir Roger Bannister who, to be fair, was long since retired from the track.

Tom caught Frederick in a few strides and punched him in the right kidney. Frederick stumbled. Tom tackled him to the ground and began asking where Sophie was. Jennifer reached them about two minutes later and Frederick looked, actually truly was, confused, surprised and scared.

"That's Sophie there, you bastard," he spluttered. "What's going on?"

Tom replied: "No, this is her sister Jennifer. You should remember her, the twin who pours coffee on two-timing bastards in bed. Where the hell is Sophie, you bastard?"

There was a lot of commotion. Frederick was cornered but, as a crowd grew and surrounded them, he began to see a possible way out. A police constable arrived and ordered silence.

"Thank God, constable, I'm glad you're here," said Frederick as he lay pinned to the ground by Tom. "These two are trying to rob me. Please arrest them."

Jennifer protested that Frederick was lying and that she wanted to know where her sister was.

The young constable, unused to such serious crime in this town—drunken students and pranks, not muggings or, worse, . . . robberies—were what the local officers were most accustomed to and, only in his first week patrolling solo, was confused.

Tom denied robbery, offering, "I have no weapon. Robbery is defined as theft with a weapon."

"Where is Sophie?" screamed the upset Jennifer into Frederick's face. Tom guessed what she'd have done with a pot of coffee right now.

"She's gone," answered the lover boy. "Haven't seen her in ages. We broke up. She's gone," stuttered Frederick.

Becoming thoroughly rattled, the constable called for back-up and was relieved when two older police officers arrived in a car.

They listened to the accusations and counterclaims, chose to believe Frederick and told the others to get into their squad car and go to the police station where they would be charged for assault, Jennifer having not helped their cause by smacking Frederick in the face in full view of all three officers. Frederick agreed to go downtown a few minutes later to press charges.

Well, they waited for Frederick at the station. And waited. And waited.

While Tom was unsurprised that Frederick was a no-show, the young constable and his sergeant seemed amazed that a high-class gentleman like Frederick, who wore a cashmere coat ("clothes maketh the man") might not be a man of his word. This was England in the 1970s, Oxford even, where gentlemen were still automatically trusted.

Jennifer was fuming, Tom was quiet but they were both behind bars, in separate and separated cells. Jennifer's many loud demands to call her wealthy parents were ignored by the officers, whose boss Inspector Yates would surely disapprove of the cost of a transatlantic phone call. Her frequently repeated shouts for her rights were also ignored. A drunk in the next cell alternated by leering at Jennifer, suggesting sex then growling at her to shut up and allow him to sleep.

This wasn't *Kojak*, it wasn't America and the constabulary was disinclined to indulge this noisy girl. Tom stayed quiet and tried but failed to develop a plan. It was his first taste of a prison cell and it was just as bleak and disgusting as they always appeared on TV. He didn't enjoy the experience at all.

Jennifer found the experience even more horrible than Tom and she'd almost lost her voice by the time of their departure but not before she'd told the police over and over again that she was, "gonna sue you lot of bastards for every dime you've got. You'll hear from my daddy's attorney."

The Oxford Police, unmoved, was not worried. They'd heard that before from other American students and they had no dimes, not on their low wages.

After six hours, it was clear even to the sergeant that the high-class victim had, in police terminology, scarpered.

No complainant meant that it was pointless to bother with any paperwork especially since Americans were involved. This could become a sensitive and embarrassing situation, so the sergeant simply ordered them to leave.

Jennifer was still outraged and complained for several days about their afternoon. Tom hadn't enjoyed it either but chose not to waste energy on a situation beyond his control and focused on the hunt. He'd nearly gotten Frederick, so close, so damned close.

"What are we going to do now?" demanded Jennifer as they walked back to their youth hostel.

Tom didn't answer for a minute. He was concentrating. Where would Frederick have gone? Where would Tom go if he were Frederick? This was how Tom searched, by trying to imagine himself in his quarry's situation.

Animals always return home, to be safe in their own dens or caves.

Humans aren't so very different from animals. The basic instincts were the same-they head for safety, home if possible. Tom was convinced that Frederick wouldn't stay in Oxford, wouldn't hole up in his apartment.

Freddy was stressed. He'd go to somewhere safe, to hide, where he wouldn't be found. He doubted that he'd run to his parents in Bula. Something told him that Freddy had outgrown his modest upbringing and that the cashmere coat wouldn't fit in with either deer herding or cleaning rooms in the big house.

He took a guess.

He played a hunch.

"Jennifer," he answered her finally, "We're going to a dentist."

"Have you gone crazy?" asked a stunned Jennifer du Pont Scott. It was a reasonable question. "Are you mad?"

"Where's your dentist? I bet he's in your hometown, right? Well, Freddy's got a dentist's appointment on the 24th in Geneva."

"What?" asked Jennifer, not understanding.

"Frederick's going home. Home has to be in Geneva. Because that's where his dentist is. He's not going to miss his dental appointment. We're going to Europe, girl, by ferry."

"When?"

"Tomorrow. It's too late to catch the ferry from Dover today."

"How do you know the sailing time, Tom? I know that you haven't had a chance to look it up."

Tom knew because he'd taken it several times but if he admitted that then he'd have to explain when and why and he didn't want to do that. His past was his secret.

"I'll bet you a hamburger that Frederick's on that ferry right this minute," Tom answered instead.

They went to the train station where they bought one-way train tickets to Dover, changing trains in London and would leave the next morning.

They'd had enough of the spires of Oxford. They ate hamburgers at a Wimpy's that evening.

Tom was too tired to run in the rain.

Chapter 5   GENEVA

The ferry trip from Dover to Calais was uneventful.

They caught the train to Paris and, as they clackity-clacked through the French countryside, Tom took a particular interest in the places where so much fighting had taken place during World War II. He'd had two teachers at school in Ireland who'd been trapped at Dunkirk and later landed on Omaha Beach.

After explaining that one of his uncles had been killed fighting in Normandy on D-Day (that was true), Tom told Jennifer about his French teacher who had worked in France during the late 1940s on the team which implemented the American conceived, financed and organized Marshall Plan, which restored a broken Europe from its post-war ashes of desperation and collapse.

His teacher had been bitter about the Marshall Plan being named after President Truman's Secretary of State General George Marshall, a brilliant man but not the man who'd created it, the businessman-turned-diplomat, Will Clayton.

Seeing firsthand the devastation of Europe, Clayton had been appalled and decided that only the U.S. could afford to—and must—address the continent's shattered economies, chaotic poverty, rubble, lost people and despair.

Clayton wrote a detailed plan, sold the idea to Marshall's second-in-charge Dean Acheson, who then persuaded General Marshall to push the plan. Marshall was the man who'd overseen the war's complex supply logistics from a desk in Washington D.C. He'd supervised all the manufacture and transport of guns, boats, planes, food and troop disbursements necessary for the planning and winning of the U.S. World War II efforts in both Europe and the Pacific.

General Marshall, a worthy hero for that, read out the plan—now his—at Harvard University on commencement day and then the American Congress had had to be bullied into agreement.

The idea cost $13 billion dollars, which sounds—is—cheap in today's dollars and proved to be worth every penny but passage of the legislation proved a close call and won by just a few votes. Preferring to leave Europe alone in its suffering, Congress nearly refused to help. That would have allowed Russia to conquer all of Western Europe and impose Communism on its population.

Mr. Clayton deserved a medal and a few statues.

Northern France and Paris, Tom thought, looked a lot better because of the Marshall Plan. What did it matter who'd received the credit? The results were great.

****

In Paris, they didn't wait long before catching the train to Geneva.

As they were so close on lover boy's scent, they immediately agreed to forego playing tourist in Paris before their next train left. Notre Dame and the Eiffel Tower would wait until after the dental appointment.

They disembarked mid-morning on December 22 in Geneva at Gare Cornavin, the city's main train station, two days before Frederick's appointment with his dentist and, with Tom again refusing to consider staying in an expensive hotel, booked into a nice small hotel on a narrow street near the Cathedral of St-Pierre.

They took the time to look around and even went on the tour of the United Nations building. Tom also ran through the city to reacquaint himself with it, having been there with his mother eight years earlier.

They went to the American Embassy, where, having been coached by Tom, Jennifer explained that her name was Sophie du Pont Scott. She claimed that she'd lost her passport but conveniently had the number (it was, she'd remembered, just one digit away from hers and she knew Sophie's social security number and—of course, this question was easy—her date of birth). She needed a replace-

ment in order to fly home to the United States in time for
Christmas with her folks.

Lulled by her innocence, the Christmas spirit and impressed by her famous name, the embassy staff took pity
on her and completed the process in record time while
Tom waited outside.

After all, a girl should spend Christmas at home with
her folks.

Tom had explained to Jennifer that Sophie might have
lost her passport and would be unable to leave Switzerland or re-enter the US without one. Both twins needed a
passport to get home.

He found it hard to pretend to Jennifer that he was
seeing everything in Geneva for the first time. Jennifer
was puzzled. She liked Tom, liked him a lot and trusted
him completely. He was strong, tough and smart. She
wanted to sleep with him, having decided that they'd do it
tonight even before finding her sister but it frustrated her
that he wasn't open.

She knew that he was hiding things from her.

Her mind was still occupied by the outrageous hospi-
tality they'd received in Oxford and the frustration of
having found and lost Frederick. The creep. Tom didn't
believe his claim that he didn't know where Sophie was.
Jennifer wanted to scratch his cheating eyes out.

They went to bed together that night and enjoyed
themselves. Later, Tom asked Jennifer how her parents
knew Dr. Stone.

"Oh, Daddy met him in the War. Dr. Stone saved
Daddy's life. Dr. Stone is my family's hero. He's a genuine
war hero."

"How?" Tom was disbelieving. "Tell me how a veterinarian saves the life of a du Pont in a war. The rich don't

let their sons fight in wars, I thought. They didn't in Vietnam, that's for sure."

"Well," Jennifer replied, "you're right about Vietnam. I dunno about Korea. I love M*A*S*H, it's my favorite TV show. But everybody fought in World War II, even Jock Whitney and even President Roosevelt's sons did."

"Back to Dr. Stone and your dad," Tom coaxed.

"OK. Well, Daddy was a co-pilot in the Air Force and was shot down over Holland in the winter. He was captured by the Germans and became a prisoner-of-war but escaped."

"From Colditz?" Tom asked, remembering the popular film, starring Steve McQueen and James Garner.

"No," answered Jennifer, "from a different prison camp. This one was in Germany. He escaped with four other men, two were shot the next day at a train station but Daddy and his friend got away ok." She gave Tom another kiss, then continued.

"Somehow, Daddy and the other man, whose name was Alan Henderson, reached eastern France, which was under occupation by the Germans of course. They were found and hidden by the Resistance. Mr. Henderson was shot dead when the Nazis discovered them in a hay barn."

"Wow," Tom said, "but where does Dr. Stone come in?"

"Just be patient, my love. Dr. Stone worked undercover with the Resistance. He organized the transfers and safety of people like Daddy and other soldiers as well as the Resistance members who were avoiding the Germans."

Another kiss.

"Dr. Stone got Daddy back safely to England. It was dangerous for everybody, especially for Dr. Stone and the people in the Resistance, who got tortured and shot by the Gestapo when captured."

More kissing.

"Anyway, Dr. Stone was undercover. He passed himself off to the Germans as a French vet, whose cover was traveling to farms to treat sick animals. He was a real vet, of course, and spoke fluent French but finally got caught at the very end of the war." She paused.

"They, the Gestapo, I mean, tortured him–that's how his arm was ruined, it wasn't bitten by a stallion–but he was freed when the Americans reached his prison. He was due to be shot that afternoon." She coughed.

"Daddy owes his life to Dr. Stone. They met up again after the war and are very close friends."

"So how come an American vet was doing cloak-and-dagger stuff?" Tom asked.

"Well, I never knew until last Christmas when Daddy said that Dr. Stone was in the SOE."

"What was that?"

"The SOE was the British special operations executive force during the war. They recruited a few Americans and, of course, French and other Europeans–all were volunteers–but most were British. In fact, the rules originally said that all members had to have been born as subjects of the British Empire."

"Why?"

"The British believed that where you were born proved your patriotism but because so many members died during operations early in the war, they needed to be replaced and the rules had to be loosened."

Tom thought that was nuts but it was another era so he shouldn't judge.

"Dr. Stone," Jennifer continued, "was a member of the OSS, the American secret intelligence agency but transferred to SOE. I guess that the two organizations worked together but I don't actually know how or why he switched. Maybe SOE borrowed him. I don't know." She paused to take a breath.

"Do you remember on the plane when you asked why my parents had asked you to find Sophie and I'd asked you why Dr. Stone had recommended you to my parents? You answered that it was because you did a bit of search and rescue?"

"Yeah," replied Tom a bit warily. He was nervous, because Jennifer had remembered that conversation, which he had hoped had been forgotten. "But I don't know why he picked me, I really don't, other than for that." He didn't want to mention Dublin, which had clearly been a trial run.

"Tom," Jennifer said. "You're a neat guy, full of mystery, so quiet, so sexy. I feel safe with you. I like you a lot but you're too naïve. It's much more than doing a bit of S and R, even though you might think that. You're wrong."

She snuggled even closer to him.

"Dr. Stone picked you because he recognizes that there is something special about you that you don't even see yourself. He knows that you can find Sophie."

Another kiss and hug.

"He knows he's right so my parents . . . and I . . . know he's right. He's right because, in World War II, he couldn't afford to be wrong. He had to be right or people would die. Daddy says that he saved many men from the Nazis. His judgment had to be perfect and Daddy says that it was."

Tom was amazed.

"But Dr. Stone doesn't know anything about me. Just that I'm an athlete, a runner."

"I promise you, Tom, Dr. Stone knows that you're determined, tough, brave, smart and a winner. He trusts you."

There was silence for a while as Tom tried to work it out. Then Jennifer suggested that they make more love. Tom was happy to agree.

When they awoke, as a grey dawn was breaking, Jennifer sensed that this was a good time to ask her other question.

"Please tell me about your mom. What was she like?"

Taken by surprise, relaxed for once, the happiest he'd been in a long time, half asleep, arms wrapped around Jennifer, snug against her warm body, well . . . Tom was vulnerable.

Tears welled in his eyes. He couldn't stop the tears. He turned away from the girl, unwilling to be seen crying. She gripped him. He cried, huge wracking sobs and lost his composure completely.

The cold-as-ice, tough, self-sufficient, self-contained young man Tom Brabazon began to cry louder and louder. He hadn't cried in years, not since the night of his father's funeral when he was eleven, hadn't even cried at his mother's funeral, had never let another person except his mother see him cry.

Tom cried his heart out as Jennifer du Pont Scott held and caressed him.

After a long time, gradually, his tears slowed and finally ceased.

Tom, who had vowed to keep his life story to himself, found himself involuntarily telling Jennifer everything. He couldn't stop himself.

He told her his real name, about his father being a police detective killed on duty in Baltimore on his birthday,
his shame at believing that his father had missed his
birthday party because he hadn't loved Tom enough.

He told Jennifer how he and his mother had moved to
Ireland, told her what had happened in Ireland, about his
hated step-father, the bleak boarding school, how his
friend the real Tom Brabazon had died at school, how he
blamed himself for that and worst of all, for his mother
being killed by a bomb in Belfast.

How he believed that her murder was his fault, because he'd been five, only five, minutes late and hadn't
run to her fast enough to save her.

How he'd watched his mother's blood flow and life end
while her crushed body lay broken in his arms, her blood
and others' blood splashed all over him, bits of skin and
clothing all over his head, face and body, how he'd had to
wipe puddles of blood from his eyes, the horrible stench
and screaming, his helplessness to save his mother, his
watching her terror and pain and then the staring-into-
the-next-world emptiness in her eyes as her brain gave
up.

How he'd watched a baby murdered the day before in
his/her pram by a gunman in Belfast, that he'd run away
from school after the real Tom Brabazon's death, forged a
new identity, how he'd escaped from Ireland, how he'd
survived alone, changed his name, arrived in America and
ended up with a forged athletics scholarship.

He told Jennifer everything.

His story took a long time to tell.

When, finally, he'd finished his story, bared his soul
and revealed everything, Tom was exhausted. He fell
asleep holding Jennifer, a rich and unworldly girl, who

was stunned and shocked by what she'd heard. She caressed him to sleep.

Tom was too upset on waking to make love again. He got up, showered and over breakfast in a café down the street, insisted that Miss Jennifer du Pont Scott promise on her grandmothers' graves and her family's honor to never, ever, ever repeat a word of his story to any person ever.

A psychologist might have believed that Tom had benefitted by "getting it all out" but Tom didn't feel pleased by any catharsis. He was shocked that he'd told someone his deepest secrets and worried what she might do. Nobody could hurt him, he'd decided years before, if they didn't know his story.

He began to panic. What if she told? He'd lose his sports scholarship, would be kicked out of the university, maybe deported from the US to . . . where? He couldn't prove that he'd been born in the United States. Jailed, maybe? He couldn't bear to go to jail. Worse, he wouldn't be able to run. He had to run. Had to. It was his compulsion.

By lunchtime, he'd thought of a solution. He liked Jennifer, admired that she was much, much more than he'd originally expected—which was a pretty but rich, shallow, spoiled girl. He liked her a lot. He didn't know if he loved her, having always been convinced that he could never love anyone after all he'd experienced.

He waited until she'd finished her sandwich.

"Jennifer, will you," Tom asked with more enthusiasm than he'd expected just minutes earlier, "will you marry me?"

Jennifer wasn't nearly as surprised as Tom expected.

"I'd like to, Tom, I think I probably really would. But I can't."

Tom asked for an explanation.

"Because you're not in the Social Register and you don't work at the Du Pont Company."

"What exactly is the Social Register?" Tom asked.

"It's a book listing all the upper class families in high society, the original aristocracy in the northeast, mostly Boston, New York and Philadelphia. The Rockefellers, Whitneys, the du Ponts of course, and so on are in it. Girls are expected not to marry anyone outside it. It's like the English aristocracy's tradition but their book is called Debretts."

"What happens if you do?"

"Well, your husband has to be approved by the people who run the Social Register or you'll be dropped from future editions. Not invited to any more society parties."

"Blackballed?" Tom asked. She nodded. Tom was used to that in Ireland.

"But what about the famous melting pot, America being a land of equality, all men are equal?"

She shrugged: "I don't make the rules."

"Are you allowed to marry someone who's outside this register?"

"Well, yes, theoretically, but that's the end of a girl being accepted as part of society and her parents will be ostracized. I can't do that to my mom and dad. I'd prefer to marry a guy who's not in the register. So many of the boys who're in it are self important jerks, losers, lazy, boring . . . not like you but I could never marry anyone of whom my parents disapproved or stand it if they got hurt socially or in business."

"What about me?"

"Sorry, my love, but I can't."

"Because I'm not rich and because I'm not in your lousy register?"

"Yes, but that's not all. My sister and I must marry either an up-and-coming executive at the company who went to Yale or Harvard or MIT or otherwise someone from another wealthy family. That's how it is, Tom. I'm sorry."

"I'm not good enough, right?"

"No, Tom, you're wrong. You're terrific, I really like you. I love you. My parents would like you too as a person but could never accept you as a son-in-law, as family."

She saw that Tom was upset.

"They would refuse permission to allow me to marry you. At least they've never said what my best friend's parents have told her. Sally's lovely and beautiful but her mother has always told her that men will only ever want to marry her for her money, nothing else and that no man will ever love her for herself. She's wrong but Sally believes it." Jennifer saw Tom's shock.

"Her parents got her engaged last month to a no account guy called Phil, who uses cocaine, dropped out of college and does nothing but get high. He's inherited as much money as her but wastes it."

"Even if," Tom corrected himself, "I mean, when . . . I find Sophie? Won't that be good enough?"

"Oh, Tom, they'll love you for that but they won't agree to our getting married."

"Because," Tom spat angrily, "I'm hired help. An outsider."

"I'm sorry but Mom and Dad don't make the rules either."

She was embarrassed, upset, sad. Tom could see this, he was sorry but he was upset, too. He continued.

"Even if I find your sister and return her home, I'll still be just a servant. Hired help. Right?"

"I'm sorry, darling Tom, I really am. I love you, I really do. I really think I'd like to marry you, get engaged anyway. But I can't do the opposite of what's expected of me. I wish I could but I just can't. I've known you for only two weeks but I've been taught the rules all my life. It's not just about love. It's business, alliances, deals."

Her eyes were full of sadness. She hated seeing Tom distressed.

"We're du Ponts. We can't marry any Smiths or Joneses. A girl can choose only from a certain group, he's got to be one of us. It's how it is and I have to obey the rules. I will never, ever, upset my parents for any reason . . . not even for love."

That rather spoiled the rest of the day and Tom was more upset that he expected. He was sorry, very sorry, that Jennifer had refused him.

He ran through the streets of Geneva that evening for two hours, too fast most of the time, uncaring where he was, angry with himself for spilling his secrets, for falling in love, for revealing himself, for crying. He lay awake in bed for most of the night and wished that she'd change her mind.

Forget the bloody frickin' money.

Screw it, screw the money, he thought angrily. All of it. Screw the bloody Social Register, Debretts, damn all those self-important bastards. He just wanted Jennifer. He didn't want a penny of the du Pont Scotts' money. He didn't want anybody's money.

He was intensely independent. He'd make it all himself. He would make enough for both of them to live well.

****

At breakfast, Tom managed to get Jennifer to change
her mind.

"Will you be allowed to marry me if, I mean when, I
win a gold at the Olympics? Would that be good enough
for the damn Social Register?"

Jennifer answered: "Well, they'll probably be okay
that, just, it's gotta be gold not silver or bronze. But yes, I
will."

She gazed into his worried eyes. "I will marry you
when you win an Olympic gold medal." She wasn't
serious. He was. She agreed only to cheer him up.

****

The next morning at 10:30, after walking over the
Pont des Bergues, they watched the comings and goings
at the dentist's office on la rue de la Rotisserie, waiting
for lover boy Freddy to arrive for his appointment.

They were south of the lake, not far from the Place de
la Madeleine and just two blocks from the Cathedral de
St. Pierre, where Calvin had preached in the mid-1500s
and there were even some Roman ruins underneath the
same cathedral.

Tom had insisted that they watch and follow Frederick when he left, see where he went, hoping that he'd lead them to wherever Sophie was. Tom was sure that Sophie was somewhere in Geneva, the postcard which the man had given him in Oxford having proved it to Tom.

He hadn't shown the postcard to Jennifer because he didn't want to have to explain what it meant, or at least what he guessed it meant. He hoped, hoped that he was wrong but he rather expected all the worst things with Freddy boy involved.

He despised Freddy and was sickened that the fake Frenchman had had sex with Jennifer, had enjoyed her, had been kissed and hugged and wanted by her, that Jennifer had given herself to him.

Freddy, you bastard, Tom thought, I've got your scent, you're in my sights and I'm going to pull the trigger on you. You're going to be very bloody sorry that you messed with Jennifer, you stinkin' bastard.

****

Freddy boy arrived punctually at the dentist's office at 11, as the postcard had instructed.

He left at 11.45 and walked down la rue de la Rotisserie as if he didn't have a care in the world, turned left onto rue de la Fontaine, then the first right which was la rue de Rive.

A few doors down, Frederick knocked on a door, it opened and then closed. His followers were careful to keep enough distance behind him to avoid being recognized but close enough to watch where he went. They kept their jackets and hats on.

After a cold half an hour's wait for Jennifer and Tom, Frederick returned to the street and walked–thank goodness there were no taxis when he wanted one–across the rond-point de Rive to the rue de la Terrassiere, turned down a narrow street, reached a door, took out a key and let himself in. This was probably the fox's den.

Tom decided to turn back to the building on la rue de Rive despite Jennifer's insistence that they confront Frederick immediately in his den.

Tom refused to agree.

He had a feeling that Frederick might hole up for a while and that the other place was important. Jennifer offered to stay behind and be a sentry but Tom argued that they must stay together–he didn't want her out of his sight, for safety's sake. He didn't want to have to tell Mr. and Mrs. du Pont Scott *and* Dr. Stone that he'd lost one twin while searching for the other.

His second reason was that he was convinced that Miss Jennifer would simply wait until he was out of sight before storming up to Frederick's door and demanding explanations. That would create a mess.

Tom won the dispute and Jennifer followed him reluctantly. When they reached la rue de Rive, Tom made her promise to stay–repeat stay–in a café on the corner while he went to reconnoiter.

Tom walked away, looking over his shoulder and was relieved that Jennifer didn't follow. He reached the door and knocked. When it opened, a man welcomed him in but just before the door closed, Jennifer burst in past Tom. All hell broke loose.

"How do you get out of here, you bitch? Get back in," shouted the man in French. Tom suddenly realized what was happening, grabbed Jennifer, dragged her out and they ran down the street out of sight.

"Why didn't you stay in here?" barked Tom when they re-entered the café. "You nearly messed everything up." He hadn't yet heard of the male chauvinist's claim that the best way to make women do what you want them to do was to tell them to do the opposite. Tom failed to be reassured or placated by her excuses.

He needed a good idea.

Fortunately, it came to him. Work alone, the voice said. A solitary creature all his life, he needed to hunt solo from now on. He asked the café's owner to order a taxi, ignored Jennifer's demands for a second assault on the angry man's door and, when he arrived, asked the taxi driver to take them straight to the airport.

On arrival at the international terminal, Tom marched Jennifer to check-in at Pan Am Airways, insisted that she be silent and requested a one-way plane ticket to New York for her. He marched her to security, gave her a kiss and wished her a Merry Christmas.

"Go home," he ordered.

"But I don't want to," she complained. "I want to stay."

"No. This is when we say goodbye. It's not safe for you anymore and I can't risk Frederick or his pal to see you again. This will get nasty and I don't want you getting hurt."

Jennifer protested but Tom pushed her through the security gate.

"Goodbye," he called. "I'll find Sophie. Enjoy your flight."

Tom was very relieved that Jennifer was gone and out of harm's way. He had a bad feeling that this hunt was about to become nasty, very nasty.

He was right.

****

Tom returned to la rue de Rive as it was getting dark that Christmas Eve. Santa Claus was never going to visit this house. He entered and discovered to his relief that the lunchtime doorman had been replaced by another doorman who'd never seen Tom.

The man demanded 250 Swiss Francs as the cost of admission and told him to go through into the next room. In the next room, a woman, who was probably no more than 40 but looked 60, showed him some photographs and asked him to make his choice. He'd never been in this sort of establishment but was quickly guessing what it was.

He pointed at one picture.

"Are you sure? I can let you have a better girl, monsieur."

Tom indicated that he was sure. The woman shrugged. She took another 250 francs from him.

"Monsieur, there's no refund if you don't like her. Ok, she's upstairs in room 3. No trouble, ok?" He followed the woman upstairs and waited while she opened the door with her key. She repeated, "No trouble, OK, monsieur?"

When Tom walked in, he felt as if he'd been kicked hard in the stomach.

What in hell was Jennifer doing here, he asked himself. How did she get here before him? He thought he would vomit. This was the worst sight he'd seen since Belfast, since his mother had bled to death in his arms.

But this wasn't Jennifer. It was Sophie, lying on the floor beside the bed, curled up in the fetal position with dirty needles on the floor, saliva oozing from her mouth, wearing only a see though nightgown, about as uninviting and unappealing a sex object as any man could ever see.

A few months earlier, Sophie du Pont Scott had been a beautiful, aristocratic, rich, fairly innocent American university girl with a happy life in front of her.

Now, on Christmas Eve in the city of Geneva where the United Nations gathered with the sincere aim of ridding the world of war and evil, where Calvin had preached his own fire against sin and evil, where bankers and chocolatiers did their business, where the Red Cross' headquarters were based, Tom Brabazon saw evil personified harming a girl whose mistake was to fall in love with a nasty fake Frenchman, who was really the son of a deer park worker and a scullery maid on an English country estate.

The beautiful aristocrat Sophie du Pont Scott had become a prostitute, a cheap hooker at 250 Swiss Francs a pop and a junkie drug addict, too.

Sophie was coherent and conscious enough to notice him, stood up with difficulty, peeled off her nightgown and lay spread-eagled on the bed.

"Come," she spoke groggily. "Have your fun. Here's a condom. You must wear it."

Tom talked to her about her parents, Jennifer and getting her home to Delaware but the girl was so dazed, so drugged that she didn't understand anything. All she knew was that this stranger was supposed to be having sex with her so she told him to hurry up.

Tom had never been so repulsed in his life and had no intention of screwing her. He tried lifting her to the door to get her out but she was almost deadweight and crumpled to the floor, jerking uncontrollably from the effect of her narcotic. He knew that he'd never get her out without the doorman stopping him.

He left her and went downstairs, outside and retched again in the street. How could anybody do that to another human being, Tom asked himself over and over again. Maybe God knew. He didn't know how but he could answer why.

For money.

That bastard Frederick. Frederick was recruiting girls in England for this brothel. He was a bastard.

His next stop was to Frederick's lair and he couldn't believe his eyes when he turned the corner to see Jennifer, of all people, getting out of a taxi just yards away on the opposite side of the street.

"What," he asked as calmly as he could, "what the hell are you doing here!?" he spluttered. "Why aren't you on the plane?"

"I'm not leaving without my sister. I told you that," replied Jennifer with a brook-no-argument attitude. Tom still hadn't learned much about women or, at least, this particular woman but he saw no point in arguing. It was too late.

"Well, now that you're back, follow me and this time, je t'en prie, I beg of you, please obey me." He added, "I've found Sophie but she's not here and yes, it's all Freddy's fault."

"Is she OK?"

"Well," Tom answered carefully, "she's in a bad way. First, I'm going to take care of your lover boy but, no joking, do what I say this time. No more damned arguing."

"OK," she agreed reluctantly.

Hoping that they hadn't been noticed, Tom knocked on Frederick's door, stood aside cop-style and charged in when Frederick opened it, Jennifer following him in.

Frederick barely had time to be amazed to see his Oxford street pals again before Tom, who hadn't actually been in a fight since boarding school but had been taught first by his dad and then by the O'Sullivans in Ireland, rabbit punched Frederick in his solar plexus.

When Frederick sprawled over, Tom then used his elbow on his left temple and then when his target hit the floor, he continued by kicking him just above his Adam's apple and under the chin. He waited until Frederick regained consciousness and told him the game was up.

Tom was taking this crime personally, having crossed the line of emotional detachment but then he wasn't a cop, he was just a very angry young man.

"I know what you did to Sophie, you disgusting son of a bitch. You screwed Jennifer and Sophie, brought Sophie to Geneva and sold her into prostitution. Did you turn her into a junkie as well?" he screamed, almost out of control. "You've made her a junkie whore, you bastard." He punched him again.

Hearing the truth, Jennifer du Pont Scott shouted and then kicked Frederick in the face, twice. Blood began pouring out of his mouth and nose as he lay in a heap. He wasn't going to go very far any time soon but Tom tied him to the toilet to keep him there.

While this was happening, a girl with an English accent ran in from what they soon discovered was the bedroom. She began screaming at them to leave Frederick alone and that she'd call the police.

Tom asked her name. When she answered that it was Lady Harriet Prescott, it rang a bell.

"Is Charlie Prescott any relation?"

"Yes, he's my brother. How do you know him?"

"We met him in Oxford. Do you know what your boyfriend's plan is, was, for you? He was going to sell you as a whore here in Geneva."

That got Lady Harriet's attention. The color drained from her shocked face.

Tom turned to Jennifer. "Right, we're getting out of here. Call for a taxi. You're taking the Lady Harriet back to our hotel and this time you both stay there. Got it? Jennifer, call her brother in England and tell him to come get her."

"What are you going to do? When are we going to get Sophie?"

"I need help but you're not coming. I can't get Sophie out of there by myself. I'm going to the police but first I'm going to tell your scumbag lover something."

Tom walked into the bathroom, lifted Frederick's head and pushed it down into the toilet bowl and flushed. Then, reckoning he'd gotten the bastard's attention, he pulled his head back out.

"You scum, you're going to jail. The cops will be here soon. I wouldn't bet much that your mummy and daddy back in Bula will be proud of you after they find out how you've been making a living, you rotten phony."

****

After dropping the girls at their hotel, where he told a surprisingly steely Jennifer to watch the English girl, Tom went to the central police station at 117 rue de Berne and asked to speak to a detective in the vice department.

A man named Sergeant Costet appeared, took Tom to his desk and asked him to talk. The detective spoke barely a syllable of English and was relieved when Tom proved fluent in French. Tom's other languages were German and Irish Gaelic, all learned at school in Ireland and during holidays with his mother.

Tom began by showing Detective Costet his father's badge—it was riveted to the inside of his belt—revealed his real name of Steve Walwyn and explained that he was the son of a dead robbery detective in Baltimore, Maryland, that his father had been killed in the line of duty.

Like all experienced and distrusting cops, Sergeant Costet needed proof.

Just to be sure, because most cops believe that all civilians and all criminals lie all the time, Costet went to another room to check the police department's list of officers killed on duty all over the world. He found the right name and date of death in Baltimore just as Tom had said.

Tom then told his story about Frederick and Sophie du Pont Scott, the brothel and the drugs and asked for help. He asked the detective to arrest Frederick and his pals at the brothel.

Sergeant Costet reflected that it would be a great bust for Christmas and would get his Inspector off the squad's back for a few days, so he agreed with enthusiasm.

"What do you want out of it?" he asked Tom.

"I want to take Sophie home to her parents on tomorrow's flight. You won't need her, will you? You'll have the other girls as witnesses and it'll be best if she doesn't have to sign a statement or testify. That way, no journalists will find out and only her family will ever know. Then, maybe, she'll have a chance of forgetting about all this."

"Deal," replied the happy cop, recognizing that this arrest would be a big winner for his career. "We'll bring all of them, the perps and the hookers back here and I'll keep your Sophie out of it. By the way," Costet was worried now, "are you going to tell the U.S. Embassy or the press?"

"No way. Absolutely not. Nobody else. Just you. It's your collar, your arrest. I don't exist."

"Good. Right, you stay here. We'll be back soon. And thanks, you son of an American cop. This is funny. I've seen Frank Serpico's film four times. He was a great cop."

"One more thing, detective Costet," Tom said. "Freddy had a fall, actually he fell a couple of times and he tied himself to the shitter. He might claim that I was involved but he's a clumsy bastard . . ."

"Don't worry, Steve. Nobody will believe a fake Frenchman who sells girls."

****

Detective Costet and the other cops returned triumphantly an hour later with Frederick, the man and woman from the brothel and six girls.

All the girls were foreigners, all American or Canadian and none of them hard-bitten professional whores. The cops would learn that they had all been Sophies and Jennifers, innocent university girls sashaying through Oxford on summer vacations, having fun until they'd met Frederick.

Detective Costet asked Tom to wait until a policewoman had tidied up Sophie, who was still only semi-conscious. Afterwards, the detective drove Sophie and Tom to the hotel.

"Are you going to go on the job, Steve? You'll make a great cop." That was a working cop's ultimate accolade and Tom appreciated it.

"No, thanks, this is enough for me. I just want to be a runner, win gold at the Olympics."

"I'll be cheering you on. Oh look, it's 1:45 a.m." The cop paused before adding with a wry grin:

"Merry Christmas."

"Not much peace and goodwill out there," replied Tom, bitterly.

"But we've won a little tonight, Tom," insisted Costet.

****

Jennifer's reaction when she opened the door was of understandable shock. She and Harriet Prescott took Sophie by the arms and then led her to the bathroom. They stayed in there for half an hour before putting Sophie into a bed. Harriet shared it with her.

Tom was asleep in the other bed. Jennifer crawled in beside him and held him close for a long time until, still sobbing silently, she too fell asleep.

****

After breakfast, they said goodbye to Harriet at the airport before boarding the Pan Am plane to J.F.K. airport in New York.

Jennifer had telephoned her parents with the news of having found Sophie, their arrival time and a Merry Christmas greeting. The new passport came in handy for Sophie and no eyebrows were raised at passport control.

After landing in New York, Tom found an excuse to lag behind the two girls after they'd all finished proceedings at Customs. He watched them go through the doors and waited a few minutes before walking out quietly.

He saw the four members of the du Pont Scott family entwined in emotional hugs and walked quietly, unseen he hoped, for the exit. He wasn't going to interrupt.

He was tired and ready to go home. Fly down to Virginia and to his apartment on campus. He wanted to be alone for the rest of Christmas.

As he was waiting at the bus stop to be taken to the terminal for his flight to Dulles airport, he suddenly noticed Jennifer beside him.

"Where are you going, Tom? My parents want to thank you."

"Thanks but no thanks. This is family time for you guys."

"Please, please spend Christmas with us." Tom shook his head. "How can I and my parents ever thank you enough for what you've done?"

"Just have a nice life, Jennifer. You're a great girl."

"But what about our getting married?"

"It can't happen. You said so yourself. You know why. I'm hired help. That's all."

Tom was insistent about not joining her and her family to celebrate Christmas. Celebrate what? The return of a daughter who was hooked on drugs and forced into prostitution in a filthy room?

Tom was tired. "Merry Christmas," he told Jennifer as she kissed him again. "I'm glad I could help, that's all. I'm just a hunter."

"And a runner," she answered. "Go win your gold medal, Tom. You're my hero." She hugged him again, then let him go.

The bus came, Tom climbed in and watched Jennifer crying as the bus pulled out into traffic.

****

Jennifer du Pont Scott went to medical school and eventually became a pediatrician.

After Sophie recovered from her addiction, she opened and managed refuges for abused women throughout the United States.

Neither woman ever returned to either Oxford or Switzerland.

Chapter 6   A PROMISE MADE

Dr. Stone listened to but refused to accept Tom's attempted retirement. He knew from personal experience back in World War II that the satisfaction of having succeeded against the odds was too thrilling for the young man to stop investigating and, more important, in his opinion, was that Tom shouldn't quit.

"I don't want to do it anymore, sir."

Tom told him this after training one evening in late January, after running in the snow, not around the track but across the infield, back and forth through the drifts, exhausting yet strengthening his cardiovascular system.

They had been the only people outside in the freezing temperature and were now, after Tom had showered, talking quietly in Dr. Stone's office in the gym building.

"I just want to be a runner, that's it."

After the du Pont Scott girl's rescue in Geneva, Tom returned to his room near campus that Christmas afternoon and had rested during the holidays. He became a recluse, a hermit in all but name and cave, hiding away except to venture to the supermarket or to run, which he did every day.

He'd unplugged the phone as he didn't want to talk to his girlfriend Sarah or to Dr. Stone. All the students had left for Christmas vacation so he was alone in the building.

But this evening was the first time that Dr. Stone had successfully cornered him into talking about Dublin and the Oxford/Geneva trips.

Tom told his stories, Dr. Stone interrupting when necessary. When he finished, the old veterinarian and undercover war hero asked various technical questions, chiefly about how the searches could have been easier, how Tom had recognized the clues that mattered and why he'd discarded the unimportant clues, how Tom had succeeded when all the private detectives and police had failed, what Tom's plan Bs might have been.

Dr. Stone heard the Dublin story for the first time that evening but he'd already listened to the other story from both Jennifer du Pont Scott and her father on New Year's Day, Sophie remaining too traumatized to talk at all. It took Sophie a long time and a lot of support to recover but she never did, completely.

Tom was scared about what Jennifer had told his coach.

"How much did she tell about me?" he asked, terrified that she'd spilled his big secret, the one about his life that he didn't want revealed to anyone. Tom had spent the weeks since Geneva worried that Jennifer would squeal.

That fear never disappeared. Tom had promised himself to never ever open up again. He'd promised himself to be better at being secretive. He'd told Jennifer *everything,* which meant that someone *knew* about him.

He promised himself never to repeat that mistake. He utterly failed to see it as a catharsis or a reasonable response to being relaxed after lovemaking. Many politicians, top businessmen, spies and ordinary men had, after all, ruined their lives after pillow talk. "Loose talk sinks ships" is a well-proven saying and now he was vulnerable, too.

Not ashamed of his past, he believed that he'd never done anything very wrong, a subjective opinion to be sure—a false identity and fake documents didn't qualify, he believed. It was too private, too personal and he'd learned the hard way years before never to trust anybody. He didn't want to be weak again.

"Jennifer's a lovely girl. She wants to marry you," Dr. Stone said.

"No, she doesn't," answered Tom, warily. "What did she tell you about me? What did she tell her father?"

"She told me a helluva lot more than you have, son."

"That, as an incentive, she promised to have sex with me when I found her sister? That we slept together before that happened? Does her father know? That she guessed why I was there and . . ." Tom was very hesitant about his final question. "Did she tell you who, ah, I . . . ?" he stammered uncomfortably.

The old man chuckled: "Your true identity? No, son. She didn't. She seems good at keeping secrets too, just not as clammy as you. She kept her word to you, swearing that she'll never repeat certain things you told her. But her father and I guessed about the sex. We were young once, you know. We remember."

"Is her father angry?"

"No, son, he's not. Like me, he's a practical man: he expected it to happen."

He smiled at Tom's shocked reaction.

"Fathers know that their daughters will be bedded by young men. We just hope that they choose wisely and don't get hurt. He saw the way Jennifer admired you at that first meeting. He's damned impressed with you, how you found Sophie. He likes you, Tom. He'd like you to marry Jennifer."

"Thanks but no thanks."

"Why not? You said that she's, and I agree with you, lovely. She's also smart, beautiful, sensible and rich. Very rich and she wants to marry you."

"Doc, the world's full of lovely girls, but she's not mine," Tom replied. "It wouldn't work out, long term."

"Why not?"

"She said it herself," Tom answered unhappily. "She has to marry the right guy, some bastard in the Social Register or a rising star at the Du Pont Company, someone socially acceptable to her parents and their group of friends, a member of their rich society. I don't qualify. I'm not that guy. I'm riff-raff to them."

Tom continued: "She only wants to marry me out of gratitude for saving her sister. And she's rich. I'm not willing to be called a gold digger."

"Would you marry her if she weren't a du Pont or rich?"

"Maybe, ah, well, possibly, yes, I dunno," Tom stammered, confused. "But I can't, ah, won't. The reality is that she *is* rich, connected *and* a du Pont. She's been raised all her life to marry to expectations. Nobody and nothing can change those facts so there's no point brooding about it." Tom chose not to admit that he'd spent a whole month brooding about it.

Jennifer had captivated him. She was smart, sensible and brave. He wanted to spend his life with her, to make her happy, to make her proud of him, to grow old together. But it was impossible.

He thought he loved her but wasn't sure as he'd never loved before. He hadn't trusted anybody since his mother's death but he trusted Jennifer. Did trust mean love? He didn't know. He was confused.

"Anyway, I don't want to marry anybody now. I'm a runner, not a wannabe husband. I don't want a 9 to 5 job, a house in the suburbs, a mortgage, 2.4 kids."

Dr. Stone laughed. "Well, son, with Jennifer as your wife you'd have no mortgage or a house in the suburbs. You'd have a mansion in the country. As for the 2.4 kids, that's out of my hands entirely. All up to you."

He handed Tom a large envelope, which the young man opened.

Inside was a $10,000 check, his agreed fee, made out to Thomas Brabazon plus a stock certificate with Tom's name on it stating that he was the owner of 100 shares of a company he'd, not surprisingly, never heard of. The corporation was called Berkshire Hathaway.

There was also a handwritten note of thanks from Mr. du Pont Scott for saving Sophie's life and saying that both his college tuition and all of Dr. Stone's coaching fees outside the college would be paid for in full and in due course, as they occurred. He would also receive another $15,000 upon graduation. Tom gawped and looked up at Dr. Stone for an answer.

"Payment for services rendered," the old man replied matter-of-factly.

"And don't worry about the taxes, this is all after tax. The du Pont Scotts have paid them all for you, federal, state, local, social security, gift tax, the whole lot. Their accountant will want your social security number so get that to me soon."

Tom didn't have one, well he had been assigned one as a child but nobody had ever told him what it was. He had faked a number for the university.

"As for the stock, it's a failed textile manufacturer in Massachusetts. That's a coincidence because my father's textile mills failed during the Depression—but forget about that. It's a winner. It's a holding name for an investment business managed by a brilliant guy in Nebraska named Warren Buffett."

By 2012, Berkshire Hathaway's shares had climbed to $125,000 each. Tom's holding was worth $12.5 million.

"Who?" Tom asked.

"I'll tell you later but I'm told that he's a star stock picker, so those shares are probably far more valuable than cash. Never sell them for any reason until I tell you to."

"Why so much?"

"Well, the easy answer is that Sophie is one of his daughters and is worth more to him than his own blood, which is all blue and very rich, richer than Jersey cows' cream. Also, remember this, boy, the du Pont Scotts are old money. Old money pays its bills, new money often doesn't. That's the difference."

"Why did you pick me for those jobs?" Tom changed direction. "Jennifer said that it was no accident that you chose me, but both times I was just lucky."

"No, Tom, you weren't just lucky over there. A man makes his own luck in this world. You've got the knack for this stuff. The right stuff. You're a hunter and smart."

Dr. Stone paused before adding: "You remind me of the young man I used to be, or the young man I almost was, the young man I wish that my son had become but didn't. What I did was by accident. There was a war on and I simply followed orders and did my duty."

He continued: "There's no war now. Dublin was a favor to me, your coach, an easy one, but you didn't have to go to Oxford and you discovered the link to Geneva on your own. You're a hunter, a damned good one. You're a helluva hunter and somebody did a damn good job teaching you." He paused, waiting for Tom to say something but Tom remained silent.

"You see yourself as a good runner, well, maybe you are, maybe not. I think that, with the right training, you might reach the Olympics, not on raw talent, because you're not the quickest out there, but on your determination. I don't know what drives you, Tom, at least not yet but in all my years of coaching college athletics you've got the most determination of any kid I've ever handled."

He paused, carefully: "So, tell me something about yourself, Tom. Where you're from, about your family, why you want to run, why running's so important to you."

"Please, sir, I'd prefer not to."

"Well," answered Dr. Stone, not offended but amused, "tell me something. You've got to realize that there'll be questions asked about you, and to your face, by officials when you're winning . . . and by journalists. They won't take the 'please, sir, I'd prefer not to' answer."

He stared at the young man.

"They'll start digging and they will discover if not everything, enough, too much by the look on your face. They're professional diggers and Americans dislike secrets, especially in their sports stars, their role models, whose faces are on cereal boxes and in ads on TV."

Tom didn't look convinced.

"So, let's start planning for the future," Dr. Stone continued. "The State Championships and Nationals will be in just a few months. When you're a track star, what are you going to say?"

Tom was uncomfortable and looked like he might bolt from the room, so Dr. Stone went over and locked the door, putting the key back in his pocket.

"First, tell me the truth or as much of the truth as you're comfortable to tell. Then, we'll work on a story that the media can't pick holes into. Always remember, son, you've got to avoid telling outright lies or you'll get into trouble."

The coach continued: "Do you know the story of *Grey Owl,* the English guy from Hastings in Sussex, England?" Tom shook his head.

"Well, he emigrated to Canada at age 18 and pretended to be an Indian, becoming so Indian that the Indians themselves were fooled, then got famous after writing a book, because he wanted to protect the environment. Somebody wondered how an Indian could write so well in English. Well, he got rumbled, somebody knew about him, blabbed and a reporter began digging. Next thing old Grey Owl knew was that his credibility was shot and people stopped listening to his environmental message.

"So, tell the media the truth but not everything and stay consistent. Don't tell any lies that can be caught. Answer their questions in sound bites, then they'll go away. But if you make them suspicious or annoy them, then they'll start digging.

"Tell me a bit, now, ok? I know that you don't want to and I don't need to know for myself but we've gotta start being prepared."

Tom knew that he was cornered by a man who was far shrewder than he was and he wanted, needed Dr. Stone to help him, to be his coach.

"Well, my father taught me how to hunt before he died. He was a police officer, a detective killed on the street in the line of duty. On my birthday. My mother remarried. She's also dead, killed by a bomb while waiting for me outside a restaurant. I was late. I didn't run fast enough to save her." Tom tried to stop but his coach raised an eyebrow.

"Somebody else, a retired con artist, taught me more about hunting, con tricks, swindles and frauds. My stepfather hated me, said I was useless and would be a failure in life. I ran away for a new life, on my own. So I run." Tom was unhappy but accepted that he must explain more.

"I have to win, have to prove that bastard wrong, have to atone for not saving my Mom, for not running fast enough to reach her in time to save her." Tom looked exhausted and Dr. Stone sensed that he wouldn't prise much more.

"Is Tom Brabazon your real name?"

"No, sir."

"The date and place of birth on your student identity card and college record: are they accurate?"

"No, sir."

"Are you the same age as on your records?"

"No, sir," Tom answered again.

"Your social security number, is that accurate?" Dr. Stone was amused at Tom's answers but kept his face expressionless.

"No."

"Where you claim to have gone to high school, did you really go there?"

"No, sir."

"Where are you from and where did you grow up?"

Tom didn't want to lose Dr. Stone's coaching. He was convinced that this was the man who could take him all the way to an Olympic medal. He respected him for his war service, his courage and his toughness. He was almost frantic now.

"I'm sorry, Dr. Stone, very sorry, but I really, really don't want to answer those questions. I don't want to lie to you but I just want to keep it out of sight, forget it. Forget what happened, as much as possible." He was panicking.

The old man replied quietly and sympathetically: "You'll never forget the bad memories, Tom. I still remember what happened in my war in Europe. We'll have to work on some answers that will fly."

Dr. Stone continued his interrogation: "Have you ever been in prison?" Tom shook his head. "Been charged or convicted of any kind of crime?" Tom continued his head shaking. "Ever committed any crime or do anything dishonest, dishonorable or wrong?" Still more shaking.

"Ever taken or are taking any drugs, been a drunk, stolen money or goods, cheated anybody, mistreated any girls, can be blackmailed or ever done anything of which you're ashamed?" Tom kept shaking. He wasn't ashamed of having taken a new name or making a new life for himself.

"Good." Dr. Stone was pleased. He believed that Tom was truthful and he was confident that he was right, because being able to decipher the difference between truth and lies kept him and many others alive during World War II. Dr. Stone was sure that his gut instinct was more accurate than any polygraph that the FBI had, or would ever produce.

"Would you take drugs to win?"

"Never."

"Would you do anything improper or dishonest to win?"

"Never."

"What do you tell your girlfriend Sarah about yourself?"

"As little as possible," Tom replied with a smile. "She's always probing and gets frustrated when I dodge. She wants openness. She's told me everything about herself, I think, to try to get me to open up."

Dr. Stone laughed about Sarah. "Why's running so important to you? Running can't bring your mother back to life. You have to answer that or I can't help you reach your best."

"To prove my bastard stepfather wrong, to make my mother proud of me, to be a winner." Tom was really exhausted.

Dr. Stone explained: "What you're trying to do is run away from your past, from your demons but you never will."

A long pause, while Dr. Stone switched gear to: "What do you want from me?"

"To coach me, sir, to help me become the best runner in the world, train me hard, hard enough to win an Olympic gold medal and be honest enough to tell me if I'm not good enough."

"Well, it's a deal." Dr. Stone was pleased to be asked. Delighted, almost ready to let out a whoop. They shook hands solemnly to seal their agreement.

He saw Tom as the best prospect he'd ever trained. He'd never attended an Olympics as a coach–it was his Holy Grail, his final ambition in life.

"OK, then, we'll do it. We'll both have to work hard but I'll tell you this truth: you'll be good enough. You're the most determined young man I've ever seen."

Tom grinned, laughed and didn't mind revealing his excitement.

"But," Dr. Stone insisted, "you've got to also promise me that after your running career is over, you'll become a hunter again. There are countless lives you'll save and improve. Promise me."

"You mean forget becoming a language teacher or optometrist?"

"Yes, son. Forget that stuff. You're a born hunter and runner. A person should do what they are supposed to do, what God put them on this Earth to do. So, do you promise me that you'll hunt?"

"Yessir," Tom promised.

Chapter 7 THE OLYMPICS

The Olympics' motto: *Citius, Altius, Fortius*
(Swifter, Higher, Stronger)
With thanks to my friends R.W. and S.W.

There she was. Tom was in love at first sight.

His head swirled and he gulped. It was hard to identify anyone in the swirling, exuberant, 12,000 member
throng of the world's greatest young athletes during the
Olympics' opening ceremonies but he felt that a stage
light was shining on her head, illuminating her, singling
her out, for only him to see, for his sake. She was beautiful.

He was already excited, thrilled in mind and body, to finally be here at the Olympics. After all he'd endured, dreaming so often of this hour and here he was walking in the stadium as a member of the American team, in an ecstasy that he'd never felt before, an intensity that he imagined was shared by all the other thousands of athletes.

It wasn't just that they were in the limelight, watched with envy and admiration by the thousands in the grandstand and many hundreds of millions watching on TV. He'd watched the opening ceremony of the two previous games, dreaming, focusing all his ambition to get here and . . . he was . . . he'd made it despite everything and so many obstacles.

He was no longer a nobody kid from Ballykennan in Ireland. He was an Olympian now.

There the girl was again, appearing then vanishing in the moving crowd. It was impossible to keep an unobstructed view of her. What was her name, her nationality and her sport? These questions suddenly meant everything to him.

What mattered, just as much as the next two weeks and the medal that he'd run his bones out to win, was . . . would she like him, would she . . . he groped for the word . . . reciprocate? His sense of reality reminded him that she wouldn't love him just because he loved her. He'd have to prove himself worthy of her love and she'd need to like him.

Would he sweep her off her feet? Or would she be already committed to another man, maybe even married? Could she accept his secrecy, his unusual demons and other faults and foibles?

He knew that he could never presume to repeat the chutzpah of what the English racehorse trainer Capt. Ryan Price had done. Price, a former commando possessing the sangfroid and certainty of a war survivor, met Dorothy on a Sunday and married her in church three days later. They enjoyed a happy 50 years of marriage.

Who was this girl? Damn, she'd disappeared again. Gently pushed in this extraordinary crowd, he knew without a doubt that this was the beginning of the two most important weeks . . . the pinnacle . . . of his life, that nothing would ever top this.

He was unable to reach her, too many other excited athletes between them in this surging, heaving crowd, unable to introduce himself and hope—more than he'd wanted anything else in his whole life, even more than an Olympic gold medal. He wanted this girl to love him.

Until twenty minutes ago, before he knew that she existed, he'd always scoffed at the idea that anyone could fall in love at first sight . . . especially him, the cold, emotionally scarred and empty, self-sufficient, rational, mixed-up guy with a self-imposed mental version of a high, surrounding, stone wall to protect himself.

He pictured himself only as the determined, focused athlete caring about just one thing: to win gold to make his mother and father proud of him, because he'd overcome all his obstacles and proven that bastard of a stepfather wrong. He had to become a winner. That's why he was here and he would show them all.

Now he had another reason to win. To win her love, whoever she was, but she'd need to love him even if he lost, if reality over the next fortnight revealed that he was slower than someone faster. He just had to find her again and he would. After all, he was a finder of missing people. That and running were his only two skills, he thought.

Oh yes, he'd find her.

****

Tom realized that the opening ceremony was very formally organized with the athletes bussed to and from the stadium, everyone subdued, waiting in national uniform before each country would march into the stadium in alphabetical order. Algeria was early on, Mauritius and Nigeria in the middle, the United Kingdom and United States, U.S.S.R at the rear followed only by Zambia and Zanzibar.

This wasn't like a university at graduation, not the end of four years of study but the beginning of a fortnight's intensity. Like Tom, whose heart was pounding, these athletes from every corner of the world would always be Olympians no matter what achievements or vicissitudes might happen during the rest of their lives.

The athletes murmured nervously among themselves, willing the time to pass before joining the longest procession in the world, passing three glacially slow hours bored and fidgeting but excited. Like all the other first timers and most of the veterans, Tom was scared yet awed by the enormity of being there.

He stared at the ceiling, then the floor, then around the room and back to the ceiling, closed his eyes and twitched his fingers, worried. He found swallowing difficult and managed only the smallest of small talk to the athletes near him. He was sweating despite the cold.

He was told later that it was tradition for some teams to break the solemnity and boredom. Gradually, as the clock ticked into the third hour, some of the Kenyans began dancing.

Tom was impressed. Then the Australians began throwing their toy kangaroos as improvised Frisbees before the New Zealand men removed their shirts and performed the indigenous Maori warlike Haka dance, done most famously by that country's All Blacks team before international rugby matches. This was followed by the Americans chanting "USA, USA, USA," before a few other nationalities produced their own ways to reduce the stress and boredom.

Finally, after officials successfully shushed the athletes back into formality and silence, the first countries were notified to stand and prepare to enter the stadium as individual teams.

****

The world's best athletes, representing more than two hundred countries, had converged on the Olympic Village during the previous week. Sixteen thousand athletes, coaches, team managers and other "accredited personnel" (physicians, physiotherapists, dieticians but no journalists) arrived in groups much like dazed university freshmen at the beginning of a new academic year. These athletes were excited down to their marrow to be present, their joy an audible buzz, youthful clean enthusiasm a credit to their ambitions for glory.

The Olympics are a far better, healthier setting for young people to congregate than the millennia old alternative of battlefields. The Olympic Games, despite the occasional and thoroughly unwelcome intrusion of politics, is simply unique . . . there is no other equivalent experience for humanity.

Nearly every athlete lived in the Village throughout the Games. Some athletes competing in events on the first day missed the Opening Ceremonies and some chose, reluctantly, to live near their locations, like the rowers who were sometimes an hour away from the Village and the equestrians whose events were usually a fair distance away as well.

Ninety-five per cent of the athletes stuck within their own teams; the huge American team in particular, while they got to know each other and, of course, focus on their performances. The teams' residences were segregated by countries, before and during competition, until their own performances ended and they could spread out to meet athletes of other nationalities.

The intense competition was hard but honest, absolute but honorable, each athlete seeking glory, affirmation, the achievement of lifelong ambition . . . money ignored, forgotten, as unwanted as chicken pox.

The large village was, Tom noted happily, comfortable enough with game rooms, movie theatres, libraries and the obligatory gyms but nobody forgot their raison d'etre. Some of the athletes watched films or played billiards to pass the time but their minds were always, exclusively, on their athletic goal: to win a medal.

Even for those athletes who recognized the improbability of their receiving a medal, just being there was enough: it was and would forever be the greatest thrill of their lives.

****

Six mornings later, while standing in the breakfast line in the vast dining hall, which seated 10,000 people, Tom saw the girl again, this time eating her breakfast at a table with five others.

The girl had beautiful, long and silky brown hair that fell loose onto her shoulders. Her fingers were thin and elegant, her face beautifully crisp, not classically beautiful like that of a Hollywood actress but full of expression, small nose broken at least once, a one-inch scar on her right cheek, teeth perfectly formed and a dazzling smile.

She looked up in his direction but didn't see him gazing at her as she was focused on what one of her companions was saying. When she and the others laughed, her eyes lit up and Tom was even more smitten.

From yards away he looked deep into the girl's sparkling brown eyes. They were so deep that he thought a man could drown in them. She was, Tom searched through his vocabulary, stunning. Tom Brabazon was even more in love.

The athlete behind Tom gave him a shove. "Hey, wake up, buddy, move along, let's eat. OK?"

Tom stammered an apology, moved along, collecting this and that without caring and when he turned to go meet her, she'd gone. He searched the room but she had disappeared. Where was she? The room was filled by athletes: he checked every head but she'd vanished. Four different people were now at that table. Her seat and another seat were empty.

Was she an apparition or was he hyperglycemic? Maybe he'd dreamed that vision. He looked at his food tray: his oatmeal bowl was empty, the orange juice glass empty, both apples and the banana, which he thought he'd selected, were absent.

"Hey, Tom," one of his teammates laughed, a blonde swimmer from California named John Hobbs, "what's up? No food, huh, aren't ya hungry? Ya gotta eat, keep up your strength."

He laughed again.

"Breakfast is the most important meal of the day, ya know what they say. Better not let the coaches see that or they'll be pissed off."

In a trance, Tom tried to say something funny but the voice sounded like a stranger's and the words nonsensical. Hobbs looked puzzled before moving away. Tom returned to the end of the line and pulled his mind back to breakfast.

Did this girl of his dreams exist or was this some kind of Olympic-newbie psychological trick by his overstimulated brain? He needed to concentrate.

Today was his first qualifier and daydreaming would embarrass him. But did today's run matter? Of course it did but all that seemed to matter, at this moment, was this girl. Who was she and would she love him the way he loved her?

****

He didn't see her again until just before his 10,000 metres final late the next week. He recognized her Italian
uniform, because he'd raced in a qualifying heat alongside
a man wearing the same uniform.

Tom was warming up, stretching, kneeing up and
down, short sprints, doing pushups and holding deep
inhalations in practice for his race in the final when he
spotted her and his world went silent. He stopped hearing
the audience or his teammates.

The young woman was lining up for the long jump. He
watched her spurt towards the wood, hit it perfectly with
her left foot and soar into the air, landing in the dirt,
crouching and rolling forward as she landed.

She stood up, stared at the screen, saw her distance,
frowned and returned for jump number two. This time,
she had a foot fault when her toes landed inches too far
over the wood. Jump number two was disqualified. She
returned dispirited to the end of the queue. She would be
the final jumper in the women's long jump.

Tom knew that he had only ten minutes before his
race so he kept warming up as he watched fascinated,
obsessed, focused, wanting her to do a Bob Beamon on her
final jump.

He knew that the American coaches would frown upon
him, get angry even but what could they do? They
couldn't stop him. Nobody could stop Tom Brabazon in a
determined mood.

What the heck, he told himself, protocol be damned.
You get only one chance in this world.

He stood up, ran over to the long jump area, up to the
girl and, knowing no Italian, spoke in two languages
saying, "Je m'appelle Tom des Etats Unis. Bonne chance.

Tu peux gagner." His French gave out so he switched to English. "Make a great jump. You can win!"

The girl stared, surprised at him, understood him, smiled a gorgeous smile, her eyes lit up with excitement and she replied, "Grazie."

She quickly switched her attention back to her jump, stared down the runway and zoomed from zero to top speed. She hit the wood perfectly with her left foot and soared again into the air as if forever ignoring gravity. She finally landed and pitched forward, rolled, sat up and stared at the screen. Her distance came up and shone like a lighthouse beacon: she'd won silver.

A Norwegian had won the gold with the bronze achieved by a Spaniard. Jubilation and total excitement caused her to leap in the air and she sprinted to her teammates, laughing and jumping for joy. She'd won a medal for her country. She was ecstatic. Tom watched as she was enveloped inside her compatriots all hugging and kissing her.

Then a hand landed on Tom's shoulder.

"You're up now. Go," a voice ordered but Tom didn't budge. "Now," commanded a coach, who was unhappy at Tom's distraction. "They're just a bunch of girls and Italians at that. Go race. Do your fuckin' job."

Tom did. He ran the best race of his life.

Even the American chief de mission, who held total responsibility for the entire American team and possessed the highly prized "infinity pass" badge, which allowed him access to everywhere–it was also called the "ultimate pass"–even he was impressed by what Tom, the same runner whom the coaches had insisted held a snowball's chance in Miami of gaining a medal, did next.

Indeed, they were already astonished that this young man had reached the finals, having predicted that this newbie would be too overawed and inexperienced to survive the second heat in his first Olympics. These coaches weren't the first men and would be far from the last to underestimate Tom Brabazon, born Stephen Walwyn.

Not an official team coach and officially ignored, Dr. Stone was allowed neither in the village nor on the track but was fidgeting among the audience, uncharacteristically nervous, up in the stands.

This was the pinnacle of his life too, except for his saving many lives in World War II.

He talked to Tom twice daily at designated times outside the village gate and the stadium's entrance for athletes, this being before the days of cell phones. He didn't, couldn't, take his eyes off Tom and wondered what the hell his protégé was doing talking to those long jumping girls, being too distant to recognize the specific girl of Tom's attention.

He hoped to God that the boy wasn't going to lose the plot over some skirt: that wasn't his Tom, the most focused person he'd ever met.

Goddamnit, he'd have been a great undercover agent in the War, Dr. Stone repeated to himself for the umpteenth time. What the hell is Tom doing?

"Refocus, son, pay attention. You're here to run . . . so run, son."

Tom felt calm despite the pressure of running in the final of the 10,000 metres, the only American left in the race. He heard a girl shout encouragement, looked over and recognized Jennifer du Pont Scott–she of the Oxford/Switzerland expedition–wave and shout:

"Good luck, Tom. Go win your gold."

She'd finagled a spot as a volunteer on the track.

Eight runners, the world's best at 10,000 metres. Elite, star athletes. One opponent was from the Argentine, another English, one was Australian, the man wearing black represented New Zealand, following in the traditions of that country's running gold medalist champion Peter Snell, one very tall Ethiopian, one Siberian with a flattened nose and one Canadian. The Australian was the favorite, Tom the complete outsider.

Nobody but Tom and Dr. Stone believed that Tom had a chance of winning but, as in horse racing, the odds don't matter once the flag goes down. Opinions no longer counted. This was all about strength of the body and, more important, the mind. Nobody cared about anything except the next 10,000 metres. Each runner possessed his own hard-earned, tenacious story of progress towards this day, this hour, this moment. This race was everything that mattered to them.

These men were all winners.

The gunshot sprang them into action and the Ethiopian took command. Tom didn't hurry, didn't panic. Strangely, he never heard the cheering crowd until after the finish line. Like all the others, he was focused. Like all the others, he was fit and ready to run for his life.

All the runners owned huge dedication, rare ability and determination but, he only guessed this bit, he was the only man newly in love. He raced "in the zone" as runners like to describe their own concentration.

Adrenalin sky-high, he somehow knew that he wouldn't fluff his lines. Winning this race was what he was meant to do on this earth and that's what he would do. No need to panic, no time to be awed by where he was. He'd never felt calmer or more comfortable.

He relaxed just as Dr. Stone had taught him, every stride was smooth while he watched his opponents. He cruised easily, without tension. He seemed to float, his shoes barely touching the track as if they and it were velvet. Everything slowed down for him mentally.

He felt throughout the race that things seemed in slow motion, the slowest race he'd ever run in, but it was the fastest. Afterwards, it always felt like a blur in his memory, the fastest competition he'd ever experienced. He raced within himself, floating through every section as the pace gradually increased. His shoes barely touched the track.

Dr. Stone thought he was running as smoothly as a cat, a mountain lion.

One of the leaders faltered at halfway and faded rapidly.

The first two alternated the lead, Tom staying on the inside–Dr. Stone had taught him to "always stick to the fence, go the shortest distance"–his stride easy and unencumbered by his opponents. The New Zealander ran alongside him humming and the Australian behind them whistled Frank Sinatra's "My Way."

Tom was as silent as the grave but his heart sang with joy. He wondered when the wall of fatigue would hit and crush him but he was on an emotional high and he avoided the wall that day, the greatest day of his life: there would be no pain today.

All of Dr. Stone's coaching had led to these few vital minutes. Dr. Stone had developed his coaching skills by combining his own techniques with the lessons taught by the great New Zealand coach Arthur Lydiard. Another maverick like Dr. Stone and equally disliked by team officials, Lydiard had coached Snell, Halberg and John Walker to Olympic running gold medals.

Lydiard was Dr. Stone's sporting hero but no coach can train winners unless their pupils have "it," the will to win despite enduring injuries, sacrifices and the determination to break through "the pain barrier." Dr. Stone knew that Tom was his final chance to become famous in the Olympic history book.

The Australian surged past Brabazon and the New Zealander as the bell rang out for the final lap but Tom was in no hurry—he knew that he possessed the stamina and enough speed to go nose to nose but only in the last 184 metres. He and Dr. Stone had measured his run and knew precisely what he could achieve and for how long. Not a metre less, not a metre more.

He'd asked a teammate to stand at the exact spot, 184 metres from the finish. His teammate obliged and that's when Tom accelerated. Dr. Stone whooped.

"That's my boy. Go, son. Run," he shouted as he rose to his feet.

That day, Tom somehow ran 22 seconds faster than his previous career best. It was his best and fortunately, of all days, when it mattered the most, rather than in an exhibition event in a small town in Virginia. That was a massive improvement that later raised eyebrows and caused searching questions to be asked. Not caused by a banned drug but by something more powerful.

It was undeniable pressure on the biggest stage of all but nobody knew, of course, what pressures Tom had faced and conquered in his weird past. While this race was the crème de la crème of his ambition, he'd survived much tougher pressures.

Except for his uniform, Tom wasn't running for his country, really, he was running for vindication, to honor and please his parents and to defeat his stepfather's insistence that Tom would always be a failure. All his demons, all his purpose for life gave him perfect tactics that afternoon.

He couldn't control his opponents but this was independence time and Tom was surely the most independent man of this group of young super fit super achievers.

Nobody was humming or whistling as they entered the home turn, where Tom was in third place, one and a half strides behind the Argentine leader. The Australian was second and then bounded into the lead as the Argentine's stride shortened and Tom swerved around him, losing not an inch during the maneuver.

The others were all beaten and knew that they couldn't catch the two leaders but nobody was gonna quit. Tom had the Australian in his sights and it was clearly a two horse race down the final 100 metres.

Tom accelerated again, one final desperate surge for victory. He gave it everything, his throat burned, his chest was at full extension as were his knees and arms. His heart was pumping at maximum pressure.

He charged down the straight, reaching the Aussie, getting ahead by a head, then half a length, but the man from the hamlet of Mulbring, population of 500, 1 ½ hours' north of Sydney in the Hunter Valley of New South Wales, was finding more reserves of strength, both men at full speed, full determination, full effort.

The Australian shirt caught up to Tom, neither of them had any extra, they were at full throttle running towards glory, Tom picturing his mother and father cheering him on and imagining the Italian girl doing the same. He'd never reached this pinnacle of running before and was producing everything his sinews and brain had to offer. His effort was as close to perfection, the perfect running machine, as he would ever reach.

It was a photo finish. They crossed the line together. The commentator predicted a dead heat while the judges studied the photograph with a magnifying lens.

Tom slowed down gradually, unaware yet of the official result but taking his time. Too many athletes had injured themselves with too quick a halt, usually causing tendon strain or a bone chip in the knee or ankle, wanting to immediately see the result flashed on the screen. Tom and the Australian, Richard Francome, eased in tandem to a walk, shook hands and congratulated each other, asking whether the other one had won. Neither knew: both hoped.

The other competitors all joined them, shaking hands, patting backs, congratulating the first pair. Everybody had finished unhurt and sound. They were for a few more blissful moments free from coaches, officials and media. They all waited impatiently for the official result.

The runners stared at the screen and cheered when the result finally flashed.

The winner of the Men's 10,000 Metres' Final:

Number 3, Francome, the man in yellow had prevailed. Australia had won the *gold* medal by half an inch.

The United States runner, *number 2, Brabazon,* in the stars and stripes, was second. *Silver.*

The Soviet Union's man from Siberia, *number 6, Kaminski,* had won the *bronze.* They raise them tough in Siberia.

The time, 28 minutes and 58 seconds, was a new record for the year but slower than Finland's great Lasse

Viren, whose quickest of two gold medals in the 10,000 metres had been twelve seconds faster.

The runners all re-congratulated the medal winners and then their special and private camaraderie was invaded by an excited man with an Australian flag who handed it to Francome. The gold medalist waved it over his head as he trotted his victory lap around the track, acknowledging the crowd's applause and appreciation for an epic final. He was sure that his family—parents, sister, wife and daughter—were cheering back home in front of the TV.

Tom wasn't disappointed, far from it. He was elated, overjoyed and satisfied. He'd given the best performance of his life, had produced every bit of his talent and determination and had won a silver medal. He'd done it, made it, he was a winner.

His parents must surely be proud of him, even have forgiven him for his mistakes, for not running fast enough that awful day in Belfast and being angry with his dad on his 11th birthday.

He'd done it. Won a medal. Did his best. He was proud.

The awards ceremony was rather a blur. He listened to the Australian national anthem for the first time, thought it odd when he—like the other medalists—was handed a bunch of flowers. ("What the hell are we going to do with flowers?" he asked himself, "Open a florist shop?")

Guys don't want flowers. He solved the problem by giving his to Jennifer du Pont Scott when she raced up immediately afterwards to kiss and hug him, shouting, "I'll marry you. I promised I would when you won a medal."

Everybody was very happy, even Tom. He'd done his best, he'd damned near won gold, he'd won silver. Any medal was a success. He had succeeded, that little kid runaway who'd escaped with nothing except for the things that mattered most . . . determination, a dream and honor.

Then they were herded off to be tested, like criminals, for drugs.

His teammates all congratulated him, an Irish journalist called Cathy O'Toole interviewed him and other journalists spoke to him. Photographs were taken and the American TV network interviewer asked him easy questions that he tossed back easily. Nobody accused him with, "Your real name is Steve Walwyn and you've falsified your age."

The coaches pretended that they'd always believed that he'd win a medal.

Even the United States' *chef de mission* shook his hand and congratulated him.

The Italian girl was nowhere to be found but she couldn't have gotten through the crowd of well-wishers without a bazooka.

After a shower, Tom found Dr. Stone at the exit gate and thanked him, tough old Dr. Stone, who was crying tears of joy, a sight no human had previously observed. They shook hands and said to each other:

"That was great. Let's do it again in four years." Tom then hopped on the shuttle bus, returned to the village, went to his room, fell into bed and slept for 12 hours, clutching his medal tight.

****

The closing ceremonies were the next day.

Gone were the formalities and nervousness of the opening ceremonies. The coaches could no longer control their athletes, who were beyond caring about rules or protocols. The athletes deliberately sought out athletes from other countries now that the competitions had ended. This was going to be one massive party as soon as the marathon ended. The athletes mixed together, pouring happily into the stadium the very moment the doors were opened.

Gone, too, was the organized alphabetical entry by country from the opening ceremony. Everybody mingled and mixed in a massive free-for-all, happy, embracing, enjoying, reveling in the next few hours of total happiness and celebration.

You'd believe it impossible in that huge crowd of 12,000 athletes and volunteers, in the darkness, that noise, happy chaos, loud music and swirling celebrations, that one person could find a stranger but Tom Brabazon was a determined hunter in search of a girl whose name he didn't know but thought he loved. He was in the happiest state of his life. In his joy, Brabazon might have found a pin in the world's biggest haystack or Amelia Earhart in the Pacific Ocean.

He found her.

She was thrilled to see him again.

She saw his silver medal hanging around his neck just as her silver was hanging around hers. From the moment they locked eyes, they forgot the party, the closing ceremonies, their teams, the Olympics, blocked out the sounds.

His admiration was clearly reciprocated and they were inseparable until dawn. They danced, talked, him in

French, her in Italian but that made never no mind. There were no barriers after each made the other understand that neither was attached to another person and that they liked and enjoyed each other.

They danced. Tom had never danced before; they danced until they were almost the last people there then walked slowly home the several miles to the athletes' village. Tom wasn't going to ask for sex that night, their first night, they didn't need physical love to prove anything, they both knew that they were in love and Tom heard the phrase "till death us do part" ricochet in his brain and smiled every time.

Once inside the village, Tom walked Katya to the Italians' section, the sun having already risen after the most perfect night of Tom's life. He asked Katya to marry him and she agreed with a huge hug. They kissed again and said goodnight.

Tom was too excited to go to bed. He walked outside, still fingering his medal (he did that for weeks), slid down to the ground, his back against a wall and began laughing.

He was a happy man. Finally.

Chapter 8   PRODIGAL SON RETURNS TO IRELAND

After the closing ceremonies and flight home, the U.S. Olympic team held its goodbye meeting at its Colorado Springs headquarters with medical check-ups and coaching debriefings for all the athletes, excepting the equestrian team who'd traveled straight home with their horses.

The gold medalists were flown to Washington D.C. to be introduced to the President, Vice President and others at a fancy meal at the White House.

Silver medalists like Tom were not invited. As one coach had explained so succinctly, albeit too bluntly for some: "You lot were losers." Either you had won gold or you were a loser. Winner takes all.

That wasn't how Tom or Dr. Stone felt about his silver medal, the result of so much concentration, dedication and focus. They were jubilant, Tom even more so because he was in love with and engaged to marry Katya, his beautiful discovery during the opening ceremonies, the most unexpected and wonderful event of Tom's life.

To him, his silver medal represented victory, not failure, while Katya was sublime: a joy that he'd never imagined possible. She was his other half. As unlikely as it sounded, he was certain that she was his soul mate, the mirror of his soul, the whole point of his existence and reason for his future.

Running had been, of course, the solution to his demons and now running had found Katya for him. Even better, his feelings were reciprocated: Katya loved him. Tom had never felt giddiness like this, had never been in love, not with Sarah Stone or Jennifer du Pont Scott, who'd cheered him on during his Olympic races, or Cathy Darraggio, whom he'd dated after his relationship ended with Sarah.

This was different, this was wonderful, great, he could imagine children and grandchildren, growing old with Katya, being faithful to her, protecting, helping, admiring, enjoying and adoring her.

Yet he didn't speak her language. On the plane home, he decided to learn Italian, to become fluent in it, refusing to require her to learn English. Oh, he'd teach and help her but theirs would be an equal partnership not one where he, as the man, would demand that she change to fit into his life, his customs, his ambitions.

Whatever Katya wanted would be as or more important, as valuable, as his desires. He wanted to make and keep her happy, to honor and encourage her forever.

After the debriefings ended, their Olympic experience over, the athletes were told to leave, to look after themselves, and that their masters would contact the chosen few in a year to consider qualifying for the next Olympic team.

Tom didn't mind, in fact he preferred to be free. Oh, he was determined to participate in the next Olympics but he wanted, needed, his independence so this suited him fine. With his college degree in business, he'd find work doing something interesting, marry Katya, they'd choose where to live and spend a while enjoying themselves while ticking over for 18 months before stepping up their training a notch.

Tom could now see a life beyond running–Katya– although he remained just as determined and obstinate as ever to win gold, for his mom's sake.

If Katya wanted to train for the next Olympics, that would be fine, if she wanted a baby, fine, if she wanted to become a polar explorer or zookeeper or pilot . . . fine.

Tom would do everything in his power to help her achieve whatever she dreamed. His only non-Katya related goal was the next Olympics but he realized, with a few nudges from Dr. Stone, that he needed to ease off his training or he'd boil over.

Tom had two plans now. The second was to marry Katya but first he was determined to return to Ireland and show his medal to his mother and show the old bastard, his ex-stepfather, that he had succeeded and that the old goat had been wrong in his many taunts that Tom was useless and would become a failure.

He was going to push his silver medal into John McKinley's face and force him to admit who was the failure. Of course, McKinley was and Tom wanted, above all, to hear the man, who'd treated him and his mom so shabbily, to say those important words.

The man had never admitted that he was wrong, ever, but acted so superior to Tom and his mother, was so cruel to both of them. He would have to admit to Tom's face that Tom had succeeded and that, despite education at Eton and Trinity College in Dublin, despite inheriting two hundred fifty acres of prime land, despite all his easily gained opportunities, that he, John McKinley, was the failure.

His upper class pedigree and superior upbringing, which had taught him to believe in his innate superiority, had failed him. Despite both grandfathers having been generals in the British Army, despite his victories as an amateur jockey, despite all of those advantages, John had failed to make the team for his Olympics. Now, he would be forced to agree that Tom was a success and he, by comparison, was a failure.

Tom also intended to collect all of his mother's money, which McKinley had stolen from her.

Tom first flew home to rest for two days and didn't even run once. He felt odd, let down after the excitement, there was nobody at college to whom he could tell his wondrous news, because all the other students were away for summer vacation. His apartment was just a place to sleep, it wasn't a home. The Olympics seemed almost a dream, because there wasn't anybody with whom to share his experience.

At college, his unusual life had separated him from the other students who'd lived such stable lives–he had distanced himself, hadn't known how to change. In Ireland, he'd been a foreigner because he'd been born in America but in the States he was an outsider because he'd grown up abroad. He had no roots, no family, no shared experiences with childhood friends. Although he always insisted to himself that those negatives never upset him, truthfully they did . . . to his core.

He hoped that, in time, he and Katya would find someplace that included them. He didn't want to stay an outsider forever. He wanted them to belong somewhere.

****

Tom had unfinished business.

He flew to Ireland, landing at Dublin airport before breakfast time on a beautiful summer's morning. The airport was much bigger than it had been on his first arrival in Ireland as an 11-year-old, emigrating from the States. Everyone had laughed when he said that he was frightened, having seen how tiny Ireland was on his classroom's world map, that he was afraid they would fall over a cliff into the sea.

The immigration officer recognized him as an Olympian because the Irish media, led by Cathy O'Toole, had adopted him as an Irishman. She was the same young woman who'd helped him at the Irish Times several years back when he'd gone looking for the lady with the crooked son-in-law minister.

Cathy had almost recognized him when insisting on an interview at the Olympics, then ignored his story of being descended from a convict—she invented a more palatable ancestry for the hero—and had appointed the American runner an Irishman. This, because he possessed the Irish surname made famous forever by the 1940s steeplechase jockey, Aubrey Brabazon, who'd ridden the great steeple-chaser Cottage Rake to victory three times in the hallowed Cheltenham Gold Cup in 1948, 1949 and 1950.

They'd become national heroes in old Ireland, the country's first post World War II heroes, when there were still more people using donkeys and carts than cars, half a century before the Celtic Tiger was invented.

> *Aubrey's up, the money's down,*
> *The frightened bookies quake*
> *Come on, me lads, and give a cheer,*
> *Begod, 'tis Cottage Rake*

Tom thanked the immigration officer for his congratulations but asked him to keep quiet about his arrival.

He'd heard somewhere that some immigration officers supplement their take-home pay with cash by tipping off the media regarding the arrivals of "celebrities." He suspected that an Olympian might represent a small honorarium, particularly on what was probably a slow news day as there were no Beatles in sight.

Tom supposed that the media would receive a call despite his request and, wanting even more than usual to be invisible in Ireland, he used a different name for the rental car.

The clever forger Mark Moulton, Tom's schoolmate, had been kept busy all those years ago for Steve Walwyn, making up different identities for the young lad who was so determined to vanish without trace.

So it was that, instead of a temporarily famous Olympian with the Brabazon surname, Tom was Michael Ferguson Dickinson, who was a month older, lived in Boston, and rented a compact car from one of the smaller rental car agencies at the Dublin airport.

He had no trouble remembering which narrow roads to take from the airport, having been driven to and from it enough times. He turned left, drove through the village of Swords–'strange name, that,' he told himself–and drove for an hour and a half along mostly empty roads through a very familiar landscape.

Along the way he passed several farms whose owners, like many cattle farmers in those days, believed in using "Long Farm," also known as the roadsides where there was plenty of grass: all of it free. Nobody complained, or would have considered doing so, and traffic was rare so there was no real danger to the cows.

Cattle were still herded on hoof to the markets during Tom's previous time in Ireland. Liability insurance and litigation were unknown in rural Ireland in those days. It was a common sight in the late afternoons to see a child or two, armed only with sticks, rounding up the cows and sending them home at a slow walk.

Passing one particular farm brought a laugh to Tom as he recalled its chief cow, known as "Bossy," an immense creature with an uncharacteristically bad temper, whose practice of lying down on the road with her tail stretched across the other lane would stop traffic while she chewed placidly, ignoring attempts to make her move until she was ready. Strangers got out of their cars and often became friendly: one unsubstantiated rumor had insisted that several pregnancies had occurred while people waited for Bossy to get up and move.

He remembered a schoolmate named Fox, who lived in Co. Meath, only a few miles from where he was driving now, not far from the Hill of Tara where the ancient Kings of Ireland had met 1500 years earlier for major negotiations and wild, debauched parties. Not far away was the town of Navan, which would become famous a few years later as the birthplace of James Bond actor Pierce Brosnan.

The Fox family endured a curious tradition: 24 hours before the death of a family member, anywhere in the world, the local foxes would appear from the woods, circle the house and bay. Although spooky, the locals insisted that it was true.

Tom was now in deepest rural Ireland, in what he considered "home," where he'd lived from just before his 12th birthday until he'd run away from school at seventeen. Where he and his mother had been strangers to the closed worlds of both the Anglo-Irish aristocracy and Irish Catholic working class, automatically distrusted by both groups (especially the Anglo-Irish) simply because of their nationality. It wasn't fair but he and his mother were both foreigners and that could never change.

He reached his destination, the front gate of his former home.

This was where he'd spent all his school holidays, on the farm down the long driveway, behind the closed but unlocked iron gate. He sat uncomfortably puzzled in his car. The scene was wrong.

This was the right place but the entrance had gone "native." It was untidy, unlike when he'd lived there, in what had been generally regarded as the most beautiful property in the district. Not the biggest or fanciest house but a reflection of his mother's determination and flair.

He hadn't been there for seven years and the whitethorn hedge, which ran for the entire half mile along the quiet road, had gone wild, clearly uncut for several years. It had been one of his many farm jobs to cut and layer this with tools like slashers and axes, because his stepfather, though happy to spend his mom's money on horses and clothes and parties, was disinclined to hire a tractor-operated hedge cutter which could have trimmed every mile of the farm's hedgerows in two days.

Why waste money, McKinley often laughed, when young Stevie was home doing nothing useful.

"Young people stay out of trouble when they're busy. Keep them too tired to cause trouble, that's what I say," was his explanation.

Of course he never paid "young Peter"—he never called Stevie by his real name—either money or a compliment for cutting the hedges, painting fences and gates, cleaning the ditches with just a shovel, building horse jumps and mucking out stalls. Tom also repaired stone walls, cut hay with a scythe the old-fashioned way, putting it into round haystacks, chopped and sawed downed tree branches into firewood.

Other tasks included carrying the heavy slate shingles, weighing 40 pounds each, back up onto the high roof after they'd tumbled to the ground during windstorms, carrying water from the distant troughs to the house in summer when the house well ran dry, digging the house well deeper with a shovel after the old man lowered him down on a rope then dropped the rope and walked off, keeping Stevie at the bottom of the hand-dug well until he remembered to return.

John McKinley didn't do much in the way of work himself during the school holidays, calling himself a supervisor and teacher, saying:

"I like to see young people at work. It's good for their souls," and "I approve of hard work. I can watch it all day."

When Stevie was at school and his half-brother was too young either to work or to be shipped off to boarding school, McKinley mucked out the stalls and did essential repairs but mostly he just rode his horses.

Tom never minded the work, preferring to be occupied, busy, doing useful activities and he had never been one for watching TV. Mind you, TV was quite basic back then: just a fledgling piece of exciting technology in black and white, showing the one Irish station, RTE, which repeated endless American cowboy soap operas while the only alternative was a grainy, wobbly picture of the BBC with its *Z Cars* and *Dad's Army*.

What Tom had objected to was being treated like a servant, at McKinley's beck and call and every whim, being ordered about, the belittling and constant criticism, never receiving any appreciation. Some may draw a certain similarity to Heathcliff in Emily Bronte's *Wuthering Heights* but that never crossed Tom's mind, even while reading the book at school. For one thing, there was no wild, free-spirited Cathy in the house and, in the book, the old master of the house had always treated the adopted Heathcliff with kindness: it was the master's son who'd started all the agony.

Most especially, Tom despised McKinley's treatment of his mother. He hated McKinley and he was now finally going to settle a long overdue score and prove that he'd become a success, despite his stepfather's criticisms and predictions.

But something prevented him from getting out of the car to open the gate and hurl himself towards confrontation.

Tom decided to go elsewhere before confronting his nemesis–he was more nervous than he'd expected–so he backed out onto the road, turned right and passed O'Reilly's Shop, which was 50 yards from the gate and had grown in the last few years. Then he drove through the hamlet of Ballykennan past the "shibeen," an unlicensed pub. That's where Mr. Fagan brewed *potheen*, a drink made from distilled potato that could remove paint from a car and possessed the kick of an angry mule. West Virginia's moonshine is the equivalent 'poison'–or joy–in the U.S.

Mrs. Fagan sold magic medical lotions, having convinced a loyal clientele that her special tonic cured warts, diarrhea, skin diseases and intestinal complaints. It didn't, however, cure poverty.

For all his unpleasantness, his stepfather could possess a wry sense of humor and gallons of charm when he found it useful, like when courting Tom's mother in the States, and he used to invent extraordinary stories about local people just for fun.

Take old Oliver Deegan, an ancient semi-retired small farmer who passed his days walking up and down the half-mile between his house and O'Reilly's shop and had most probably never traveled further than his local church. McKinley claimed that Deegan was a CIA spy, whose hearing aid connected him directly to the White House and who frequently traveled through Europe on vital espionage missions.

Another local farmer, a man whose only possessions in this world were an ancient donkey and rickety cart, was reclassified by McKinley into an international business mogul who, like John Pierpont Morgan decades earlier, regularly terrified the traders on Wall Street.

McKinley once placed an order for striped paint at the hardware store in Mullingar, saying that his mother-in-law sold it to barbers for their flagpoles.

Full of memories, Tom drove past the small national schoolhouse that educated the local Catholic working class kids until the age of 14, when they were pushed out into the world to fend for themselves. He took a left and drove two miles to Rathincree Church for Protestants—Church of Ireland—where his family had gone every Sunday morning to church.

It was an important weekly social get-together based on a calm, gentle belief in God rather than hardcore bible-thumping religion: very far from Lutherism or, a few decades later, Jimmy and Tammy Faye Bakker in North Carolina.

The current church had been constructed in 1788 on the site—going back far enough—of the original religious church founded in the 7th Century by a St. Eltan. An ancestor of Elton John, perhaps?

As a boy, Tom/Steve had been fascinated by the local history told to him by Mary O'Sullivan, who had included a story about a religious synod held there in 804.

Unfortunately, for 9th century property developers hoping to make a quick profit by capitalizing on Rathincree's certain increase in property values, it never grew into a regional city or even a village.

Hamlet was as large as you could stretch the description: it was simply a crossroads with an ancient pub, a church 50 yards away and nothing else. The year 804 was the apex of Rathincree's excitement and it had been rather quiet since, except for church services on Sunday mornings and the occasional marriage and funeral.

Back in 1788, having used the church in Rathincree for centuries, the Catholic priests built a new and bigger church one mile away in the next parish and gave the land and building to the Church of Ireland. Catholics were still buried on the right hand side of the driveway while the left side was reserved for Protestant parishioners.

St. Eltan had used a holy well less than a hundred yards away that was still in use by the locals for their drinking and bath water almost 1400 years later. People had lived here for 60 generations but there was very little trace of them.

Tom parked at the closed gate, which led up a short, steep driveway through the old graveyard to the grey stone church. There were no people in sight—the only other living humans would have been inside the pub.

The scene was thoroughly peaceful, empty rural Ireland in mid-afternoon at its best, far from every maddening crowd, but this spot hadn't always been so relaxing.

Well known for their human sacrifices, the Druids had spent time here in pre-Christian and pre-St. Eltan days, while Tom could see a small hill named Cnoc na Liu (Gaelic language for "hill of the crying") where in 1642 British troops had massacred 230 innocents, who were working in the surrounding fields, just for fun. Cattle were grazing there now, chewing bloodstained grass.

Tom reflected as to how the local scene hadn't changed a jot since his last visit. He'd changed enormously but this spot was identical. Except for the paving of its roads, this spot in rural Ireland was unchanged for many centuries. Did the pub customers change, he wondered. How old was the thatched pub: hundreds or maybe a thousand years?

The last time he'd been here was the day of his mother's funeral. He walked slowly towards the church and found his mother's grave all alone on the left side, about 40 yards from the door, near the stone wall. It was a modern tombstone with clear, unfaded lettering unlike most of the other unreadable tombstones, some of which dated back many centuries.

It was quiet and he was alone. He stood at the base of his mother's grave and, even though there was nobody alive to hear him, spoke quietly.

"Mom, it's Stevie. I love you. Here is my silver medal that I won at the Olympics. I won it for you."

He began crying.

"I'm still so sorry, so very sorry, that I didn't run that evening. I just walked. If I'd run, I'd have gotten there sooner and we'd have been well clear, down the street, when the bomb blew up. It was my fault: not the bomb, of course, but my fault that you were still there waiting for me. I'm sorry, sorry, sorry. I've been running everywhere, ever since. I'm now living back in America."

He continued:

"One day, I promise, I'll arrange for you to be moved from here, where you had no friends, back home to be with Daddy in his grave in Virginia. I don't know how to do it yet but I promise that I will. You've been here too long, seven long years. I've thought about you every day, every single day."

He looked around to make sure that no people were watching. Only sheep in the next paddock and they were taking no notice of him.

"I've graduated from college, represented our country in the Olympics and I've met Katya, the girl I'm going to marry. She's lovely and I'm sure that you'd approve of her. I'll treat her like a princess, the way Daddy treated you, the way McKinley never did.

"I suppose that if it's true that there's an afterlife, and I don't know, that you're in heaven and you know what I've been doing, that you're watching me. I hope that you can hear me. If not, then you're just lying here. I hope that you're up in heaven, which is what you deserve, and that you're with Daddy and Billy, happy and pro . . . " he stuttered, choked with emotion, "proud of me."

He stuttered for a while.

"I'm doing my best in life to make you proud of me. I'm gonna win a gold medal or two or three. For you, Mom, for you. Haven't figured out my career yet but I'll fight injustice somehow, do something valuable and useful. I'll never do anything improper to anyone but I'll improve my corner of this world, somehow, like Daddy did before he died."

He paused, failing to control his weeping.

"Right now, I've got unfinished business to take care of at Barclay House. I'm going to see that bastard. He's going to apologize for having made you unhappy and then I'm going to punish him to make him sorry that he treated you so badly. I'll get back the money he stole from you and use some of it to have you transferred to Virginia. Goodbye, Mom, for now."

Sobbing uncontrollably, Tom walked back down the driveway to his car.

Forcing himself to cheer up, he remembered the time when, oh he was about 13 or 14, an important member of the community named Henry Marsh who trained horses had been at a party nearby with his wife and young assistant Noel.

After having too much to drink, Marsh ordered Noel to drive when they left at 2 a.m., after several happy hours of whiskey and poker. The young man peered nervously through the dense fog. Young Noel was desperately tired, struggling to keep his eyes open and somehow stay on the unfamiliar roads, which had deep drainage ditches on both sides.

There was suddenly a bump, then a crash and the car stopped, all forward progress prevented by some invisible obstacle. When Noel got out for a closer look, he saw that the car bumper was pressed up against a tombstone in the Rathincree churchyard, somebody having inconveniently left the gate open.

Henry jumped up, suddenly awake and shouted, "Where are we?" When Noel replied that they were in a churchyard, Henry answered, "Let it graze," and returned to sleep. Noel reversed nervously and crept home.

****

Tom drove back to the front gate of Barclay House, opened it and drove slowly down the long driveway. He was nervous but this was home. He shouldn't have been frightened but he was trembling all the same.

How can anyone be afraid of home?

He wasn't scared of a fight, because he was prepared for nothing else. There were no animals in the 22-acre front field. As he turned the 45-degree bend, he hit the brakes in shock.

The house, his home where he'd grown up, was a roof-less ruin with empty windows, the front doorway gone, its former beauty vanished.

Nobody could be living there now. Nobody could ever live there again, either. After passing the huge and ancient beech tree on his right, he parked outside the front yard gate, switched off the ignition and climbed slowly from the car. The place was silent, no sign or sound of horses and cattle, not even any birds singing, everything was eerie and the house was clearly empty.

He walked slowly, carefully, shocked to see his mother's beautiful rose garden gone to waste, a car in the main garage with its windows broken, slashed tires and bullet holes in its sides. The monkey puzzle tree and the small golf putting green on the right lawn had vanished amid grass four feet tall.

Everything was a mess.

The house, built in 1702 with local limestone rock and three-feet-thick external walls, was a wreck.

As he stepped through what had been the front door and noticed the glassless front windows that had adorned the living and dining rooms, he realized that the house had burned and very recently.

The floors and the wood paneling were gone, there was rubbish strewn all over and plenty of water—presumably from the fire brigade—everywhere, compounding the mess. It was warm and the fire was clearly recent. His feet crunched on the broken shards of glass scattered every-where.

Tom retched, partly from the rancid smell but also from the shock of losing what had been perfect. A beauti-fully designed house that could, should, have been fea-tured in *Country Life* or *Luxury Houses of the World* magazines was now a ruin and surely impossible to restore to what it had been when his mother had been in charge.

She had ensured that the house was innovated and updated in every way—she had put her foot down at the beginning and gotten her way, using her own money for the improvements.

She'd been unimpressed when her new husband showed her the house, which he'd lived in alone. The place needed many improvements and a woman's touch.

Aghast at the idea of keeping coal and wood burning in the fireplaces in every single one of the 15 rooms—the Aga stove kept the kitchen the warmest room in the house, as was typical in Ireland—she'd demanded central heating.

Finding that no house in Ireland had it, she had imported a specialist contractor from London tout de suite. She wasn't going to freeze in this old house in winter. It was cold even in summer.

The wool carpets, wires and pipes, old paintings, framed photographs and the magnificent elk head trophy were twisted together in heaps. As he progressed painfully and with huge sadness—his mother not being alive to see this, was his only consolation—down the hallway, peering into each room, he was ever more shocked by each new sight of desolation, destruction and ugliness. He arrived expecting an argument and a fight, probably including blood, but he'd never expected this.

There was obviously nobody living here. How, why had the house burned down and how could it be restored to his former glory, Tom kept asking himself. Insurance would surely pay for it but it couldn't ever be the same.

The house was a ruin.

Ireland was full of burned-out mansions, historically burned by locals rebelling against their masters living in the "big houses." These formerly beautiful houses were now beyond restoring, open to all weathers, rotting away, permanent dark shells, reminders of oppression.

But that was in the past and had mostly stopped by the time of Independence in 1922. That couldn't be the cause here. Only Germans were burned out of their houses in Ireland these days.

The turning staircase was mostly destroyed. Tom decided not to risk climbing it even though he wanted to see what his old bedroom looked like, to discover whether any trace of him remained.

Under the stairs, he looked into the small toilet room with its secret passage in case of attack. The toilet had been installed by order of his mother, the house having no internal plumbing during its first two and a half centuries before he and his mother had arrived. Refusing to live in a house without toilets or running water, she'd gone immediately to the hotel in Mullingar, a largish town a few miles away, until civilization had been installed.

Oh yes, guess who had to clean out the septic tank with a shovel and bucket: yes, it was Tom.

More memories crowded into his shocked brain. McKinley had refused, Tom now remembered, to allow him more than three inches of water in his weekly bath and woke him every morning at 6 a.m., slashing a cold wet towel across his face.

On mornings when his mother was away, his stepfather would pour the contents of a bucket over Tom and refuse to allow the bed linen or blankets to be changed until the day of his mother's return. John McKinley would have presumably failed "sensitivity and good step-parenting" classes.

No wonder Tom never minded the discomforts of boarding school where, no matter what else happened (and plenty did), he always slept in a dry bed.

He looked into the narrow library where many tense evenings had been endured while McKinley drank whiskey and sniped at Tom and his mother. This room was unrecognizable, even worse than the dining and living rooms at the front of the house.

The beautiful wood shelves with ancient books were dissolved into a mess. The portrait of his mother at age 18 at her debutante's party in Philadelphia, a lifetime ago, was in tatters, her then-innocent face only just visible. Tom retched again. The other paintings, mostly of horses, the leather furniture and carpet had also been destroyed by the fire. There were bottles and broken glass on the floor.

Brabazon turned into the kitchen, which, like all the other rooms, was a complete mess. He remembered many happy times in this room when just he and his mother would relax while McKinley was out riding his horses or away doing errands or visiting relatives and friends. He never took his wife along.

They'd sit together, usually sipping hot chocolates, with his mother telling her son about her childhood and first marriage "to the greatest, kindest man I've ever known"–his father the police officer–and Tom telling her his dreams of winning an Olympic medal and saving her from this hell.

McKinley never actually hit her–he was proud of his code of honor of "never hitting a woman because that's wrong"–but his verbal abuse, arrogance and lack of affection were more than enough to have drained all joy from his mother's life. But mother and son used to sit there in the kitchen, ignoring the present, remembering the past, dreaming of a better future.

Tom's shock at this devastation became horror when he saw what could have been—but surely it wasn't—five Olympic rings, the Olympics' symbol of peace and unity. They had been sprayed—splattered in shaky shapes rather than circles—on the wall above the old Aga stove with the words, "They stink" and "Peter's a bastard" on another wall. Tom literally staggered.

"Peter" had been his stepfather's nickname for him. The graffiti was obviously referring to him.

This was all too much.

He ran out of the house into the back courtyard where he used to play rugby by himself, both teams, thirty players, with himself as the impartial but fair referee. His much younger half-brother, George, had been too young to play with him but had often acted as his enthusiastic audience and unreliable scorekeeper. He'd always liked George, never blaming the son for the father's sins. He wondered where George was and where the hell was McKinley, the old bastard.

Tom wondered whether McKinley had remarried.

Tom felt that he'd had all the stuffing shaken out of him by now and that he'd be hard pressed to outpunch either Pooh Bear or Mickey Mouse. He was relieved that the house was empty.

He was determined to find McKinley but he needed to calm down for a while so he went out to a field and sat down, mentally exhausted, leaning against an old oak tree. He fell asleep and didn't wake up for an hour, finding himself covered in drizzle. He got up, wiped his face with his handkerchief and, mission unaccomplished, walked to his car, got in and drove away, shutting the road gate behind him and heading to O'Reilly's shop for information.

The shop had been enlarged since his last visit. He remembered the owner, an old woman, with the quickest, sharpest brain of anyone he'd ever met, including his college professors.

She'd left school at age 14 armed with only the basics but had begun this grocery shop from scratch after her husband's death. She and her two sons had grown it into what had obviously become a prosperous, high quality food store and petrol station at the center of the scattered community and the only shop of any kind within a large radius.

The old lady could quickly add and subtract in the old currency in her head—pounds, shillings and pence, 12 pence in a shilling and 20 shillings or "bob" in a pound, with farthings, ha'pennies, thruppences, two and sixes, half crowns and guineas tossed into the currency's melting pot before decimalization and inflation were forced on the citizens.

Without using a calculator or paper and pencil, Mrs. O'Reilly calculated the amounts more accurately than any computer, which hadn't yet been invented or, at any rate, hadn't reached rural County Westmeath.

She was invariably accurate no matter how often her customers checked the numbers. She'd also short-change the customer, just to ensure that the buyer was paying attention, and always provided the balance upon request.

But the customer had to ask and for the correct amount or Mrs. O'Reilly won the contest and kept the change. Tom's first off-the-farm job had been stocking the shelves, pumping petrol and carrying the milk bottles inside from the sun. He'd learned a lot about the local people while working there.

All these years later, Tom wanted to remain unrecognized–it was such an ingrained instinct in him. He walked in, still shaken from what he'd seen across the road and was relieved not to find Mrs. O'Reilly or her son, Sean, whom he knew would recognize him. He saw a young man in his upper teens.

He introduced himself as Ciaran O'Reilly, Sean's son. Sean and his mother, he explained, had gone to the races in Galway about 40 miles away and had left him in charge.

"What can I do for you? You're a stranger around here, aren't you?"

"Yes, I'm just passing through," Tom began as he chose a chocolate bar, a bag of biscuits and a bottle of blackcurrant juice. "A friend of mine at school, Steve Walwyn, used to live on the farm across the road. I haven't seen him for years, we lost touch, so I thought I'd drop in and visit."

"Have you been over there yet?"

"Yes, what happened? Where are Steve and his family? When did the house burn down?"

"Well, we were told that Steve died at school."

"Well," Tom answered carefully, "he didn't. We finished sixth form together and he started at Trinity College in Dublin."

"Well, that's not what we were told. Mr. McKinley told me Da and Gran that he'd died playing cricket at school."

"Well, that's wrong. I know he didn't and, besides, that's ridiculous. How can anyone die playing cricket?"

At any other time, they might have laughed. People sometimes died playing hurling, which was Ireland's national sport—but never on the cricket field.

"Well," said Ciaran, "that's what Mr. McKinley told us so we believed him. We have to believe the McKinleys because they own this community. They're the local royalty." Tom knew that was true.

Having been the big local landowners for generations, with most of them British Army officers and all of them successful horse riders, they behaved like royalty and tolerated the local citizenry with undisguised condescension. Ireland was changing quickly in this decade and the traditional power structure with it. The McKinleys' power was ebbing and would vanish before the end of the millenium. Ciaran sounded petulant, like he didn't agree with the status quo. He had good cause.

"So, Steve must have died at Trinity which explains why he didn't stay in touch," replied Tom. He'd wondered how the bastard had explained his absence. Death rather stopped all need for supplying further updates.

"Well, what about the house?"

"Well now, sure it's funny that you're visiting now," Ciaran answered. "It burned down on Friday last week. It's hard to believe, sure enough. The fire began after dinner. I was the first one who saw flames when I went outside to switch off the petrol pumps. I shouted to me Da and we rode our bikes down to the house. The house was blazing. We rushed back here and called Emergency and the fire brigade came but it was too late. They were there for hours, until dawn, but couldn't save the house."

"Wow," Tom said when Ciaran took a sip of tea.

"Then it got worse. The firemen found Mr. McKinley's body. He was dead, found in his library, burnt to death by the fire."

"That's terrible," was Tom's verbal response but inside he was unsympathetic, furious, swearing silently: The fuc- . . . cheated me. He died before I could kill him. Damn him, damn him to hell. I'll never win now.

"Well, it was and it wasn't. You shouldn't speak ill of the dead, I know that, Father Cleary and me Da and Gran say that but Mr. McKinley always treated me bad."

Tom encouraged him to continue.

"Always a sneer, always rude. He used to snigger that my mother had abandoned me, used to step on my toes while I was pumping his petrol and push me. Didn't pay his bills, either, to us or a lot of others. He drank too much and was often drunk when he came in here. Oh, I shouldn't being saying this especially to you. I don't know you."

"It's ok, don't worry," Tom told him. "I believe you and it's ok, really. Steve used to talk about his stepfather a lot. He was nasty to him, too."

Ciaran's anger was stronger than his diplomacy and he couldn't know that Tom was experienced at getting strangers to open up and reveal their real feelings.

"Well, he owes us a lot of money. Always said, 'just put it on my account,'" Ciaran said in a fake Anglo-Irish accent. "He used to say: 'Oh, I don't bother paying cash for little amounts.'"

"How did he get away with it?" Tom asked gently.

"He's a McKinley and Anglo-Irish, that's how. I'm leaving here soon, I just can't stand being treated like dirt by the McKinleys and some of the others. We're shopkeepers, middle class, we work hard, we're not rubbish."

"Well, what happened?" Tom was keen to direct Ciaran away from his future plans and back to Tom's preferred subject.

"The fire chief told us that Mr. McKinley began the fire with a can of petrol, bought but not paid for from us. There were lots of empty whiskey bottles, Mr. O'Donovan said, so he thought that the squire had lit petrol or dropped a match while drunk." Ciaran drank more tea.

"He'd been drinking awful hard for years, ever since his American wife died. She was a lovely, beautiful lady, who died in a bomb blast in Belfast, such a terrible thing. Did you know her?" Ciaran asked innocently.

"Yes," replied Tom and agreed. "My mom . . ." he slipped but corrected himself, hoping that Ciaran hadn't noticed. "Steve's mom, yes, she was lovely."

"Well, she was always very kind to me, never looked down at me or any of us, treated us all well. She used to tell me stories about America. I want to go there, you know? Everybody loved her and . . ." his voice trailed off for a while, remembering, "and her older son Stevie. They also had another son named George, my age, but he's living in England now with his aunt. Been there for a good few years now."

Another customer came in, paid for petrol and left.

"Stevie was a nice lad. He helped here in the shop, did you know?"

Tom knew, of course, but didn't comment.

"And he was fast. One time Stevie caught a thief—Jimmy Connolly, it was, a bad piece of work. His brother Mick was at school with me."

Tom had forgotten this event.

"Jimmy grabbed twenty quid from our money box, we didn't have a cash register then, we'd never had any thefts. He ran out of the shop when me Da saw what he'd done. Jimmy jumped on his bike and took off towards Ballykennan. Stevie came out of the storeroom when he heard Da shouting and took off on foot after Jimmy, who had to 've been 100 yards away by then. Steve was so quick that he caught him and pulled him off his bike, got the money and brought it back to me Da. Yeah, Stevie was fast." He paused.

Tom recalled that Jimmy's head start was really only about 20 yards but was pleased with the fish-got-bigger story.

"Ya know, Mr. McKinley came in last week cussin' and swearin' that he'd seen Stevie on TV, but he always called him 'Peter,' I don't know why. He shouted that he'd seen Stevie running in the Olympics and winning a medal. We thought he'd gone mad for hadn't Stevie died at school all those years ago?"

Tom suddenly understood the graffiti in the kitchen. He'd been recognized by the man he hated most in this world. He felt a glimmer of satisfied revenge and slightly less cheated, because he now knew that McKinley had watched him become a winner. He felt not an ounce of sympathy for the man who'd perished in the fire. He tried to keep a straight face but failed.

"What is it?" Ciaran asked.

"Ah, nothing. You're right, the man must have been mad."

"Well, that was the last time we saw him. He'd told Da to 'put the petrol on his tab'–again. After Mr. McKinley left, Da told me that he owed us 1,600 quid and that, until we got his money, he couldn't afford for me to go to the chefs' training school in Dublin and that was final." Ciaran tidied up the magazines on the counter.

"I want to be a chef with my own restaurant in America some day. New York sounds good. I knew then and there that I'd go down to the house and demand our money that evening. Thanks be to God that Father Cleary came to supper with us that evening or I'd be accused of killin' Mr. McKinley. I have an alibi. Father Cleary is my witness."

So, Tom thought with considerable relief, so do I. His alibi was cast-iron solid for he'd been surrounded by dozens of people at the Olympic Center in Colorado Springs that whole day and the next, five thousand miles away in the Rocky Mountains. Not even a silver medalist could move that quickly.

"The funeral was yesterday. None of us locals went. We all disliked him and he let that good farm go to pieces, too. Me Da says that's a crime for that lovely farm."

It was time to leave. Tom didn't want to risk being there when Ciaran's father and grandmother returned from the races, because he knew that they'd recognize him: no doubt about that. He thanked Ciaran and drove off.

Where to now, he wondered.

Unusually, he had nowhere to go, a change from his always tightly planned schedule. He'd had enough emotional battering for one day. He'd expected to return to the airport after confronting John McKinley and fly back to the States, satisfied with having settled an old festering sore and probably with a murder on his conscience. That had been his plan for seven years. He didn't feel like getting on another plane today and knew better than to check into a hotel room and stare at the wall with only his demons for company.

He drove idly off, making a turn here and there without purpose or conscious effort, lost in memories good and bad, wondering how his life would have turned out if his dad hadn't died in Baltimore, if McKinley had been loving to his mom and decent to him, if his best friend Tom–the real Tom–hadn't died, and most of all, if he'd run faster and saved his mom from being blasted to death outside that restaurant in Belfast.

Tom awoke from his reverie and discovered that he was at a familiar crossroads, beside a public tennis court. Turning right would take him to his only remaining friends in Ireland. Serendipity or not, he could see the O'Sullivans' two-storied modest grey stuccoed house only 100 yards away. Their house had been his refuge for many years.

Old man O'Sullivan was a blacksmith, while his older brother Sean had returned from the States as a retired and never-arrested con man with a fund of stories that fascinated all the boys, especially Steve.

Jolly Mrs. O'Sullivan believed that good food–and she was a great cook–solved all ills and, despite no money, with five sons and two daughters, there was always laughter, lots of jokes and fun in their house. Tom had learned in their home that wealth didn't equal happiness and that families could be happy without money. What Tom needed now was laughter and Mrs. O'Sullivan's mothering. They had been his refuge many times and he needed the O'Sullivans now.

He expected considerable surprise when they'd open the door to see the long lost prodigal son on their doorstep. He felt as if he were truly home. Nothing had changed: peat smoke was leaving the chimney, the tiny lawn was mowed and tidy and it seemed that at least here nothing had changed. He knocked.

"Come give me a hug, Stevie Walwyn, right now," instructed an amazed, slightly greyer and a much heavier Mrs. O'Sullivan, who must have been in her 50s by now. And, by God, despite an unyielding lifelong hatred of obeying orders, Tom obeyed her instantly and with relief. He felt like a child again as she pulled him into her enormous bosom and called out to her family.

"Oh my Lord, Jesus Christ, everyone come see whom our Lord has brought home to us. Stephen, you've grown up so much." Now this was a warm, well, hot, welcome as six members of the O'Sullivan family abandoned whatever they'd been doing to greet him with undisguised joy.

"Well, the prodigal son has returned," laughed Gary, the biggest mischief-maker and joker of the children. "Come on in, we never believed that story that you'd died at school."

Everybody chimed in a question or three. It was all a jumble and Tom was thrilled to be welcomed so heartily. He had spent many happy hours in this house.

"Where have you been, Stevie?"

"My, you've grown up a lot. Tell us what you've been doing."

"We've missed you. Come on in and sit down right here at the kitchen table and tell us everything."

"You look exhausted. Why?"

"Here, you must be starving. Have some tea and supper."

"Are you married? Any children yet?"

"Are you alone?"

"You look grand, lad, Stevie, look how big you are now."

"Where are ya living and what are ya doing with yourself?"

"We've prayed for your soul and your darlin' mum's soul many times and thought of you often."

While old Mr. O'Sullivan said the best line of all: "We've all missed you, lad."

****

Tom fell asleep right after finishing supper, called 'tea' by the Irish but a meal rather than simply a beverage. He slept for almost 24 hours, his next conscious thought appearing the next afternoon at 3:30 when he woke to find himself in a bed, wearing his own pajamas and holding an old, threadbare teddy bear. After a shower and a shave, he went downstairs to find Mrs. O'Sullivan in the kitchen, cooking him a lovely snack. Ravenous, he ate all of it. He relaxed before supper, taking a walk, reading a book, napping.

That evening, over dinner and feeling much better, he explained his past seven years to the O'Sullivan family. They were proud of him for having improved himself and especially for his Olympic medal, asking repeatedly to rub it. They required many answers about the Olympics, being in awe of his having competed.

Gary O'Sullivan asked if Tom remembered old man Stirling, who'd had four sons at school, when Tom was still Steve. His eldest boy, Walter, was a brilliant athlete, the best ever seen at the school, the champion teenage athlete in the whole of Ireland and a certain future Olympian. However, his father had insisted that Walter refuse a sports scholarship offered by a top American university, which would have fast-tracked him to the Olympics and a professional athletic career afterwards in any of the dozen sports in which the young man excelled.

Why had old Stirling denied permission? Because, as a professional paid athlete, considered unacceptably vulgar to the stiff Anglo-Irish, his son would no longer be eligible for membership to the county's fishing club. Walter obeyed and, sadly no scholar, became a local potter, evidently a more socially acceptable occupation.

"What a waste of talent," everybody agreed.

"He was the first brilliant athlete I knew," said Tom. "He was where I got the ambition to be an Olympian. Later, the world champion squash player Jonah Barrington came to my school to teach squash."

The O'Sullivan clan knew nothing of psychiatry but plenty about life and had first-hand experience with suffering. They realized that Tom was at great risk of depression, having in such a short time reached the very heights of ecstasy before crashing into the depths of despair. They also knew the cure: plenty of hard work and laughter plus, above all, no time for brooding. Their treatment worked.

Gary and Tom returned the rental car to Dublin airport, Gary driving because Tom was too shaky and exhausted, and caught buses to return home. They rode one from the airport terminal into the main bus station in the centre of Dublin, then hopped onto a provincial bus to the nearest village, walking home the last two miles.

Tom stayed for three months, repairing himself by helping with the horses, assisting in the blacksmith shop with the making of iron gates and repairing farm machinery brought in by the locals, shopping with Mrs.

O'Sullivan, rounding up the cattle and herding them to the cattle market on foot. This was a long way from the Olympics and his problems.

He laughed as the O'Sullivan family reminded him of the many funny events which had happened over the years. As a clan, they were determined to make him enjoy life for a while.

"Do you remember the time Gary visited Barclay House after you'd just carried two buckets of water in from a cattle trough and placed them on the back door-stop during a drought, when the house well was dry? Your mother would boil the water for the family to drink it. Gary looked at the mess and told your dear mother, God rest her soul, 'Missus, there's more eatin' than drinkin' in there.'"

"Your first girlfriend, Ellen Wilkinson, ah she was a special one even though her mother, a German princess, insisted that the Germans had won the War. Ellen was the most beautiful girleen I ever saw," said Mrs. O'Sullivan, "and Olly fixed that dangerous pony of hers."

The phone rang. Mrs. O'Sullivan answered it and had a brief conversation before resuming her tale:

"Ellen rode over to see you when the pony was finally safe to be ridden, just a girl of 14 or 15, and at your front gate took off all her clothes—all of them except her panties—and rode down your driveway like Lady Godiva, almost as bare as the day she entered this world. She slid off her pony when she saw ya' and gave you a big kiss and hug. That John McKinley was envious of ya that day, so he was."

Tom remembered. That had been a great afternoon.

"Sure, and didn't ya meet Mick Jagger at her house one day—he was Ellen's mother's boyfriend for a while—

and when we asked you if you'd gotten his autograph, you hadn't a clue who her man was? Jeez, that'd be worth a lot of money now, ya know."

"Ya remember Major Thomas, who was McKinley's half-brother, same mother, different father? He's entertained people around here for years. He used to drive backwards after church through town all the way home, that's two miles, every Sunday morning. Nobody minded as he never hit anyone."

Dermot asked: "And remember that day when he tucked the edge of his overcoat underneath his race-horse's girth before the race and the jockey galloped off with him hanging on, himself shouting, being dragged, flinging his arms about with his feet clattering on and off the ground?"

They all laughed.

"Don't forget the time," said someone else, "when he left a fancy party at the McNamees' house, all dressed in his finest. Must have had 200 quid's worth of clothes hangin' on him and he was also wearin' fancy shoes. He drove down their driveway, sure your lovely mother was there watching, and instead of turning right or left he went straight ahead into the bog. His car sank into the swamp, of course. When he scrambled to the surface about 10 feet out in all that filthy mess, dripping all over, he climbed onto the roof of his car which was barely visible and called out:

"'Will someone throw me a rope, please. I think . . .' *think,* he said, sure to God, as if there was any doubt about it at all, but there wasn't—he said, 'I *think* I'm stuck.'"

"Remember the time," another O'Sullivan chimed in, "when he was in third place in the national show jumping championships and decided to look at the course before the final round and jumped a fence without his horse? Next day, he was on crutches with a broken leg in plaster. No wonder the British lost their empire, him being a Major and all. I wouldn't fancy him leading me into a battle."

"And the Brig, Brigadier McKinley, blind as a bat . . . but refused to wear glasses when he drove. The old man insisted that he'd driven a tank in the war in North Africa so people should stay out of his way."

"Remember that doctor from Dublin who was an alcoholic and your mum rented a cottage to him?"

"Yes," Tom replied.

"Your cat Tarzan used to sleep at the end of the branches on the row of trees in your back courtyard. Remember?"

"Yes." Tom smiled this time. "He was a funny cat."

"One night when yer man the doctor was walking over to use the phone and couldn't see anything 'cause of the dark, Tarzan dropped onto his shoulder from a tree and meowed. Yer man let out a howl that could have been heard in Australia. Sure, he didn't touch another drop for a whole week."

"And your school friend whom his dad told to get rid of the rooks and so he did, when they were sitting on the TV aerial. Shot the birds alright . . . and blew the aerial to bits."

Someone mentioned the Northern Ireland Tourism Board's desperate plea for tourists during the time of the "Troubles," the civil war in the late 60s and throughout the 70s and 80s, when the NITB advertised in American magazines: "Come to Northern Ireland for a shooting holiday."

The laughter was quickly extinguished by discomfort when everyone remembered how Tom's mom had died.

"Oh, I'm so sorry, Steve."

"That's OK. Really, it is," he answered, although it wasn't, of course.

"And Miss O'Connolly, who was Mr. King's housekeeper in Rathbridge," Olly said into the silence, making everyone laugh again.

"A few months after the old man died, she told the minister that he'd come to her in a dream and complained that his knees got wet when it rained so he wanted to be reburied but deeper next time. The minister said ok, so his men got their shovels out, dug him up, made the hole deeper and replanted him. Right enough, a few months later the old biddy told the minister that he was dry and happier now."

Everyone laughed.

"You know, she fills her house up with potatoes or turnips every winter, betting there'll be a shortage and the price will jump and she'll resell at a huge profit."

"Does it?" Steve wondered.

"Not yet," came the reply, everybody laughing again.

"Don't forget the Danish lady who bought the big house in Rathbridge and you know those Danes are a bit different," said Joe. "That lady's friends stripped nude at her parties so the local fellas would shimmy up those big trees inside her road wall. Big fuss when Tommy Lenihan lost his grip, fell out of his tree and landed in her swimming pool."

Laughter.

"Sure and wasn't his missus madder than Mrs. Danish Lady when she found out?"

"What about the time when your mother's maid decided to bake a cake?" Mrs. O'Sullivan asked. "It came out so hard nobody could eat it and it ended up being given away to the lads at the soccer club. They used it as a football."

"And Stevie, what about that holiday you and your mum took to Wexford and stayed in a collapsed castle? Do you remember?"

"Sure," Tom answered. "The old place was a wreck but was full of tourists. The only toilet was on a staircase landing."

"Not good for privacy, right?"

"Right."

"And they served you jellied soup for dinner? That was all they served for the children."

"Yes," agreed Tom.

"When you refused to eat it, they took it away and dropped a boiled potato in it, didn't they?"

"Yes," repeated Tom. "I ate only the potato. That soup looked awful. They returned it to the kitchen, then served it up again for breakfast and dinner again the next day. I never took a bite of it."

Olly asked: "Do ya suppose that they're still offering the same bowl of soup to children today, all these years later?"

"Probably," Tom laughed. "Nobody with eyesight would eat it."

"What about that young Englishman, what was his name, who bought that house down the road from your farm? He had a very pretty Spanish wife, she was a real countess' daughter who'd always lived in the lap o' luxury and had her own maids in a palace in Spain." This was Michael's contribution.

Tom remembered the oddly-matched couple.

"She didn't know a word of English and he brought her here all the way from Spain on the back of his motorbike to live in that filthy house and she had to carry a bucket a whole mile to get water from the village pump. He made her use a ladder to the upstairs bedroom when he concreted the floor during winter. Sure, it took until summer to harden." He paused. "Somehow she got to the airport and flew home."

"What happened next?" asked Tom.

"The Englishman took his bike back down to the palace in Spain and brought her back here."

Everybody laughed again but only out of sympathy for the young woman.

"Your wonderful mum, God rest her blessed soul," added Sheila O'Sullivan, "she visited her often and was her only friend here. Your mum paid me to clean the Princess' house every week and help her with a vegetable garden. I think that your mum stopped the poor lady from going stark raving bonkers mad."

"Sure, he was a real English Lord, or so he said, but had no money," said Gary with disdain, "and he claimed that he was also a writer. Remember when he got you to help him load his donkey into the trailer which was way too short and the donkey refused and eventually ran off down the road?"

"Yes," Tom recalled, "and on a Sunday night in winter, so it was. My dinner was cold when I got home hours later. He told me to chase the donkey down the road and catch her but I told him to get stuffed, then turned around and walked home instead."

They all laughed.

"And the same fella, he was a real eejit, he caused an accident driving in Dublin one day. He complained about it being the other driver's fault but admitted after a while that he'd been reading the Sunday newspaper at the wheel."

More laughter.

"And, of course, there was the time he went to buy a horse after dark," Gary began. "The gelding was a real pig in a poke and the seller had him in a stall with straw up to his crippled knees and a blanket to cover the rest of what was wrong with him. Anyway, yer man kept striking matches to see whether he should buy the nag, never thinking about waiting until daylight. He was an eejit but a funny one at that."

"That same fool," Olly remembered, "took his horse over to Barclay House one day for a jumping lesson. He asked Stevie to ride her. Do you remember that drainage ditch that runs across the front field?" Olly had ridden McKinley's racehorses many times around the farm.

"Yes," replied Tom, Michael and Gary.

"I had to clean it by myself every summer," remembered Tom, "with an adze and shovel. Lots of wasp nests and nettles."

"And, sure, the Englishman wanted his mare to jump the ditch back and forth," Olly continued. "But he insisted that she and Tom jump it *backwards*."

"But the mare refused, of course," Tom recalled. "I thought that he was daft."

"You weren't the only one to think that," Michael observed, "and we still agree."

"Remember the old vet," said Gary, "who upset the new priest by announcing at church that people are contrary, because everybody wants to go to Heaven but nobody wants to die."

Everyone had enjoyed the old vet.

"Yes and that same young Father," added Gary, "full of new ideas, said that if ya stayed home from church ya were a sinner but if ya went, then ya were a hypocrite, so people stayed home to avoid hearing more of his nonsense . . . and yer man was so worried about babies drowning during their baptisms that he proposed that they wear tiny little life jackets."

"Sure and, Stevie," asked Mick, "do you enjoy swimming now more than you used to?"

He grinned. "Why, bejasus, what was wrong with learning to swim in that big cattle trough in your front field while the cattle were burping and slobbering and shitting all over ya there in the water?"

"And," Olly contributed again, "when you rode your good mare at the Dublin Horse Show, your mare who hated men and whips. When you told the judge not to use his whip on her, he told you off, then rode the mare down the ring, then turned back, giving her two smacks. She stopped dead, jerked her head back and grabbed his ankle with her teeth, yanked him out of the saddle and stomped on him. You'd almost swear she was telling him, 'You should've listened to the boy.'"

They all laughed again when Tom said with a grin that he'd often wondered why the judge hadn't given them the winning ribbon.

"That mare Poochie was amazing." Tom continued. "She thought she was a queen and she was so smart. Do it her way and everything was great. Stand in her way and she'd flatten you." Tom had loved her independence and courage.

"She hated the rain getting on her face: ok on the rest of her body, just not on her head but she was a great mare. I won many competitions on her and she was a great polo pony too, so brave. She loved the speed of polo and eyeballing the other horses."

"D'ya remember when a cricket ball was hit into your mouth at school, ya lost two teeth and bled like a pig?" Gary asked. "Your cricket master was furious at you for bleeding on his grass."

"Yes."

Mrs. O' Sullivan remembered a quiz at school when Stevie's class was asked: What are the four countries that border Czechoslovakia? And Stevie's answer was, "Unlucky."

Someone again mentioned old Brig, Brigadier McKinley, Tom's step-grandfather, saying, "People should get out of the way of my tank," and how he had once pushed a tax man's car off his driveway with his jeep, claiming that he hadn't seen it.

Gary reminded the group about the weekend driving test.

Soon after Ireland voted to join the European Economic Community (now called the "EU"), some politician realized that to satisfy their new fellow citizens in France and Germany, the Irish would probably be required to switch from driving on the left side of the road to the right.

This was a quandary that required delicate consideration. The democratic, typically quirky, Irish decision was to allocate a weekend during which the people could drive on their preferred side and tabulate the results. Chaos was anticipated but there were no more accidents than during a typical weekend. The Irish still drive on the left although down the center is common practice in the countryside.

"And your darling mother . . ." Mrs. O'Sullivan began to say.

"God rest her soul," everyone quickly added.

"Your lovely mother, may she rest in Heaven, that story she told about the golfer."

"The one about Fred, Mum?" asked one son.

"Yes, that's the one," she confirmed.

"Tell it again, Mum."

"Well, this fella Jim loved his golf and played every Saturday with his friend, Fred, and was always late getting home. One morning his wife told him over breakfast, 'Jim, the Armstrongs are coming to dinner tonight and you must be home in time. Dinner's at 7 so get home before 6 to help me get ready, ya hear me?'

"'Yes, dear, I promise,' sez Jim. So off he went, repeating his promise. Well, of course, he didn't return on time. Their friends arrived, still no Jim, seven o' clock came and passed, they waited until 8 to eat, still no Jim. The Armstrongs left at 10, still no Jim.

"By the time Jim returned at 10:30, his wife was fittin' to be tied, she was so angry. She started yelling at Jim before he'd removed his jacket. She was spittin' tacks.

"'Stop, woman,' Jim interrupted. 'I'm sorry about being late but this has been the worst day of my life and I'm exhausted.'

"'Why?' she asked, suspiciously.

"'Well, everything was fine until the third hole when Fred had a heart attack and dropped down dead. As dead as Aunt Sarah, God bless her soul.'

"'Oh, that's dreadful,' cried his wife who'd liked Fred, too. 'So what happened after that?'

"'Well, that's why I'm exhausted and so late. We al-ways play 36 holes on Saturdays, you know that. So, after Fred died, every time I hit the ball, I had to pick Fred up and drag him. Hit the ball and drag Fred, hit the ball and drag Fred, hit the . . . .'"

****

One afternoon at a local horse show, Tom realized that it was time to return to the world when the local queen, "Lady Mary" McKinley herself–his step grandmother–had handed him a twenty pence tip (about half a dollar) for holding her horse, failing to recognize him, thinking him to be nothing more than a local yob. Gary quipped that she'd gotten a bargain: "She'd a paid ya five pounds if she'd realized you're an Olympian."

He felt healed and ready. It was time to marry Katya and time to start training for the next Olympics. He packed his bags the next morning after breakfast and said tearful thanks and goodbyes to the entire family.

The whole family spoke in unison, inviting him to re-turn, "Whenever you want. We'll always be here. Bring Katya and, God willing, your children to see us and . . . don't forget now . . . go and win your gold medal."

He loved these people and they loved him. He did, really did, finally belong to somebody. He wasn't an outsider here, in this happy house, in this remote spot of Ireland. They were . . . family . . . his family.

Tom climbed into his car and drove away reluctantly, watching in the rearview mirror, the family waving at him until he went around the bend heading back towards the airport.

Chapter 9   THE WEDDING AND HEIR HUNTING

After the O'Sullivans had restored his spirit, Tom flew back to Virginia to discover that Dr. Stone had arranged a job for him in the Pennsylvania office of an English company that tracked down heirs in the U.S. and Canada to unclaimed estates in the United Kingdom.

****

The wedding took place in Como in northern Italy, just south of the Swiss border north of Milan, one year to the day after the Olympics ended, a date carefully chosen by Katya's parents to eliminate any gossip of a pregnant bride.

Como is the biggest town in the area, famed for its stunning lake and silk industry. Silk is still woven in the town by skilled artisans and then exported around the globe, despite the need to import silkworms since the death of the town's mulberry trees a century ago. A few miles north of Katya's lifelong village, which was near the town of Cantu, Como is home to two cathedrals. Katya's favorite was the marble-clad Piazza del Duomo, begun in the 1300s, but not completed until the 18th century.

Fit for an Olympian princess' wedding, the cathedral is topped by a high octagonal dome reputedly visible from Mont Blanc but only by those with a falcon's vision.

The Cardinal, sensing favorable publicity and feeling more than a little pride in having baptized the future Olympic silver medalist when he was just a young cleric, quickly agreed to the request by Katya's mother. He agreed that Cantu, the family's parish church, wasn't grand enough for the local heroine.

Katya was thrilled because beautiful Lake Como lies in front of the great cathedral and she had always dreamed of saying her wedding vows there, not in the little church in Cantu where she'd been baptized and gone to mass every Sunday of her life.

The twelve months had given Katya's mother and aunts enough time to organize the wedding day thoroughly, even though they didn't meet Katya's betrothed until two days before the big event. Katya had become famous throughout northern Italy because of her Olympic success and was feted in many towns in the region.

Tom and Katya kept in contact with daily letters. Phone calls were rare thanks to the chaotic Italian telephone system. Tom and Katya were both smitten, any idiot could tell that and her parents were happy too because they believed that their youngest daughter was far too good for any of the local boys. And, even better, she was going to live in America.

The legal economy in their region of Italy was poor enough–the illegal underground economy was booming, as is traditional throughout Italy. Her parents believed that the United States was a Promised Land, its streets paved with gold, a place where anyone could climb the ladder and become a millionaire.

Two of Katya's uncles lived in New York City, one a shoemaker and the other a dentist. Both were instructed to visit Tom *in situ* in Pennsylvania, an order that they obeyed. The shoemaker and dentist, with their wives, drove to Tom's new home in Lancaster to spend a weekend examining him. Tom passed inspection with flying colors.

Charmed by Tom, the uncles recommended him as a suitable husband for Katya and their report was met with relief by Katya's parents. Her parents were also pleased to learn that Tom was studying Italian so seriously that he had insisted on speaking the language throughout the weekend.

Refusing to say a word in English, he was determined to learn from the rare opportunity to converse in Italian rather than just practice by watching Italian films on videotape and listening to cassettes.

Tom began his job at the heir hunting company while only running twice a week, because Dr. Stone, concerned about overtraining, preferred him just to "tick over."

He realized that Tom wouldn't cope mentally with a complete vacation from running, so he prescribed only very light training one day per week and Sunday afternoon hikes across the fields and undulating countryside as a whipper-in for a pack of hunting beagles in nearby Chester county. The beagles chased rabbits officially, and deer unofficially, when they hit a line and they had considerable speed and stamina. The whipper-in's job was to keep the hounds together, round them all up at dusk and chase after them when they peeled off at top speed towards deer.

This was another part of Dr. Stone's unorthodox system for Tom's training development. Running with the hounds was valuable athletic training. Dr. Stone wasn't a coach who believed 100% in slogging round and round and round an oval track.

The hunt was a social affair with the local, very wealthy gentry in Chester County, southeast of Lancaster. Tom was happy to bask in praise when somebody mentioned his Olympic medal, but since the main conversation around the hamlet of Unionville always centered on horses, hounds and more horses, this wasn't usually an issue and for once it didn't faze him.

He was in love.

****

On a beautiful summer's day in Como, Tom and Katya were married in front of her family, friends and hundreds of locals, who honored their own Olympic girl in the Piazza del Duomo.

Tom's "side" was outnumbered almost 200 to four because the only people present on his side were Dr. Stone and his running friends Pauleen Farrell and George Mason, both of whom had represented the U.S. in track events at the previous year's Olympics.

The reception was held on a boat, floating on the beautiful, serene waters of Lake Como and their wedding night was spent in a small hotel in the gorgeous small town of Bellagio. Bellagio rests halfway along the lake, at the tip before the inlet, which tapers south to Leggo, with its many groups of stone steps.

They spent their first 48 hours of married life walking through the Villa Serbelloni's gorgeous gardens, riding boats on Lake Como and strolling slowly arm-in-arm through Gravedona and several other villages that dot the shoreline of Lake Como.

After saying farewell to her parents three days later, they took the train to Milan and then switched to another train that took them to Venice. Tom told Katya about the Dublin city council's gondola-in-the-park plan and she laughed until tears rolled down her cheeks.

They enjoyed four days wandering around Venice, happy, enraptured, besotted, giddy, swimming in love, oblivious of the other tourists, noticing only each other. The old Tom wouldn't have recognized himself. The demons were finally, at very long last, absent.

But were they gone forever?

After Venice, they slowly meandered in a one-way rental car through Switzerland and France, spending

three days in Paris, including a day exploring the ultimate in rich vanity–the Sun King's Versailles–then
hopping the train to Calais and the ferry to Dover. Tom
remembered the last time he'd been on this ferry, at
Christmastime, with Jennifer du Pont Scott, heading in
the opposite direction to Geneva.

From Dover in England, they headed to London to follow the usual tourist route, even getting their photo
snapped in front of the Buckingham Palace gates.

Tom wanted to make one special trip before returning
to the United States as a married couple: to the
O'Sullivans' house in Ireland.

They took a train to Holyhead, Wales, and ferry to
Dun Laoghaire, a few miles south of Dublin city, as this
was much cheaper than flying back in those pre-
deregulated days and they had a long transatlantic flight
awaiting them. Tom loved trains but hated the plunging
ferries on the rough English Channel and Irish Sea
crossings.

From Dun Laoghaire, Tom's natural penny-pinching
was temporarily thwarted when they rented another car
instead of riding the buses. They drove to the O'Sullivans
by the back roads via a very long and indirect route
through the windswept and barren Wicklow Mountains.
There, they walked to the 6th century round tower and
monastic centre in the emptiness of Glendalough, then
drove to Kilkenny city the next morning.

They wandered through the 12th century Kilkenny
castle, built by Strongbow, the first French Norman
invader of Ireland. After a lunch of salmon caught that
morning by the chef in the river Nore, which runs
through the city, they drove down to Waterford to enjoy

the Waterford Crystal factory in the southeastern corner of the country.

Tom bought a beautifully cut lead crystal glass bowl with matching glasses and the sales clerk wrapped it up to be mailed to America to the home of "Mr. and Mrs. Brabazon."

This was the first time that a stranger had called them "Mr. and Mrs. Brabazon" and the most marvelous sensation flowed through Tom's veins. He was so proud that Katya had married him. They really were married now. It was real.

The reception the O'Sullivans gave Tom and his wife dazzled them both and he floated though the next week. They spent nights in the tiny room where he'd lived after the Olympics, days helping the family, and evenings talking in front of the peat-fuelled fire.

Tom never took Katya to Barclay House or told her any of his ugly memories. He'd taken care to ask the O'Sullivans to call him by his new name and not to refer to his past life. He felt that Katya wouldn't understand and, since she couldn't change what had happened to him, that all of it would be best unrepeated.

The past couldn't be changed but the future was fresh. He could, would, make a great life for them, day-by-day, starting anew.

Each morning allows everybody to make a new start.

The only seam he allowed her to peak through was showing her his mother's grave and he simply told his wife that she'd died in an accident. Well, the bombing hadn't been an accident but his mother waiting for him for too long outside on the street and being in the wrong place at the wrong time was an accident.

He whispered to his mom and was sure that he could hear her answer. Tom hoped that she was proud of him and impressed with Katya. He also hoped that she could finally forgive him for being late on that dreadful evening in Belfast. If only he'd run faster . . . .

****

The odds for Tom and Katya having met were so long.

Had Tom's fake identity been revealed, he would have never been allowed into the Olympic squad, and if it had come to light once he was on, he'd have been thrown off and forbidden to represent his country. His unusual circumstances would never have been tolerated, despite his triumph over pain.

If discovered, his false name, fake SAT scores and forged high school diploma would have ruined his chance of being an Olympian, despite his many track victories at the local, state, and regional level.

As for Katya, she had been a double reserve in the long jump team, luckily gaining her place after not one, but two dropouts: the first girl through a surprise pregnancy and the second girl having been defeated by the flu the day before the first round, the illness making her too sick to sit up straight, let alone jump for Italy.

Little of his past life mattered so much now to Tom, not the bombings or the secrets that had kept him on tenterhooks for so many years, fearing his real identity and past would be unmasked.

All that mattered to him now was his darling Katya for whom he'd do, endure and risk anything, ignore any hardship, fight and protect, keeping her happy until death did them part.

****

Back in Lancaster, Pennsylvania, Tom began introducing Katya to American life and was the happiest he'd ever been. Katya was thrilled at the many novelties that America offered, from the massive supermarkets to the Amish people to her and Tom's hikes along the Appalachian Trail, which passed nearby.

He returned to his job as an heir hunter, where his colleagues made a fuss over Katya, and made them both feel welcome socially.

The system in Britain was such that when someone died intestate—without a will or known family in Britain—the government claimed the deceased's assets until an heir made a claim. Several companies specialize in the strange job of finding legally rightful heirs, the best known being the long established, London-based Fraser & Fraser.

Each Thursday morning, the Treasury Department of the British government released a list of names of intestate dead people for whom no heirs had yet claimed the estate and then the heir hunting companies began searching. Their reward was a commission in the form of a percentage of the inheritance.

Tom and his colleagues arrived at the office by 4 a.m. on Thursdays. His firm believed that having a branch office in Pennsylvania was to their advantage and that they would be quicker in signing up American heirs than if they were contacting people from England. The time difference was just one factor.

The best time to reach people is in the evenings and calling them at midnight from London, 7 p.m. in the Eastern U.S. and 4 p.m. in California, was increasingly unpopular among the staff. Tom's bosses decided that having an office in the U.S. would give them a big advantage over their competitors, who usually out-sourced the jobs to Americans, and therefore had to split the profit.

The intestate often left behind a house and belongings and their neighbors sometimes didn't know of any relatives.

Neither the house nor other property could be sold or otherwise disposed of until the rightful legal processes were completed. The government would, after a certain period of time without any claims from heirs, simply sell the assets and put the resulting money into the government's general account.

The inheritance hunters tracked down relatives, competing with rivals from other companies to reach and sign up the heirs first. This, Tom learned, was done in the old days by tracing births and family trees in old files and microfiche and more recently was done with computers.

The people in the inheritance hunting business searched electoral rolls, looked for birth and marriage certificates, checked telephone books and developed family trees. It's an awkward job in today's modern, very mobile society where few people live or die near their birthplaces.

Until the eighteenth century, before easier travel, most people spent their earthly existence near the villages or in the counties where they'd been born.

The last 300 years have, of course, seen enormous emigration, flight from the countryside to cities and, more recently, the ease of car and air travel. A more recent factor has been the switch from lifelong employment with the same company to multiple job changes—and necessary moves—during a career plus the increasing number of divorces and name changes.

All these and other factors, including the many people with identical names and sometimes even the same ages, made Tom's job of tracking down the correct heirs to an estate difficult. He found a comfortable groove with increasing experience as the months passed and felt that his job was useful and satisfying.

In many cases, the legal heirs—sometimes, in small families, third cousins twice removed—never met the deceased and were often ignorant of their existence. They were surprised at the sudden and unearned windfall that came with a knock on their door or a strange phone call from the representative of an heir hunting company.

The laws were strict about the order of inheritance and about the splitting of assets, while taking no consideration of whether the deceased would have been pleased to have their worldly goods end up in the pockets of total strangers just because they were distant relatives.

Most people were delighted, though suspicious, when Tom and his colleagues told them of their unexpected windfall. Many of those conversations required convincing their heirs that the good news wasn't a scam.

His boss, complaining that people should be more considerate by dying at their birthplace, just like salmon, enjoyed telling the staff the story of the wise California-based billionaire investor Charlie Munger, the long-time business partner of Warren Buffett, who was quoted as saying:

"I don't want to know when I'm going to die, just where, so that I can ensure that I'll never go there."

Tom had worked part-time during university and before the Olympics as a learner in an insurance adjustor's office, working on claims ranging from car accidents to house fire to damage and theft of household items to business claims. He'd learned a lot.

Tom was comfortable with working odd hours and found his new job convenient for training for track and field. He learned his basic lessons there and Dr. Stone, proud of his protégé, continued to be pleased with his progress in Lancaster.

West of Philadelphia and an hour's drive in easy traffic but three hours during rush hours, Lancaster is an old town with much history. It was the nation's capital for one whole day in September 1777 after the defeat at the battle of Brandywine and is now world famous for the Amish, who live without electricity or other modern comforts in Lancaster County.

The newlyweds had a lot of fun exploring this beautiful, historic area and getting to know the community.

The popular film *Witness,* starring Harrison Ford, was filmed in the area and gave the public a glimpse into the Amish's unique and old-fashioned, 18th century way of life.

The Amish are famous for refusing to use electricity and hundreds of thousands of tourists flock annually to the county to stare at how their own ancestors lived centuries before. The tourists cannot comprehend how anybody can live without electricity. Thank goodness for the inventions of the light bulb and the telephone.

One January morning, the temperature was 28 degrees below zero. On his Tuesday jog on a country road, next to banks of packed snow four feet high, Tom was stunned to see a helicopter fly to each pylon on one Amish farm. A rope dropped and a man climbed down the rope, holding a hammer. Tom watched the man hammering ice off the wires before being flown to the next pylon.

Hammer-man needed to trust the pilot not to drop the rope or get too close to the power lines. Tom wondered what hammer-man had done to his boss to deserve this.

That was surely the worst job in the country that day.

****

Tom discovered that the Amish hate attention and that they believe that being photographed is a sin.

They crave being left alone–fat chance–by the tourists and the U.S government, both having made their lives a lot more difficult than their ideal. The 20,000 Lancaster County Amish, still living in their original settlement from the 1720s when their ancestors immigrated from Germany and Switzerland, is the best known group of the old order Amish, who are scattered through 20 American states, one Canadian province, and one Central American country. Ohio has the largest group.

Excellent farmers, the Amish use Belgian horses to pull their wagons and equipment. The men milk cows and raise crops while their wives make quilts and sell food outside their front entrances. They live plain, hard, honest, comfortless, old-fashioned, luxury-less lives, raising large families, often with a dozen or more children, and they are religiously devout, independent, debtless and credit card free.

What looks idyllic on a hot summer's day is actually a brutal life, particularly in winter, something no modern, non-Amish person could survive for even a month.

Because of being pestered by the outside world, the Amish are exceedingly cautious about allowing outsiders into any part of their lives but those living outside the oddly named village Bird-in-Hand, east of Lancaster, not far from Paradise, another small village, got used to the unusual sight of Katya and Tom on the side roads off of busy Route 340.

The Amish work way too hard to need to exercise in gyms or by jogging. A young Amish woman named Matilda overcame her shyness one afternoon when the young couple stopped to buy apple juice from her roadside stand, finally giving in to her curiosity and blurting out the question on the lips of many of the puzzled Amish living in the area:

"Why are you running?"

The Amish try desperately to avoid the modern world and aim to live like their ancestors, as prescribed by their religious beliefs. They don't watch television or read newspapers except their own but, despite all that, even they know about and admire Olympians.

A week later, Matilda invited them into her kitchen and from then on Mr. and Mrs. Brabazon were privileged to learn some of the Amish way of life. Tom helped with the farm chores for a few hours each week, while Katya helped Matilda with housework. The elders wouldn't normally have permitted that, but their being Olympic medalists eased the way.

Matilda and her husband, Otis, were both 20 years old, farmed fifty acres and had already produced two small children. A few months after they'd become friends with the Brabazons, Otis announced that Matilda had been diagnosed with cancer by the group's non-medically trained medicine man, after she failed to become pregnant again–an annual expectation for Amish wives.

The Amish didn't have health insurance policies and couldn't afford to pay the local specialists in cash. The elders–and all the elders are men–decided that a dozen elderly ladies would accompany the frightened Matilda and an older woman with breast cancer on a long train ride to San Diego, California. The ladies would then cross the border daily for treatment at a mysterious medical center.

None of these women had ever traveled more than 15 miles from home, so it was a big adventure.

What the border police thought of this group of Amish ladies, none possessing driver's licenses or any other photographic or normal identification, is unknown but the unsophisticated women returned safely a fortnight later with amazing stories of a huge, bewildering and unexpected America.

When Otis asked Tom to buy them a dozen large jars of grape juice every week from the supermarket, too far away and dangerous for their buggies to go, he explained that the 'doctor' in Mexico had prescribed weekly, cold grape juice baths for Matilda. Of course, Otis reimbursed Tom with cash for the juice. Three months later, Otis reported that his wife was pregnant and that the grape juice had cured her cancer.

The experts at the Mayo or Sloane-Kettering cancer clinics don't prescribe grape juice baths. Should they?

Chapter 10   VIRGINIA

Tom worked for the heir discovering company for two and a half years, gaining valuable experience finding people and doing much painstaking but necessary research.

This was investigating and hunting and he learned a lot, but was ready now for a new challenge, believing that heir hunting could teach him no new skills.

Dr. Stone, who had a grand plan for Tom—a scheme, if you prefer—recognized the signs of change in Tom, having deliberately planted the seed of restlessness. He found a suitable new job for his protégé and arranged for a certain money management firm's managing director to make Tom an offer.

The job was at a brokerage firm located in Remington, Virginia, about 55 miles southwest of Washington D.C., 25 miles south of Manassas University and 35 miles from Middleburg, where Dr. Stone lived.

Dr. Stone had coached them from 150 miles away while they lived in Lancaster, but this would be more convenient for everyone now that the Olympics were getting closer. They still had one and half years before the Olympics.

Tom and Katya knew they were on borrowed time with Dr. Stone, expecting the U.S. Olympic Committee to issue an order that could only be disobeyed if they won every race and long-jump in the build-up to team selection. That order would be to return to Colorado Springs for intensely supervised training, but without Dr. Stone.

Katya loved and admired Dr. Stone nearly as much as Tom. Neither wanted to train a day without Dr. Stone and the feeling was mutual. Katya hadn't yet decided whether to represent Italy again or her new country.

Dr. Stone loved Katya. Everybody did.

****

So they moved to Virginia and settled into a rented cottage on a big farm out on Fauquier Springs Road near the country club, only a few minutes drive from Remington and about five miles from the bigger town of Warrenton, the county seat of Fauquier County.

The Springs road splits into three roads a mile outside Warrenton—one going downhill towards Fauquier Springs country club, Lee's Ridge, which heads uphill and the cul-de-sac road on the right called Shipmadilly Lane, leading alongside the high wire fence of the 'secret' CIA communications and satellite center, which was in the old girls' school property.

Oh, it was all supposed to be top secret, very hush-hush, but all the locals knew and didn't particularly care. They weren't afraid of any Russian invasion so long as they could continue to ride their horses without interruption and the spooks kept to themselves on their base.

The country club's golf course possessed some local fame due to the exploits of a temporary golf coach. He had a problem one day with wet golf balls that he needed to use quickly: to dry them, he went into the kitchen, plopped them into the microwave and turned the new machine on. The balls smashed through the microwave, ricocheting throughout the kitchen while the cooks dove for cover.

Katya loved living on a beautiful farm in upper-class, old-fashioned, pleasant Virginia. This was not an Italian's typical image of America of teeming immigrants in the noisy New York City boroughs of Queens and Brooklyn, or scuffling around in New Jersey.

It was beautiful countryside with lots of history, backed in the distance out west by the lovely Blue Ridge foothills, which were silhouetted on every sunny evening by bright sunsets. There was no need for Mafia membership or huddled masses here.

Katya had fallen for Tom as completely as he had with her. She knew that she'd picked the right man and adored Tom with passion. She loved his reliability, trusted him, saw his complete integrity and decency and admired his determination. Most of all, she felt safe with him protecting her.

She'd qualified as a physiotherapist in Italy and had no problem finding good jobs in Lancaster, and later in Warrenton, after passing the state board exams.

Fauquier County was wealthy, quiet, Old World, genteel American South, populated by landed gentry and wealthy professional people, who lived for their horses.

Contented people who welcomed the young Olympians into their big homes and huge parties in the evenings, hunt breakfasts in the afternoons after hunts ended and hunt balls during the dark winters.

For Katya, this was all new, exciting and enchanting, while for Tom, living just a few miles from his grandparents' farm in neighboring Culpeper county, it was a welcome relief after being excluded all those years in Ireland.

Warrenton was fun. Tom and Katya both loved it. The young couple was welcomed warmly with honest invitations and accepted, even though Katya couldn't ride at the beginning. She would learn: It was *de rigueur* in that community to ride and ride well.

Horses were loaned to them both and Katya took lessons from a lady whose family had owned her farm since 1825 and, many years before, had dated the county's greatest hero since the Civil War. Crompton Tommy Smith was the local lad who'd gone to England with the gelding Jay Trump and ridden him to triumph in the world's greatest steeplechase, the Aintree Grand National, back in 1965.

Tom remembered easily enough how to ride—nobody forgets how—and their first foxhunt was a thrilling experience for Katya, Tom having hunted countless times on horseback back in Ireland.

From February to May, there were weekly point-to-point and official steeplechase meetings with "tailgating" picnics behind parked cars, the locals rode their horses behind foxhounds in winter and entered the show rings in nearby Upperville in June and the local show in Warrenton on Labor Day weekend in early September.

Winters were cold with plenty of snow but dazzling blue skies, summers as hot as an oven with almost daily afternoon thunderstorms and plenty of humidity. Springtime was gorgeous and the autumn colors beautiful.

The outside world never seemed to push into historic Fauquier County, where the locals remained upset only at having lost the Civil War to "those damned Yankees."

The young couple ran, loved and played together while continuing their training for the next Olympics. Tom avoided mentioning to anyone that his father's parents' farm was just outside nearby Amissville and Sperryville, to the west of Warrenton, heading towards Luray's magnificent limestone caverns. He hadn't had any contact with them since his father's funeral and, for reasons unknown, his mother had ceased contact with them after moving to Ireland.

Tom absolutely didn't want to open old wounds for either himself or his grandparents, although he had fond memories of them and the fun experiences on their farm, having learned from his father to hunt deer and track them and other animals on and near that farm.

A few times, he found himself driving slowly past it, wondering if his decision was fair to them but each time drove on, uncertain of the right choice. He reckoned that his uncle would be running the farm now. He did visit his father's grave in Sperryville and, four months after arriving in Virginia, he fulfilled his promise to his mother by secretly arranging the transfer of her remains from Rathincree to Sperryville, where she was interred next to Tom's dad.

Besides, the cost of revealing himself would have ripped apart his new life and absolutely ended his chance of competing in the next Olympics, while he would no doubt be stripped of his silver medal. So, he satisfied himself–and this was easy–with his beloved Katya, doing his job and dreaming of gold at the next Games for them both.

Tom's finance courses at university qualified him to work at the brokerage, which, of course, bought and sold stocks and bonds for their clients, mostly individual investors who lived locally, but also had a department that managed investment accounts.

Management wanted somebody young and untarnished by Wall Street to investigate companies in which they had invested and companies they were considering for their clients' money. They had a financial analyst who tore apart annual and quarterly reports, while the money managers spoke to company bosses and chief financial officers daily, watched the trends on Wall Street and, like every other money manager, strove to be in the top decile of their divisional race.

Tom's job was not to look at the financials as such but to check that the companies were honest, doing what they claimed they were doing and not manipulating sales and earnings results.

This idea was born after several publicly traded companies had imploded due to fraud, embezzlement and damaging diversification. Several years later, the Canadian-based Bre-X gold mining fraud would swindle many savvy top money managers on Wall Street and at leading investment firms around the country, resulting in a stock fiasco. However, there were frequently mercifully smaller company frauds that caused investment professionals minor heart attacks. The guys at Tristram Brokerage in Remington preferred to avoid heart attacks.

Wall Street loves fads and quick riches more than ordinary people and has a tendency to plunge into investments—using other people's money, not its own—without always first exercising complete due diligence.

There are too many true quotes from big-time money managers to the tune of, "I don't care what a company does so long as I can make money trading its stock."

The guys at Tristram were, to their great credit, especially prudent and prescient. They didn't want to have to answer the embarrassing question, "Why didn't you check the company properly?" from clients when a company went broke or, worse, was charged with criminal action by the S.E.C., the Securities and Exchange Commission. The Tristram team were honorable people, looking out properly and carefully for their clients' welfare and they welcomed Dr. Stone's recommendation of Tom.

Dr. Stone's suggestion that Tom investigate public companies delighted the firm's directors and the deal was struck with the understanding that Tom required time off for training, events and the Olympics.

The reflected glow of an Olympic-competing employee, and increased numbers of impressed clients paying money management fees, made it easy for Dr. Stone to negotiate a good deal for his star runner.

****

In his first few months, Tom scored a notable victory, impressing his bosses and the firm's clients. The company was a highflying Wall Street 'darling' with stock prices heading to the sky.

It was easy for stockbrokers to talk clients into buying shares of this kind of boom company, so easy that some clients almost–but not quite–argued in the waiting room over who got into the brokers' offices first to place their orders.

William Simpson, a recently qualified broker and nephew of the senior partner Jim Simpson, who was close to retirement, asked Tom to investigate the company, a long distance telephone service company. William had a nagging suspicion, just a hunch, that perhaps this firm might be too perfect.

He believed in being cautious. After all, his clients were his and his uncle's friends and neighbors, not long-distance strangers.

Possessing a well-deserved, stellar reputation in the community, the Simpsons were conscientious, careful and dedicated to performing as well as possible for their clients.

Tom's investigation into the long distance phone company provider required a trip to the bleak and dusty plains of Texas, far removed from the glamorous world of the TV series *Dallas*.

AT&T had recently lost the monopoly of its American telephone service and was broken up into bits. Numerous companies had rushed into the void to set up competition against what became known as "The Baby Bells."

MCI and Sprint quickly developed into quality leading rivals and were well run, satisfying their shareholders with steady stock price gains though not doubling annually, like this new firm trading on the NASDAQ/over the counter.

Tom had earlier checked out all the publicly traded telecommunications companies and found most of them satisfactory but, from the six he researched, one company kept bothering him.

This company was one of several which boasted cheaper calls as a result of buying in bulk from AT&T, copying some travel agencies that sell heavily discounted seats after buying in volume from airlines. It's a risky gamble but plenty of entrepreneurs play this dice.

Why the airlines and AT&T allow a middleman to reap their profit is strange but, then again, the bewilderingly complicated variety of the pricing of airplane seats is a mystery, which would have outfoxed both Albert Einstein and Isaac Newton.

Tom's first question was why the company hadn't moved its headquarters from a small town of 2,500 souls to the metropolises of Houston, Dallas or Ft. Worth, but he was warned by his boss Mr. Simpson, Sr. not to make a hasty judgment based just on that.

"Remember," Mr. Simpson pointed out, "that the mighty Wal-Mart itself has grown into a giant while staying put in its founder Sam Walton's hometown of Bentonville, Arkansas."

But Tom was still dubious, so he flew to Dallas and drove three hours to the small town to check the company on-site. He wanted to observe the business as a simple tourist, without making an official visit. When he arrived, he discovered that, despite its star, home-grown success, the town still looked more like a starved 1930s dustbowl than a prosperous center of new technology.

He checked in at the town's only motel where it felt that he was the only customer, excusing the inevitable question about his presence by explaining he was in town to visit a friend who was sick. Since Tom invented this phantom pal's name, having checked the local phone book to ensure its absence, the motel owner unsurprisingly hadn't heard of the guy.

"But I thought I knew everyone in town." He paused, frustrated, wanting to show off his local knowledge. Fishing, he asked, "Hell, ain't he the new dentist?"

"No," lied Tom evenly, "he's a truck driver."

Tom realized that his arrival would be broadcast around town quickly in the likely absence of more exciting news—the town was very sleepy—so he decided to start work immediately.

He drove aimlessly around town to confuse any of the motel manager's friends, parked two blocks from the telephone company, changed his shirt and baseball cap and walked to the office.

Surprised that it was above an ordinary grocery store, having expected fancy modern offices, he double-checked the address.

This can't be right, he told himself, but his brokerage's secretary, Caroline Wilson, was efficient and simply didn't make errors. Tom was nervous, because this was his first trip to a company in his new job and naturally he wanted to impress the Simpsons.

He walked upstairs, feeling that if these ordinary premises were typical of the company's frugality, a trait which Tom admired as he was half-Scottish, then he might buy shares. He'd already learned that those companies that saved money on the non-essentials, like chauffeurs and limousines for the senior executives, were better bets than those that didn't.

Businesses with expensive art in the corridors were almost invariably losers for shareholders, the rule being the more expensive the artwork, the quicker the stock price's death spiral.

Still puzzled as he opened the door, he found no receptionist. Perhaps she was running an errand. He called out an "hello" and two men, aged probably in their late 20s or early 30s and wearing casual clothes, appeared from a back room, looking surprised to receive a visitor. They introduced themselves as Wayne Williamson and Dean Breasley, the two senior executives.

He introduced himself as a stationary salesman, having practiced his spiel on the plane, after spending a day learning the ropes in the stationary supply store in Warrenton. He added that he was a shareholder, who happened to be visiting a friend here in town on his way through to San Antonio and he had decided to drop by and meet his investment.

"Sorry not to have called first. Just an impulse to visit and see how my money's doing."

Neither man looked overjoyed. Perhaps, like many in their position, they restricted their time to Wall Street analysts. Few public companies expect small shareholders, the so-called "Mom and Pop investor," to visit or call. It isn't common practice and while not quite discouraged, public relations being important, seldom are individual–"non-institutional"–shareholders actually encouraged.

Big companies typically have their own shareholder services unit who chat with bigger investors, brokerage firms and mutual funds, which control thousands of shares. Only big mutual fund and hedge fund managers, analysts from the big stockbrokers and financial journal-ists receive the big welcome from most publicly traded companies.

Managers from Fidelity and Vanguard, controlling tens of billions of investors' money, get to talk to the C.E.O. and C.F.O. Mom-and-pop minnows don't.

Still, it's bad form and bad public relations to ignore a small investor as maybe they'll inherit $10 million tomor-row, so nearly every company will go through the motions of treating the 100-share-owning caller as if they're important. It's perfectly legal for any shareholder to ring and ask questions, being a co-owner, although few do. Just don't expect to talk to the C.E.O. or to stay on the line for too long.

Tom asked for a coffee and said he had some ques-tions. The men glanced at each other and prepared to be interrupted for a while, explaining that they were very busy.

"That's fine. I'm sure glad that you are. Making more money for me. I won't take up too much of you fellers' time. First time I've visited a company in which I'm a shareholder and it's exciting, you know. I hope that you're going to be the next WalMart." Tom put the brakes on saying "golly gee" and "gosh." He didn't want to overdo the bumpkin act.

These guys weren't stupid. According to William, back at the office in Remington, they were now worth $20 million each on paper, based on the leaping share price.

Coffee came and Tom asked vague questions, acting like he didn't quite understand high finance or big busi-ness, let alone long distance telephone billing. He tried to understand how these guys made a profit, how many customers they had signed up and their expansion plans.

Diplomatically saying that he disliked AT&T, he praised the men for standing up to the former monopoly as competition. He asked how they entered the business, whether they had been telephone repairmen or executives at AT&T.

The men gave answers that sounded unconvincing to Tom but, then again, he wasn't a trusting, gullible guy. Their replies were plausible and obviously well practiced from previous conversations with sophisticated institutional investors and the financial media. Chatting with uninvited visitors wasn't their forte.

"How many employees do you have?" Tom wondered.

The men glanced at each other before the smaller guy answered, "Eighty-six and we're hiring more all the time."

Tom noticed that nobody else was in the office and no secretary returned from mailing letters. He saw no work being done. The men said that Wednesday was the staff's day off and that they worked in eight hour shifts round-the-clock, this was really a "back office" and that most of the work was done in their office in Houston.

"And what's its address? Maybe I could go take a look."

He was discouraged politely but firmly.

"Thought you said you're heading to San Antonio," he was reminded with raised eyebrows. "There's nothing much to see except our associates working. Not worth your time. Just offices, that's all. We split our time between Houston and here."

The men were enthusiastic about sales and promised a great future with many new customers signing up monthly.

"We anticipate outselling Sprint and MCI in less than a year. We're more innovative and, because of our team

approach and corporate ethos, we respond faster to changing market conditions."

Tom chose a new angle, asking to quote on the company's stationary needs.

"How much do you guys use monthly?" he asked. "I'm
sure that I can offer you a better deal than you're getting
now. We're very competitive and our service is the best."
He paused. "Who's your supplier now?"

The men looked at each other, shrugged and said that
an "associate" named Martha Clancy handled office
procurements.

Tom continued his charade by offering his business
card, not his real one, of course, but a 'front' address of a
North Carolina post office box 200 miles from Remington
that forwarded again to Tom's office in Remington.

One of the men accepted it and said he'd give it to Ms.
Clancy.

The taller man went to another room every time the
phone rang. Tom stayed just 25 minutes, recognizing that
his welcome was running on empty, then said his goodbyes after receiving the latest quarterly report to shareholders. The glossy brochure was impressive, full of nice
pictures and prominently featuring both men.

The joint C.E.O's of the company thanked Tom for visiting and recommended that he buy more shares and
advise his friends and customers to do the same.

Their parting statement was: "We're going to be huge
in five years, we're going to go international soon and the
sky's the limit for the stock price. Get in now while you
can."

As he left, Tom fancied that he could overhear the men
agreeing with each other that:

"Thank God that there's a sucker born every minute," but perhaps he was imagining it.

****

He missed Katya enormously, this being their first night apart since their glorious wedding day. This was before mobile phones, so Tom loaded up on quarters and found a pay phone, talked to her for half an hour, missing her so much that he ached. He promised to return as soon as possible. Given a choice between cuddling Katya in front of a log fire or being in an empty, barren, dusty Texas town, well, that was a no-brainer but this was his job.

He went to a diner for dinner and got to chatting, or rather listening, to the waitresses, owner and other customers. He was lucky to possess the skills to get people to talk unselfconsciously and was smart enough to stay quiet.

"You never learn anything when your mouth is babbling. You already know what you know. You only learn things when you shut your mouth and open your ears," had been the advice given to him many years before.

So he shut up and listened. People love talking, even to strangers. He knew how to press the right buttons without seeming nosy.

In half an hour, he learned a lot about the company's founders and reputations and decided it wiser to leave town, staying the night in some motel far away, than to stay and be their target when they inevitably heard about his dinner conversation.

Tom loved field research but he was lost and alone in Texas, without backup, in unfamiliar territory, a long way from the glorious Virginia countryside. He needed to be particularly careful here. He felt like a fish out of water. This town was as dry as dust.

This was hunting, which he loved, using almost the same methods as he did in the woods when hunting quarry with hounds, but now he was dealing with people, a much wilier species than any wild animal.

Animals don't lie, cheat or destroy.

Nature's law in the wild is survival of the fittest but humans operate differently than wildlife. Tom still had much to learn and he enjoyed this new job more than the heir hunting, although that had been satisfying at many levels.

But those people were simply missing, the process of finding them needed to be quick, methodical and structured, while these companies required cunning detective work. He was no accountant but he'd been hired to investigate the bolts and screws of companies, to determine whether they were honest or greedy, playing con games, working fast and loose with proper business behavior and cheating investors.

One Bre-X or Enron scandal can permanently destroy a stock brokerage's reputation and wipe out its clients' assets. The Remington brokers, good honorable people, wanted to protect themselves and cared a lot about the welfare of their clients and friends.

Brabazon was suspicious but, he reminded himself to recognize this, he was suspicious by nature and his job was all about being suspicious.

That didn't mean that everybody he met was lying, shady or dishonest, so he mustn't jump to conclusions without proper hunting and information. If he advised, "Sell, because they're crooks," and he was wrong, what would happen if clients sold but the stock price continued to climb?

Clients would lose money and his employers would be embarrassed. You get very few second chances in life to make amends. One mistake and zoom, out the door, silver medal or not. Survival of the fittest is the oldest rule of nature.

Clients and his bosses would then have legitimate cause to gripe. He was being paid to report the correct answer not jump to premature conclusions. He had to be right but, as a patient, methodical perfectionist, that wasn't a problem.

Just take your time and sift through all the clues and evidence, he reminded himself.

****

His first call the next morning was to Caroline Wilson, the efficient secretary. He asked her to check up on Martha Clancy and then gave an interim progress report to William. He was encouraged to keep digging.

When he rang again at lunchtime from Houston, Caroline announced that she'd found no record of any Martha Clancy in Texas. She wasn't in the phone book, wasn't a customer of any utility in Texas, wasn't listed as an executive of the company in SEC records, held no Texas-issued driver's license and filed no Texas tax return for the past three years.

Now, Martha could have an unlisted number or her number listed only in her husband's name, she might be a recently hired employee, she might have moved from another state or possibly be a recent return to the workforce after being a student or staying at home raising children.

And maybe not.

Tom rang the company's Houston office directly to speak to Ms. Clancy, using his cover of a stationary salesman. An answering service picked up. This struck Tom as weird for a publicly-traded, multi-million dollar company. Like everything else, frugality can be taken to excess. He left a message and rang back an hour later. This time he spoke to one of yesterday's bosses, who said that the lady was on vacation.

So, Brabazon got lost in the city streets for ages until finding the address that Caroline had found for him. It was in a light industrial mall, functional, unglamorous, the dirty and sweaty side of wealth creation, not where you'd expected to find a modern technology company. A laundromat was on one side and a printer on the other.

A sign naming a different company was on the small lawn out front. He went into #87, which was busy with lots of people entering and leaving, but had a different company's name on the door.

He asked the cheerful receptionist for help.

"Oh, they moved out about six months ago," she informed him as friendly as could be.

"Do you know where they are now?"

"No, sorry, I don't know anything about them. You could try the post office for their forwarding address."

So he followed her recommendation. The postal clerk gave him the address he'd visited in the small town the previous day. No hiding behind privacy laws, thank goodness.

Tom had had enough. He drove to the airport after getting lost yet again–he wasn't a city boy–hopped on a plane and returned home to Warrenton, where his beloved Katya was waiting.

****

The next morning, he spoke to Jim and William Simpson and followed up his conversation with his usual written report. He concluded that he strongly doubted that the company was worth an investment, telling his bosses his findings and that the townspeople disliked the men running the company.

They'd told Tom that both men–first cousins–were "wide boys" and "shady," always into some devious mischief and scams, "even as kids," but their charm and their uncle the sheriff always combined to help them avoid punishment.

Wayne and Dean had no technical skills and the people in the diner believed that this telephone venture was just another of their scams.

The cousins refused to hire any locals, didn't associate with the town, had long since stopped going to church in this very religious community and nobody trusted them. "Not as far as I could throw a Brahma bull," one woman had said.

Wayne and Dean were considered as cheapskate hustlers, who hadn't shared any of their millions with anyone in town, instead showing off with fancy cars, helicopters and imported girls on their newly-bought ranch a few miles outside town, and refusing to make any donations for the public good.

Tom distrusted the men's answers and thought that the "office" and Ms. Clancy in Houston were simply camouflage. He had observed no workers, or working, and had decided that it was a scam.

"I recommend selling all shares," concluded Tom to his bosses and they agreed.

****

Unfortunately for Brabazon, the company's stock price continued to soar and some clients grumbled.

He concentrated on other companies—there were many to investigate—and found a few exciting, some dull but all were honest. He worried about his job but remained convinced that the Texan cousins were not safe investments.

Three months later, with the share price up 32% since Tom's visit, there were palpable chills whenever Tom chatted with Simpson senior. Then, Tom got lucky when a mutual fund in New York hired an independent auditor to investigate the Texan outfit and, after completing its investigation, called the S.E.C. who called the IRS.

Manure hit the fan, as they say on a farm.

Not only had the cousins been "cooking the books"—Wayne's accounting degree proving helpful in inventing sales and income—the pair had used knowledge of sexual indiscretions to blackmail a respected auditor in Houston into lying about the firm's financial status in all its public reports.

There were only two employees, let alone eighty-six. The cousins had faked everything: there were neither long distance purchases nor sales, no customers and no real business. Their lawyer, also a company director, was another cousin.

All the firm's income was faked and so were the claimed expenses, all the expensed furniture, salaries, retirement and health insurance plans. Everything was phony.

The only legally deductible expenses were the high salaries, which Wayne and Dean had awarded themselves, the cars, helicopter rentals and office rent. They were also discovered to be selling their shares through a third party without reporting their insider sales to the S.E.C. as per the law.

The share price collapsed immediately when the S.E.C. made this information public.

Wayne and Dean decided to elude capture by rushing to Las Vegas but, silly boys, they took one of their own cars and were quickly found. They were caught and arrested by the local police. It was a long time before they drove another automobile or tasted freedom.

Chapter 11   KATYA

Tom had never been happier than with Katya in Fauquier County. Madly in love, they enjoyed each other enormously, led a satisfying social life and their jobs fulfilled them. They both began increasing the intensity of their pre-Olympic training with Dr. Stone in Manassas and Tom participated in one race each month.

Eight months before the Olympics, Tom was surprised and delighted after Katya went to her doctor one morning with a question.

She announced her pregnancy that evening to Tom, which meant that the next Olympics would require a pass by the long jumping mother-to-be. Tom expected her to be really upset about missing the Games but Katya insisted that she was thrilled and preferred to be pregnant. The only worry was her surprisingly high blood pressure, which her doctor informed them was nothing serious to worry about.

Life continued very happily for Katya and Tom. Their lives were good.

Three months before the Olympics at the final trials for team selection, Tom was the favorite for the 10,000 metres and widely expected to solidify his place as number one on the Olympic team for that event. He was also a strong candidate for the 5,000 metres race. He'd comfortably won both at Nationals both that year and the prior year and was regarded as a serious contender for a gold medal. He'd won seven of his last eight races.

He was training well, was a better runner, had never been happier and was finishing with good times in his prep races. His win in South Carolina a month earlier had been particularly impressive when the typically oppressive summer afternoon, with temperatures in the high 90s and near 100 percent humidity, had the athletes literally wringing the sweat from their clothes.

One athlete suggested, and the others agreed, that an inventor should devise a way to air condition outdoor tracks with mini air conditioners that could be stuck to a shirt. The humidity caused plenty of dehydration but the medical staff prevented any serious problems.

Tom and the National coaches—Dr. Stone hovering, as always, not too far away—were as confident as they should be: 'not o'er much but just enough for their self-esteem,' as one journalist wrote. Tom was facing four regular opponents as well as three new ones, including a youngster named Oliver Rimell, with a big reputation, who'd just graduated from UCLA and was considered a probable for the team.

The race began as all races do, with a bit of barging but, after a quarter of a mile, settled down into a predictable rhythm.

Two other runners, including Tom's friend George Mason, were practically already on the Olympic team, unless they performed poorly in this important trial, while the others were hoping to achieve enough that afternoon to fill out the remaining spots. The pace was strong but not silly as the runners completed the first circuit, led by Mike Berg from Florida, back from a foot injury.

Passing the line to begin the final lap, Rimell rushed past Berg to establish a decent lead.

Since he was a fresh, unknown tactician, the others accelerated to be closer, to avoid trouble in the event that the Californian was as sharp as his reputation. They'd have been embarrassed if the newcomer outfoxed them. Tom was in third place, alongside George in fourth. The time was good but not quick enough to set a new track record unless the last lap were to be really hot. Tom felt very comfortable, in the swing, in his groove, running smoothly—he was plenty fit—and he was growing more confident of success as he decided to pass Mike Berg and settled in just two strides behind Oliver Rimell in the second lane.

He wasn't taking the chance of being tripped by Rimell if the youngster stumbled or slowed unexpectedly, although that meant that he wasn't in his slipstream, which is usually the better place to be. There was no wind to worry about anyway. Harry Donovan began to make up ground from the rear, George and Mike were still comfortable but they, as did the spectators, thought that Tom was moving with the most ease and was likely to win the race.

Tom quickened just after Olly Rimell made his move 200 yards from the tape, George and Mike losing a length, not from surprise but because the leading pair had the quicker turn of foot. They still had a chance but when Tom joined Rimell 120 yards out, the race was definitely settled between the two leaders. The others were running only for third. Tom had watched tapes of some of Rimell's previous races–just as Rimell and his coach had studied Tom's victories–but his new rival's tactics were now his problem to solve alone.

This wasn't going to be easy, it wasn't supposed to be easy. Tom realized his opponent would be formidable.

Anything less than a victory for Tom would be disappointing for the coaches: the pressure was on him but he still possessed plenty of strength. As they turned into the straight, Tom and Rimell were side by side with George three lengths behind and Mike Berg laboring in fourth.

Rimell still had plenty of speed but, with 60 yards to run, Tom gained the upper hand, still not going full stride but realizing with familiar joy and satisfaction that he would win comfortably–job done, almost–though the Californian wasn't quitting.

Forty yards from the line, Tom had gained a one-length lead and he looked all over the winner but 15 yards out, his right ankle landed awkwardly, a tendon tore or a bone cracked, his head went up and he sprawled in pain. Rimell regained the lead just before the wire and won by four feet.

Tom pulled up in pain, hobbling, refusing to cry out, facing his last stride defeat in undisguised and wretched recognition that his fracture or ruptured tendon might prevent him from running in the Olympics.

He could cling to the hope that it was just a twisted ankle but that would be, he knew at once, delusional. The tendon hurt like a hot knife had scythed through it. A cracked bone would be preferable to a torn tendon in terms of recovery time and the Olympics. An athlete can race, and plenty do, with screws in various bones but only time, and plenty of it, heals damaged tendons and ligaments.

He knew enough from his horsy friends in Warrenton how very serious a damaged tendon was to their racehorses—"Either they retire from the track or the vet shoots them. They're never as good after a bowed tendon as before." Tom never seriously expected a bullet through his brain as the cure for his tendon injury but he knew this was serious.

The timing stank. He could barely walk over to the coaches. His lower leg was quickly wrapped, even though Tom insisted—and was promptly ignored—that there was nothing wrong, and an ultrasound was taken to determine the amount of damage in his tendon.

Was his Olympic dream over? He didn't know yet but there was undoubtedly some tarnish and doubt now on his place in the team.

All his rivals were concerned and consoled him: while they knew that there would now be one more of them going to the Olympics, replacing Brabazon, there was too much of their well-founded "there but for the grace of God, go I" belief to allow anyone from saying a word. They all knew how close to catastrophe—injury—they were in every day's training, let alone races. One injury can finish anyone's career in sport, removing them from their love of competition, making them just ordinary people again, members of the public, no longer stars on a mission.

The team doctor quickly arrived in the changing room to examine Tom and ordered a trip to the nearest hospital for X-rays. There was no point in Tom's arguing, because the decision wasn't his and he knew that a fracture or minor strain was his only hope of staying on course for the Olympics.

X-rays showed no fracture or chip and it was definitely not a sprain as his tendon swelled up quickly. His Olympic dream was over, for another four years at least. This was a huge blow, not only to Tom and Dr. Stone, who so badly wanted to win gold to add to their silver medal from four years before, but also for the U.S. team since Tom was one of the favorites to win. But "that's life," as they say, and certainly there are billions of people in this world with worse problems than a tendon injury. Yet, Tom's dream was punctured and the doctors told him that he couldn't run for at least ten months.

Doctors don't know everything, they don't understand, Tom consoled himself. They aren't athletes, they're too conservative. I'll be winning races in six months, he told himself. But he accepted bitterly that this year's Olympics would occur without him.

"You're still young enough to race in the next Olympics in four years' time," the doctors tried to console him. Perhaps but he'd have new opponents a decade younger and therefore fitter and fresher than him. Four years seemed as long as a century to Tom. A runner is usually retired from top competition before the age of 30. He'd be 35 by then.

The scythe of old age swings sooner for athletes.

The team coaches were more realistic and unemotional. Immediately, they mentally placed him permanently on the bench, finished as an Olympian and they decided to seek elsewhere for new, younger talent. They were running a business and Tom, whose distant personality they'd never warmed to on a personal level, despite his many successes, was now history as far as they were concerned.

Rimell, Mason and Berg were named to the team along with three others, who hadn't raced in the final trial for various reasons. Jim Campbell had missed due to the flu, Sam Jarvis had missed his flight and Mark Biddlecombe's wife was delivering their first child in far away New York. All these excuses were grudgingly accepted by the squad's selectors only because they had shown good enough form in recent competitions.

Jarvis and Biddlecombe were the only runners who'd defeated Tom (when he'd been third) all year and Campbell had set a new American record in a race, which Tom had missed. It was a strong squad but without the acknowledged best runner.

Tom could have attended the Olympics as a spectator but chose not to. He would stay home for the birth of his child. He told himself that he would try again for the next Games while Dr. Stone kept his opinion to himself–that Tom's career as a top flight runner was over. If he was wrong, great, but only time would tell.

****

Deeply unhappy about losing out on his second Olympics, Tom focused on Katya and their unborn baby. Her blood pressure remained stubbornly high, so she saw her obstetrician Dr. Keller once every month but her pregnancy was otherwise comfortable and as a "prima" (first child) she was in good condition, with a low chance of complications. Her mother flew in from Italy, her first time on an airplane, two weeks before Katya's due date.

Nine days out, Katya felt awful and her mother called Tom at work to drive Katya to her doctor who, after examination, sent her straight to the hospital to be admitted. Dr. Anne Keller was worried. She'd diagnosed pre-eclampsia and that was serious.

At the hospital, the nurses and attending obstetric resident all tried to reassure Katya and Tom that all was well but, if that were true, why was everyone fussing over her?

Out of his depth, unable to understand what was happening, Tom had to keep quiet, hold Katya's hand and trust these complete strangers. Trust in others wasn't an attribute that Tom possessed in abundance, or at all, but these people were fully trained, experienced professionals, whom he hadn't even known existed as recently as breakfast.

Now he was dependent on them. He realized that this was serious, as serious as anything could be, far more important than crying over spilt Olympic milk and he wished there was something he could do to fix this, ensure Katya's health, but there wasn't.

All he could do was comfort his wife and let her know that she was his 100 percent priority and that she was in good medical hands. Her mother hadn't been helpful, bursting into tears in the emergency room and babbling incoherently in rapid Italian when her daughter was whisked upstairs for an emergency Caesarian.

It was decided that Mama should wait in the family room near the delivery room, on the third floor. For reasons long forgotten in the mists of time, operating rooms in hospitals are traditionally located on the third floor.

"What's eclampsia?" Tom asked the medical team.

Katya's symptoms, came the nurse's reply, were classic eclampsia: high blood pressure, abnormal swelling of the hands and feet and a terrible headache, which for her had begun during breakfast. A nurse sent a urine sample off for diagnosis and the result showed protein in her urine. As time passed, Katya retained fluid and there was pressure on her kidneys.

The C-section was quick and a lovely, healthy baby girl was delivered with practiced precision. Tom was relieved that she had everything she should: hands, arms, fingers, two thumbs, legs, nose. The obstetric nurse told a skeptical Tom that the baby was fine, despite his opposite impression. To him, their baby presented with a dreadful red and contorted face, bald skull and a loud crying. Tom had never seen a newborn human before and was astonished.

Katya was still asleep, having received a general anesthetic rather than an epidural, which would have lowered her blood pressure but would have delayed the surgery since a localized anesthetic takes much longer than a general to take effect, but the anesthesiologist quickly brought her back to consciousness while her afterbirth was removed. It was an exciting moment for all when Katya held and kissed her baby. Everything was fine.

The baby was then whisked off to receive an Apgar testing and be washed before being taken out of the room for whatever unexplained purpose.

"What's an Apgar?" Tom asked but everybody was too busy to explain. The Apgar test, named after Dr. Virginia Apgar, tests a newborn's health.

Katya was wheeled away to ICU, the intensive care unit, before she would be taken to a semi-private room. Tom missed the anesthesiologist's quiet chat with Dr. Keller but he noticed that the former, a small, efficient and focused lady named Dr. Schmidt who stood just five feet in height, stayed very close to Katya as she was wheeled into the ICU. He followed. He didn't know what else to do.

He supposed that this close attention was normal but, twenty minutes later, all hell broke loose.

Katya had a fit, which eased after Dr. Schmidt injected a drug but ten minutes later, she had another seizure, her arms and legs again shaking uncontrollably. She wasn't an epileptic, which had been one of the anesthesiologist's first questions before entering the OR, so that wasn't the cause. What was happening, Tom asked.

The post-op nurse, a middle-aged man named John who'd seen nearly every complication in a long career, unsuccessfully reassured Tom that all should be well and informed him that Dr. Schmidt was a top flight doctor— "She's the best anesthesiologist we've got here. She's brilliant. I picked her for both my kids and, please, try to relax, everything will be OK."

Dr. Schmidt advised Tom that eclampsia caused the seizures and that usually they could control and end them.

"Usually" wasn't the reassurance that Tom wanted. What he wanted was a definite, "She's in no danger. She'll be fine. Don't worry, your wife will be OK. She'll recover from eclampsia."

Die? No, that must be impossible, mothers don't die in childbirth any more, Tom thought urgently, suddenly more scared than he'd ever been before. He wondered where their daughter was, then re-focused on his wife. Then Dr. Schmidt politely but firmly asked him to leave and wait outside. This frightened him even more but he obeyed. He was in the way. He was a nuisance to the doctor and nurse.

When pressed by a panicky Tom, Dr. Schmidt again refused to give an absolute assurance that all would be well. "We'll do our best and I'll come out to speak with you after she's out of danger."

Danger. "Oh no, Tom barely breathed, "that's a bad word" but he left as ordered and stood outside in the corridor, alone and shaking. Three hours earlier, he'd never heard of the medical condition "eclampsia" now it was threatening Katya's life. He thought of going to find his mother-in-law and telling her that she had a grand-daughter but chose to stay outside the post-op door. Time passed ultra slowly for Tom. A curtain had been pulled around Katya so that he couldn't see anything.

The door was suddenly pushed open and Katya was rolled out as the same nurse explained in a hurry that she was being returned to the operating room. Dr. Schmidt was silent, focused on her patient.

"Doctor, what's happening? Will Katya be OK? What's wrong?" Tom pleaded but received no reply.

Dr. Schmidt was alongside Katya, didn't seem to see Tom and pushed him out of the way in her rush. They went straight to the OR and this time another nurse forbade Tom from entering. A surgeon and a third nurse rushed in.

Tom waited some more, his emotions stretched, at his nerves' end.

He knew that the situation was grim. He was frightened, terrified. What was happening to his wife? This wasn't normal childbirth activity. Why was Katya obviously in trouble?

Didn't millions of mothers in the third world safely deliver their babies in rice paddies or in dirt huts and get up to immediately plough the fields or milk the goats and cows with no post-operative complications or scares? Well, most do but some of them and many of their babies die from lack of medical attendance. Childbirth remains a hazardous activity and is one of the riskiest activities in suburban America.

Time passed in trickles.

Tom leaned against the wall and swore that he would never impregnate Katya again, never cause any chance of another risk like this, no more babies if this was what would happen every time. He felt guilty for his role in this scare. No more babies, this was his final decision, he would insist to Katya after this nightmare was over, when they were back home relaxing with their daughter.

If she wanted more children, then they'd adopt. There must be plenty of lovely babies or toddlers needing loving parents. He wondered how much red tape and bureaucracy would be involved. No matter. What did matter, *all* that mattered, was Katya's good health and recovery. He hadn't thought of his exit from the Olympics for hours, since the moment when Katya's mother had called him that morning.

More time passed, as it must, but none of the medical team went out to give an update or encouraging report to Tom. He was sure that the longer Katya was in there, the worse her condition. He knew nothing about hospitals or medical care, he hadn't let himself believe for a moment that childbirth could harm Katya.

What was happening in there, Tom wondered constantly. His fear was sky high and the inability to *do* something was frustrating, utterly nerve wracking. Where was their baby? Oh no, a sudden thought, is their baby OK? What if she's in trouble as well?

What were the two doctors doing in that room?

Why did Katya have eclampsia? Dr. Keller had said that nobody knew for sure why a few expectant mothers got it but high blood pressure wasn't abnormal and was seldom a high risk issue in a young, otherwise healthy woman like Katya. The obstetrician had not warned them about what was happening now, presumably it was rare, maybe one in a thousand but why was Katya that "one?"

What could he do now to help? Nothing. That was worse, knowing that there was nothing he could do to help. He possessed no medical training—he was a runner, ah, make that he was probably a retired runner. He supposed that if they needed blood from the blood bank, he could run and get it for Katya.

He heard the overhead page: "Dr. Schmidt, please go to OR 2, stat. Dr. Schmidt, please go to OR 2, stat." Dr. Schmidt was in OR 4 and not leaving. Another doctor entered the corridor a minute later and went into OR 2, presumably to cover for Dr. Schmidt.

Tom walked to the nurses' desk and asked inane questions, none of which the friendly nurses could answer.

"How much longer will my wife be in that room?" "What can you tell me about what's happening?" "When will the doctors come talk to me?"

The nurses only gave pat, reassuring, unhelpful answers to those and other questions. "How bad is eclampsia?" "Will my wife be OK?" "When will I be allowed to see my wife?"

The nurses knew a great deal about eclampsia, its complications and prognosis but they decided to let the doctors field and parry his questions. They weren't going to stick their necks on the line and maybe say the wrong thing and get in trouble. They'd all dealt with husbands and parents of eclampsic patients before and they were going to be cautious with Tom. They knew what could happen. Usually the patient recovered fine, but once in a bad while . . . .

Tom lost track of time, didn't feel hunger or thirst and felt awful. Not knowing what was happening was worse than knowing, he decided.

His imagination went to the nasty outcomes: what if Katya became a permanent invalid, what if somehow she became paralyzed, or . . . of course, he thought of this, with horror, what if she d– . . . . He didn't want to tempt fate although fate was out of his hands and in those of the medical experts in that room. What would he do with the baby without Katya? He knew nothing about babies except that they cried a lot. Why, what reason would he have to bother carrying on living if Katya di– . . ? What would be the point of existing if Katya didn't survive?

He knew that very few mothers died in hospitals any more but he guessed that some did, maybe just one in a thousand or in two thousand maybe but he didn't know the statistics. They were all women loved by somebody;

they were women like Katya with a husband like Tom or a mother like Katya's mother.

Some people do die in hospitals, surprisingly few considering the many accidents and ill-health in modern society, although most recover and walk out the door.

Modern medicine creates miraculous cures these days with antibiotics, cardiac surgeries, cancer treatments and all the rest of the modern cures that were unknown and impossible just half a century ago. He knew that penicillin was first used during the Second World War, only a decade before his own birth, millions of years after the first humans were chased by woolly mammoths. The astonishing medical advances were so recent and, too often, taken for granted.

He wondered whether his own mother had suffered complications during his birth, how long her labor had been, whether he'd been a difficult or sick baby. He didn't know, would never know. He remembered when he was thirteen and she had given birth to his half brother in Ireland: everything went smoothly then, or at least he hadn't been informed of any problems. The school hadn't permitted him to visit her in the hospital as he was on the rugby team and they were playing matches against other schools that day and the next. He was needed on the rugby field.

His gut informed him that the longer Katya was in the operating room, the worse the problem but, alternatively, maybe the worst case . . . that she was dea— . . . (he refused to tolerate the "d" word), would have meant that they'd given up ages ago, so maybe the long wait was good news.

Why on earth had Tom thought that the Olympics were so important?

Well, yes they were . . . they had been his goal, had been his purpose and career—he was a professional athlete and one of few who had a full-time non-athletic job in this modern era of professionalism.

Nothing, even the Olympics, had ever been more important to him than Katya and a bowed, torn tendon was nothing, pathetic even to complain about, compared to Katya's struggle on the other side of that door.

He wasn't a religious man but there's that old saying that there are no atheists or agnostics in foxholes—and he found himself praying for Katya. Being Italian and raised Catholic, Katya was religious and attended mass every Sunday but Tom couldn't believe in any God because of all the bad events he'd seen, like holding his dying mother after she was blown apart by that bomb in Belfast.

He prayed—a new convert if only temporarily, until Katya was safe again.

Tom tried to change his focus, to think about their baby, about the unknowable changes in their lifestyle once home with their daughter, about his job. Nothing succeeded in banishing Katya from his mind for more than a few seconds.

He waited and waited. He'd lost track of time, didn't remember when Katya had been taken to post-op recovery, how long she'd been back inside the OR. His watch showed the time was 12:22 p.m. That phone call from his mother-in-law seemed a century ago, a lifetime—their daughter's lifetime ago.

The door opened. Both the surgeon, name unknown, and Dr. Schmidt, the anesthesiologist, came out into the corridor and removed their surgical masks.

"Hi," said the tall man with an unreadable face. Tom thought a smile would mean good news so his stomach lurched. "I'm Dr. Berry. You've met Dr. Schmidt, I know. You're Mr. Brabazon, Katya's husband, right?"

"Yes," Tom replied uneasily.

"Your wife had eclampsia, as I understand you know. It's a rare condition and we don't know exactly what causes it but . . . "

"Is she all right?" Tom interrupted desperately. He was in no mood to hear a scientific lecture.

The doctors' faces remained impassive.

"Are there any other family members here?" Dr. Berry sideswiped his question.

"Just Katya's mother. She's in the family room, waiting, like me." Tom repeated his question with urgency. He wouldn't tolerate another question, he wanted an answer, a straight one, but it must be the only one he craved. "Is Katya all right? Is she safe? Can I go in to see her now?"

Dr. Berry looked uncomfortable and Tom felt sick.

"I'm sorry, Mr. Brabazon," answered Dr. Berry. "We did everything we could but we couldn't revive her. I'm sorry but she's passed on. We're all very sorry. You can go in now, if you like."

Tom Brabazon crumpled, disbelieving, refusing to accept the surgeon's statement.

"But she can't have, she's young, she's healthy, just had a baby, never been sick, just a little bit of high blood pressure, what happened?" He pleaded to both doctors who were genuinely upset and sorry.

"She had several seizures," Dr. Schmidt replied gently. Telling bad news to family members was the worst part of her job no matter how many lives she'd saved and there'd been thousands of successes in her 30-year career. Each death hurt hard.

"We did everything we could," she continued, "but she just couldn't survive the pressures put on her heart and we think that an aneurism burst deep inside her brain. We'll explain more later, as often as you want, whenever you want. We're really, really sorry.

"Your wife is our first death from eclampsia this year in over 2,000 deliveries. We don't yet know why she didn't recover like other patients with eclampsia but we hope to discover why."

She paused, touching him on his shoulder. "Go on in now, ok? You can spend as much time as you like with her."

The surgeon asked for permission for an autopsy, to be performed by the hospital's pathologist. "Any information your wife provides us might save other patients in the future." Tom nodded, tears flowing down his face. "We're sorry, very sorry. One of the nurses will help you with everything. Just ask and the staff will do their best." Dr. Berry then excused himself but Dr. Schmidt walked back into the OR with Tom to see Katya, who was lying on the table.

"There," the anesthesiologist said sympathetically, "we'll leave you alone now but I'll be on duty for another six hours so if you want anything, ask a nurse or have them page me. I'll talk to you so long as I'm not with another patient. Take all the time you need."

"Doctor," asked Tom clumsily, "did she suffer?"

"No, I don't think so. She was never in conscious pain," she answered. "Her final memory was holding your baby."

Tom absently thanked Dr. Schmidt and was left alone. He kissed Katya many times, held her in his arms and talked to her as he sobbed. He was devastated.

Chapter 12   A PROMISE KEPT

When the immediate shock of losing Katya wore off, Tom sank into a clinical depression that lasted for many months. Horrified by Katya's death and, to a much lesser degree, the likely permanent end of his top level running career, he became a mentally fragile hull of himself. It was awful to watch.

He was in a daze for a long time and very grateful to his friends George Mason and Pauleen Farrell, who'd married just before the recent Olympics.

Pauleen had been his advisor from day one at Manassas University whenever he'd had doubts: he'd had none about Katya, or Dr. Stone, but Pauleen had always been there for other important decisions. George was a good pal, too. They'd loved Katya, too. Everybody had loved Katya.

Tom couldn't cheer up even when holding his baby, whom he'd christened Catherine Frederica Stone Brabazon. Frederica was Katya's mother's name. Stone commemorated their coach and hero, Dr. Stone, who'd made everything happen for Tom and Katya. They'd agreed early on about naming their child after him.

After returning from the Olympics—each with a bronze medal, despite their shock at the news—George and Pauleen took care of all the hard details with which Tom couldn't cope, like a lawyer to deal with Katya's estate. She'd saved only a few thousand dollars in a joint account with her husband and had died without a will.

Tom didn't understand why a lawyer was necessary when Katya had basically no assets but his friends insisted that the laws must be obeyed, many documents had to be filed and the bureaucracy fed. For that, a lawyer was required.

Truly, all that Katya had was love (not taxable . . . yet . . . but the government has plans), but the various government agencies had to be satisfied.

Her birth certificate was in Italy, which upset the American bureaucrats inordinately and she'd had dual citizenship, which duplicated the paperwork. Tom saw no justification to amuse the bureaucracies but was overruled by George and Pauleen, who moved in to Tom's house. He was too apathetic to refuse them and they were worried that he'd never look after himself properly if left alone with his sadness and all-too-brief memories of Katya.

His bosses at Tristram Brokerage realized that he was in no condition to do quality work and that any work he'd do would be full of gaps, below his usually high standard, and thus worthless, so they gave him a three-month leave of absence on full pay. He was useful to them and they wanted him back but only when fully able to concentrate on his job.

Busyness is an important form of treatment for depression–perhaps the most important after hope–but his employers required quality work. While hugely sympathetic, they weren't babysitters. It wasn't their duty to nurse him back to life.

"That's life . . . and death," was Tom's oft-repeated response to the tragedy but everyone knew that he was far, far more troubled than that. Still waters and so forth.

Forty-six lawyers contacted him urging a lawsuit against the doctors and the hospital. Tom ignored their letters and told those who telephoned to: "Go to hell and the quicker the better." The hospital sent flowers to the house and funeral and several of the staff attended the funeral.

The woman who'd taught Katya to ride horses arranged the funeral, held in Warrenton's Catholic Church where Katya had worshipped. Over 250 people attended, a large number given how brief a time Katya and Tom had lived in the county, their local celebrity because of their Olympic medals. The tragedy made the front page of the local and state newspapers. None of their Olympian friends could attend, because the Games began five days after her funeral, but they all sent cards and flowers. Katya had been very popular in the world of track athletes as well as in Virginia.

Few of the locals had met her but they knew about her and felt sorry for the young mother's death. The day after the funeral, Katya's mother traveled back home to northern Italy with her daughter's body, which was laid to rest in her hometown cemetery after another service, held in the church where she'd been baptized. Tom had agreed that that was best. Her father had stayed at home in Italy. Tom stayed in Virginia.

Katya's friend from prenatal classes, Carol Murtagh, who had her own six-week-old child, had taken baby Catherine into her home in Warrenton and looked after her, because Tom was clearly in no condition to look after his infant. He didn't know how, anyway, never having been exposed to babies.

The hospital's only psychiatrist suggested to Dr. Keller, although without knowing Tom's character—he'd never met him—that a man in Tom's mental state might harm his child, blaming the infant for Katya's death. This was nonsense in Tom's case but Tom accepted and appreciated Carol appointing herself as the baby's foster mom. He was too apathetic to arrange anything himself.

The autopsy confirmed that the seizures had pressurized Katya's internal systems so much that she'd suffered an uncontrollable bleed in her head, to be precise, an aneurysm in the middle cerebral artery of her brain. She hadn't suffered any pain other than a crippling headache and never knew that she would die that day. She had passed away peacefully and, despite many CPR attempts, she could not be resuscitated by Dr. Berry and Dr. Schmidt.

After several meetings with colleagues, in what are called M&Ms (morbidity and mortality meetings), the two shaken doctors were reassured unanimously that not only had they not done anything wrong and that they'd done everything right, but that there was nothing anybody could have done to save her life. Some patients die and doctors can't change that. They must accept it.

The doctors speculated on the possibility that Katya's lobe might have previously been compromised during a childhood illness such as influenza and that was why her seizures killed her, or that she may simply have been born with the weakness. Nobody could be sure. Aneurisms, the doctors explained, were mysterious. They struck without warning. The only good thing about them is that they are usually instantaneous and Katya probably felt no pain or knew what happened.

Death, of course, comes to everyone: lights on, lights off, black curtains, time to discover humanity's biggest mystery—if there's really any afterlife, any truth to heaven and hell, St. Peter and the Pearly Gates, eternal life or nothingness or reincarnation. Nobody alive knows for sure . . . and dead people tell no tales.

Tom couldn't sleep, except for two-ish hours after taking Temazapam, a sleeping tablet. He'd lie in bed feeling wretched, guilty, without hope. Hope was essential for recovery but he'd lost all of his.

Sleep was impossible without drugs, which he hated. He tried counting sheep, but they all looked alike to him and he'd lose count. He tried penguins, ditto. He counted backwards; he tried to think happy thoughts but none lasted for more than a few seconds. He drank pints of hot chocolate but then had to get up and go urinate.

Only the Temazapan succeeded in temporarily knocking him out but he gained no rest and certainly didn't dream. When he got up he'd sit morosely in a chair, staring at the wall, unresponsive and uncaring. There were many times when his friends dragged him out of bed insisting, "You're not allowed to mope in a day bed," and ordered him to get vertical. Nothing interested him.

He lacked energy or interest, cared about nothing, held his head bowed in his hands, grieving and feeling guilty, convinced that his future wasn't worth living. He welcomed death, begged silently for it, but he knew that George and Pauleen would prevent it.

He tried starvation but his friends forced him to eat and drink. Nevertheless, he lost weight and became gaunt. He didn't bother exercising even though everyone told him he should, that it would reduce his misery. But he didn't care. He was miserable and no amount of exercise would change the fact that Katya was gone and he felt hopeless. So he refused to exercise most days.

Pauleen and George went with him on rare walks and traveled with him into town, ready to save him from harming himself.

The sleeping tablets were recommended by Dr. Keller, who'd told them that she'd no personal experience with the drug because, as a very busy obstetrician, she seldom had time for sleep or sleeplessness and hadn't enjoyed an eight hour sleep like normal people since her last vacation. The sleeping pills were addictive, sure, but they were the only solution to his insomnia.

Lying in bed for hours, feeling huge guilt, suffering panic attacks, shivering, feeling lousy, awful, hopelessly missing Katya, realizing that he'd been partly responsible for her death, knowing that he'd never see her again, touch her, hear her voice, feel her love, hold hands, enjoy her, watch her with joy and love.

He was alone again. He missed Katya so very much.

A loner since his mother's death, he'd loved sharing his life with Katya, adored his wife and now she was gone forever. He knew that he'd never forgive himself for getting her pregnant, the first step towards her death. He blamed himself no matter how many friends disagreed with him.

What was, he tortured himself, the point in continuing to live? He was eating—when forced by his friends—with dullness, with no appetite, no interest, just swallowing what Pauleen ordered him to eat. He cared about nothing. His vow of "til death us do part" with Katya was, he thought, meant to imply *his* lifetime, a proper lifetime together, 60 years or so, with him dying first, a grandfather. He was older than Katya . . . didn't most men die before their wives?

He wasn't safe to drive and so was either driven to see his daughter or Carol would visit his house with the baby but, after the briefest talks to Catherine, Tom would simply stare mechanically into the distance, his own thousand yard stare, scaring his friends. He refused to see a counselor, let alone the idiot psychiatrist in town, or any other "shrinks" elsewhere.

George, Pauleen and Dr. Stone, the three people who knew Tom the best—even they couldn't get him to talk much.

George and Pauleen agreed never to let Tom out of their sight for more than a minute, except for the bathroom and his bed and, just in case, they placed concealed audio and video monitors in both rooms.

His recovery, at best, would take months. Time seemed the only healer since Tom had lost all interest in sport, his job, the weather, his future. He watched the Olympic videos out of politeness for Pauleen and George, without any interest and only because of his innate good manners did he congratulate them on their medal-winning performances.

Tom was, most definitely, profoundly and clinically depressed. He never smiled or laughed, even when Pauleen made him watch *The Two Ronnies, M*A*S*H* or Bob Hope.

His two former teammates were in awe of him, because they'd always admired his grit and determination against the odds and they were perfectly happy to put their newlywed lives on hold to help him. They knew that he'd have done the same for them since his friendships, though rare, were profound.

They didn't know about his strange pre-university life—Tom was so relieved that the media hadn't found out—but admired his integrity and success in finding people and his devotion to Katya.

Dr. Stone had told them about Tom's "hunting" exploits and the people at Tristram Brokerage were not quiet about telling of his successes in investment investigations. Pauleen and George had also gone hunting with Tom and Katya in the woods, with cameras not guns, and were astonished at his ability to track and predict what the deer and other animals would do.

They believed that Tom and Katya were both very special people.

****

Dr. Stone decided that Tom needed to end his depression—six months of mourning was enough—and it was time for his protégé to return to the world of social productivity. While he appreciated George and Pauleen's babysitting, he doubted that they could spur Tom back into the saddle.

"Life goes on, come what may," the old coach said one afternoon to the three friends in Tom's living room, "and it's time for all three of you to get back into living. You two need to make babies." Dr. Stone was always blunt and tactless but never rude. He looked at the newlyweds.

"The Olympics are over for all of you and you need to start normal lives like all the other rats in the rat race. What," he asked George, "are you going to do? I mean, starting next week?"

"Well, we'll return to Louisville, where I've got a job waiting for me as a dentist."

"Can you switch to Lexington?"

"I don't know," came George's response. "Why?" They knew their coach never asked a question lightly. He always had a good reason.

The others wondered why, too, but Dr. Stone ignored them.

"Pauleen?" asked Dr. Stone. "What are your plans other than becoming a broodmare?"

She answered, blushing, "Well, not yet, coach. We want to wait a year or two."

"Why?"

"Why not?" she replied. "It's none of anyone else's business, is it?"

"Well, yes, it's technically none of my business when you get off the pill but us old folk need young folk to pay for our old age retirement and medical costs and if nobody's having babies, then gawd help retirees in 20 and 30 years." Dr. Stone huffed. "Social Security is great in theory but won't work without young'uns working. Anyhow, it's neither social nor secure. The fund'll run out of cash the day after I retire."

They laughed, except Tom.

"So, what're you gonna do, Pauleen?"

"I'm going to become a computer expert," she replied. "Everything's becoming computerized now, that's the future. I took a course this year and enjoyed it. I'll work for a big company until the babies, I mean, your rescuers of Social Security, come along. Then I'll start my own consultancy and repair business."

George asked what Dr. Stone was planning for himself.

"Will you keep coaching?"

"No," came the bombshell they half expected but dreaded to hear. "I'm hanging up my whip, retiring to sit in my rocking chair." Coaching had been his life for over 30 years, all he cared about.

"Why, sir?" asked Tom, shocked.

Dr. Stone only gave half an answer, hoping that they hadn't noticed the first tremors of Parkinson's disease that had begun the day after Katya had died.

"Because you, Pauleen and George got me as close to my holy grail, a gold, as I'll ever get. I've never coached four finer athletes or better young people than you and, God bless her, Katya. I'm proud of all of you and I know I'll never find anyone better, so it's time to quit. I've had my day in the sun. Time to move on. Time for all of us . . . ." He paused, then stared. "You, too, Tom."

The three retired athletes gave Dr. Stone a standing ovation and a "Three Cheers." They later swore to each other that they'd seen a tear or two drop from his left eye.

"What about you, Tom?" barked Dr. Stone. "Back to Tristram Brokerage? Do you want to work there forever? Is it satisfying enough for you?" He hoped not.

Tom stared without interest past his coach and hero.

"I don't know. I don't care," he added forlornly.

Dr. Stone was determined to snap Tom out of his stupor.

"You're too talented to give up, curl your toes and quit, young man," he announced bluntly. "You are going to get your act together and obey me." Dr. Stone had quietly planned Tom's career for years without Tom realizing it.

"You need to do what you were put on this Earth to do. You're a hunter, you're smart, determined and great at catching your quarry. Right?"

They all knew that. They all remembered the Sophie du Pont Scott story and Tom's other successes finding missing people.

Tom agreed as the others insisted he must. Out loud.

"You have a bright future at Tristram and could become CEO of a top brokerage firm even though you couldn't sell stocks or, for that matter, lemonade to a man dying of thirst in the Sahara." Dr. Stone paused. "You could get an investigating job at the SEC. But you can, should, do more good for society than that."

They guessed that Dr. Stone had something specific in mind.

"Do you remember," asked Dr. Stone, "your promise to me in my office at the college that January evening after you rescued the du Pont Scott girl in Geneva?"

Tom nodded: of course he did. He'd hoped that his coach had forgotten. He'd only promised because it was the only way he could convince Dr. Stone to keep coaching him to win a gold medal at the Olympics.

"You made me a promise. Remember that?"

"Yes," he answered reluctantly.

"What was it?"

"I promised you that I would become a hunter after my running career ended."

"Well?" The old man stared hard. "Your running days are now history. That tendon will never again bear the pressure of top-level racing. Today, now, right now, is the first minute of your new life. Time to make good on your promise to me: a promise is a promise, son."

Tom still looked miserable and uncaring but Dr. Stone continued.

"I coached you so now you need to fulfill your side of our deal. Go catch bad guys, find missing people, help society. You'd make much more money at Tristram than chasing criminals, sure, but so what, you'll be repaying society much better if you reduce the crime rate."

"Do you mean, sir, become a cop?"

"Like your old man? Hell, no," Dr. Stone replied. "That's no good for you. Police forces are like the military. Chains of command, you have to take orders, sometimes even do what you disapprove of. That's not your style. You'd hate it. So would I. We're independent, disobedient guys: you and I."

"Then what?" Tom asked.

"Meet a friend of mine. He'll offer you a job. Accept it. He'll teach you what you need to know." Dr. Stone suddenly grinned. "You'll love his job. It'll suit you. I've waited many years to introduce you to him."

Tom looked dubious.

"You were a star, Tom, on the track and you'll be another star hunting and catching bad guys."

"I don't know," Tom answered. "I'm not ready yet. I think I'd wash out, it's too soon after Katya. Maybe in a few months time. I'll talk to him then, if I'm feeling better."

"No, Tom, now. I've arranged for him to meet you tomorrow morning at 9 at the Red Fox Tavern in Middleburg. It's only 45 minutes' drive." He turned to George and Pauleen. "Will you drive him?" he asked.

Pauleen answered that she would.

Tom insisted that he wasn't ready to launch into a job, any job. He would wash out, he insisted. Dr. Stone disagreed and repeated, "Do what I ask, keep your promise." Then he asked Pauleen to speak to him as he walked out to his car.

"Pauleen," he urged. "Make him go. Talk him into it. Make him accept the offer. He's ready now. Left to himself, he'll sit on his butt, moping for the rest of his life."

She agreed. "Tom's got to get busy. Busyness and hope are the best cures for depression, aren't they, sir?"

"Yes, girl, they are. He's had enough time now." Dr. Stone got into his car, rolled down his window and said, "Make him do it. Twist his arm, kick him, get him to accept the job. It's what he should do. He's a hunter, not a stock market guru."

He then added one word, a word which none of his athletes had ever heard him utter: "Pauleen, please. Please make him accept. This is his destiny. I've gotten him his jobs in Lancaster and Remington as training steps for this. He'll be brilliant. Our sick society needs him to do this." Her coach repeated that strange word: "Please."

Pauleen Farrell had never disobeyed her coach.

"But you know how depressed and stubborn he is, sir."

He nodded. "Yes, of course I do. Please."

"Yes sir, I will. I promise."

"Thank you, young lady." The old man climbed back out of his car, hugged and kissed her on her left cheek. "You can't know how many lives he'll help but it'll be a lot."

"Yes, sir," she replied. "Just one more thing, Dr. Stone, where's this job?"

"It'll be everywhere, all over the world, but mostly here in the States. He'll be based in Lexington, Kentucky, just down the road from you in Louisville."

"OK, sir," she said.

"Keep an eye on him, will you?" the old man asked. "I'll miss you, my running crew."

"Yes, we will, sir, and we'll miss you, too. Just one more thing, sir."

"Yes?" asked Dr. Stone.

"Do you think Tom'll let us adopt Catherine? George and I love her and we'd like to."

"I can't think of better parents than you, young lady. You have my blessing." Dr. Stone hesitated. "I'm proud of all of you. You're great kids and I've enjoyed coaching you. Take care of yourselves or I'll have to fly down to Kentucky to kick your behinds."

"Please visit any time, sir. You are our hero. Thanks for helping us win our medals and for so much more." Pauleen believed that she saw more tears from the old man as he drove away.

****

So, after talking hard on the drive to Middleburg, Tom and Pauleen found themselves meeting the former Olympic champion, George Hancock Alexander. Tom listened to Alexander, sealed their deal with a handshake and entered the world of investigating most kinds of frauds. Danger traveled with him down the new road.

The same road that would eventually lead to the day when Tom was knifed, close to his heart.

Chapter 13   KENTUCKY

It took Tom quite a long while to get to know people in Lexington, outside of his new work colleagues. There were only seven of them and no customers ever visited, so the office atmosphere was markedly different from that at Tristram Brokerage with 12 employees and dozens of daily visiting customers.

Two weeks after meeting George Alexander, he'd said goodbye to his colleagues in Remington and friends in Warrenton and driven to Kentucky. Pauleen and George adopted Catherine, which Tom agreed was best for the baby, and moved to Louisville, just 80 miles from Lexington.

Tom's depression eased slightly each week but it took several more months before he smiled and laughed again.

He sold his Italian-made Alpha Romeo to reduce (in a tiny way) memories of Katya, finding that he constantly turned his head to look at her and every time was struck by sadness at her absence. He bought a Saab, made in Sweden, as a change and trained himself to stop turning his head towards the front passenger seat. He never stopped talking to Katya, though—in his head when he was with people and out loud when alone.

After three nights in a motel, he rented a satisfactory apartment in an attractive complex, built off of Versailles Road on a former horse farm with many trees. The complex was in a long-established neighborhood. He could run to and from work, two miles away. Two months after he moved in, he still had no furniture and slept on the floor in a sleeping bag. Pauleen appointed herself his furniture buyer, guessing correctly that he'd never bother and winning her $5 bet with George. Housekeeping and nest building weren't foremost in Tom's mind.

He deliberately made an effort to drive around Kentucky to discover its beauty and heritage. While he loved the great scenery and beautifully manicured horse farms, where money seemed limitless, that surrounded Lexington, Midway and Versailles, his favorite location became Pleasant Hill at Shakertown, about half an hour's drive south of Lexington, across the river.

Shakertown was home to a religious group during the 19th century. Founded in 1805, the settlement reached 4,000 acres and its special furniture and agricultural seeds became nationally famous, but the group slowly died out. The limestone buildings were restored in the 1960s, the farmland now totaling about 3,000 acres and the property receiving thousands of tourists annually.

He met Barbara Frost while eating lunch in the quaint dining room at Shakertown, inside an inn with extraordinarily beautiful twin spiral staircases. They were assigned places at the same table and began talking. After lunch, they walked through the beautifully restored buildings and bought a few knickknacks in the village shop before walking to their cars.

They said goodbye, Tom assuming that he'd never see her again. He wasn't ready for a relationship, thought he never would be, and that was that, but it had been pleasant to talk to such an attractive stranger.

But neither fate nor Cupid had given up on him and that evening, when he took his laundry to the apartment complex's shared laundry room, there was Barbara, doing the same chore.

They hadn't revealed to each other where they lived in Lexington. They began talking again and, gradually, very gradually, they became good friends.

Divorced from a jerk, Barbara was feeling very gun-shy about another relationship: she was carrying baggage and needed time to heal. Tom revealed his love of Katya in nearly every sentence. Barbara admired his faithfulness and devotion but didn't want to compete with Katya.

Barbara was the opposite of Katya in looks and personality. She was taller and a natural blonde, while Katya was five inches shorter with long brown hair. Barbara had been a successful horsewoman in show jumping but now restricted herself to pleasure tennis and her favorite game was chess. Her personality was a lot closer to Tom's than Katya's had been.

Katya had been innocent of the big world, while Barbara was worldly and did not believe that a woman should be subjugated to "her man," the wife doing the traditional donkeywork and the housecleaning role. Barbara owned plenty of cynicism from her experiences in business and particularly from her ex-husband, a Mr. Bill Bailey. She was determined not to repeat that error of judgment. From now on, she'd vet any man thoroughly no later than the second date.

Fiercely independent, now that she'd gotten rid of Bailey, who had became an unacceptable pain in her neck the second she'd discovered his real occupation of con artist. He'd certainly conned her. She'd dropped him like a toxic rock and walked out immediately. Fortunately, there were no kids to complicate matters. The divorce was fast but left Barbara without a penny. She soon discovered that delightful Bill had wasted all of her small inheritance.

Zero cash was a shrewd settlement, she felt with relief, when Bill was arrested six months later for fraud. He was as guilty as hell, having swindled three old ladies out of their life savings. He'd cheated his former employer, also, by selling stolen merchandise to the black market.

She decided she needed a man as much as a cat needs a bicycle, as her mother used to say and stayed away from the dating market while taking time to develop a hope that not all men were crooks.

After the divorce, she kept her interesting job wholesaling jewelry to high quality retail jewelry stores in order to earn cash for survival. She also sometimes bought rare pieces as an agent for a museum. She quit the wholesaling job when she felt she had enough of a cash cushion to become a self-employed agent with the museum as her only client. It was time, she decided, to recreate herself as an inventor, following in the footsteps of her dead father, an air conditioning repairman and part-time farmer who'd created gizmos in his barn in his spare time.

The big difference between father and daughter was that Dad was a babe in the woods when selling his inventions. Not bothering to secure patents and too trusting, he never received more than a pittance, while most of his buyers made tens of thousands, sometimes millions.

Much more business-like, Barbara refused to make the same mistake. She loved inventing but was a hard-edged businesswoman. After college many years before, she'd completed an apprenticeship in jewelry design, learning how to make and sell pieces, before gaining a business degree from the University of Pennsylvania and then working as a jewelry wholesaler.

After ending her brief marriage, she'd arrived in Lexington two months before meeting Tom. Just before meeting him, she'd bought a house in the Lansdowne suburb off Tates Creek Road and was waiting for the house to be refurbished before moving into it. Her new house had a double garage that would be ideal for her workshop.

She'd moved to Lexington because an old college friend, Sally Young, raved about the better quality of life there, especially the beautiful horse farms surrounding the city.

One visit to see Sally, who was an emergency room nurse, and Barbara agreed.

Barbara had always loved helping her dad with his creations and her business plan was to make prosaic but profitable inventions, useful for everyday small needs, practical but not earth-shatteringly important. She wasn't aiming to copy Edison and his telephone or repeat Hewlett & Packard's growth. Her heroes were her dad—though not because of his failure as a negotiator—and Russell Carrier, the inventor of air conditioning.

Buying pieces for the museum was a job she enjoyed and good for cash flow, so she kept it: regular cash flow being critical for all businesses, especially start-ups and most particularly an invention company where dependable income by definition is usually years away.

Barbara wasn't going to burn any bridges, although she had happily quit wholesaling, because she needed the time to devote to her passion—inventions. Her long-term goal was to make top-quality jewelry, which fascinated her, after her plain vanilla inventions had made her rich enough to semi-retire.

Her first big winner was a better rear-view mirror for cars, eliminating all blind spots completely, for which she'd just that week obtained the essential patent. Her expected royalties from that would keep her debt-free for years as long as she didn't get silly: and silly wasn't in Barbara's vocabulary.

Barbara preferred to work on several projects simultaneously, believing that cross-pollinating her ideas was her best research strategy for inventions. The working on one idea forever wasn't her style. Her best current idea was a new patch with a quick local anesthetic that didn't hurt like bandaids when removed, which she thought would be valued by mothers with injury-prone kids—another huge market for royalties.

She was also curious about inventing sensors with plenty of applications. She was determined to control all the manufacturing and marketing herself by carefully licensing them out or managing the whole process. She wouldn't allow strangers to siphon off all the profits as her dad had.

As it was, she'd only licensed the manufacturer of her car mirrors for eight years. She would maintain tight control of all her patents by working alone, taking no chances that an employee would steal or sell her notions or distract her. When working, she was as focused as Tom was when he did his investigations.

Barbara didn't really bother with small talk but that didn't prevent them from becoming pals and, later, lovers. Both were self-sufficient, independent, worldly, totally honest and reliable. Barbara didn't follow sport and had never heard of Tom's achievement at the Olympics: while suitably impressed, her interest in Tom was him not his celebrity or trophies. Tom liked that.

For his part, Barbara's skills impressed but didn't overwhelm him. He didn't know a thing about jewelry, had no technical skills, could barely make an omelet let alone an instrument and knew nothing about inventions or gadgets.

Barbara's friend, Sally, introduced Tom to her boyfriend, a retired English steeplechase jockey named Charlie Scott, who had begun a bloodstock agency in Lexington. His job was the buying and selling of racehorses, broodmares and the occasional stallion, on commission for clients around the U.S., to and from England and Ireland, and fillies to an agent in Australia, where they would become broodmares.

His specialty and main trade was buying young racehorses in England to be imported to race in the States for clients. An expert on British racing, he'd made some smart selections, including a future winner of a Breeders'

Cup race who had only displayed modest form back in Yorkshire. Charlie had spotted his potential, taken a risk and been right. His career trajectory and reputation improved after that winner.

He and Tom became friends at Sally's house and both worked on the three million dollar Humorist horse case a year later. Charlie introduced Tom to the backstretch of Lexington's Keeneland racetrack and taught him the basics about racing and training, while they watched the Thoroughbreds galloping in the early mornings.

A cat adopted Tom one morning in a trainer's barn. He shadowed Tom all morning then followed him to his car, hopping in when Tom opened the driver's door and settling down on the front passenger seat.

"She's yours, if you want her," called the assistant trainer. "We've got two other barn cats. We call her 'Lady.'"

That's how Tom obtained a flat mate, whom he renamed "Pinky" when, on checking, he discovered that Lady was actually a Lord. They quickly became best friends. Pinky enjoyed snoozing on Tom's lap, shared his pillow at night, tapped him on the nose with his paw at wake-up time and lay on his left shoulder and neck when Tom drove. His purr was as loud as tinnitus.

Charlie often took Tom with him when inspecting the great stallions, like Triple Crown winners Secretariat and Nijinsky, who lived in luxury at famous farms in central Kentucky. Tom loved the area and slowly began to enjoy life again without, however, forgetting Katya for even five minutes. She was always in his heart.

****

Tom enjoyed his new work and it eased his depression. Alexander and the others liked him immediately and they taught him the tricks of their odd trade. He learned many new lessons, with them first assigning him small, simple cases.

Each case was different and called for a fresh approach. There was no such creature as "routine" at The Alexander Agency. Everyone discussed their cases in a half hour meeting every morning.

Their caseload included finding employees who'd skipped town just before a lot of money was discovered missing from the company's checkbook, or soon after complaints began filtering in from customers suddenly nervous about their previously much-trusted financial advisor, or after the customers had been conned out of money because of a great variety of scams or . . . the list was almost endless.

Difficulties were brought to their attention from small and large businesses, families, individuals, brokerage firms, insurance underwriters with awkward claims from policyholders, and CEO's with personal problems. The agency refused to work for lawyers. Alexander's did, however, investigate and pursue lawyers.

Other cases involved investigating investments of all descriptions; lawyers and real estate agents who'd disappeared, hiding money stolen from trust or escrow accounts; accountants who had quit accounting and were suddenly living lifestyles way beyond their salaries; bank employees who were suddenly driving expensive cars.

Discretion was vital for the clients—no media was ever to get word of any stories. The Alexander Agency usually solved the frauds or whatever without needing to get the police or the courts involved, or lawsuits. Cases came in via word of mouth. There was no advertising and never any publicity.

Bob McCutcheon quickly made friends with Tom. With the agency for three years, Bob's specialty was corporate espionage, having been a consultant to large corporations for a decade.

Tiring of the politics, (Bob told people: "Big companies are minefields without grass."), he'd joined The Alexander Agency, where in his first job as an undercover executive, he discovered that it was the chief financial officer, not the suspected chief assistant to the vice-President, who was embezzling $100,000 every month by inventing inventory purchases in overseas offices.

McCutcheon specialized in finding executives possessing corporate secrets and sometimes corporate cash, who disappeared or joined competitors without notice, violating their non-compete contracts.

Technology companies, in particular, objected to the latter behavior and hired Alexander's to solve these headaches, wanting to avoid lawyers and to keep quiet with the media. The first hint of spilled secrets would damage the company's stock price and, of course, the value of the executives' stock options.

"This job," Bob told Tom, "is more fun than catching salmon in a river with a grizzly standing 20 feet away wanting to share it with you."

Tom's first case was finding a secretary who, angry at her boss, had walked out of her job at a non-profit association, stealing money and all the accounts and membership files as her final goodbye. She'd also switched the outgoing mail, placing thank you letters to new members into envelopes destined for debtors . . . and vice versa.

The irate members drove her former boss crazy and demanded a slew of apologies for the switched mail.

Tom easily tracked the secretary down, finding her boyfriend and asking him where she'd gone. The boyfriend gave Tom her phone number. After she heard how embarrassed her boss had become, she reckoned she'd had her fun and told Tom where the documents were.

She insisted that she hadn't stolen any money, proving to Tom's satisfaction that she'd had no access to funds and that if any money was missing then to look straight at her former boss. She added that she hoped her lazy ex-boss would treat her replacement better.

Believing her, Tom explained the situation to her former boss, who grudgingly admitted that no money had fled with the ex-secretary. Tom then told him where she'd claimed the bag was, hidden behind the office's refrigerator, and closed the file.

Tom's second solo case was a lawyer who'd invested friends' money in a real estate transaction but had bought the building only in his name, pretending that his friends were co-owners. He had only paid out a third of the rents for three years before one investor, his brother-in-law, got suspicious after reading a newspaper article about one of the tenants who named the lawyer as the sole owner.

Just a stroke of bad luck for the lawyer. Publicity isn't always better than none.

****

Tom enjoyed Barbara and Lexington, was fascinated by his new job and learned a lot every day. His depression lifted and, after so many horrible months when he'd wanted to die, he finally felt hopeful for the future.

Dr. Stone had, as always, been right.

Tom was fulfilling his potential and his destiny. He was a hunter, a fraud catcher.

Chapter 14   ANNE EDDERY

It was the trips home that Tom dreaded, returning from the nursing home where his mentor Dr. Stone lay suffering in a bed, at the end of his life, simply waiting to die and wanting to die soon. On this rainy afternoon, Tom wasn't expecting to discover another fraud case needing to be solved, this time affecting the old vet.

Four years after his retirement from coaching, war hero Dr. Stone lay feebly in bed, with no control over his body, battling both rheumatoid arthritis and Parkinson's disease. He'd lost many vertebrae, had shrunk in height by a foot and was gaunt, desperately weak, his hair white.

Bedridden, wracked with pain, wrists and arms shaking involuntarily and unable to lift a cup or turn the pages of a book, he needed everything done for him. His teeth were brushed for him, he was raised up into position to watch mindless, witless programs on the TV shackled high up on the opposite wall and needed to be taken to and from the toilet, everything. He usually wet the bed before the nurses could reach him.

As Brabazon stood by the old man's bedside, he was always embarrassed and horrified to see the tough old World War II vet and his former athletics coach in such misery.

The old man's fingers were curled up uselessly and he was constantly rubbing them to ease the pain but nothing helped, not even his medication, which he usually spat out. Dr. Stone was too tough, too rigid to accept the weakness implied by pain medication.

It was appalling. At times, against his will, the nurses simply injected him. Embarrassed at the indignity, he couldn't stop them. The bedpans were the ultimate embarrassment.

"Well, Tom, it's come to this, broken, battered, old," said Dr. Stone in between gasps of pain.

"Never expected this. We're a long damned way from the Olympics and the Nationals but we've done a few things together, boy, haven't we?" This was how the conversation always began.

"The Nazis couldn't defeat me but I can't beat this. Would have been better off dead in France than with this."

Tom nodded. He knew he'd be crying by the time he reached his car: it happened every time. He visited Dr.

Stone every other week without fail, no matter where he'd been.

Nobody knew how long the old man would have to wait for death. Tom knew that he owed him such enormous gratitude for everything the old man had done for him that, despite his busy schedule and many files full of frauds and swindles, he always made the trip, in addition to telephoning every evening.

He'd never be able to repay Dr. Stone for giving him the life he'd had since meeting him on the athletics pitch at Manassas University all those years before. He knew that he owed him, quite simply and truly, everything.

"Yessir," he replied. "We sure did."

And then, because the old man's memory was also in and out, remembering the old days but unable to remember the last several minutes, so sometimes forgetting what he'd just said, they'd reminisce as if for the first time about their track victories and their first missing persons cases.

They also chatted about the cases that Tom was working on now but Dr. Stone kept forgetting whole sentences and Tom would need to gently repeat himself.

It was painful to realize that this was the same Dr. Stone whose judgment of people in wartime Europe had been so accurate that he survived working undercover, despite intense pressure in dangerous situations, rescuing Allied soldiers and getting them safely back to England.

He'd identified and nurtured Tom's talent both as an athlete and as an investigator. Tom had become an expert in two very niche areas thanks to Dr. Stone's tutelage and encouragement.

As Tom left, upset that he couldn't solve this problem—he'd have given anything for Dr. Stone to be pain free again—he said a polite hello, as usual, to the busy nursing aide, who was wearing a tag that sported the name "Anne." She nodded back and Tom continued down the corridor and out the door to the parking lot.

Already concentrating on his caseload in order to try to forget Dr. Stone's misery, he heard a woman calling him and looked around. It was Anne.

Anne was in her fifties, with a major speech impediment, which slurred her words. She had scars across her left cheek and forehead, bad teeth and tired eyes. She had clearly led a hard life but possessed a heart of gold and the patients at the retirement home were as devoted to her as she was to them. Even Dr. Stone gave her credit.

The other staff at the retirement home looked down on her but, though she noticed and it hurt her feelings, she never let them know that she'd once been both a doctor and a beautiful young woman.

A car accident during her last year of training to be a surgeon had robbed Anne of a great future. It happened just two months before she was to complete her surgical residency, while she was fielding several offers to be appointed an assistant professor of surgery at the best hospitals, including the Mayo Clinic, Emory in Atlanta and Johns Hopkins in Baltimore.

She'd gained both her degrees with honors, first through the four years of college and then another four in medical school, before receiving her medical degree. Then she'd coped with the year of slavery and lack of sleep, the rite of passage known as the "internship," then another five equally hard years of surgical residency.

The experienced clinicians and her peers all predicted that Anne Eddery would have a glittering career as a brilliant surgeon. She was a golden girl with brains, great hands, courage, skill and beauty. She had it all.

Until a hit-and-run car driver knocked her off her racing bike. The driver was never found.

After the accident, it took a while for her brain to recover and the scars and physical pains to subside. The emotional scars never healed. Her fiancé had vomited after seeing her in the hospital bed then cancelled the engagement, saying that he was sorry but couldn't look at her face again and he walked out of her life. Her parents tried so hard for their only child but eventually descended into their own hells. They died many years ago.

Between her inability to express herself clearly and, because, for the first decade, both hands were numb, preventing her from writing legibly, nobody could understand that her brain still worked perfectly. Thus, she couldn't finish her training, pass any state board exams, write anything, speak properly, be taken seriously or be allowed to provide advanced care to patients.

Hospitals were too afraid of litigation to employ her; to be fair to them she seemed hopeless, so the best she could do was work in a series of nursing homes at minimum wage.

Even now, all these years later, her handwriting still resembled a bicycle tire skidding on ice in a blizzard but she had managed finally to make it legible if she worked slowly and held her breath.

She had no friends or family anymore, no male admirers, hadn't since the accident, all having vanished from her life.

Her brain worked perfectly well yet acquaintances assumed that she was stupid, retarded and ignorant simply because she was unable to express herself clearly. It frustrated her constantly. She desperately wanted to prove to others that her mind was healthy and that she was safe . . . and a person, not a mental cripple.

She loved taking care of patients—she'd wanted to be a doctor since third grade—and had worked in this nursing home for seven years.

Anne had long resigned herself to a lonely, frustrated, empty existence—you couldn't call it a life—and her two cats at home were all she still had, except for playing chess.

Sometimes she played chess with neighbors in her apartment building. You don't need to talk during chess other than saying the word "checkmate." She nearly always won but was afraid to play in competitions, for fear of more ridicule. She lacked much in her life but suffered plenty of ridicule, having endured more than enough of that.

"Meester," she called out to Tom. "Meester, havvvaya-hha ggggotta a mi-nnnnute?"

Upset about Dr. Stone, late for his flight back to Lexington, Tom hesitated. He knew nothing about her, having only noticed her floating around the retirement home looking after patients' needs. He was off duty, off guard, not expecting trouble, troubled about his mentor. He really didn't have a minute to spare and he nearly blew her off. Much later, he reflected how relieved he was that he'd ignored his first impulse to ignore her.

"How can I help you?"

"Meester, I ah like Meester Stahn." She meant Dr. Stone.

"So do I."

"I ah like Mrs. Wall . . . ace too."

"Good." Tom nearly walked off.

"I ah don't a like thaht man who talk . . . tak . . . who talked to ah 'dem yast . . . er . . . day."

Tom was now bored. He'd been polite long enough and had plenty to think about. He said goodbye and had already forgotten the woman when, 15 seconds later, she stuttered again as he was unlocking his car door.

"I ah theenk he ah is st . . . st . . . stealing thems mo . . . mo . . . ney."

Tom snapped to attention, turned back to her and asked for details. He really wasn't at all amused at the idea that anybody would dare steal from Dr. Stone.

He had difficulty understanding Anne's speech but he recognized that this woman's simple mind was telling a truth. Tom usually agreed with the grizzled old detective who'd told him, "Everybody lies, all criminals lie, all citizens lie and everybody ranked above sergeant lies," but he'd been around enough to believe that he was able to identify the rare exceptions.

The woman continued, of course, to have difficulty expressing her thoughts to Tom but her gist was that this visitor talked to various residents, persuading them to sign documents. Tom felt the old shiver up his spine.

He disliked what he was hearing and wanted to know more but he simply couldn't understand her. He led Anne back inside to look for a translator but the first nurse he found told him to ignore her.

He persisted and, by luck, saw the manager—with a name tag identifying him as such—walking across the sitting room.

"Excuse me," Tom began. "May we talk, please?"

The manager stopped, believing Tom to be a son of one of the patients, giving a wide smile and a handshake. After the social niceties and Tom's explaining that he had just visited Dr. Stone, Tom asked if the manager knew anything about a young man who was getting residents to sign documents.

George Gifford, the manager, changed his attitude from customer greeting to annoyance.

"What have you been saying, Anne? I've told you before to leave people alone. Now get back to work."

He turned his attention back to Tom. "I'm sorry about her, sir. She should mind her business and do her job. She's a pest. I don't know why I keep her on. Well, as far as Mr. Stone," he changed the subject, "that's just routine policy, nothing to worry about, just some forms to update our guests' information. I trust that you are pleased with your father's comfort?"

"Actually, no, I'm not. He needs to get his medication every time. He's in a lot of pain. And I'm not his son but I've known him for many years. I used to work for him."

This was the first time he'd met the manager despite having visited every other week for four months—where had the man been, he wondered—and he was irritated about the arrogant manner in which the manager had dismissed Anne and then badmouthed her to a stranger. That got his back up. Tom had developed a theory that good bosses and managers were courteous to everybody, especially to their lowest level employees.

The flip worked too. When a manager was rude to the staff, then he or she was more likely to be dishonest. He'd also discovered that the best companies treated their staff well and bad companies didn't.

The more the manager assured Tom that there was nothing to worry about, the more Tom did. Gifford refused to give any details about the young man whom Anne suspected of "st . . . st . . . stea . . . ling." Tom shook his head and walked away, planning his next move.

Dr. Stone's daughter Ellen was a nice enough woman and a faithful daughter but she and Tom weren't friends. A radio station manager in far-off Milwaukee, she'd chosen this retirement home for her father, made all the necessary arrangements and had visited a few times.

She felt crowded by Tom, occasionally resentful of his closeness with her dad and thought that he should accept that she was in charge of making decisions for his old coach. Tom hadn't liked this place, feeling that it was too down-market and that his mentor deserved a lot better, yet Ellen refused to reconsider.

This retirement home was part of a large public company that traded on the New York Stock Exchange. Tom had, of course, checked out the company's management and finances, finding it to be a solid enough, honestly managed company expanding rapidly across the country, with a share price traveling upwards.

Whatever anyone's personal feelings about the ethics of investing in health care companies and profiting from other peoples' pain and suffering–Tom understood both sides' opinions–Tom had found no cause to be alarmed about the method of operation of this business, its balance sheet or its treatment of patients. It was not going to close its doors anytime soon and its patients were well looked after.

Still, he'd preferred a better home for Dr. Stone: ideally, five star luxury like the Greenbriar or a Waldorf-Astoria. But then, they'd have been even more expensive and Tom wasn't paying the bills, Dr. Stone was and Ellen Dennard intended, needed, to inherit more money rather than less. Retirement homes are expensive.

Tom had missed his plane but decided that the next one would be satisfactory. He walked outside again and waited patiently in his car for two hours until Anne walked out in street clothes, having finished her shift. He offered her dinner.

This had been the first time since her accident that Anne had been invited by a man for dinner—love had been another casualty of her car accident—but, though surprised and wary, she accepted.

"Do I haave too . . . do you expp . . . ect me . . . or ah want . . . me . . . to ha . . . ve sex with ah . . . ya . . . you?" She was nervous.

"No, absolutely not, Anne. I'm faithful to my girlfriend at home. This is just going to be dinner so that you can tell me about this man who is bothering Dr. Stone and the other residents."

Over dinner, Anne tried time and again to explain but eventually gave up. She took a pen and notebook from her pocket and wrote her story down with difficulty. Tom typically wondered about peoples' motives for giving information but he was certain that Anne Eddery's reason was honest and that she could be believed.

This man, Anne explained with difficulty, had been going around to some of the residents recommending that they allow him to invest all of their money. The majority of the patients lived off interest from their investments, usually municipal bonds rather than company stock, because they needed regular, guaranteed income to pay their rent and a few personal expenses like books and gifts to their grandchildren.

During their high income earning years, most people invest their spare cash in shares of fast-growing, well-managed companies because there's plenty of time for their nest-eggs to grow, yet they're young enough to recover from the inevitable, frequent and sometimes gut-wrenching tornadoes of Wall Street's price fluctuations.

But old people need safety, not growth, for their money.

Because the economy was doing well at the time, interest rates were falling—good news for businesspeople and borrowers but disastrous for investors with bond investments—these retired people were worried about their falling incomes.

Even though the interest rate stays the same because the fixed monthly income from bonds remained static, municipalities sometimes redeem—"call"—the bonds, returning their investors' money to them, offering them the chance to reinvest at a lower yield.

One of the world's worst investments for investors is a callable, long-term 20, even 30-year term bond at fixed interest. No upside, no growth, capital locked in the bond, destroyed by inflation.

Needing, of course, to reinvest their capital, the lower interest income would be a lot less plus, during times of inflation, bonds lose market value.

Tom learned most of this information later from talking to Mrs. Wallace and Mrs. Harris, because Anne's handwriting covered only her basic worries for her patients.

This "nice, honest looking young man" visiting Dr. Stone's retirement home had explained to Mrs. Wallace and the others, including his former coach, that because their income was dropping, they needed to boost their income or they stood a chance of being evicted for non-payment of rent.

But, conveniently, he knew a way that they could increase their income and make big profits at 'no risk,' so
that their money would be safe and they could leave even
larger nest eggs for their families.

Naturally, he knew just the right investment for them,
which was profitable but 'safe'–that word was repeated
often, with emphasis–for them and offered great tax
advantages, too. He called it currency trading.

That was not a 'safe' investment for anyone, least of all
dying old people, but rather a complex battle of wits for
sophisticated expert professionals like George Soros and
the Irishman J.P. McManus.

This 'nice young man' with the winning, persuasive
smile assured the pensioners that their money would be
particularly safe in a foreign currency since the U.S.
dollar and economy were both doomed and that the government was planning to reduce Social Security payments
to the elderly. Maybe true but a tactic designed more to
scare than anything else.

His solution was to use the Australian dollar as the
core currency–none of these customers knew anything
about Australia, let alone its 'hot' currency–and that his
team of experts would trade in and out of English ster-
ling, French francs, Deutschmarks and the drachma
based on his bank's specially-developed proprietary
system.

He claimed that this system could predict weaknesses
and trends in the U.S. dollar and Japanese yen, that the
bank retained a Nobel Prize winner in economics and that
his wealthy clients in Florida were already making large
profits from this 'esoteric and unique' trading.

Recommending a quick decision, the young man
pointed out that he was restricting new investment to

only 50 more investors before closing the fund so that it remained exclusive and the profits wouldn't be diluted. He added that his mother and grandmother were both investors in the fund.

Anne told Tom that Dr. Stone and several other patients had given him checks.

Tom smelled a rotten fish, a con of the first degree, so decided to investigate but Dr. Stone clammed up, insisting that his finances were his business and none of Tom's, hissing "mind your own damned business" before returning his attention to the hilarious adventures of Tom and Jerry on the TV.

Interview time was over.

He went searching for Mrs. Wallace but as she was asleep there was nothing more to do other than drive to the airport. He would check out the investment guru but as it looked like just another scam, it would have to wait.

He had plenty of other cases. In detective and TV shows, the heroes only seem to ever have one case to solve and they always succeed in the last 15 minutes before the final credits. In real life, there are dozens of files on a detective's desk, all studied simultaneously.

****

Tom's oddest file at the moment was a wealthy and smart businessman who'd done a very silly thing and wanted his money back.

Richard Brackenberg had landed on Omaha Beach on D-Day as an 18-year-old and was forever grateful to have survived this first European visit. He was no mug in business and had become CEO of a Fortune 500 company but, like many other successful businesspeople, he'd floundered in the horse business after buying a farm and hiring a farm manager.

It took little time for his farm manager, Jimmy, to supplement his salary by convincing his boss to buy half a stallion in, of all places, Chile, and sending $200,000 down to South America as payment.

The deal was that the stallion would be flown to the U.S. after the Chilean breeding season ended in December and would travel back and forth between the countries to cover mares in both hemispheres in a process called "shuttling."

This enterprise became very popular particularly between Kentucky and Ireland in the northern hemisphere and Australia and New Zealand in the southern, allowing the stallions to double their breedings and their income instead of standing around idle and earning nothing during the non-breeding seasons.

Mr. Brackenberg didn't receive his horse.

His phone calls and faxes to Chile went unanswered. Becoming uneasy, he consulted a bloodstock agent, Tom Brabazon's friend, Charlie Scott, for an appraisal. Scott researched the horse and told his client the unsettling news that the horse's market value had been just $10,000 alive—for the whole horse, not even half—but that he had died one month before Hackenberger had made payment.

Scott explained gently, for his client was upset, that the stallion's pedigree would have had no appeal to American broodmare owners and that his value as a stallion in the United States was therefore a nominal $1,000. The farm manager had bought a totally inappropriate stallion for his boss.

It was no surprise, therefore, that the sellers didn't answer their mail. Charlie's advice was to take a total tax loss and fire the farm manager and require a refund of $200,000 from Jimmy. To his surprise, Mr. Brackenberg replied:

"No, I'll never fire him. He's a nice fellow and he'll be my farm manager for as long as I own this farm. I'll just not let him buy any more horses for me."

And it came to pass within the fullness of time and much patience, that when Brackenberg decided to quit, having wasted many millions with scant joy, the Irishman was still farm manager on the day the farm was sold. Having arrived penniless in the U.S. five years earlier, Jimmy quickly drove to Kentucky and bought a decent-sized farm with cash. He'd had no need for a mortgage.

Scott had also recommended Tom at The Alexander Agency. Brackenberg asked Tom to fly to Chile to retrieve the money if not the corpse. Tom's reinforcement of Scott's recommendations again fell on deaf ears.

Since this was the era of General Pincochet and his disappearing citizens, Tom reckoned that a dead horse worth $10,000 alive and less "as is," i.e. dead, wasn't sufficient to tempt him to visit Chile, despite a favorable exchange rate and no tourists.

General Pinochet's methods of causing people to disappear might have been the reason for the scarcity of tourists.

Tom remembered the famous Northern Ireland Tourist Board's advertisement in American magazines during the 1970s, during the peak of the civil war there, when the nifty slogan was "Come to Northern Ireland for a shooting holiday." Perhaps the Chileans could try: "Come to Chile to disappear."

Tom decided not to fly to South America for a dead horse.

As the plane flew toward central Kentucky on its way to Bluegrass Airport in Lexington, Tom chose to recommend multiple pieces of advice: the principle of "caveat emptor," independent qualified valuing in advance and serious due diligence the next time Mr. Brackenberg wanted to buy a stallion and reinforced Charlie's advice to fire the farm manager.

He wondered how some people could be so smart in business but hopelessly naïve when buying horses.

Tom closed the file and asked Elizabeth to send a final invoice attached to his written recommendations.

****

Tom woke up the next morning deciding to place the nursing home case as his first priority. All his cases were important but some of these patients were going to die soon and they couldn't wait.

Besides, Dr. Stone telling him to mind his own business irritated him and then there was the manager's haughty treatment of Anne and his general attitude. Tom owed everything to Dr. Stone and, though his debt would never—could never—be fully repaid, he wasn't going to delay checking into this currency trading business.

He certainly wasn't going to allow Dr. Stone's stonewalling to keep him from doing his job and Dr. Stone from being cheated. He told Elizabeth where he'd be and why: standard procedure in the easy-to-disappear business.

The office always knew where he was and on what cases he was working. The same went for his colleagues. They all gave daily reports and schedules. Just in case.

A year later, for safety's sake, Tom's boss George Alexander asked his investigators to begin wearing a tracking device, made in New Zealand of all places and invented originally to track wild deer in mountains and fish in oceans. It was inserted under their skin, just like identifiers for dogs and cats and was ideal for parents to keep track of where their teenagers were.

He advised Elizabeth that the retirement home's case would likely be charged to the "Open fund" account. This was funded by their centi-millionaire benefactor Ronald Barry for "charitable" cases where there was no billable client but was a case that benefitted society in general or pro-bono clients, who couldn't pay or whom the agency preferred not to charge for a variety of reasons.

Tom wasn't going to send a bill to Dr. Stone or the sweet old ladies in the retirement home.

So, instead of flying, because all the flights were full that morning, he drove back to Roanoke in his green Saab, the first two hours through nothingness on Interstate 64 to the West Virginia border and five more hours after that. He occupied these boring hours by listening to his favorite music: Simon and Garfunkel, treating himself to the rare joy of singing out of tune loudly with the windows down and without harming anybody's ears. His favorite S+G melodies were "I Am a Rock" and "The Boxer."

He was a lousy singer. Any singing career ambition had been thwarted at school when the music teacher had always ordered: "Walwyn, just move your lips, don't make any noise." That was for his audience's benefit but his young ego was punctured. Sensitivity wasn't the music teacher's best virtue.

Then the landscape improved just a little past Huntington towards the state's capital, Charleston, where interstates 64 and 77 merged for a while before 64 became independent again. An hour and a half later, he crossed the Virginia border, smiled at the welcoming sign reading, "Virginia is for lovers," and stopped at a restaurant, at an I-81 exit, near the small town of Bective.

While eating soup and a sandwich, he saw the strange apparition of a middle-aged man entering the restaurant wearing a kangaroo suit complete with, in keeping with authenticity, a long bouncy tail.

His amazed reaction was equaled by two pole-axed, jaw-dropped Virginia state troopers, who were eating their cheeseburgers. The man, accompanied by another man dressed normally and a girl about six or eight years old, was greeted warmly by the staff. He was clearly a regular and eccentric customer.

The cops finished their meals but watched the apparition warily, never taking their eyes off the man until they left the restaurant. If being dressed as a kangaroo was illegal in Virginia, the state troopers didn't know about it but it was obvious what they were hoping.

There are lots of peculiar laws in America. Tom had been told that it was illegal to catch a giraffe's neck in Chicago or hunt a whale in far-from-any-ocean Utah or to bicycle through a swimming pool in California.

He finished his lunch, took another look at the kangaroo suit and left.

It was another hour's drive to the nursing home near Roanoke.

Tom reached it in mid-afternoon.

He was sure that this currency trading was a scam but didn't yet know how. He would solve it. Even if legal—and it probably was, but only *just*—it was a thoroughly inappropriate investment for elderly people. Currency trading is high risk for any age group and should only be a small percentage of anyone's investment portfolio.

Dr. Stone was surprised to see him again so soon and didn't hide his pleasure.

Lying in a nursing home bed, unable to do anything, was boring and he had always admired Tom for being the type of man that he'd hoped his own son would have become. Tom knew better than to raise the subject of the earnest young investment counselor again so, after a while, he went and talked to Mrs. Wallace and two other residents, who were all delighted to pass the time talking with someone new.

All three ladies had been approached by—"oh, here's his tri-color business card,"—J. Anthony Webber, III, Vice President and Investment Counselor at a bank in Miami, Florida.

Tom had never heard of the Twenty Five Global Bank but his first thought was why J. Anthony, *the Third*, etc., etc. would need to troll for clients in far-off Virginia when there were millions of retirees living in Florida from whom he could earn enough commissions to avoid the need of taking his investment pitch on the road.

He'd promised the ladies, not the 5% they were receiving from their bonds but "at least 25% and usually 50% profit every year with less risk than a certificate of deposit." That was doubtful, to be sure.

Brabazon had learned long ago that listening was his best skill. He listened quietly and sympathetically: that was his method. A con artist he'd caught in Chicago had told him, "People trust you. They open up." Then paying him what the crook regarded as the ultimate compliment:

"Tom, you'd make a great con artist. It's too bad that you're honest." Seeming to be trustworthy is the most valuable weapon in all con artists' bags of tricks.

These ladies were lonely and were delighted to speak with somebody new. They knew everything about their companions' grandchildren. Tom was a fresh face for these old ladies.

So Mrs. Wallace and Mrs. Harris opened up, discussing their investments, their worries about their bonds and their relief when the nice, young Mr. Webber had visited them.

"He told me," Mrs. Wallace said, "that his own mother is in a nursing home, so he understood our situation. He's made 44% profit on her money since he invested it just 10 months ago."

"That's certainly better," Mrs. Harris piped up, "than 3.5% per year on a 30-year municipal bond or the 5% earning GNMA that my stockbroker invested my money in *and* he charged me hefty commissions."

"Young Mr. Webber isn't charging us anything," Mrs. Mackenzie pointed out happily, "because of his mother. He's such a delightful young man."

The elderly ladies hadn't wondered yet—didn't want to wonder—why Mr. Webber was spending his time visiting them without profit. Brabazon had heard this same story sliced into dozens of translations but with the same bottom line. These ladies were being conned but he knew better than to tell them that and upset them.

People, Tom realized for the umpteenth time, believe what they want to believe and nice, honest people like Mrs. Wallace, Mrs. Mackenzie and Mrs. Harris were convinced that everybody they met was, like themselves, nice, decent and honest.

He needed to move quickly to rescue their money.

What Webber was doing was not illegal, Tom realized, if he were a licensed investment advisor but it was improper.

Elderly people requiring regular income need asset protection not growth investments. Currency trading isn't suitable for most people, certainly not for the elderly and nobody of any age should risk all 100% of their assets in anything. Careful diversification was better than putting all their eggs in one basket, no matter how tempting the basket.

Time to go hunting for Mr. Webber.

Tom rang Mr. Webber's number three times, getting a cheerful voice recording each time, but chose against leaving any message.

He then rang Elizabeth Hogan, explained what he was doing and asked her to run checks on Webber: registrations in Virginia and Florida, SEC history and complaints, driver's license, credit history, criminal background and to do the corporate equivalent on the bank.

Elizabeth rang back two hours later. Tom spent the time with Dr. Stone.

Mr. J. Anthony Webber III had a spotless record, scarcely a parking ticket, no homicides or embezzlement charges, no infringements, was properly licensed and no complaints against him, nice house, wife and two kids, a man who might become a bank's C.E.O or a town mayor someday. Nobody had yet to say a bad word to say about him.

His employer Twenty Five Global Bank was a me-
dium-sized, growing bank with a solid history, no scan-
dals, a good reputation with many branches in Florida,
privately owned by a group of respected Florida businessmen, doctors and a famous actress married to one of
the doctors.

Tom was unconvinced.

A reputable investment advisor wouldn't be targeting
these people for currency trading, let alone convincing
them to sell their assets, collecting commissions, of
course, and reinvesting in something oh-so-risky. Soros in
New York and McManus in Ireland and Switzerland were
about the only guys to consistently make money doing
major currency trading.

Tom asked the ladies Wallace and Harris to describe J.
A. Webber and all the rest of his name. Mrs. Wallace, a
former artist, found it easier to sketch him. After half an
hour, both ladies were satisfied with the drawing but Tom
went to show it to Anne for confirmation.

Anne recognized the investment advisor immediately.

When Tom told her that he would find Mr. Webber,
Anne beamed:

"Thh . . . th . . . ank you ah, sir. Plee . . . ah . . . se stop
him. He's a b . . . baad mm . . . man."

                              ****

A man infinitely patient, Tom disapproved of procras-
tination.

He felt an urgency about Anthony Webber, who was
likely to be trolling other nursing homes for customers

but who needed to return home to his lair sometimes in order to deposit the checks.

So Brabazon drove to Roanoke airport after telling Elizabeth his plan. He bought a ticket on USAir and, after changing planes in Charlotte, North Carolina, flew to Miami. He'd never been there before but didn't have time to enjoy the pleasures of the city. He was on a mission.

Tom took a bus from the airport to the center of the commercial district in downtown Miami. The front door of the Twenty Five Global Bank building was only a block away from his bus stop.

Outside and inside, the bank looked thoroughly appropriate and respectable. So it really did exist, Tom sighed with surprise. It wouldn't be his only surprise that day.

He asked the clerk at the information desk for the office of J. Anthony Webber III, and was pointed to an elevator.

"He's in office 509 on the fifth floor, sir," the helpful young woman said as she pointed to the elevator. Tom never rode in elevators, feeling unsafe, trapped and claustrophobic in them, a moving oven—and instead rationalized taking stairs as good exercise.

A friend had once told Tom about his then 74-year-old father, who'd discovered himself trapped in the elevator inside a five star hotel in Liverpool, England. The door had closed quickly after his friend had exited it, too quickly for his dad to leave.

The door jammed shut despite his dad's pounding on the buttons when he noticed a fire in the long metal ashcan.

While smoke quickly filled the elevator, his dad—who'd been a boxer in his youth and had remained immensely fit—tore open the door, walked to the reception desk, where, while smoke was billowing out of the elevator, he calmly told the staff that the elevator was on fire and quietly suggested calling the fire department, before walking outside.

After the fire had been doused, the doors looked as if they'd been torn apart by a marauding herd of buffalo. The hotel had the chutzpah to put the repair cost on his dad's account, who refused to pay up. The charge was cancelled after he threatened to "tidy" the front lobby in similar fashion.

Ever since hearing that story, Tom had been afraid of elevators. He trotted up to the 5th floor, two steps at a time, and found a secretary apparently in charge of the entire floor.

He explained his desire to meet Mr. Webber, admitting that he had no appointment and he only had to wait 10 minutes before being ushered in to the man's inner sanctum.

There was a great view of the city.

Mr. Webber was friendly, understandably surprised but there was no hostility or fear in his expression. Short brown coiffed hair, clean-shaven, in a medium-priced, good quality business suit with a sensible tie, Webber looked every inch the prosperous, conservative and respectable banking executive.

He looked in his late 40s or early 50s despite the nursing home's elderly ladies' descriptions that he was a "young man" but Tom supposed that anyone without grey hair probably fell into that category from the perspective of anyone living or working in a retirement home. He looked a lot older than in Mrs. Wallace's drawing.

Tom was puzzled but determined. He introduced himself, as he always did when working cases, as Tom Mercer.

"Well, what can I do for you, Mr. Mercer, would you like a coffee?" asked the banker. "Please sit down."

After the coffee had arrived and the secretary left, Tom was direct:

"Please explain why you're selling a currency trading investment to elderly residents in retirement homes."

Webber looked surprised but there was no hint of wariness in his eyes.

"I don't know what you're talking about. I'm an investment advisor but do nothing of that sort. I don't recommend currency trading for any of my clients. What makes you suggest it?"

Tom was also surprised. Webber looked like he was telling the truth.

Barbara often reminded him that decent people didn't lie, at least not often, to which Tom always answered that he seldom met decent people in his line of work. He thought that he was good at identifying when people were lying to him.

"Well, you've sold your investment spiel to several, no doubt many, old people in at least one retirement home in Virginia and I don't approve of inappropriate investment advice for people like that."

Webber still didn't look defensive or even angry as he answered:

"Neither do I, Mr. Mercer, but you must have the wrong person. Why don't you explain why you're here in more detail and I'll try to see how I can help you."

Tom, still surprised at Webber's relaxed facial and body posture, complied carefully.

"Based on what I've been told by several people, you have been convincing old people, in at least one nursing home, to sell their current bonds and, with the proceeds, open new accounts with your bank in order for you to invest in currency trading for them."

Tom continued: "These are old people, dependent on regular income and rock solid safe assets to pay their rent and daily expenses, who should not be taking any risks with their money. Currency trading is inappropriate for these people, so why are you doing it?"

Webber's expression was confused but still not defensive.

"I thoroughly agree with you that currency trading is inappropriate for elderly customers such as you've described but I repeat that I've done nothing of the sort."

"Are you J. Anthony Webber the Third?" Tom persisted.

"Yes, of course I am," came the reply. "Listen, somebody's made a mistake but I'm not your man. Are you sure that these elderly people are . . . well . . . I mean . . . totally, um, coherent, that is, you know, fully competent, ah, . . . in full control of their faculties . . . what about Alzheimer's and dementia?" Webber was trying not to be rude.

"Yes, they are all sane and coherent. Their stories are the same and three ladies have given you at least $240,000. I don't know how much the man has given you as he was too embarrassed to admit the amount."

Webber was still not angry or defensive.

"Well, my only guess is that somebody is impersonating me." Tom had heard that line before, too many times and it had never been true. He didn't believe it now.

Webber continued politely: "May I ask how you're involved in this? You're not a police officer or from the S.E.C., because you've not shown me any identification. You'd have said if you were a lawyer, so you're just an ordinary citizen. What's this got to do with you?"

"I happen to be a friend of one of the victims and have been asked to look into this. It's obviously a fraud, dishonest and unethical, and I want their money returned to them today and with an apology."

Webber answered in the same level, carefully measured tone of voice as before:

"I repeat that it's not me and that I've got nothing to do with it. I agree that it sounds fishy and I want to help you if I can, but don't know how. Have you gone to the police?"

"No," replied Tom, "because of jurisdiction. These people live in Virginia and you're quite obviously in Florida."

"How about the F.B.I. then?"

"I don't have a great amount of faith in their skills or speed. These people don't have many years left. I just want their money back and a promise that they'll be left alone. This is your business card, isn't it?"

Webber leaned over the desk, glanced at it and replied:

"No, it's not. Wrong colors. Mine is blue on a white background. The one you've got has my name on it, yes, but it's black . . . Here, I'll show you mine," and he did so. "This must be identity theft. Somebody's using my name."

"And harming your reputation," Tom added.

"I'll call the police, get them working on it." His eyes showed annoyance but still no fear or dishonesty. "I'm sorry but I can't help you and I've got an appointment downstairs in five minutes so I must ask you to leave now. I'm sorry. I'd help you if I could."

He stood up, offered a handshake and expected Tom to leave, so he did.

Thrown off kilter and still puzzled, convinced now that Webber was innocent despite his certainty, just fifteen minutes earlier, of the man's guilt, Tom walked past the secretary, wondering what to do next and feeling that he'd taken a one day's excursion and an expensive airfare into a dead end.

He remembered suddenly that he had Mrs. Wallace's drawing in his pocket. He pulled it out and showed it to the secretary, not knowing why.

"Excuse me, Ma'am, do you recognize this man?"

"Why, I sure do, sir, that's Mr. Webber's nephew, young Tony, Tony Gifford. He works here in the bank, in the printing department. Why do you ask?"

Anthony Webber was still in his office and on the phone when Tom strode back in, showed him Mrs. Wallace's drawing and announced:

"Your nephew is the one. He's impersonating you, using your identity. Where is he?"

Webber looked at the drawing, gulped and nodded. "Yes, that looks like Tony but it can't be him. He's a good kid."

"No such thing as an innocent coincidence, Mr. Webber. Now where is he?"

Webber told Tom to follow and this time Tom had to ride down in the oven as Webber showed no inclination of taking the stairs. Tom hoped that his sweat didn't show. They went an extra floor, Tom's nerves gulping again, to the basement.

Webber turned left into the corridor with Tom following, walked 20 yards and turned into what was obviously the printing department. Webber explained later that printing statements were done in-house as a protection against fraud.

There was only a young woman there, in her early twenties. She looked startled when an angry Webber asked where his nephew was.

"He's quit, sir."

"What? Why?"

"He's getting his, I mean our, yacht ready for the weekend," the girl answered. "He's working for himself now." Tom believed that. From a printer at a bank to a financier. The American Dream come true.

"We're getting married on Sunday in Bermuda, see, look at my ring."

Webber wasn't in the least bit interested in the ring or his nephew's impending nuptials.

"Yacht?" he spluttered. "What yacht? Where the hell is he now?"

The flustered young fiancée continued, realizing that something was badly wrong but not understanding what. "He got back last night from a business trip to Virginia and is spending today tidying the yacht. We're sailing to Aruba on Saturday."

"Where is this boat . . . yacht? What the hell is he doing with a yacht on a $25,000 a year salary?" Webber demanded and was given an address at a marina. "If he calls you, don't tell him you told me."

The baffled, frightened girl nodded as the men turned and walked back towards the elevator. Tom's nerves pounded again. They rode up, the doors opened, no fire within and they walked out of the bank with Webber hailing a taxi.

He barked an address and the two men climbed into the back seat, Tom relieved that there were likely no more terrifying elevators in the near future.

Tom was lost because he'd never been in Miami before, but all was well. He was intrigued how quickly impressions can change: first he believed that Webber was a lousy crook, then an innocent victim and now his comrade in battle. He could almost hear the footsteps of following soldiers as he imagined Webber and himself leading them into an attack.

He was finally back in control of his pulse as the elevator receded into the distance.

Webber asked to look at the business card again and examined it much more carefully this time. There were other errors, deliberate errors, on the card.

First: the bank's real name was slightly different from the name on the business card. Second: the direct phone number of the real Webber was wrong. Third: it had a different telephone prefix, which was not the bank's prefix. Fourth: there was a P.O. Box number on the card, which probably didn't belong to the bank and, fifth: the zip code was different. Webber explained that it was a suburb several miles away.

It was, Tom reckoned, a drop box for Gifford.

Webber asked Tom what he thought was happening and Tom was happy to guess, based on much experience gained during his career, to fill in the blanks with plausible answers.

Tom reckoned that the entrepreneurial young Webber was using his thoroughly respectable uncle as his cover since he knew his uncle's date of birth and work history, and had simply gone to a print shop and had 500 business cards printed . . . and paid cash probably without keeping a receipt for a tax deduction. It was likely that young Tony wasn't filing his proper quarterly estimated tax payments like a good boy.

Tom continued, whispering to Webber so that the cabbie couldn't overhear them, that Tony had probably learned how to print improvised statements on bank template, which he sent monthly to his customers and had them mail their checks to the fake P.O. Box.

"Your nephew," he suggested, "is most probably not risking his clients' money in currency arbitrage but hiding it offshore in his personal bank account somewhere in the Caribbean on an island that, conveniently, has no extradition treaty with the U.S."

Webber agreed. Tom continued whispering:

"He's presumably remitting a small amount to each customer every month, which reassures their faith in the young investing mastermind."

Tom paused. "I'll bet you, just to keep them hooked, that he writes a quarterly report discussing his successful trades just like the real players do at brokerage firms and mutual fund companies."

Webber asked: "Do you suppose that he'll keep visiting retirement homes for new customers while the happy existing ones add to their accounts?"

"Yes. It's a classic Ponzi scheme, leaving plenty of money, after travel expenses, to buy a yacht."

"Wait until I get my hands on my nephew," announced Webber firmly and rubbed his hands together.

"I've come across this type of scheme several times," Tom told Webber. "Few people ever do any checking out, any due diligence, before parting with their money and they usually say the same things.

"'He was so likeable. I trusted him immediately,' is said so many times by the victims." Tom shrugged. "It's so easy, too damn easy."

"Yes," replied Webber grimly. "I'm afraid you're right."

Anybody checking would find a clean, glowing record on J. A. Webber *the Third* with the Securities and Exchange Commission and Twenty Five Global Bank also had a spotless reputation for integrity and financial soundness.

That's what Elizabeth had discovered and she was a professional. An ordinary investor, innocent and trusting, would have discovered nothing suspicious.

It was Tony Gifford's pure bad luck, not bad planning, that Anne Eddery wasn't as stupid as she looked.

When they reached the marina, Tom was stunned by the opulence he saw—little yachts, big yachts, conspicuous displays of wealth. No one was hurting in this part of the United States, no matter how precarious the lives of the unemployed in the big, rust belt cities up in the colder latitudes of the nation.

Tom was reminded of the old, unsubtle joke on Wall Street:

"The stock market goes up and down,
Customers are rich, then poor
But commissions are forever.
Brokers have yachts but their customers don't.
Where have all the customers' yachts gone?"

Anthony Webber, the real investment broker, was clearly accustomed with this marina. He marched to the right section and found the correct berth without much difficulty.

Two young people in their twenties, one male with a crewcut and the other a blonde girl, were on deck. The male was their quarry, young Tony Webber the fourth (by distaff, not male, line) but he wasn't pleased at their approach.

Young Tony looked alarmed as he called out, "Hi, Uncle Anthony, how are you?" with a big smile. "Do you like my yacht? Isn't she a beauty?"

"I'm fine but what are you doing here and how can you afford a boat? When did you quit your job at the bank? How can you afford a boat? Your mother is working two jobs just to pay her bills since the divorce."

Tony decided not to answer those questions as he countered with one of his own.

"Who's your friend?" looking straight at Tom.

"My friend," said the elder Webber most carefully, "says that you're a thief, that you're stealing from widows and widowers in retirement homes in Virginia, that you're a forger and . . . last but not least . . . you're posing as an investment manager and posing as me. You've stolen my identity. Why?"

"Your friend," replied Tony, "is a liar." Tony was looking frightened. The girl, whatever her name was, stood transfixed.

Uncle Anthony turned to Tom and asked, quite calmly, "Well, are you?"

"No, I'm not," replied Tom politely.

"He is," yelled Tony. "He's making it all up. I don't know what you're talking about." He then reached under a jacket, which was lying on top of some rope, pulled out a gun, grabbed the girl and pointed the gun point-blank at her head.

"Go away or I'll shoot her. I'll shoot Mary. I will."

Mary shrieked.

"Who is she?" asked Uncle Anthony after the noise receded.

"My girlfriend, that's who."

Uncle Anthony was shocked, his face had turned white and he stepped back. "Don't do that, Tony. Come on, there's no need for violence. Put the gun down."

Tom asked whether Mary, the girlfriend, knew about the bank employee fiancée. Then when Mary, who didn't, screamed and twisted, switching Tony's attention away from the men towards her, Tom seized the opportunity, jumped at Tony and tackled him to the deck, yanking the gun from his hand and punching Tony between his Adam's apple and chin.

He threw the gun into the water, safely out of harm's way. Mary performed some violence of her own, slapping and kicking and more yelling, which resulted in Tony wrapping himself into the fetal position and begging for help. Sympathy levels running at zero, nobody helped him.

Mary kept kicking. Tom stood up and rejoined Webber.

"Will you call the police, please?" Webber asked. "I think I'll stay here and keep an eye on my nephew until they arrive."

"Sure," Tom answered and began to turn away.

"Just one thing before you go," Webber said. "That took a lot of courage. Why did you run the risk of getting shot?"

"The risk was minimal. Your delightful nephew hadn't turned off the safety catch. He couldn't have fired. Besides, I bet that he lacks the guts to shoot anybody. But, I'll tell you something. I doubt that he'll be marrying anybody this weekend."

Tom found a pay phone and rang the police. He then walked until he saw a taxi, hopped in and went to the airport.

****

The next day, back in Lexington, he wrote a report for George Alexander as per protocol, before phoning the CEO at the company headquarters of Dr. Stone's retirement home to reveal the story, praising Anne Eddery for her insight and explaining the involvement in the fraud of the manager, George Gifford, and his connection with his son, Anthony. George Gifford was fired and arrested. He went to jail.

So did Anthony Gifford.

The CEO called his counterpart at Twenty Five Global Bank in Miami.

Both companies, after agreeing to pay the Alexander Agency for Tom's success in stopping young Gifford's independent profit-making, split the bill 50/50 but reimbursed by insurance, also hired the Alexander Agency to tighten and supervise financial security at their companies. Tom and his boss were relieved that this wasn't a pro-bono case after all.

To preserve his own reputation and protect that of his bank, the CEO in Miami made sure that swift repayment was made to the victims of Dr. Stone's retirement home.

As reward for his swift action, Webber was promoted.

The bank's lawyers sold the yacht, which covered some of the repayment, and the bank's shareholders ate the rest of the loss. This because, following his own lawyer's advice, young Tony refused to divulge the location of the money he'd deposited off-shore and was disinclined to refund it. He also refused to name any other customers at other retirement homes.

Tom sent Anne a bouquet of flowers every week for a year.

After an I.Q. test showed a result of 148, enough to qualify to join Mensa, Anne Eddery was promoted to be the new manager of patients at Arvagh Joelle Nursing Home. The company paid for intensive speech therapy and an interpreter, which improved Anne's communication skills by a lot.

Tom began taking Barbara to see Dr. Stone and, discovering their shared love of chess, Barbara and Anne often played while Tom talked to Dr. Stone. Gradually, as her trust grew, Anne told her life story to Barbara.

Mrs. Wallace died from a heart attack before her refund arrived. Her estate received the check.

Dr. Stone got all of his $100,000 investment back.

*****

This chapter is dedicated to all the 'Anne Edderys,' whose indomitable courage and goodness in the face of cruelty and unfair bad luck are inspirational.

CHAPTER 15   BALTIMORE BEAR

It was time to find out. Tom shouldn't postpone it any more. He needed to know and needed to discover how and why his father had died 24 years earlier back in Baltimore on little Stevie Walwyn's 11th birthday.

So much had happened to him since then: Ireland, his mother's death, Dr. Stone, the Olympics, his marriage to Katya and her death, their daughter Catherine, his strange career investigating frauds and crimes and finding missing people.

What could be more important than investigating his own father's death?

It was time to go, time to open that long-closed door, time to drag out and banish those demons which he'd always refused to confront, time to end his shame at having been angry at his dad for missing his birthday when shot and bleeding to death in a gutter on one of Baltimore's worst streets.

So he left, telling Barbara that he needed to take another trip with the usual "no idea" when he'd return . . . if he'd return. He always told her and his office where he was going and, if he didn't return, how to start looking.

This was nothing new and Barbara hugged and kissed him, saying, as she always did, "Don't break a leg. You promised to go with me to Louisville next week. So, drag your sorry ass back and do it. And, as Sergeant Esterhazy of *Hill Street Blues* told his crew at the end of roll calls: 'Remember, let's be careful out there.'"

Tom laughed, as he always did. This time, though, was different: this wasn't a case, so he told her now—in a move so out of character she knew it was important, not routine—why he was going to Baltimore.

She always pretended to be blasé about his trips and, though this one worried her, she knew better than to show any concern. She realized there was no point trying to talk him out of it and saw that he must go.

"Don't waste your money going to a baseball game. The Orioles always lose. More predictable than knowing it's going to snow in winter."

He was relieved that Barbara never asked what, when, where, how and why. She wasn't openly inquisitive but she cared in her own way, which Tom understood. Tom didn't care for emotion, for scenes: there was no hot Mediterranean blood in either of them.

They were right for each other but wrong for probably most everybody else. He was glad he'd found Barbara and didn't want her to change: independent, tough, self-sufficient, sensible, unemotional, didn't need him or any man for survival, but he knew that she liked him. Loved him, maybe, Tom didn't know. They were comfortable together, supportive but not clingy, independent. Both preferred it that way.

He knew she'd be upset if someday he didn't make it home, got killed on the job or disappeared. He was confident that she'd track down the bastard responsible and use one of her inventions to make the guy wish he hadn't harmed Tom. Then, mission accomplished and misbehavior punished, she'd return to her shed and invent something new.

****

Tom arrived at Baltimore airport in mid-afternoon and hopped on a bus to take him to the city center.

His first port-of-call was the library at *The Baltimore Sun*'s office. He loved newspaper and public libraries as they were treasure troves of free and abundant information. The life of a librarian, though, wasn't for him. He loved research and while, sure, it was kind of like hunting—but without the mud and blood—it was too slow for him. He needed adrenalin rushes.

He loved, craved, needed action and speed. He always appreciated how librarians would drop their tasks in order to help customers who were friendly and acted a bit haphazard or clumsy. Based on his long experience, librarians were unfailingly patient and helpful. Helping a customer find something unusual created a nice diversion between re-shelving and categorizing. Not for them the chaotic, uncategorized, untidy, out-of-order outside world.

This librarian was a middle-aged woman whose name-tag read "Sandra G." She told Tom that she'd been a teacher in her previous life before the escalating school violence and unappreciative students—some of whom had scared her—finally caused her to put away her chalk for the final time.

Without asking why, she searched her microfiche files for the story of a police office slain in the line of duty in Baltimore on May 12, 1963. There were, she said sadly, too many police officers killed even way back then, though the streets were so much worse nowadays, weren't they? Tom nodded.

She found the story. It wasn't the lead story but it still made the front page.

Tom felt weak, his blood seeming to have drained in an instant. Feeling dreadful all over, tears flooding his eyes and having the sensation that he'd been kicked in the gut, he was suddenly nauseated, choking, dizzy, cold and hot. He asked to use the restroom where he retched and waited until he stopped sweating and shaking.

When he returned a few minutes later, the nice, genuinely concerned librarian asked nervously if he were all right. He wasn't, quite obviously, so she rushed off to get a glass of cold water for him. Tom knew it would cause him hours of emotional pain and a sleepless night, but he had to read the story published on May 13 and the follow-up article on May 14.

By the 15th his father had been forgotten by the newspaper, Baltimore being a city hardened to murder even back then, even the murder of a decorated police officer, with subsequent murders lining up to replace the previous week's. By 1988, the number of official murders in the city would reach 305 a year, plus countless other unrecognized or unreported victims had been killed.

Murder by homicide was increasingly common everywhere, but particularly in Baltimore.

Baltimore and Washington D.C. were vying to be the nation's leading homicide city and the area had become a growth industry for undertakers, florists and coffin makers, offering job security for pathologists and a new generation of homicide detectives, all grimly carrying out the flipside of the American Dream.

Tom tried again to read the stories. His father had made the front page on May 13, the story detailing the killing and then Tom read the editorial, which deplored the murder and extolled the policeman's "ultimate sacrifice," more in terms of a soldier defending the great city of Baltimore than in personal terms. There was brief mention of a wife, now a widow, named Helen and their son, 11-year-old Stevie.

The poignancy and ill-timing of Detective third grade Richard Walwyn's death on his son's birthday merited a sentence in the editorial but the majority of the editorial concentrated on the 'thin blue line' becoming thinner and the deteriorating respect towards the police.

May 1963 was just a year after the first black officer had died in Baltimore and five years before the racial riots erupted in 1968. One officer's death was sad but not, in the scheme of the American experience, an epic tragedy.

Although the newspaper's stance was officially pro-police, in reality much of the community of Baltimore–

white and black, especially the blacks, rich and poor, judged their police department in the 1960s as corrupt and racist, and far too often excessively violent, often downright brutal.

The riots in Los Angeles were just over the horizon while Frank Serpico, whose life actor Al Pacino made famous in the film *Serpico*, was beginning his lonely struggle against corruption in the New York Police Department, which climaxed in his being shot in the face while his fellow police officers stood back and let him bleed on a tenement floor.

Like its counterparts L.A., New York City and Chicago, old Baltimore city had a police department which in the 1960s didn't resemble any town in which the actor Jimmy Stewart would choose to live in a reprise of his best movie *It's A Wonderful Life*.

So, while the murder of a police officer was officially a sad day for the city, unofficially, many citizens didn't mind too much. What comes around, sticks around. The cop had probably gotten what he deserved. He was probably a racist, trigger-happy, nightstick-toting thug with a badge.

Tom was unaware of all of that. To him, his father was a hero, a barely remembered honest detective and great dad, who was doing his duty while dying in a gutter and missing Stevie's birthday, missing his party, never getting to again say, "I love you, son," or, finally, "goodbye . . . son."

Tom read the related articles in the next two days' papers before the story fizzled out, forgotten as the citizens returned to the baseball results.

Five days later, an article on page six described an honor guard brass band saluting the fallen hero with the police brass and mayor solemnly declaring how much the department appreciated the ultimate sacrifice of Detective third grade Richard Oliver Walwyn, a "great police officer slain in the course of protecting the city."

Naturally, neither speaker–neither the mayor nor the police commissioner–had ever heard of or met Detective Walwyn and they soon forgot him. He was simply a foot soldier whose memory would be maintained by his photograph hung on a corridor hall in the Western Precinct, where he'd worked as a patrolman for his first year and then back there in plainclothes for the last 22 months of his career. But, except by his co-workers and the new patrolmen who always looked at the pictures on the wall, Detective Richard Walwyn was soon forgotten by the police department and the city.

Tom's mother struggled for compensation and survivor's benefits. After a few months, she stopped trying. The Baltimore police department's bureaucracy was implacable.

****

Tom wanted to see where his dad had died. That wasn't easy as the corner of Appleton and Mosher streets was in a slum where no taxi driver was willing to take him even in daytime. Each driver warned Tom that it was too dangerous and refused, advising him, as a white man, to stay away from there.

"They'll chomp you up and down but good, man," he was warned. "Have you got a death wish, got cancer, want to have a quick death by letting those gang members cut you up? You must be crazy, a white man going up there.

Forget it unless you've got a badge or you're an ambulance driver and even then, best ask a priest for last rites before you go in there."

Another taxi driver told him: "Even the police dogs travel in pairs up there and wear bulletproof collars, it's that bad."

Having not grown up in America, working in the racial free zone of frauds and swindles and never having lived in a big city, Tom had no experience or understanding of racism in the United States. He supposed that it couldn't be more dangerous than Belfast and Londonderry in the '70s. He was wrong.

A white man didn't go into the Western district, didn't even think about exploring the limited amenities of Appleton.

Tom just didn't understand the racial divide between whites and blacks in urban America; he never felt any unease when blacks followed him down a street or walked into a shop. He didn't recognize the signs of tension. He didn't have a racist bone in his body, didn't discriminate or favor anybody based on race, religion or ethnic origin. He rated people as individuals not as representatives of a group.

He divided people only as honest or crooks, cheats or decent and he'd seen enough of life to know that there were bad and good people everywhere. With one exception: while working for the heir-hunting company, he'd lived in Lancaster, Pennsylvania where the majority population was Amish. The Amish were honest, never broke the law and were God-fearing avoiders of the modern world. They refused to use electricity or cars. They were peaceful.

When he'd get gloomy about the people he investigated, ranting about all the crooks he dealt with, telling Barbara, "There are a lot of bad people out there, you just don't understand," she enjoyed telling him there are lots of good people, too.

"Yes," Tom would answer glumly, "but you don't have to worry about them."

"I see your point but without crooks you'd have no job, no work and no income. Be grateful to them for they pay your bills," Barbara would joke.

"Well," Tom replied sometimes, "The Bible says that the meek shall inherit the earth. Maybe they should but they won't. Besides, if somehow they do, some swindler will steal it off them."

"And you'll catch the swindler."

"Yeah, that's what I do."

"Come on, let's play chess."

****

Thwarted by the taxi drivers and one bus driver, who'd shaken his head in disbelief before closing the door and driving off, Tom walked to the headquarters of the Baltimore Police Department, founded in 1845.

Tom had read that that the first Baltimore police officer killed in the line of duty in poet Edgar Allan Poe's hometown was Sergeant William Jourdan, back on October 14, 1857 and that on average one police officer was murdered and a dozen seriously wounded, per year.

Tom explained to several officials downtown that he was researching the 1963 death of an officer, a relative, before someone took him seriously and decided to help. A secretary said maybe old Sarge O'Brien might help.

"He's been on the force forever. If anyone knows anything about that detective's death, it'll be him. Sarge is an institution around here: too honest to be promoted, too old to work the streets and too ornery to take his pension and go fishing. The Department is his life. He's got a memory better than a blackmailer. I'll go find him. Wait here. Don't move or you might get arrested. It's the last day of the month and the patrol officers need to fill their quotas."

After about 20 minutes, an old man with white hair, shrewd eyes, a nose broken at least twice, a back as straight as a ramrod, in full uniform and with half a dozen medals on his chest appeared in front of Tom, who was waiting impatiently in reception.

"I'm Sergeant O'Brien. What are you after and what's your name?"

Tom countered: "I'm looking for information about an officer who was killed on duty in 1963, Detective Richard Walwyn, out on Appleton. I want to find out what happened."

"That was a long time ago. Why and why now? Are you a reporter?"

"No, officer, I'm not. He was a relative."

"Let's go into my office." He gestured for Tom to walk in front of him. Sergeant O'Brien never allowed anybody to walk behind him.

When they'd settled down in the sergeant's untidy office, Tom relaxed a bit. He'd once been told never to trust anybody with a perfectly tidy desk, the same advisor having bizarrely also warned that a woman without a handbag was a spy. That advice still baffled Tom, who'd never, as far as he knew, met a spy. And wouldn't a spy be shrewd enough to know about the handbag theory?

"I remember him. We were friends," said the old cop. "I was his training officer when he came out of the academy. Why do you want to know?"

Tom gasped. He'd just met someone who'd known his father, worked with him and been his friend.

Tom had never correctly identified himself in his many years in America and he hadn't used the name Steve Walwyn since school in Ireland. However, Andy Winter, the cynical old former homicide detective now in Alexander's in Lexington had told him about the war horses in his old precincts in New York, whom street officers knew they could trust.

Tom realized that he wasn't going to successfully bamboozle or fool this old cop, whose eyes could bore through him and read him better than an X-ray. If he lied, or twisted, the old cop would throw him out.

Tom identified himself as Detective Richard Walwyn's son.

The old dinosaur asked for identification in the form of his driver's license, which unhelpfully showed the name of Tom Brabazon. Before handing it over, Tom explained that he'd changed his name and proffered his belt with his father's badge sewn inside. The last time he'd shown his belt to anyone, it was to a cop in Geneva, Switzerland, on Christmas Eve so long ago, before the Olympics . . . before Katya.

From his wallet, he pulled a crumpled black and white Polaroid photo of his parents and him taken just a week before everything was ruined.

He told some of his story, leaving out many details but revealing enough to win the old cop's wary belief.

Tom answered questions which only a son would know
. . . his mother's name, their exact address, his father's
birth date, descriptions, habits, details and memories that
surprised him, because they'd been so hidden for so long.
The old cop asked about family pets and Tom apparently
answered correctly, because the old cop slowly relaxed.
The last question was what Dick had called Tom's
mother, whose name was Helen.

"Sopha, because he said that Sophia Loren looked like
Mom, not the other way around," Tom replied.

Finally convinced, the old cop relaxed, smiled and
leaned over to shake Tom's hand.

"The last time I did that, son, was at your daddy's funeral. You wouldn't remember me, though, huh?"

Tom did.

He remembered every moment of that hideous day and
that night, after his mother had kissed him goodnight
through his tears and sobs, staying awake all night
unable to sleep, listening to his mother scream in pain in
her room. He had gone to her as the clock struck midnight
and they curled up together, crying all night until dawn
and all the next day and the next.

He'd never returned to his school, because they moved
to live in his grandmother's house in Chestnut Hill, a
fancy suburb in Philadelphia, where his mother would
meet McKinley, who was visiting for a polo match. The
move to Ireland happened later.

Oh yes, Tom remembered the funeral far too vividly.
He remembered many men in uniform coming to shake
his hand after his father's burial, though, naturally, he
couldn't specifically remember the younger version of the
man sitting across the desk right now.

"What're you doing now? Are you on the job and, if so, where?"

"No, sir, I'm not."

"Why not? If you're a chip off the old block, you'd make a great cop."

Tom was flattered but said, "I won't take orders and hate paperwork. I'm a business and insurance fraud investigator, working for a private company. Do my own thing; my own boss, almost. I was an Olympic runner before that."

"Win a gold medal?" Everybody asked that.

"No, but I brought home a silver."

"Well done. Somehow I never had time to watch any Olympics, too busy here, saving the good citizens of this great city." Sergeant O'Brien had dedicated, devoted, his life to being a cop. There was nothing else he wanted to do; nothing else that he could consider would be as satisfying . . . as good . . . as worthy.

"Married, I see." Tom still wore his wedding band out of respect for Katya. "And kids?"

"My wife died giving birth. Our daughter is five and has started kindergarten."

The sergeant switched back to the purpose of Tom's visit and told him about his dad and his career.

Dick Walwyn had been a good partner and a good, honest cop's cop, refusing to take bribes or accept favors, didn't curry patronage from the bosses and didn't want a "rabbi" to help his career. He just wanted to protect and serve, reduce crime, help the community, ignore the politics. He despised defense lawyers. He had the right instinct as a street cop, even though he'd grown up in the country a long way from any city.

O'Brien added that Dick was observant, brave, reliable, a great partner and a born hunter, who loved nothing better than to chase and find criminals. Despite being too much of a straight talker and too lousy at paperwork to please the brass, Walwyn was sure, predicted O'Brien, to make it to the pinnacle of a street cop's career–the homicide department. O'Brien reckoned that he was only a year or two away from that.

"Your dad was a damned good cop, one of the best partners I ever worked with and a good guy, too. We caught lots of mopes, so we did, more than our share. He looked after you and your mom well, made sure you had a good safe home out in the country, out near Woodbine, so you'd never have to live in the city. Am sorry about your brother, son."

Tom's older brother Billy had died of pneumonia four months before their dad's death.

"I'll order up a copy of the file on your dad's case, but it'll take an hour."

"Thanks. I'd like to see where he died on Appleton Street but all the taxi drivers refused to take me there, because they said it was too dangerous." He pulled out his two knives. "I'll go there now and be back in an hour or so."

"Sure, son, in a body bag in the morgue." The old man was serious.

"I can take care of myself," came Tom's stubborn but naïve answer.

"Not in that neighborhood, son, you being white. Arnold Schwarzenegger wouldn't survive alone up there. They'd chop up your guts for garters." The old cop laughed.

"Would you really take a knife to a gun fight? Those punks don't play by the rules, any rules. You'd be dead in less than five minutes, tops." He looked amused.

"I'll take you there in a unit, a squad car, sirens on, piece out. Let's see them try their sales pitch on this old cop. Hell, I'm sure that I busted their not-so-great grandfathers. Let's go. It's time to be a real cop again instead of being a desk jockey." He stood up, getting ready to leave.

"I'm a role model, you know, the antique. They bring the new rookies in to gawk at me and I scare them by telling them they'll end up looking like me unless they grab their pension after 20 years."

O'Brien hurried Tom out into the corridor.

"Lemme show you our lovely version of the great American Dream. Come see Bawlmer's huddled masses, the delightful and young tax-evading entrepreneurs of the flourishing drug culture. I warn you, it's a long way from Miami and the glamour on Miami Vice. "

O'Brien signed out a squad car and drove Tom to the very spot where his father had died. Tom was shocked at the decay that he saw in the city streets once they'd left the cocoon of downtown, where the business leaders, politicians and tourists flocked, a far cry from the reality of poverty, crime and failure nearby.

It was worse than Derry in Northern Ireland after the bombs had blown that city to bits. Before every election, Sarge O'Brien explained, every politician swore to revitalize Baltimore, changing the ghetto by providing jobs and "investments." Did renewal ever happen, Tom asked.

"No, son. Don't be naïve."

Mayors of some cities, which he didn't name, were sometimes guilty, O'Brien then said, of prodding their police departments to fudge on crime reporting by listing a few homicides as, say, traffic violations, to make it appear that, "We're winning the war on crime and if you voters will re-elect me, there will be no more crime or poverty."

Yet, after every election, regardless of which politician won, nothing ever changed for the better in the ghettoes.

On their way out to nobody's idea of civilization, O'Brien remembered that Tom's father had grown up on a farm in Virginia before joining the Army and later the Baltimore Police Department in the late '50s. It had taken Dick Walwyn a while, he recalled, to adjust to the asphalt jungle of the crowded city.

Tom remembered trips back to his grandparents' cattle farm about 60 miles from Washington D.C. That's where his dad had taught him hunting, tracking and surviving skills in the woods in the nearby Blue Ridge Mountains, west of Sperryville in Rappahannock county, where both his parents were buried.

O'Brien parked on Appleton Street, outside a boarded up store that had been a drycleaner's which also offered formal wear rentals. It had probably been decades since any teenage boy in this neighborhood had rented a "monkey suit" to attend his high school prom. The street looked awful and it stank.

Small groups of young black men scattered as the patrol car was driven past them, only to regroup quickly after they'd realized that these cops weren't going to bust *them*, right *now*. This generation had lost its fear of the police. Tom was relieved that he wasn't alone.

They got out, Tom stunned by what he saw.

Sergeant O'Brien walked over to the gutter ten feet in front of his patrol car, which he locked, pointed down and said: "This is it. Where your daddy died."

Tom hadn't expected a statue or memorial, exactly. It looked like the street had seen plenty of deaths, still this decrepit urban thoroughfare looked like the last place anybody should have to die. There was rubbish, broken bottles, empty food wrappers and a child's shoe. Looking around, Tom couldn't believe that anyone would raise a child in this hellhole slum.

How—why?—how could any parent do this to their child? The cost to escape to a better life was just the price of a bus ticket.

These streets didn't resemble the battlefields at Waterloo, Guadalcanal or anywhere in Vietnam, but they were a battleground nonetheless.

Tom felt a million miles from the Olympics. To realize that his father died here, bleeding into this gutter, just another soon-to-be-anonymous soldier lost in America's never ending war on crime, instead of being at Stevie's birthday party.

****

The file was waiting when they returned, Tom chastened and quiet while the old cop told him his memories of "what went down that bad day."

O'Brien had been recovering in Johns Hopkins Hospital, the city's biggest hospital, from a bullet wound that had pierced his neck three days earlier. He refreshed his memory of the official report before handing it to Tom: "Here, read this, while I go do a few things."

The old sergeant returned 20 minutes later, having allowed Tom some time to reflect on the report.

"What happened to Victor Brown, the bastard who killed my father?" Tom asked.

"Lasted three days on the street before being found in a girlfriend's apartment near Pimlico racetrack. Brown was shot while attempting to evade capture. He died at the scene. Suicide, in other words."

"What were Detective Walsh and Lieutenant Mullins like?" Tom wanted to know. "Where are they now?"

"Walsh was your dad's partner but never recovered from your dad's death. He ran foul of Mullins during the investigation. Mullins oversaw it. Nowadays, the rule is that two homicide detectives and a lieutenant jointly investigate all police-involved shootings, those cases when cops are shot and also when a civilian is shot by a cop. It was different back then. Mullins was the shift lieutenant in robbery and was your dad's boss."

"So what happened to them?" Tom repeated.

"Walsh got sidelined, transferred out to another division. I see him sometimes–his daughter is married to one of my sons. He's a part-time drunk and full-time security officer at a bank out in Bethesda now. He blamed Mullins for what happened and they had a fight one day in the locker room. Mullins was shouting about your dad's empty shells."

Tom looked oddly at the sergeant, who continued:

"Next day, Walsh was gone. Nobody high-up listened to him. That happened a lot back then. Mullins had the power to stop any independent investigation. Most of us agreed with Walsh even though he was excitable, we thought Mullins was involved somehow, knew more than he said in his report but . . . to be honest . . . we disliked Mullins anyway. Maybe we agreed with Walsh because we disliked Mullins."

O'Brien paused before adding: "I never trusted Mullins on the street and he was a bad boss."

Mullins concluded in the report that Brown, who was out on bail, started firing at Detective Walwyn after a chase that began in an alley, and Tom's dad went down.

"They'd gone to arrest him for a hold-up of a liquor store," O'Brien said. "They had witnesses: it was a simple slam dunk, normal case. Brown didn't need to shoot. He'd been inside before, it was a second home for him, somewhere to relax and not worry about making rent or remembering to meet his parole officer.

"Andy Walsh wanted Mullins off the case, said Mullins had had it in for your dad, I don't remember why but Walsh said Mullins was responsible."

"Why didn't the higher-ups listen?"

"Well back then, it was different than today. Strict rule of authority just like the army. Enlisted men in the army get ignored when they complain about officers, just get ordered to dig more latrines. Same in the bad old days in the BPD. Your dad, Walsh and I were just ordinary cops with no connections or 'rabbis,' as we cops call them." He took a swallow of coffee.

"Mullins was connected and knew the right people. His first wife was the daughter of an inspector who was the mayor's brother-in-law and he got promoted faster than he deserved. None of us who worked under him liked him but he made the rules." O'Brien had Tom's complete attention.

"The bosses wanted your dad's file closed once the punk was shot. They didn't want any independent grand jury looking for excessive use of police force pushed on the department by the newspaper or community leaders.

They didn't want to open up any cans of worms. Your dad knew nobody downtown, none of the brass."

"Brass?" Tom asked for a translation.

"The bosses," O'Brien explained. "I never liked or trusted Mullins. You never felt that he'd back up what you did on the street and he was a stickler for paperwork being right. He was on the take but many cops were, back then. There was lots of corruption." He paused.

"Your dad was clean; I was too, so was Walsh, almost, and a handful of other officers but we were a minority. I never took a bribe or a bent dollar in my career.

"But Mullins was different, always wore expensive suits, silk ties and drove a fancy car but never put in overtime. He was corrupt–but nobody ever went after him, neither Internal Affairs nor the brass downtown. He always avoided trouble."

O'Brien continued: "There was one time he slipped out of a solid rape charge, back when I was stationed in what we call 'Billyland,' the southern district full of ex-hillbillies from West Virginia and Tennessee. He was always on the make, a politician with a badge, not a true cop. He made assistant police commissioner before leaving the department. Good riddance. Don't know where he is now."

Tom felt he should leave. He asked for retired Detective Walsh's contact details.

"What are you going to do, Steve?" asked the old warrior.

"Talk to Detective Walsh and find Mullins."

"Why? It's been a long time. What can you do, Steve? It's over. Let it go."

"You see, Sergeant, I appreciate everything you've told me but it's what Detective Walsh said about dad's empty gun. Dad was a hunter, always prepared. The empty shells bit doesn't make sense. My instinct tells me to investigate dad's empty gun. I've got to ask Walsh about it."

"Make sure you catch him sober."

"Okay," Tom agreed.

"Then what?" The sergeant had been a cop for a long time. He knew that Tom wouldn't let it go.

"I'm going to find former Assistant Police Commissioner Mullins and ask him some questions. My instinct tells me to."

"What do you hope to achieve?"

"Justice."

O'Brien snorted. "In this world? Never. It's plea bargained down every day."

"That's why I'm not a cop, sir. In my small corner of this world, I make real justice happen." Tom stood up and thanked the gnarled old veteran twice.

"Would your instinct say the same if this were somebody else's death and not your dad's?" It was a question that surprised Tom but needed to be answered honestly.

"I think so but I'm not sure. I know that I can tell the difference between real scent and a dragline—where the scent is fake, when a person drags an artificial scent to mimic a fox or deer. This smells real to me."

The old cop held out his hand, wished him luck and offered his help anytime.

"Lemme me know what happens." He added, "Your dad was a good cop and my good friend. Good to meet you, son. Good luck."

****

Andy Walsh was easy to find—a potbellied, balding, tired guy in a security man's uniform at a bank in Bethesda, a wealthy and upper-class neighborhood that probably hadn't seen a bank robbery in decades, because the police station was next door.

Still, the bank manager reasoned that having a security guard, though expensive, was good for business, assuring the customers that they were important enough for the bank to worry about.

The most strenuous job Andy did was opening the door for customers and looking for robbers when the armored Brinks truck arrived.

He'd spent 22 years on the force never doing better than routine cases, which he blamed on Mullins. After Mullins had permanently wrecked his chances, he knew he had no hope of promotion and had worked in uniform in a patrol car after Mullins had transferred him from the division for insubordination and with threats of corruption charges.

He hated Mullins for that and hated the uniform on hot days in summer. Ironic that nowadays he wore one every day, but didn't mind. The income helped his pension a lot: he couldn't have survived on only his police pension and he knew this was the best job he'd get, though boring as hell.

Not for him the glamorous life of a private detective or being bodyguard to a big shot businessman or running a bar. He was a bar's best customer, he'd have drunk all his profits. He belonged on the drinking, not the pouring, side of the counter.

This job would do him until the booze rotted his gut, until his liver surrendered and hardened in despair. He was alone, lonely, broke and usually drunk.

And he hated Mullins.

Mullins had ruined his career and life, just because he'd discovered that Andy had shaken down a grocery store owner and screwed a lying hooker, for free, in exchange for not booking her for prostitution. Two lousy misdeeds in 22 years, well, there were a few others but Mullins hadn't discovered those. They were nothing compared to what Mullins had done. Meanwhile, Mullins had sailed higher and higher.

On this Thursday morning in July, retired police officer Andrew Walsh got his wish at last: Untouchable Mullins was going to go down.

Tom offered Walsh a cup of coffee at the café on the corner, explaining for the second time in two days that he was the son of Detective Richard Walwyn and asking to hear Walsh's story. Walsh was stunned and thrilled to meet Tom—and overjoyed to tell his story to someone who'd listen. It had been 24 years.

After deleting all the many "fucking" and "cockhead" and "bastard," "cun–" "shi–head," "as–ole," "scum–g," "motherfuc–," and many other unsuitable-cocktail party style descriptions of Mullins' personality, this was Walsh's story, which, in its original and unabridged form, took nearly 35 minutes.

Andy Walsh alleged that Mullins had removed live bullets from Walwyn's service revolver, switching them with empty shells at the beginning of shift the morning of Tom's dad's death. Walsh claimed that he'd seen him do the switch in the changing room after roll call while Dick had gone to the toilet, but he hadn't realized what had happened, until too late.

If only . . . .

"Anyway, we went out to investigate some new robberies. Just before lunchtime, we saw the perp Victor Brown, whom we wanted to pick up and arrest as our prime suspect in a recent liquor store robbery a few blocks away.

"Brown ran so we chased him," Walsh was thrilled to be telling his story at long last.

"I fell back, too many burgers and beer even back then," he explained, looking down at his large belly.

"I watched as your dad, who was faster and fitter, started catching up to Brown. They ran down an alley then turned left on Appleton. I heard shots before making the corner, then I saw Brown standing with a gun in his left hand. Your dad was down with blood pouring out of him, his gun held tight in his right hand. Brown saw me, turned and fled.

"I checked out your dad's wounds, told him to hold on, that I'd get help. I sprinted as fast as I could to a call box 50 yards away to report shots fired, officer down, then ran back to hold your dad. I didn't understand until later, that your dad was groaning that he'd fired but nothing happened . . . he'd fired, he repeated, he'd fired.

"The first cop," Walsh continued, "on the scene was none other than that bastard Mullins, which was strange as he seldom left the precinct. Your dad died in my arms and the only words I could hear coherently were: 'I fired but nothing happened. Tell Sopha that I love her and Stevie.'"

He saw that Tom was shocked.

"He had no pulse when the ambulance arrived, I was shaking him, begging him to reopen his eyes, that he'd make it, to hang on. He tried but couldn't. That was the worst fuckin . . . day of my whole life."

Walsh added that the bastard Mullins had insisted on being the only investigator of the murder–as he was their boss, none of his troops could demand anybody else–and closed the file as soon as Brown failed to report his version of the event, having been exited from this world by means of bullets fired by two officers, who received citations.

"I didn't know why Mullins showed up like he did. He must have been following us. I asked why and he told me to fuck off."

Mullins was congratulated on solving the case and the department moved on to await the next police killing. There were plenty of cops shot even back then, Walsh said.

"I was shot at several times but fortunately they all missed me."

The fight in the locker room occurred when Andrew Walsh accused Mullins of removing bullets.

Walsh returned to the street every day for a week after getting off duty and searched for casings or any evidence. He never found anything. He would have if Richard Walwyn had fired live rounds and, he added, Dick was a fuckin . . . good shot, he wouldn't have missed Brown. Something stank and Walsh reckoned it was Mullins.

"That bastard. I got transferred and demoted with a bad mark in my employee file. No comeback, no appeal, nobody would listen to me, just to Mullins.

"That f . . . bast . . . motherfu . . . shith . . . fuc . . . cun . . . scumba . . . fuc. . .dipshi . . . Mullins murdered your dad, as sure as I'm sitting here talking to you," former detective Walsh fumed. Tom recognized that Walsh was biased, his hatred of Mullins being unconcealed, but it was enough to convince him.

Tom promised himself that he would bring down Frank Mullins, wherever he was, somehow. He would punish the monster for causing his dad, a fellow cop, to be gunned down in a ghetto. On Tom's birthday.

Depriving Tom of his father for the rest of his life, ruining his and his mother's lives.

Walsh told Tom where the bast . . . prick Mullins was. The bastard was living the life of the fuc . . . rich and pampered in fuc . . . Middleburg, Virginia, and was a motherfu . . . goddamned state senator.

After they parted, Tom swore that Frank Mullins would be sorry for the havoc he'd caused. Now, he just had to figure out how.

****

Middleburg, Virginia, is a rich village about 40 miles west of Washington, D.C., near the homes of Paul Mellon, Jackie Onassis and Jack Kent Cooke, and very far from the squalor, dirt and hopelessness of much of Baltimore, where Patrolman Frank Mullins had once precariously and nervously earned his paychecks before climbing the ladder in the Baltimore Police Department to become assistant police commissioner.

He'd retired from the department to marry Amy, an awe-struck heiress—he was her brave knight in shining armor—who'd inherited 400 acres on Zulla Road several miles from Middleburg. He then concentrated on becoming a local "identity."

Ambition fueled, aided and abetted by too much adulation from his wife and new neighbors sent him into politics and won him a senate seat in Richmond, the state capital. He was now scheming, pulling in numerous favors, to become Governor of Virginia.

Someday, perhaps, he dreamed, he'd reach the ultimate, the Mt. Everest of an ambitious man's ambition: the White House. "Mr. President" had a nice ring to it. He'd come a long way since breaking up fights, or not, between drunken ex-hillbillies in south Baltimore. In his rosy memory, he'd done it singlehandedly. His wife craved the limelight and her tens of millions helped buy publicity and votes.

His two political opponents for the governorship knew that the majority of middle class voters were enchanted by his "ordinary police officer defending the citizenry" credentials that they couldn't top.

One candidate was a professor of economics, while the other had a law practice, specializing in drunk driving cases. They were no match for a former top cop skilled in the machinations of real politics inside a large police department.

He was untouchable, he proudly told himself, because he knew too much dirt on too many important people. He'd reveled in a lifetime's obsession of digging for scandal and letting victims know what he knew and that he would one day require a favor, or three. He knew that nobody dared risk harming him. Most important people he met inevitably became his victims. Mullins was an expert at twisting, blackmailing and frightening his victims, who didn't dare criticize him publicly for fear of retaliation.

Mullins didn't believe in ghosts and thought he was safe.

He didn't realize that, no matter how many years pass, sometimes the next dark cloud has your name on it and you might get your comeuppance. His black cloud was approaching after two decades and in the shape of an obsessed investigator with a personal vendetta.

Mullins hadn't had the stomach to be a good street cop, was downright afraid, but he possessed the ability to play politics in spades. He could manipulate the truth, charm and blackmail people with impunity.

He'd begun divorce proceedings from his first wife the day after she'd buried her father, struck by a heart attack, because she was of no further use to Mullins' career ambitions. Hoping to humiliate her so that she'd surrender without fighting his terms of divorce (he wanted everything), Mullins alleged that their two kids, both daughters, didn't look like him and claimed that they were the results of an affair.

Blood tests disagreed with his pretended outrage, forcing him to pay alimony and child support.

****

He then discovered polo, the game of the rich by the rich.

A man named Clifford Odets said that sex is the poor man's polo.

While Frank hated horses, he paid for expensive lessons to learn how to ride well enough to play a decent standard of polo. As a factory worker's son, horses and pony clubs had been absent from his life but he pictured polo ponies as his ticket upwards.

Polo, as Mullins knew it would, introduced him to the world of the rich, especially the many rich ladies looking for a husband. Being well off for a cop but by no means rich, in terms of the wealthy elite, he learned the second secret of the polo world: if you aren't rich, just pretend to be.

His scheme worked.

He'd bagged Amy and along with her, as his prize and her dowry, came the 400 acres of prime Virginia country-side, close to President Kennedy's former home, Wexford Farm, plus houses in Vermont, Kentucky and Chantilly, France plus a 'cottage' in Bermuda for each Christmas, because Amy disliked cold winters.

She had inherited money from her grandfather, a rich trader on Wall Street. Amy was all right but Mullins needed more sex than her post-first-baby mood preferred. So he had a few affairs, one with a rich but lonely married woman in Middleburg and others elsewhere, either when he could use a false name or impress women by his status as a senator.

He'd become a state senator using his same old tricks. Mullins loved being a senator and reckoned that being governor would be even tastier. Billyland was ancient history. He shivered every time he remembered the place.

****

Tom returned to Lexington to work on various investi-gations while he planned how to interrupt Frank Mullins' cozy lifestyle.

Over the next few months, in between cases, he made more trips to Baltimore, where he read plenty in the public library about Mullins' stellar career in the BPD and, by digging, discovered that two 15-year-old runaways had reported rapes by Mullins but they, as well as several other people alleging instances of corruption, had all been ignored by the Baltimore Police Department.

Nothing ever stuck to him. Mullins was bulletproof.

Tom also made several trips to Virginia, to Middleburg, to identify Mullins, follow him carefully, asking the locals about him—he was a local celebrity so it was easy. It was there he discovered the affair with the local married woman and watched from a distance as Mullins cut the ribbon to open a jewelry store next door to the Red Fox Tavern and played golf near Marshall, a town six miles south.

Tom followed him to Richmond, watching and listening while Mullins gave pompous, self-serving speeches in the senate house, 110 miles from Middleburg. He disappeared into crowds as he listened to speeches given in other towns around the commonwealth, listening to the applause, certain that the same people would cheer less loudly if they knew the truth about Mullins, appalled at his listeners' enthusiasm for the man.

Mullins was sure to become governor. All the polls agreed. The election was soon. Tom needed to move quickly.

Tom developed two plans, plan A and plan B. Neither was legal, neither was nice but Tom didn't care. As events turned out, he didn't need plan B. None of his cases were ever personal but this situation was.

He was avenging his father's death.

Barbara noticed the change in Tom's mood, was told it was simply a case, nothing personal with her and so gave him enough space. She realized that he'd tell her when and if it were necessary.

He appreciated her keeping her distance and not requiring answers for everything. Their relationship was built on trust and staying out of each other's work. She didn't demand to know everything ticking in Tom's brain.

In return, he tried to understand her method of making inventions but lacked the technical artistry to understand. She loved making gadgets. He loved solving crimes.

****

Patience was a gift that Brabazon possessed but he got his chance sooner than expected.

He'd bought a taxi cheaply, paying for it in cash, naturally, complete with working meter. He paid a mechanic to add some extras to it, including putting locks on the rear seat seatbelts. Then he borrowed–stole, to be precise–two Maryland license plates from two cars of the same model and color parked in a shopping mall in Bethesda. The thefts would be reported in Maryland, not in Virginia, so he put one new plate on his taxi.

On the next day, Tom waited patiently in the parking lot of the golf club near Marshall where Frank Mullins was playing his regular Wednesday morning round.

When the place was quiet, the members out on the course, Tom walked up to his quarry's Mercedes and slashed two tires. He grinned as he listened to the air sizzling out and watched the tires flatten as he returned to his taxi. He waited.

Mullins finally returned to his car, hefted his golf bag into the trunk and then noticed, with appropriate annoyance, that his tires were flat. Damn. Must be some punks from the village.

He looked around, not knowing what to do. One thing he wasn't going to do was to change his own tires. That was undignified for a big, important man like him. Besides, he only had one spare. He wasn't a member of AAA and he owed the garage owner in Middleburg, so both those options were out.

Then he spotted the taxi, walked over and asked for a ride home.

"Please get in, sir."

"Damned punks slit my tires. Did you see anything?" Mullins asked.

"Oh no, sir, but I haven't been here for long. Where do you wish to go, sir?"

Mullins gave his home address, got in, shut the door and put on the seat belt, which clicked loudly.

That was the last action Mullins made as a man free in spirit and happiness. His visions of governor and, if he got lucky, president, were about to implode. Frank Mullins made a big mistake getting in Tom's taxi. His luck had run out. The black cloud had arrived from his distant past. There was no way out.

He was in Tom's trap, caught. He's mine, Tom smiled, all mine.

Mullins fell asleep quickly. He'd always been able to take catnaps in cars. Tom checked in the mirror before deliberately turning the wrong way out of the golf course and, avoiding the town of Marshall, drove through tiny

Delaplane and into what the locals called "The Free State" of Fauquier County. A few miles later they went through the empty hamlet of Orlean to reach route 211, which went west from Warrenton towards the Blue Ridge Mountains and the Shenandoah Valley. He wasn't far from his grandparents' farm. He had carefully chosen to take the back roads, having re-learned them the previous day. He drove past Sperryville cemetery and nodded his respect toward his parents' graves.

Mullins was perplexed when he woke up 40 minutes after leaving the golf course and didn't recognize his location. Tom was driving down a dirt road through woods, about four miles from Sperryville. Mullins realized that he wasn't at home.

"Where the hell am I? What the fuck are you doing? Take me home now or you'll be fucking sorry. Don't you know,"–politics had convinced Mullins that he was famous, at least in Virginia–"who I am? You're in a shitload of trouble," he spluttered.

Tom stayed silent. The doors were all locked and Mullins had no form of communication with the outside world.

Mullins' seatbelt was jammed, operable only by a switch on Tom's dashboard. The windows had a special tint, darkened after turning on the ignition, so nobody could see in. Mullins could only observe the outside world in a bit of a dark blur. The rear windows were closed, powered only by a switch beside Tom's clutch. Tom kept driving, ignoring Mullins' shouts, unmoved by his passenger's distress.

"Stop this fucking taxi," Mullins demanded to no avail. "Let me out. I have to piss."

Tom broke his silence.

"Then pee in your pants, asshole. You're going to have worse than that happen to you tonight."

"Kidnapping of a state senator is illegal, it's a felony," Mullins hissed furiously. "You'll go to death row. I'll get you executed in the electric chair." Mullins was most definitely upset.

Tom was unconcerned.

"By tomorrow morning," he told Mullins, "your chances of ever being governor will have vanished. The good news is that you're probably going to die tonight. Pee if you like but don't wet the seat."

Mullins continued to shout threats mixed with obscenities but Tom was unmoved, uncaring, determined to bring justice. He drove for another few minutes then stopped and switched off the ignition. He kept on his surgical gloves and got out.

Later, when returning to the car after saying goodbye to his victim, he would remove the taxi sign and change the license plate. It was no longer recognizable as the taxi at the golf course. He wasn't too worried about being remembered at the golf course, because he doubted that anybody would have noticed his taxi.

He'd learned that trick from his colleague Andy Winters, who'd worked undercover on the mean streets of New York City, sometimes using a taxi as his prop. He'd told Tom that taxis, like pandas and penguins, all look alike to people and were seldom noticed.

Tom opened the back door, stuffed a thick sock into Mullins' mouth, put a hood over his jerking and shouting head, hit him with a hammer, scaring the man into silence, tied his victim's arms behind his back and tied his ankles, unlocked the seat belt and hauled him out and shoved him onto the ground. Tom was in no mood to observe Mullins' constitutional rights or any other rights, or lefts.

He put a rope around Mullins' neck and told him to get up and walk in front of him. Mullins refused, so Tom walked around in front and started pulling. Mullins then got up, unable to see through the hood and peed again.

The man was scared. Tom pulled again and Mullins began stumbling in Tom's direction.

They proceeded about 200 yards, weaving around trees and bushes. Tom wanted to be far away from the car; he didn't wanted visitors or hikers to interrupt them. He knew this piece of woods and had selected it deliberately. He'd checked it out the previous day. He and his father had camped here the last time they'd spent a night together in the woods, a lifetime ago.

Tom wasn't going to kill Mullins himself. He hoped that a bear would do it for him. A hungry bear. Bears are always hungry. There are many bears in the Blue Ridge Mountains.

He tied Mullins by his neck, wrists and ankles, to a tree with binder twine and then removed his shoes and socks. Binder twine was easier to handle than wire. Mullins tried to shout despite his mouth being full of sock. Then Tom picked up Mullins' shoes and socks and threw them downhill as far off as possible. They landed in a large pile of brambles, far enough away to make an uncomfortable walk for Mullins if he ever got away from the tree. Next he pulled off the hood.

"Shut up and listen to me, you creep. Nobody is going to come along and save you, lock me up and elect you to anything, not the governorship, nothing. You're finished, you bum."

He waited for Mullins to stop struggling.

"Save your breath. Listen. You're going to get your comeuppance, you're going to finally—and it's taken 24 years, so it's long past due—finally get what you deserve. This is going to be the worst, and I hope, the last night of your disgusting life."

Mullins stared uncomprehending at Tom, who continued: "I know a lot about you and none of it is appealing." He definitely had Mullins' attention.

"Don't bother threatening me or asking for mercy as I'll give you none. You're bear bait, dead meat, you bastard, and I'll tell you why. You'll probably die tonight by being mauled by a bear or maybe several bears but maybe you're lucky and they've gone to another piece of woods to hunt, but you can see their fresh marks on that tree, can't you?"

The marks were old but Tom was betting that Mullins wouldn't know the difference.

"They were here this morning. They should be back tonight. They'll enjoy eating you. Do you know how bears describe humans? 'Soft on the outside, crunchy on the inside.'"

Mullins peed again. He was petrified.

"Black bears take their time killing their prey, tearing off chunks at a time. They're in no hurry. They'll enjoy ripping you apart. Like cats playing with mice except that bears are bigger and their claws are longer." Tom paused.

"Do you like snakes?" he asked chattily, suddenly cheerful. "Lots of copperheads in these woods."

Mullins couldn't turn his head far enough because of the binder twine tight around his neck.

"There's a nest about 20 yards away. Well, at least you won't be lonely after I've left, what with the snakes and bears to keep you company."

Mullins didn't cheer up. Tom had more to say.

"If you survive tonight and somehow free yourself from this tree and crawl barefoot out to the road and catch a ride back to Middleburg, you'll find frosty receptions from your wife and buddies. I've mailed reports about you to your devoted wife.

"She'll be less devoted after she reads about your raping those underage girls back in Baltimore and your recent affairs. I've discovered two women this year and two others last year. Did I find all of them? I bet that you've given a STD or AIDS to your wife. That judge's secretary you screwed in Richmond has AIDS, did you know? She thinks that you gave it to her."

He paused.

"Remember Baltimore, do you? . . . . Good."

Mullins was apoplectic. But Tom was just warming up.

"Then there's Amy's wrong image—and the voters' image—of you as a brave, good police officer, protecting the citizenry against criminals. You were a fucking criminal and a lousy cop. You had no courage, no guts—you were afraid—and nobody you worked with respected you."

He let that sink in before continuing:

"My letter reports many bits of corruption, which you performed while an officer sworn to uphold the law and all that other sugary, noble stuff. Income addition, like taking cash from unwilling citizens—you called it 'protection'—and pay-offs from business people and bookies, big stuff like blackmailing your former father-in-law the police inspector and taking drug money from dealers."

Mullins peed again. His pants were soaked. He was trembling with fear. His pupils were dilated, his eyes blinking rapidly.

"Then I spent more postage, sending more copies of your transgressions to the newspapers—papers in Richmond, *The Washington Post*, *The New York Times* and *The Baltimore Sun* and, of course, you love being on TV so I sent copies to CBS, NBC and ABC in New York. You have no influence up there. Another envelope has gone to CNN in Atlanta. My reports are about your felonies, blackmailing and sexual activity. You're going to be headline news, mister, but not all publicity is good publicity."

Tom continued: "You're going to hope, pray, beg that the bears eat you tonight, you bastard." He paused. "You're never going to be governor now, you shithead."

Mullins was terrified now. His eyes were pleading for mercy, for a way out. He'd always escaped before but he'd never before met anyone as determined as Tom.

"If somehow you survive tonight and I certainly hope that you don't, but if somehow you return to civilization and everybody still loves you, well, they won't for long.

"I've also been busy sending copies to the homicide department of the Baltimore Police Department and to your first wife. Now there's a woman who already hates you just for what you did to her. Other copies have gone to your daughters, to the Mayor of Middleburg, the Governor of Virginia, to the FBI and to the committee of your golf club. I spent a lot of postage on you, you sonofabitch."

And to Sergeant O'Brien of the BPD, he added silently to himself.

"I now offer my pièce de résistance. You caused the murder of a Baltimore police officer, Detective Richard Walwyn, on May 12, 1963 by removing the bullets from his .38 revolver and replacing them with empty shells."

Mullins kept blinking.

"After his murder, you assigned yourself as the case investigator–you were the precinct boss so nobody could overrule you–declaring the case closed when Victor Brown was gunned down by two uniforms before he got to sing. When Walwyn's partner, Andy Walsh, was suspicious and openly confronted you, you had him transferred and demoted back to uniform under a cloud by accusing him of corruption.

"Guess what, Walsh still dislikes you. In fact, he hates you. He wants to piss on you. So will everybody else after they read their mail. You, Frank Mullins, are doomed. Death by bear tonight and wrecked forever back in the human world. And it serves you right."

Tom pulled a sealed plastic bag from his pocket and pulled out some raw meat and Snickers bars. He'd read somewhere that bears adore Snickers. They enjoy raw meat, too, even human meat when available. He removed the plastic from the meat and the Snickers bars, scattering the food on the ground around Mullins' feet. Then he removed the rag from Mullins' mouth. He wanted Mullins to ask the right question.

Mullins did. The fight was gone from him but the terror was complete.

"Who cares about Walwyn? He was a stupid nobody, a fool."

"I do."

"Why?"

"Take a guess," Tom parried.

"Why, you fucker, why are you doing this? I never did anything to you, you scumbag."

"You're wrong. Because Detective Richard Walwyn had a wife and son. I'm his son. He was my father. I was only

11 years old. Dad was 35. You ruined his life, my mother's life and, you filthy degenerate bastard, my life.

"You destroyed my family and I lost my dad because of you. You wrecked my life."

Mullins began choking. "You can't prove anything, it's been too long, beyond the statute of limitations. Any judge will throw out all your hearsay." Tom noticed that he hadn't denied Tom's allegations.

Tom replied: "I don't have to prove anything in a court of law. You'll get your punishment tonight. Out here, alone, in the darkness, just you and the bears and snakes. You thought you'd never get what you deserve, that your past, that justice—real justice—would never catch up with you.

"I bet," he added, "that you thought you were home free, you bastard. Guess what, you were wrong. It's taken 24 years but the consequences of what you did and justice, real justice, have finally caught up with you . . . and you'll suffer for it tonight."

Mullins caved in, terrified. His eyes revealed that he knew he was in unfixable trouble and that Tom was not going to let him go but begged for mercy, anyway. He began begging for a final chance, promising to make it up to Tom. How could he? Tom felt no pity for the man who'd ruined his life.

"Why," Tom needed to know, "did you do that to my dad?"

Mullins replied: "He was going to rat on me. Report me for being dirty. I warned him to mind his own damned business. I was making good money and not hurting anybody. I was helping society by making the crooks pay me fees."

"Tell me more."

"Your dad was stupid and holier than thou, a fool for not taking money. Everybody did it, you know, back then. He refused. Wouldn't go along with the rest of us, the sanctimonious jerk. We got paid so lousy, so little. We needed the money to pay our bills and we got piss-poor overtime pay back then."

Tom squeezed his victim's throat hard, then let go. Mullins gasped and choked for breath. Tom stuffed the sock back into his mouth.

Then, to attract the bears even more, he picked up a long stick, sharpened it with his penknife and told Mullins where he was going to stick it.

"Bears can smell human blood from miles away," Tom reassured him.

With the sharpened stick, he jammed it up Mullins' left nostril.

Mullins screamed from the sharp pain but very little sound passed through the sock.

First a trickle, then a stream of blood fell from the nostril, reddening his expensive silk shirt and designer golf trousers. Tom pulled out the stick and jammed it into his left ear canal, piercing it. That would cause little blood but lots of pain and tinnitus, constant agonizing ringing. Then he threw the stick away.

"Rot in hell," Tom finished and walked away, back to his car and out of the woods.

Being a hunter, Tom knew how to hide his tracks and that's what he did, carefully.

Tom put the second license plate on the car, drove back to route 11, drove to Warrenton, taking its bypass north half an hour to an empty street in a run-down industrial section of Manassas, far away from any security cameras, where he guessed the car would be stripped overnight by street kids and rendered unidentifiable.

That's why he didn't park it at Dulles airport. He didn't want the car found intact. He walked for five minutes, dropped the car keys and both license plates down a manhole cover before walking another five minutes to a high-rise parking lot beside a shopping mall, where his own car was waiting for him.

He drove down to the street and, still wearing two pairs of gloves, found a mailbox on a deserted street without any CCTV cameras into which he fed many envelopes.

Then, too wired to be tired, he began driving to Lexington, threw the gloves into a rubbish can outside an empty store in Charlottesville two hours later, turned on I-64, then reached I-81 near Staunton and got back onto I-64 west outside Lexington, Virginia, keeping just below the speed limit. It was a long drive in the darkness. He checked regularly that nobody was following him, paid cash for gas to avoid a credit card charge and arrived home for lunch the next day.

****

He'd left his cat Pinky with Barbara.

He let himself into his apartment, took a shower, went to bed and slept until dawn the next morning, Friday. After another shower, he first reported his return to his office then rang Barbara and invited himself to breakfast at her house.

Barbara had her TV on and Mullins was one of the major stories on the news. Tom watched intently. The reporter, speaking from Marshall, Virginia, was saying that the would-be governor of Virginia was missing and that the police were searching for him. He'd disappeared two days before after playing golf.

The reporter added that she had lots of embarrassing questions to ask Senator Mullins, which pleased Tom because this meant that the contents of his envelopes must already have been read. He hadn't told anybody where to find Mullins, figuring that the longer he spent in the woods, the better. Fresh air should be good for Mullins.

His wife, Amy, was reportedly distraught. I bet she is, thought Tom, if she's read my letter.

"Ever been there?" Barbara wondered.

"Where, Marshall?"

"Yes," Barbara answered.

"Sure, it's near Warrenton, where Katya and I lived."

The news switched to a scandal on Wall Street.

"Have a successful trip?" Barbara asked, handing him a coffee. "Did you do anything interesting?"

"Yes," Tom replied with a smile. "Solved another case. Biggest and most important case of my life. Created some justice and took a walk in the woods." He drank some coffee. "Fresh air makes a man feel good. I feel great."

"Tell me about it," she urged.

"Better not. Why don't you describe your latest invention instead?"

And so she did.

His office rang his pager an hour later. He phoned back. Tom had been assigned a new fraud case to solve, involving a missing company executive and a lot of missing company money. He ran out of the house.

To another hunt.

EPILOGUE

Barbara's phone rang at 5:25 that afternoon.

"Hi, Barbara, it's me, Elizabeth, at the office. Tom's hurt." Her voice was high-pitched and frightened.

"How?"

"There are two detectives here. They say he was stabbed outside a supermarket. He left here, the office, I mean, at 3:30."

"How badly is he hurt?" asked Barbara. She'd guessed that this would happen someday although Tom had always laughed off her premonition.

"The detectives won't say. He's been taken to a hospital."

"Which one?"

Elizabeth named it.

"I've got a friend who works in the E.R. there," Barbara replied, meaning Sally Young. "I'll call her now and meet you at the hospital in 20 minutes, ok?"

"OK, Barbara," Elizabeth answered sadly. "I hope that he'll be ok."

"Who did it?" Barbara asked.

"The detectives say that they don't know. They asked me if anybody has a grudge against him and who would want him hurt. They want to talk to you."

"Please ask them to meet me at the hospital. What did you tell 'em?"

"That there are lots of people. There are at least ten people who've threatened him, like all our investigators, you know, they all get threats sometimes but I told the detectives that it's more likely to be one of the dozens who want Tom hurt but kept quiet. I like Tom, this is awful."

Barbara hung up, then looked up the hospital's phone number, dialed and asked the receptionist to patch her through to the emergency room, where she asked to speak to Sally.

Sally came on the line.

"What's up, Barbara? Why are you calling me at work?"

"Tom's been stabbed."

"Oh, no!" Sally said. "How bad is he?"

"I don't know. I'm hoping that you'll know. He's been taken to your E.R. Have you seen him?"

"No," Sally replied. "I'm working on six patients, a GSW, broken leg, overdose, kidney stone, concussion and a fractured jaw. It's busy here, as usual. We've got two other gunshots, one burn from a house fire, several car accidents, the usual broken bones, a failed suicide, sore throats, two noisy drunks, sick babies and normal stuff. Just a second, I'll ask."

Thirty seconds passed until Sally spoke again.

"He's here," she confirmed. "He's critical and was taken up to the O.R. fifteen minutes ago. Lost a lot of blood. Some moron pulled the knife out at the scene. It looks grim, Barbara. Get here fast. Go straight upstairs. I'll call Charlie."

"Thanks, Sally. I'll keep you posted."

"I'll see you upstairs after my shift ends at 8 or so," Sally replied. "I've gotta go now."

Barbara grabbed her keys and handbag, turned to Tom's cat Pinky and, on her way to the door, told him the news.

"Do us a favor, Pinky. Give your dad some of your nine lives. How about seven? He's going to need them."

THE END

www.ingramcontent.com/pod-product-compliance
Lightning Source LLC
Chambersburg PA
CBHW051132030726
47504CB00004B/834